HIDDEN

Gods Among Us Triquetra Prophecy
Book One

Melody Grace Hicks

HIDDEN

For information contact :
http://www.melodygracehicks.com

Book and Cover design by Melody Grace Hicks

Paperback ISBN: 978-1-0689324-2-7
Hardcover ISBN: 978-1-0689324-3-4

10 9 8 7 6 5 4 3 2 1

CONTENTS

DESCRIPTION

After a steamy encounter with Asgard's Black Prince unlocks her genetics, an unsuspecting scientist discovers not only are gods real, she is one. Can she survive mythological worlds that hold dangers she's never imagined?

When Shannon boards her flight to London, she's stunned her seatmate is a famous singer/songwriter and actor Tod Corvus. Their rawly sensual union forges an unbreakable connection, triggering her dormant genes, while uncovering his hidden identity as Loki, Asgardian God of Chaos, Story, and Song. With her worldview and sense of identity shattered, Shannon reels at the destruction of everything she's worked to build in her life. How can she trust her heart to another after her painful past? But more than her feelings are at stake. Mastering her awakened goddess powers presents its own challenges as anger generates a wall of fire or fear spawns a tornado. With mythology coming to life around her in an expanding universe beyond Earth, adjusting to her new reality requires time she may not have.

Loki never expected to be blessed with a soulmate, especially after the murder of his Valkyrie wife and the tragic death of his oldest brother. Finding Shannon, then losing her within hours of her goddess transformation is devastating. And it's his fault. As a new immortal of unknown background, she has yet to learn the range of her abilities, how to protect herself, or even what threats await her. Asgard's powerful Black Prince has never feared his enemies.

Until now.

Now, he has everything to lose.

PREFACE

Welcome to the Gods Among Us Universe. It's inspired by an amalgamation of world mythologies including Norse, West Coast First Nations, Mesoamerican, Celtic, Greek, Roman, Mesopotamian, Egyptian, and Asian, blended with our current modern world, and expanded to other worlds across multiple solar systems within this created universe. I take copious liberties with world mythologies, twisting them as needed to serve the interests of my stories. No disrespect is intended to any original ancient sources, cultures, or religions associated with these world mythologies.

World mythology pre-dates modern usage in popular culture. Characters in my fiction created from these mythologies share some traits and occasional backstory elements with popular culture characters since both are sourced from the same ancient material. Reference to popular world culture provides a sense of the *real world* in the Earth-based scenes and would be familiar to characters living in a version of our modern world. Points to readers who catch my pop culture references and specific mythology legends.

The Gods Among Us Universe is diverse, with a wide range of abilities, appearances, mental states, and gender expressions, and sexualities, including a shapeshifting genderfluid race. While the main romance in the Triquetra Prophecy is predominately heterosexual, with the ability to shapeshift, genderfluid characters transition physically in addition to socially such that their chosen gender identity and biological sex assignment matches. This author's choice to present gender fluidity tied with shapeshifting should not in any way be construed as disrespecting real world individuals of their gender choice, whether cis or trans to their biological sex.

This first trilogy, the Triquetra Prophecy, is focused on three main characters, two of whom you'll meet in this book, and the third will appear in book two. The story starts quickly. This is no slow-burn fantasy romance, but more of a rollercoaster, with a fast upward climb, then lots of twists, turns, peaks, and valleys right through to the end of the third book. Additional tropes include: he-falls-first, altered heroine, ancient-being-finds-love, soulmates, dangerous secrets, unplanned pregnancy, touch-her-and-die, and fish-out-of-water. For information on trigger warnings within *Hidden,* please see my website (www.melodygracehicks.com).

PART 1

The Faces We Wear

"The Japanese say we have three faces. The first face, you show to the world. The second face, you show to your close friends and family. The third face, you never show anyone. It is the truest reflection of who you are."

Unknown

Chapter 1

TEMPTATION

Of all the days for Shannon Murphy's controlling ass of an ex to show up and harass her in her driveway, Trent just had to pick today. Three years since she'd broken their engagement, but the bastard wouldn't take a fucking hint. Stifling her frustrated groan as he stalked closer, Shannon fumbled for the keys in her pocket with suddenly sweaty fingers, longing for the nearby safety of her Toyota RAV4. No way would she be fast enough.

Damn it. Why hadn't she left just five minutes sooner?

Rage twisted Trent's deceptive blond and blue-eyed Nordic features—an outwardly handsome man, he'd fooled Shannon for a few years before she'd recognized the sadistic predator lurking inside. Faster than she could evade, the two-hundred-pound former hockey player lunged, and like a striking viper, those iron-like fingers cut into her upper arm as she reached to open the SUV's door. She bit back a pained cry. It would only encourage the bastard.

"Where are you going?" Trent snarled, yanking at the dark-blue backpack hooked over her shoulder.

Shannon struggled to keep her feet as his tug arched her back and threw her off balance. "To work—"

"Lying bitch!" His fingers squeezed tighter, and a pulse of agony shot up her arm. "This is your *travel* backpack. What poor sucker did you con with an inept, frigid fuck between your fat thighs? Or was it your traitorous tongue sucking his cock that got you the grant money for this trip?" A disgusting spray of spittle hit her cheek as she leaned away from his venomous words.

Closing her eyes, she tried to tune out and endure, to not respond. It was the only way to keep from further inflaming him. He'd usually leave when he didn't get the reaction he wanted.

Not today, though.

No, today he ground the muscle of her arm into the bone, and she fought her rising nausea. Towering over her and using his far greater strength, Trent was damn determined to make him impossible to ignore. His smile sent chills down her spine when unwilling tears betrayed the pain she refused to acknowledge.

"Let her go, Trent. I've already called nine-one-one," called a familiar voice from the street.

With a snarl, Trent shoved Shannon away. As she caught her balance against her vehicle's mirror, muscles sagging in relief, her best friend approached, phone held to her ear. Thank gods.

Lynda murmured into the cell and repeated Shannon's address, nodding at whatever she heard.

"I'm going, you fucking scag." Trent swung a fist at Lynda's face and she side-stepped him quickly, despite her four-inch heels and tight pencil skirt. Glaring at him as spots of colour appeared on her pale cheeks, she continued talking into her phone. Swearing, Trent hurried down the driveway. Tires squealed as he floored his black Mustang, fishtailing down the road.

Good fucking riddance.

Skin crawling, Shannon yanked open the door of her SUV, dropped her backpack, and dug in the centre console for a wet wipe. Damn it. Damn it. Damn it. With shaking hands, she cleaned the spit from her face. A shudder wracked her. Despite repeated scrubbing, the foul sensation lingered. Gods, she had to get him *off* of her.

Lynda's fingers closed around Shannon's, halting her frantic scouring and drawing her into a hug. The embrace was a quick pat on the back that left a good six inches of air between them before Lynda released her, but it was enough to disrupt the creeping sensation in Shannon's flesh. No way would her best friend let the clasp wrinkle her perfectly coiffed appearance.

Lynda rolled her eyes. "So much for that restraining order."

Used to Lynda's lack of affection, Shannon didn't hide her small smile at the stilted attempt at comfort. Nor did she muffle her snort as her friend brushed manicured fingernails through a stylish blond chin-length bob and smoothed a hand down her mauve suit jacket. Lynda never presented anything but an immaculate appearance to the world.

"Thank you. Perfect timing on your part. Are the cops on the way?" Shannon frowned when her friend tucked her iPhone back into her purse. *Aren't you supposed to stay on the line when you call nine-one-one?*

Lynda waved a careless hand. "What are best friends for? No, I didn't actually call anyone."

Despite the spikes of pain throbbing up and down Shannon's arm as she shifted her backpack into the passenger seat, a small burble of amusement emerged. Trent wasn't the smartest, but he made up for it by being a vicious bully. Good thing he hadn't seen through Lynda's ruse or he might have gone after both of them. At just over six feet tall and made of solid muscle, the former athlete-turned-academic was more than either woman could handle. Even if Shannon had taken a couple years of self-defence lessons after breaking up with him.

"Let's get you to the airport." Lynda held out a hand. "I've got just enough time to drop you off and bring your car back before I need to head to a meeting. Another potential client," she said with a satisfied twist of her lips and an excited gleam in her cornflower-blue eyes.

Shannon dropped the keys into Lynda's outstretched palm and moved around the vehicle. "Thanks. I'll keep my fingers crossed for you. Anyone I know?" As they drove off to Lynda's rapid-fire chatter about the wealthy businessman she hoped would hire her marketing company, Shannon murmured occasional encouragement while trying to stifle the shaking in her limbs, adrenaline still surging through her system.

Two hours later, Shannon's gaze lingered on the beautiful wood-carved artwork of Raven on the concourse wall. The trickster was a cultural hero across the First Nations Peoples of coastal British Columbia, and his stories were her favourite. She couldn't help but smile at the connection with her heritage despite the tension wound around her spine—a constrictor ruthlessly choking the life from her. If only Raven would turn his mischief against Trent.

The image of the carving coming alive, taking flight, and bursting from Vancouver airport to chase down her ex-fiancé had Shannon biting back an unexpected laugh as she held out her boarding pass and passport. Gods, if only.

The gate attendant returned the documents with a polite nod. "Welcome aboard, Doctor Murphy."

"Thank you." After heading through the doorway and down the ramp, she reached the plane. The first-class section had large, deep seats with alternating rows for privacy. She'd almost cried at the complimentary upgraded ticket when she'd checked in, and now, as she searched for her row, Shannon practically skipped through the aisle. About damn time her luck changed today.

Releasing a long sigh, she sank into the luxury window seat, shoved her backpack underneath, and closed her eyes, trying to ignore the mental replay of Trent's latest visit. Ugh, as if work hadn't been stressful enough this week. Trent's nastiness was the shit icing on her already crappy cupcake.

She rolled her shoulders to loosen the knots, drew in a breath and let it out in another slow exhale as she opened her eyes to the window and view of the coastal mountains. It had been a gorgeous August day, warm but not hot, yet bright and sunny. The clear skies were darkening, with the sunset reflecting off the few clouds near the north shore mountains. Brilliant reds and oranges contrasted with the rich emerald green of the coniferous forests that surrounded her home—her sole source of solace these past few years. As much as she loved it, fuck, did she need to escape, to get away for a while.

"Pardon me, love. I believe I'm your seatmate for this journey," a British-accented baritone voice stated.

Turning from the window with a smile, Shannon froze as she recognized the face of the man lifting a guitar case into the overhead bin above her, a face she'd only ever seen on the big screen or album covers.

Holy shit. No way.

With the ruthlessness of flame devouring dry tinder, heat crept up her cheeks. She took in his tall, athletic build, his beautifully tailored black blazer, and soft white Henley. His bright auburn hair was cut short on the sides and slightly longer on top, setting off his handsome face. A scruffy start to a beard surrounded a pair of narrow lips, currently pressed together in apparent concentration.

Not noticing her reaction, he removed his jacket and handed it to the flight attendant standing beside him with a hanger. Shannon hadn't even noticed the airline crew. Instead, her thoughts stuttered at the identity of her seatmate. Was he really sitting next to her? Could she truly be that lucky?

As he shoved up the sleeves of his shirt, revealing leanly muscled forearms, he looked down at her with a curious tilt to his head, smiling as their eyes finally met.

All the moisture disappeared from her mouth. "Hi, I'm Doctor Murphy, I mean, I'm Murphy… Shannon… Shannon Murphy," she corrected. She blinked a few times then got a hold of herself enough to offer her hand as a mental voice sounding suspiciously like her mother's chided her. *Good gods, Shannon. You'd think you'd never seen a handsome man before with the foolish way you're acting.*

His smile widened, revealing dimples, as pale-blue eyes like an early spring sky twinkled with mischief. "You don't know for sure?" When he sat, he took her hand and kissed the back of it with a gentle caress of his thumb across her fingers. "Nice to meet you, Shannon. I'm Tod."

Was her blush visible? Please, no. Surely the light was too dim?

He stroked his thumb over her fingers a second time before releasing her. Holy hell, it had been years since she'd responded to anyone, but his light touch sent shivers up her arm and through her body with an entirely different, much more pleasurable tension than had troubled her minutes before.

"Yes, I'm aware. My brother is a fan of Raven's Chaos. He has all your albums, and I re-watched *The Assassin's Quest* a few days ago," she said in as even a voice as she could manage, despite the rapid heartbeat thundering in her ears.

"Ah, I'm found out then." He smiled with a self-deprecating twist of his lips. "So what kind of doctor are you?"

His response had her blinking, at a momentary loss for words. While she enjoyed his songs, and yes, admired his fine form from afar—okay, so she'd totally drooled at those shirtless scenes in his movies—she'd never considered him as an individual. Shannon would have expected someone as outgoing as the lead singer/songwriter of a chart-topping band and a popular actor to *want* to talk about himself.

"An ecologist, a professor at one of the local universities. I study climate change effects on our regional environments, like the coastal temperate rainforests and the drier pine forests of the British Columbian interior," she replied when she got over her surprise.

"A scientist then. Which university? There are a couple in Vancouver, correct?"

"Victoria Charles," she replied. "The one on the mountain." She pointed through the window.

As he shifted closer, bracing on the seat in front of her to peer where she'd indicated, the fragrance of orange, leather, and wood enveloped her. An intrinsically male scent, it sank into her skin, dove deep inside and woke long-buried instincts.

She caught herself leaning in to inhale, halting abruptly.

Smooth, very smooth, Shannon. Just blurt out how long she'd been out of the dating game, why didn't she? Or that she hadn't had sex in... good lord, over four years.

At her aborted movement, his gaze met hers, a slow smile quirking up one side of his lips. Those playfully intense blue eyes ensnared her. She couldn't look away, even as her breath escaped in little pants. He slowly raised his right hand, and the backs of his fingers brushed lightly along her cheek. Her lungs froze on a gasp.

Time halted for one beat of her heart, then a second, and at the third, her body finally remembered how to breathe.

"You had an eyelash," he said as she remained captivated. "What's it like, being a professor?" With a featherlight touch, he skimmed his fingertips over her cheek a second time and sat back in his seat.

"I... um... well."

Shannon struggled to gather her thoughts. Famous or not, his in-person charisma was nothing short of divine. This man did not need to rely on any movie magic or sound mixers. Not with that purring voice, those mesmerizing eyes. Incredibly distracted, she stifled the completely inappropriate impulses that kept popping into her head, like licking that little divot in his chin below those expressive, kissable lips, running her fingers through his hair, or feeling the scruff of his beard on her skin. Maybe her inner thighs. Damn it. Fuuuck.

"It's great." Her voice squeaked, and with a quick clearing of her throat, she forced her tone back to its normal range. "I love being outside in the forests with my grad students. It's the research that drives me, discovering how the world around us works, and contributing to saving it in practical ways." As she told him the details, he nodded with every appearance of listening intently. If only her thoughts would stay on track instead of being hijacked by her suddenly lively libido.

"Is that why you're travelling to London?"

She released a shaky breath, fighting to calm her rapid pulse, and nodded. "It's a week-long conference starting the day after tomorrow. This meeting only happens every four years between the Europeans and North Americans." It would be a blend of scientific talks, social mixers, and prospective job offers, and by all the gods, Shannon had been looking forward to the much-needed escape from the day-to-day stresses of grant writing, publishing, entitled students, difficult colleagues, and—especially—misogynistic administrators.

She was burned out. Even research didn't bring the same joy anymore. Not with everything else weighing her down.

Shannon desperately needed a break, some time and distance to think about how to fix her life. A serious change was in order, but only if the right opportunity came along. Changing universities was a big step, and she wouldn't jeopardize her success. Not after dedicating so much of her life to her career.

Her career was all she had.

After her engagement to Trent died in spectacular fashion with a screaming row at a faculty event, she'd buried herself in work, in the success of her science, and avoided romantic entanglements—men were too much effort and *way* too much drama. Any time she forgot that lesson, it was reinforced by Trent's periodic reappearances.

This trip was her mental salvation and an excellent chance to explore new possibilities.

Although holy moly, she'd not expected her flight to start like this. Her palms damp from titillated arousal she hadn't felt in years, Shannon rubbed her hands slowly over her black jeans. The Fates were *certainly* having fun with her today. Or was Raven messing with her? If her mom's stories were to be believed, that damn trickster would enjoy this kind of mischief.

A little smile curled at the edges of Tod's lips as his gaze flicked down to Shannon's restless hands then back to her face, and he tilted his head slightly. "You are an intriguing woman, Doctor Murphy. I don't often meet scientists. Do you teach in addition to your research?"

What thought put that wicked smile on his lips? She blinked and pulled her attention back, even as she flexed her fingertips over the denim covering her thighs. Gods, she wanted... *Stop fantasizing, Shannon!* No way was he actually interested in her. Not that way, at least. "Yes, three courses per year. When students want to be there, teaching is great. It's awful when they don't participate. Just standing in front of them, delivering information, isn't my cup of tea. Ideally, I'd like my courses to be interactive, interesting, and dynamic."

He wrinkled his nose. "Yes, from my student perspective at uni, I did *not* enjoy purely lecture courses nearly as much as those that required a more active role. What do you teach?"

"What did you take—" A crackle over the speaker cut off Shannon's question as a flight attendant started the preflight briefing and the crew demonstrated the aircraft's safety features. She glanced from the nearby steward back to Tod.

He was watching her, not the crew.

When Shannon's gaze met his again, nerves squirmed in her belly. Damn, he had such beautiful eyes. Like a wolf, maybe... definitely some kind of predator. Yeah, he could eat her all up. A wave of heat rose in her chest and face as the fantasy image sent her heart thundering, and she bit back a whimper. Holy crap, she couldn't believe she'd just thought that. In front of him. Fuck.

Trying to not fidget or reveal her racing lascivious thoughts, she turned and reached for the seat belt that had fallen between the seat and the window. She fought to hide her wince as she bumped her arm. Damn Trent and his iron grip. No doubt she had a ring of bruises to remind her of his unwanted touch.

But all thoughts of her ex fled when she sat back with the buckle in hand.

Tod held the other side of her seat belt. Eyes wide, her breath caught as he slowly took the buckle from her clasp, giving her every chance to stop him. She was unable to look away, and his mesmerizing gaze stole every thought from her head while he connected the two sides then tightened the strap snugly.

Yet, not too tight.

No—*oh my gods*—he used his fingers between her body and the buckle as a guide. Those long graceful fingers in her lap had heat pooling, her thighs pressing together, and her pulse thrumming an eager dance she'd been sure her body had long forgotten. She didn't dare move, frozen, snared by the erotic potential hanging in the air.

His perusal flicked from his hands to her eyes, back down to his hands, and a quick grin twitched at the corners of his lips as he met her gaze again. Sitting back, he said, "You're all set" as he buckled himself in.

Shannon exhaled a shaky breath. He had to be flirting. Surely, she was reading him right? Holy moly, it had been so long. She wasn't certain if her sex-starved brain was misreading what seemed to be clear signs of interest. If she woke when the flight landed in London to find this was a dream, she was going to be so pissed.

Her voice was husky when she thanked him quietly. Had he heard her over the flight attendant announcement?

"My pleasure, I'm sure," he replied, winking.

"Not just yours," she muttered.

"I'm sorry, I didn't catch that?" he inquired with a slight smirk, his blue eyes dancing.

She narrowed her gaze. He was playing games, the sexy bastard. "You know exactly what I said."

But why her? Was he toying to see if she was interested or... oh gods, please tell her she didn't have *sex-starved nerdy professor* stamped on her forehead like she was some bloody internet meme. She wasn't beautiful like those perfect slim twenty-somethings with big boobs he was usually seen with. She was boring, normal, with dull olive skin, plain brown hair, and on the border of having to shop in the plus-sized clothes section. She fought back memories of the numerous insults Trent had made about her body over the years.

No, there was no way Tod's interest was sincere.

His smirk spread into a wide smile that lit his expression, and he laughed. "Yes, you are definitely intriguing. This is going to be a very enjoyable flight."

As the plane accelerated down the runway, Shannon squirmed and pressed her legs together tighter. How was she going to survive a nine-and-a-half-hour flight next to this man? She was going to make a fool of herself, for sure.

Chapter 2

CONTROL IS OVERRATED

Good stories were definitely one of Tod Corvus's weaknesses. As the first few hours of flight time passed in delightful conversation, Shannon's tales of her graduate students and field research mishaps didn't disappoint.

"We had the choice of walking several kilometres into the site, or attempting to get the truck through the mud." Her lips twitched as she held back a laugh.

"What did you do?" Tod asked, grinning as she continued the tale of mayhem.

Intelligence and amusement gleamed in Shannon's green-gold hazel eyes. "I jumped out to see how bad the mud was. It can get quite deep when the ground thaws. The road looked dangerous—covered in water—but it was only a foot deep. My two students had never been on logging roads during spring breakup, so they didn't know how to judge it. I made sure the truck had enough momentum before we hit the mud to carry us through, even as we slid somewhat sideways."

Her deceptively nonchalant expression had him chuckling. "I suspect your version of 'somewhat sideways' is actually a lot sideways?" His gaze caressed her flawless olive skin, her long silky brown hair with red and gold highlights, her pert nose, and those lush full lips.

And whenever their eyes met, a spark of connection hummed.

With a bright tinkling burst of sound, she laughed. “Yeah, okay, so I was driving straight while looking through the side window, with mud and water spraying up like a geyser on either side of us, but my grad students are now convinced I’m a goddess when it comes to four-wheeling.”

An unexpected flash of longing pierced him, almost stealing his breath as he laughed with her. Norns knew it had been some time since someone caught his interest in anything more than a superficial way. The people he met wanted his money or body but didn't want him. They had no depth. Unable to resist the need to touch her, to feel that connection, he tugged a lock of her hair playfully. “Well, of course you are a goddess. It’s good they recognize your greatness,” he teased, trying to keep the wistful note to himself.

A light flush came over her golden skin when she met his eyes, smiled, and looked down. Yeah, he wanted to glide his fingertips over that soft, supple skin again, to feel her—

“Anything to drink?” the flight attendant interrupted, staring at Shannon's chest. Fucking asshole. Tod clenched a fist, forcing down the urge to flick the puny male away. This was the third damned time the bloody man had come by to leer at her since their flight had levelled off.

“Red wine, please. What do you want, Tod?” Not seeming to notice or reciprocate the attendant’s roving eyes, Shannon met Tod's gaze.

Yeah, she's not for you, you mangy git. Tod relaxed his fingers even as fire raced through his veins. The image her question brought to mind was in no way related to an innocent drink order. Reluctantly, he wrenched his wayward thoughts back under control. “I’ll have the red as well, thanks.”

The man poured two wines from his cart. When he reached over, ogling her cleavage, Tod took the glass from him and handed it to Shannon. “Here you go, darling.” Her eyes shot to Tod’s as she took the drink from him, pupils dilating as their hands touched.

So very responsive.

An image flashed in his thoughts—her curvy body under him with those expressive eyes glazed with passion, cheeks flushed, and mouth open as he drove himself inside her. Yggdrasil’s roots, it was hard to hold back, to not take what he wanted immediately. Rarely did he deny himself once his interest had been piqued.

But something told him Shannon would be worth savouring, a possibility or knowing that flickered to life deep within his soul. She was a fascinating rare gem—more than a quick, energy-boosting fuck in a first-class airplane bathroom, only to be forgotten at the end of the flight. Some instinct had him holding back, taking his time to delve into who she was as an individual, despite how frequently his mind taunted him with the desires he held in check.

Although he was *not* a patient creature, delayed gratification had its benefits. Taking his glass from the flight attendant, Tod raised it in a toast. "To a most interesting flight," he said, before taking a sip.

A half smile on her face, she tilted her head slightly. "Wait, is that like the Chinese curse *may you live in interesting times* because I don't think that's supposed to be a good thing!" She laughed, eyes alight with mischief.

"No, interesting is better. Boredom lacks any appeal, and I definitely wasn't implying a curse in this instance. Getting to know you is an absolute pleasure." Not the pleasure his body craved, but his mind was certainly stimulated in ways he'd missed of late.

She sipped her wine. "Well, I have to admit I'd normally be tuning out my seatmate to read a book by now. I'm very much enjoying getting to know you as well. Still, I've been rambling on about myself for hours. Let's talk about you."

He shrugged a shoulder. "What do you want to know? There is so much about me already in the media."

"True, but that's your public persona." She squirmed in her seat and gazed up through her lashes in a way that had him fighting to not drag her into his lap so he could satisfy the desire in her eyes. Did she realize how much she gave away when she looked at him with such need? "Maybe you could tell me about the you that is hidden, the parts that only peek out in the songs you write and the various roles you play."

Her insightful comment reinforced his impression of her intelligence, both her mind and body attractive to one such as him. All his lyrics, the melodies he created, even the roles he chose... in some way, they each contained an expression of his soul. Norns, but she drew every aspect of him.

Appeasing his growing need to touch her, he took her hand, rubbing his thumb over her fingers. Her breath caught, a flush rising on her cheeks and the skin revealed by her silken blouse. Yes, she wasn't indifferent to him. Smiling at her reaction even as it heated his blood, Tod met her gaze. "Not many recognize that each role I play must resonate within me. You are an insightful woman. What parts of me are you most curious about?"

Even with his half-hearted attempt to behave, he had no doubt she'd hear the double meaning behind his words. Nor did he hide the wickedness in his eyes. As her mouth dropped open and her cheeks flamed, the spots of colour deepening, his lips twitched, a smirk appearing.

"Bloody hell, Tod. If you're trying to get me so hot and bothered that I need a change of panties, it's working!" Her eyes widened, her free hand flying to her mouth.

A rolling laugh burst from him, so enchanted he was with her reaction. "Oh darling, you are such a delight to tease. I just can't resist."

"I... I didn't mean to... that was blunter than I—"

Without conscious thought, Tod's hand was at the back of her neck, tilting her head up to his. He leaned over to capture her lips as they parted with some apology he didn't care to accept. There was nothing to forgive. At her instant surrender, an electrifying bolt of possessive instinct roared through him, stiffening flesh and demanding he claim her now, seduce her regardless of their surroundings. Caressing his tongue over hers gently, he reluctantly pulled back. It wouldn't do to lose con—

A needy moan escaped her mouth, and the sound broke some of his restraint. He kissed her again, more passionately, his other hand holding her cheek. She tasted like rich wine, far more succulent than that which had been in their glasses. Drunk on her taste, he sipped from her as her hand slid up into his hair, tugging and pulling him closer.

Heat swirled, swelled, and expanded within him. By the Nine, she was perfect. He drew her closer. Something halted her progress, preventing him from pulling her into his lap. When he released her lips to remove the obstruction, she exhaled a soft mewl.

Shannon met Tod's gaze as their lips parted. His eyes flared brilliant green with such blazing carnality she found herself leaning, straining towards him. Hadn't they been a pale blue? Her thoughts scattered as his hand tightened, pulling her hair in sinful demand and his mouth descended again to plunder deeper and more thoroughly. Fingers cupping her cheek, he nipped, teased, and stroked her arousal higher.

When his head lifted, she couldn't completely stifle a protest, biting her lip as she caught her breath. Gods, she was burning up from the inside out. Never had a first kiss been like that before. Holy hell, she'd never had *any* kiss like that before.

With a ghost of a smile on his lips, his tongue flicked over her abused lower lip, then his mouth shifted to her neck, exploring his way along her throat to her ear and leaving devastating waves of gooseflesh in his wake. Shannon's pulse throbbed, molten fire in her veins, and she tilted her head to give him better access.

After nipping her earlobe, he whispered, "As much as I greatly desire to test your claim of soaked knickers, darling, if I don't stop now, I won't be able to until I'm buried to the hilt inside your hot, wet quim, ravishing you thoroughly regardless of our surroundings."

A wave of heat flared over her skin, her spine arching, and a whimper escaped even as she choked it back. Fuck, that was the most erotic, most arousing thing any man had ever said to her. Would it be wrong to crawl onto his lap? Did she care if others saw them? Her breath shuddered, and when he drew back, his eyes darkened to pin her with his sultry gaze. Blue... like the hottest flame of a gas stove.

She blinked.

That kiss really *had* scattered her senses.

Before she could reply or surrender to her wayward desire, the flight attendant arrived with their dinners. Shannon couldn't decide if she wanted to curse at the interruption or sigh in relief that she hadn't flung herself at Tod. Still, whatever insanity had possessed him to flirt with her, gods, she prayed it continued... at least for a little while. It had been so long since she'd felt this carefree, like she might actually be a desirable woman and not a mousy academic almost too old to have kids, too chubby and mature to interest a gorgeous man who had his pick of female attention. Surely, she didn't need to return to reality quite yet.

As if her wish had been granted, Tod didn't stop his teasing.

Instead, he stole her fork with a smirk and fed her as "payment for her crime" when she snapped her teeth at him in a mock bite. After moving the armrests out of the way, he tucked her chest into his shoulder and curled an arm around her, letting it rest on her ribs, so temptingly close to her breast. Damn, it was fun. Somehow, everything was so easy with Tod, no topic off limits, no teasing awkward. Shannon had never enjoyed a meal more.

A bite of broccoli fell from his fork into the scooped neckline of her royal-blue silk blouse and landed on the top edge of her black lace bra.

"Oops," he taunted, eyes wicked. "Would you like me to get that?"

Was that a trick question? She peeked at him through her lashes. "You make the mess, you clean it up." Her voice didn't even sound like her, a breathless huskiness to it. Who was this woman who dared to tease and flirt? Where had she been for the past decade?

"Mmm... darling, I do like how you think," he purred as his long fingers dipped down to pluck out the green floret, fingertips teasing along the lace edge before he popped the bite into his mouth. "Although, when it comes to food, I think it's fair that whoever cooks shouldn't have to do the dishes."

Seriously, could this man get any hotter? "You cook?" She enjoyed cooking and baking, but sharing it with someone after a long day sounded amazing. Not that Trent had ever offered. The reminder of her ex broke through the desire clouding her thoughts like poison ivy sprouting on her favourite picnic spot. Yeah, she wasn't in any emotional state to be looking for anything... although—she perused the spectacular man beside her—perhaps a vacation fling might be in the cards. Hell, she'd take even just one night.

Tod's smile was slow. "Yes. There is something to be said for playing with your food."

Why did she get the impression he wasn't talking about actual food? Still, he didn't try for anything more as they discussed favourite recipes, and she couldn't help but be disappointed. Heat churned within her abdomen, skin prickling with sensation, and the lace of her bra scraped against taut flesh with every shaky breath.

When he held a bit of cheesecake, she licked it slowly off the fork, taking her time until he groaned. "You wicked temptress! Playing with fire, darling." As he removed the fork from her mouth, his other hand slid up to cup her breast and pinch her nipple through the thin barrier of silk and lace.

"Tod!" she gasped, the sharp flare shifting to warm honey flowing down her body into her soaked core. He put down the fork and wrapped long fingers around her throat in a hold so carnal, her sex clenched and she couldn't restrain her whimper. Her pulse fluttered under his fingertips with frantic butterfly wings, and her chest rose and fell with each rapid breath.

"You like that, don't you?" he breathed into her ear in a low, rough voice.

"Yes," she moaned. Gods, she had no intention of denying it. This primally sensual man had her closer to orgasm with them fully clothed and sitting beside each other than her ex had after an hour of naked play in the bedroom.

"Would you let me fuck you right here, in front of all these passengers?" Tod growled, temptation in every sinful syllable. His thumb flicked over her peaked nipple again and a tremor quaked her body in a sensuous ripple. The imagery he evoked had her thoughts melting into heat, low and deep. She was a being of want, of animalistic instinct, of desire. A low whine escaped that she attempted to stifle, unable to form words to answer him.

Chapter 3

CARNAL INVITATION

The submissive sound made Tod's unruly cock jump. *Wait*, he reminded himself, thankful her curvy ass was against his outer thigh so she couldn't squirm against his rigid length. Never had it been such a fight to control his desires. Even with the cramped space of the lavatory right there, taunting him with possibility only steps away. He could have her locked in there within moments, bent over with her hands on the back wall as he satisfied the ache in his groin.

Tempting... so very tempting.

Gritting his teeth, Tod worked to dampen his fierce arousal, fighting his need. Reluctantly, he forced his hand to release her breast and returned his palm to her ribs. Despite her dilated pupils, he watched her rebuild her control as they panted, their faces only centimeters apart. Her pulse fluttered under his fingertips, each frantic beat a siren's song to the inferno within him.

As her eyes lost the dazed, desire-drugged appearance, she murmured, "Talk about lightning in a bottle."

Stiffening at the mental image, Tod growled. No way was he sharing her. Shannon was *his*. Instinct and reason fought for supremacy within him as he squashed his rumble. What was it about her that created this surge of unusual possessiveness for someone he'd met only hours ago?

"Sorr—"

Tod relinquished the soft flesh of her throat to cut Shannon off with a finger to her lips. "No, no apology. Let's watch something on the entertainment system, if that's acceptable?" A distraction was definitely in order if he was going to get through this flight without satisfying his increasing desire for this woman.

She nodded against his finger.

He shifted her until she spooned against his torso so he could put his back to the aisle. Thanks to the location of their wide and deep first-class seats, they had relative privacy, even without Tod's shielding. So easy. It would be so easy to take her, to have her ride him as he thrust up into her sweet curves. Forcing the seductive images from his mind, he wrapped his arms around her, holding her pressed tight to his chest and breathing in her vanilla-and-lemon scent.

As she scrolled through the entertainment choices and they discussed their likes and dislikes in movies and television shows, the talons of clawing need eased somewhat. How it had burned so deep, so fast, he wasn't sure, but he absolutely did not want to let her go. Not this woman who seemed to share his love of stories and grew more interesting the longer he spent with her.

"How about this movie?"

The amusement in her voice had Tod shifting her long hair to one side to see the screen on the seat back. It also provided a perfect view down the scooped neckline of her blouse to lush flesh restrained in black lace. Silently cursing the continued torture, he reluctantly dragged his eyes from the mouthwatering sight back to the monitor.

Her choice had him snorting a laugh. "Wanting to see me get smashed, bloody, and beaten, do you? Wicked woman."

"Well, you know, you let out that adorable groan when you hobble off after the nuns whack you for invading their sanctuary."

"Dangerous territory, darling, as it makes me want to hear more of your adorable moans." Tod lifted a hand from her lower ribs to under her breast and her breath caught. Not cupping that gorgeous curve again took restraint he didn't know he possessed. When had he gotten so noble? His palm still tingled with the remembered erotic weight.

"Okay, I'll behave and pick something else."

"No, I don't want you to behave. Go ahead and watch it. It's a great story." There was no way he would spoil her fun. Indeed, Tod wanted to encourage her to misbehave with him, as long as he could restrain his raging passions.

The idea of how embarrassed she'd be if he caved to his desires in front of the other passengers had him building back more of his frayed control. She didn't know no one would see or hear them unless Tod allowed it. Which he wouldn't. Ever. Not her. She was *his*. Unfortunately, he couldn't explain without potentially scaring her away. And allowing her to escape before he got to fully explore the depths of her intriguing personality? Not a risk Tod was willing to take. Not with the way something in her called to him.

She started the movie, and they shared a pair of headphones. He'd never enjoyed the action-adventure more. Her reactions enriched every aspect, and he found himself revealing parts of the assassin's character that resonated with him, the elements of actual history woven into the fantasy plot. As they debated the merits of various plot choices, he puzzled over his unusual response to her, his continual need to gain insight into her mind even as carnal images invaded his thoughts, holding him on the razor edge of desire.

When she squirmed against him with her fingernails digging into his forearm at the scene where he emerged from the aqueduct shirtless with a knife in his mouth, Tod grinned. He stifled a laugh at her satisfied "Hmpft!" in the scene where the nuns pulverized him. It seemed his darling sexy Shannon was decidedly frustrated with being unsatisfied. She had adorable kitten claws she wanted to sharpen. And by all the realms, he was more than willing to feel their bite.

As the movie ended, the flight attendant came around to collect their dinner trays. After handing out blankets, pillows, and eye masks, the crew dimmed the lights to allow passengers to sleep the last five hours of flight time.

Wrapping the two woven throws around them, Tod cuddled Shannon to his chest in the faint light from someone's screen several rows up. A few snores surrounded them as more passengers fell asleep. Yet Shannon didn't relax into sleep. With her thighs fidgeting and every squirm of her ass against him firing his blood, there was only one conclusion. Arousal thrummed too heavily in her lush little body. Tightening his grip on his desire, Tod slid his hand down under the blankets to play over her jean-clad sex. She gasped, jerking in his arms at the contact, and he muffled his groan at the tantalizing warmth detectable under his fingertips. Bor's beard, but he wanted to tear away the interfering fabric layers.

"Let me help you, darling. I can feel your frustration," Tod murmured.

Her hand covered his and shifted his fingers slightly. She bit her lip, trying and failing to hold back a whimper, but it didn't matter. He'd muffled the little sensual sound before it escaped their secluded bubble. Only he got to enjoy her mewls.

"That's it. Let go," he encouraged, as her hips moved restlessly against his circling fingers. Her breathing shortened, turning choppy, while he relentlessly drove her arousal higher. Despite his raging instincts, Tod continued to talk to her, kiss her neck, and describe the darkly erotic things he wanted to do with her, some of the fantasies that had tormented him over the last few hours.

She writhed in his arms, nails biting into his forearms in carnal demand. Fuck, he wanted her clawing his back with those little fingernails as he... *Stop torturing yourself, you Norns-cursed idiot.*

Tod's other hand shifted to her breast, pinching the nipple between thumb and forefinger.

Her breath caught, held, and he bit her neck as he clung to his control with fierce determination. Knowing she was on the cusp, he forced the seam of her jeans to apply the pressure she needed. She trembled, the orgasm shaking her within the cradle of his torso. Fuck, she was glorious.

After almost five hours of keeping her in a state of frustrated arousal, he wasn't surprised when she fell asleep. With the intoxicating heat radiating into his cupped hand and the hints of her warm scent tantalizing him, he couldn't force himself to release her.

So near, yet so far.

Leaning his head back against the seat, he tried to convince his body to follow her into sleep. Still, Shannon's soft, warm form plagued him, keeping him hard through the next four hours as he considered the different ways he was going to enjoy her. It didn't help when her hands covered his, holding them to her as if she craved his touch, even in her slumber.

Of course, when she woke, she lifted her fingers in a sudden startled movement that had Tod chuckling. "I don't mind you showing me exactly where you want my hands, darling."

She twisted around. "Tod! Oh my gods!" She blushed, and he had to restrain the overwhelming urge to kiss her.

"Yes?" He smiled, raising a finger to gently brush the hair back from her face.

“I... uhhh.” Hazel eyes dazed, she appeared both sleepy and aroused. Beautiful.

“I think we could both use something to clear the morning fog. They will start the tea service shortly. We aren’t too far from landing now.” Tod continued to stroke her soft cheek and silky hair. The overhead lights flickered on as the flight attendants began moving along the aisles.

Tod shared a couple cups of strong tea with Shannon, and the last of the sleepiness disappeared from her expression. While she pulled out her phone and checked the time, his internal clock told him it was early afternoon in London.

“Please put away your large electronics. Raise your seatbacks and tray tables into their upright and locked position for landing. We will be coming around to pick up any last service items, and expect to be on the ground in the next thirty minutes” crackled over the speaker.

Shannon shifted back fully into her seat, a light flush on her cheeks as her eyes flickered to Tod, then away. Yggdrasil’s roots, she was adorable. Yet the loss of her warm body cuddled against his opened a dark pit inside him, an emptiness that had him flexing his hands, fighting to not yank her back. Instincts screamed he couldn’t let this woman escape him.

She was his.

With a teasing grin, Tod reached over and fastened her seat belt, then wrapped his arm around her, playing with her hair as he considered how best to ensnare her. She had her conference tomorrow, and he had a red-carpet event tonight. Was it fair to expose her to that? Being seen with him, she’d be photographed, hounded, and harassed by the paps. Not that it was unusual for Tod to bring dates to these events. He rarely went solo.

But damn it, he wanted her for longer than a quick shag. And there were advantages to having her linked with him by the media.

Holding her in his arms as she’d slept had been torturous, but also satisfying in a way he couldn’t define. It had been so long since he’d wanted that connection with someone, so long since he’d dared allow himself more. At a minimum, he desired her in his bed the full week that she was in London. She... pulled at him, drew him, more than any other had in ages.

Yes, she was his. Decision made, the only question remaining was how best to convince her to spend that time with *him*. If he had to seduce her repeatedly to get that, well, he wasn’t above deviousness to obtain what he wanted.

After a few minutes, he took her chin, turning her to face him, his stomach twisting. "I know you have your conference starting tomorrow, but would you spend the rest of today with me? I've got a special movie preview showing to attend if you are interested?"

Chapter 4

BUSINESS OR PLEASURE

Shannon wanted to make changes in her life, and well, here was her first opportunity, gift-wrapped and handed to her. Tod's eyes planned some devilment, clearly, but she also caught a hint of vulnerability as he waited for her answer. What on earth did he have to worry about? Was he seriously thinking she might say no? After *that* demonstration of sensual mastery? Heat surged through her body, curling her toes with the intensity of her interest in everything his invitation suggested.

"Yes, I'd love to spend the rest of today with you." And night, too.

She had no idea why he'd chosen plain old her, but she was no fool to refuse. While she didn't want the emotional tangle of a real relationship after her ex-fiancé's nasty games and the unwelcome reminder yesterday, there was no risk of that with Tod.

He only wanted a smoking hot fling.

It was the perfect solution to her prolonged sexless stretch. After several years of a progressively toxic relationship with Trent, and another few years of keeping men at a distance, Shannon was fed up with doing without. It seemed Tod was of a similar mindset if his flirting and invitation were any indication. He was aware she was only in London for the week, so whether he only wanted the single night or the week, she was going to hit that.

Plus, the man definitely knew his way around the female body. Oh my gods. If the orgasm he'd given her was a demonstration of his skills, sign her up for the *full* lesson.

Tod smiled, his expression brightening at her answer. As the plane made its final descent, they settled the logistics of getting to the event and Shannon's hotel afterwards, then discussed their favourite breakfast foods. Although they agreed on eggs, bacon, sausage, and shredded potatoes by the time the wheels bumped down, they were in a heated debate over the merits of grilled tomatoes, baked beans, and black pudding when the plane finally pulled up to the gate.

Her nose wrinkled. "I might be willing to try black pudding."

"I'll make it worth your while," Tod teased, nibbling on her fingertips.

"Perhaps, but there is no way I'm eating baked beans. I've always hated beans!"

He laughed as he tugged her to her feet. "We'll see."

Tod stepped out into the aisle, retrieved his guitar, and took his blazer from the flight attendant with a polite acknowledgement. After unrolling his sleeves, he drew on his jacket.

Despite the hours in the air, he appeared so damn hot, Shannon wanted to jump him right there. Just take a nibble out of that sexy lower lip and slide her fingers over those broad shoulders and that steely chest she'd cuddled against.

Much to her chagrin, he caught her devouring him with her eyes and those tempting lips curved.

She glanced away as she lifted her backpack to her shoulder. Even the pain as the strap scraped over her bruised upper arm didn't dim the warmth colouring her cheeks.

He reached in to take her elbow and help her into the aisle. As she stepped in front of him, he leaned down, brushed the hair off her neck, and said in a deep, low voice, "If you don't stop looking at me like that, I'm going to haul you off into this airplane lavatory beside us to fuck you until you scream my name."

The tremor that rippled through Shannon's body had her catching the seats on either side to keep upright. Tod growled against her neck, and she bit her lip to stifle a whimper. Gods, maybe she should have joined the mile-high club.

On uncertain legs, she set off down the aisle with his hand a fiery brand on her lower back. She nodded farewell to the flight attendants, ever conscious of Tod behind her.

Once off the plane, he moved beside her, offering his arm, and presenting the image of a perfectly respectful English gentleman. The rock 'n' roll sex god who'd been growling and threatening to ravish her minutes earlier again hidden from sight. Yet being dangerous and dominant fit his reputation, his flirtatious playboy persona, far more than this portrayal of impeccable old-world manners. There were hidden depths to this man. Each glimpse was intriguing, drawing the part of her that was endlessly curious, always seeking answers.

He quirked an eyebrow at her hesitation. A slight smirk played at the edge of his lips. Clearly, he had himself under control, a control he hadn't demonstrated on the plane when he'd been kissing her senseless or, gods, turning her boneless with pleasure. When she remained undecided, debating the wisdom of accepting, Tod chuckled.

"You are safe for the moment, darling." His wicked wide smile taunted her.

But hell, it wasn't just *his* control Shannon worried about. Despite the clear insanity of it, *she* might be the one to drag them off to a dark corner at this rate. Something about this man had her wanting to fling off all convention and jump him like a hormonal teenager, regardless of anyone around them. Her fingers itched to reach out to him, to touch, to explore. Never had she had such a hard time restraining herself. Not even when she'd *been* a hormonal teenager.

What was it about him that drew her so strongly? With another long look, she wrapped her arm around his elbow. His body heat sank into her, and she couldn't help but lean into his warmth. As he led them through the airport and to customs and immigration, she considered the question. His attentiveness on the plane had been refreshing—a mix of pertinent questions that demonstrated he'd listened to everything she said, but still, there was no doubt he'd appreciated her as a woman. And perhaps that was it. The headiness of a wildly attractive man recognizing both her intelligence and her femininity, with no ulterior motive.

Unlike her ex, Tod didn't gain any career advancement from sex with her. He didn't want authorship on her papers or grants, or to steal her research. Instead, Tod seemed to want sex with her for herself and his motive to ask her questions about her research was just his interest, not what he could get from her. And yeah, she liked it... a lot. Holy hell, he had a way about him that made everything else drop away, like they were the only ones present. It had been a long time since anyone had looked at her like she was the most important person around.

"What's the purpose of your visit to the United Kingdom? Business or pleasure?" the customs official asked, drawing Shannon's attention.

"Bit of both, I suspect, if he has his way." Shannon nodded towards Tod, who was not inconspicuously waiting for her to clear. Although he drew plenty of admiring attention and some requests for autographs, security continued to move the fans along. And amazingly, Tod's eyes remained on her whenever she glanced toward him. Why he wanted her when he had so many younger, more beautiful, thinner options attempting to gain his interest, she didn't know but she sure wasn't going to complain. Fuck's sake, she could almost feel the heat of his gaze travelling over her body. It didn't help that her mind kept replaying Tod's wicked words. She shifted her weight and tried not to fidget.

"Ah, lucky fellow then," the agent said, an amused half-smile as he stamped her passport, then returned her documents. "Enjoy your time in the UK, Doctor Murphy."

"I believe I will. Thanks." She bit her lip as a lick of erotic heat shimmered down her spine.

Proffering his arm again as she reached him, Tod led her outside as security prevented his fans from following. Although distracted by him, she still blinked at the camera flashes as they passed. No doubt he'd be featured in some gossip rag. Her lips quirked. What would they make of her? Likely not the usual flattering stories she'd enjoyed when the media interviewed her about her research. Not with his reputation. No, they'd probably tear her appearance apart. She almost sighed. Not like Trent hadn't already picked her apart thoroughly over and over.

When they arrived at a white Aston Martin, he took her backpack and placed it with his guitar in the trunk before opening her door. His gentlemanly actions had her wondering which was the real him. They seemed to be unconscious acts, like he'd not thought about the small courtesies, despite their incongruity with his impatient rock god reputation—snarling at pushy fans and paparazzi. Did he take such care with... everything? Shannon's thoughts wandered into fantasy as she recalled her dreams and his devilishly sinful whispers.

He pressed the ignition switch, and a throaty roar rumbled.

"Nice car," she said, running a fingertip over the sleek black dash. "I'm surprised they haven't asked you to be their spokesperson."

His eyes gleamed. "Who says they haven't? I just haven't said yes, yet." He backed up and eased out of the lot.

Shannon grinned at the wink he gave her, then laughed as she was pressed back into her seat with the acceleration onto the highway. She'd never been a bad girl. She'd never ridden in fast cars or dated the bad boy. The idea of having a fling with Tod, the epitome of a bad boy, had bubbles of excitement bursting within her chest. Yes, this week, she'd be wicked, flirtatious... explore her inner hussy. She'd buy those magazines when she got home, laugh at the images and stories no matter how much they tore her up, and make herself a scrapbook to remind herself that she could let loose once in a while. She was done being good, being responsible. She was a tenured full professor, and damn it, her choices in her personal life were her own. Maybe she didn't need to change universities and risk setting her career, her research, back a year as she transferred. Maybe she just needed to have some godsdamn *fun*.

Tod wove expertly through traffic. After a relatively short thirty-minute drive, he exited the highway onto London city streets. Soon, they were through a gated entrance into another small parking lot. Before she could think of opening her door, Tod was there, helping her out of the low-slung vehicle. With her backpack on his shoulder and his guitar in hand, he wrapped his free arm around her waist to direct her to the elevator.

Pressed against his leanly muscled form, Shannon had a hard time paying attention to her surroundings, especially in the wake of her resolve to enjoy herself. She eyed the elevator stop button, tempted to give in as he swiped his card. A bad girl would do it. Before she could decide, the elevator rose to the top floor and opened to an entrance foyer with a single white door. Another swipe of his card and they were inside.

"Welcome to my flat," he said with a sweeping bow.

Distracting herself from the desire simmering through her veins, she took in his home. Soaring ceilings and a back wall of windows, with few interior walls made it bright and open concept. To the right, a large white wall stretched the length of the space, with only a single break for a doorway. On the closer portion, a large TV was mounted above a stone fireplace. Several black leather couches were organized in a seating area facing the fireplace, and past it sat a gleaming black baby grand piano, a small desk, a music stand, and a few backless stools.

Shelves with electronics filled the far wall, maybe some kind of sound system, until it met the windows of the back wall.

In front of her, the entrance tiles gave way to an open kitchen, with green marble counters and rich wood cupboards below. There were no upper cabinets, just a backsplash that appeared to be smoothed river stone, and open shelves with dishes, glasses, and mugs. It had the feel of bringing the outdoors inside. The temperate rainforest aesthetic reminded Shannon of her home, and her shoulders relaxed, losing a tension she hadn't realized she'd been carrying.

Beyond the kitchen, dining table, and a well-stocked bar, French doors led out into an expansive green roof area, complete with small trees and an infinity pool. As nice as it was, she wouldn't trade it for her ocean view or the forest surrounding her home.

It seemed they also shared a love of books. Through one of the doorways to the left, she glimpsed a library, with floor-to-ceiling bookshelves and a comfy couch or two. What authors did he like? If she got the chance, she'd browse his collection.

Tod watched her take it all in, a little smile on his face.

"I love the earth tones. It's similar to what I would have chosen."

Smiling more broadly like he was pleased with her assessment, he took her hand and led her to the open doorway between the wall of electronics and the fireplace. It was a bedroom. His bedroom, she realized after taking in the clothes laying across a chair, books on one of the nightstands, and the massive king sized bed dominating the space. Her pulse began to race. Was he planning to fuck her senseless before they left for the movie? Her sex clenched. Gods, yes please.

"As much as I want to ravish you, we only have ninety minutes to refresh from our travel, eat, and then get to the show's venue." He stepped into a walk-in closet and returned seconds later with a couple of folded white towels. "Why don't you shower and change, and I'll whip up some food. Sound good?"

Shannon's inner wanton suggested discarding her clothes and demanding he take her up against the wall. To hell with waiting. Yet, her logical side insisted there was value in delaying until they could take their time and explore each other. Be thorough in their ravishment.

Restraining her pout, she said, "That sounds fabulous." The smile she beamed at Tod was as much for him as it was in amusement at her own suddenly demanding inner bad girl.

Ugh. She was so ridiculously horny for this man. Maybe she should just—

After handing her the towels, he reached for her hair but halted. "Nope, I better not kiss you or all my good intentions will vanish. We wouldn't make the show at all." With a long exhale, he stepped back while lowering his hand. "Off you go, darling, before I regret my decision more than I already do."

Warmth curled through her, coiling in her abdomen. He seemed to be walking the same conflicted tightrope of desire between rushing and waiting. A shiver raised gooseflesh on her skin, and she revelled in the heady feeling of her awakened femininity. Swaying her hips, she glided into the bathroom.

Oh my gods. She pressed the towels to her face. Had he really groaned as she walked away? She grinned as she closed the bathroom door between them, barely muffling her squee of delight.

The rainforest colour scheme continued with the large emerald green marble sunken tub and separate walk-in river-stone shower. While admiring the spaciousness, Shannon placed the towels on the matching marble counter. Ferns sat on stands throughout the room and along the side of the tub. Comforting and familiar, it was like she was about to jump into one of the many creeks around her home.

After stripping off her travel-wrinkled clothes, she gratefully stepped into the cascade pouring from the waterfall-like spout in the shower's ceiling. The soap smelled of oranges—a scent she'd forever equate with Tod now. While washing from head to toe in the heated flow, and trying to resist imagining him in the shower with her, she stretched muscles that had tightened on the long plane ride. Refreshed and excited, she shut off the flow and wrapped herself in the fluffy white towels.

Drying her almost waist-length hair was usually a pain, but the towels were amazingly effective, leaving her hair only slightly damp. Curious, she flipped the towel around, searching unsuccessfully for a tag. She'd have to ask. Wherever it was he shopped, Shannon wanted some.

With another towel tight around her body, she halted. Shit. She'd left her backpack in his bedroom. After blowing out a nervous breath, she opened the door and her bag fell over into the doorway.

Damn, Tod continued to impress.

"How formal is this shindig? Are we talking jeans or dress?" she shouted as she picked up her backpack and unzipped the centre section.

"Definitely dress," Tod called back.

Her options were limited, but she wanted to wow him. At least, as much as she was capable. Damn it, why hadn't she packed her Spanx? Although, maybe she didn't need them. She recalled his groan and bounced on her toes, excitement bubbling within her like champagne. Gods, she loved the idea that he was lusting after her. If she could make him lose that rigid control, tempt him into misbehaving with her, all the better. A thrill of electricity sparked through her. Could she tempt him into making out with her like horny teenagers in the back of the movie theatre? She'd never done it, but as she pressed her thighs together, she couldn't deny she wanted to.

As usual, her strategy had been to pack light with things she could mix and match. She'd brought one basic black dress with a cowl neckline, calf-length with a slit up to mid-thigh. Instead of the all-purpose flats she'd worn on the plane, she paired the dress with silver stiletto heels. A royal-blue and silver wrap provided a pop of colour and helped hide the dark-purple bruises on her upper arm.

Damn that asshole Trent. Embarrassing enough she'd fallen for his shit. To still be dealing with his crap years later... She scowled and dug into her backpack. Fortunately, she'd packed foundation and used a practiced dab to cover the violent marks, a skill she'd gotten far too good at.

But she wasn't going to focus on that. Not now. Not when she had a smoking hot man waiting for her to stretch her wings with. Platinum and sapphire drop earrings, bracelets, and a necklace completed the look. She added smoky eyes and her favourite ruby lip balm from her small supply of cosmetics.

Done, she wrinkled her nose at herself in the mirror. It would have to do.

Shannon left the bathroom and returned to the main area in her bare feet, shoes swinging from the tips of her fingers. Tod didn't seem to hear her over the sizzling of the frying pan. Taking advantage of the chance to watch him unnoticed, she leaned against a nearby couch back.

That characteristic seductive purr of his voice rose and fell with devastating effect on her senses—the song lyrics emerging as he moved back and forth, dancing between the pan and the plates he was filling. She was spellbound, a shiver rippling over her skin.

He'd removed his jacket and rolled up his sleeves again. Seriously, the man knew how to move his hips. Damn. That ass should come with a warning label, like *caution, may cause spontaneous panty combustion in the State of California.* Hell, every bloody US state and Canadian province, too.

It was all she could do to fight to keep her hands and the rest of her body parts to herself, like a moth irresistibly drawn to a flame even though it might burn to ash. Her fingertips tingled with the intensifying need to reach out, to touch him. Down low, her centre heated, melted, and flowed like honey. If someone told Shannon she was literally drooling, she would have believed them in that instant.

Tod turned, and their eyes connected.

Time stopped.

Her heart skipped a beat, then picked up again at a rapid tempo. She was frozen in place, immobilized by his smouldering gaze.

Without glancing away, Tod flipped off the gas burner.

She tried not to stare as he prowled over. Really, she did. He moved like a jungle cat, smooth, dangerous, and with purpose.

Chapter 5

RED CARPET AFFAIR

At the first glimpse of Shannon wrapped in slinky black fabric that caressed her full curves, Tod forgot the lyrics he was composing. Instead, the melody he'd heard was reduced to a drum beat, his heart thundering with need, cock punching to full mast in a primal reaction to the sensual vision before him. With irresistible magnetic force, he moved closer—as unable to deny the motion as to form a rational thought. That silky skin that so tempted him had his fingers reaching, stretching... Greasy smears on his fingertips, the sensation slick, halted Tod a mere fraction from touching her. Eyes closing, he clenched his fists and lowered his arms, fighting the need to close the distance between them.

Jaw flexing, he gritted, "Darling, you are absolutely stunning. I need you to go into the kitchen and eat, out of my line of sight, so I can go get ready without completely losing my head." Every breath drew her scent in, surrounding him with that delicate warm lemony vanilla mixed with the body wash he favoured. Instincts roared, a flare of heat washing over his skin. Yes, he loved his scent mixed with hers, marking his claim on her.

Shannon might not know it yet, but she was his.

Every moment she hesitated, his pulse pounded harder, hotter, building like a pressure within his chest, in his groin. Almost at the point of damning the consequences, his muscles flexed to—

She stepped away. Light footpads on the hardwood floor led behind him to the kitchen, followed by the slight scrape of a stool changing position. At the first clink of her fork on the plate he'd prepared, a shudder shook him and he strode to the bedroom without another word or backward glance. He didn't dare look. Not yet. Not until he'd gotten himself under control.

Clothes gone with barely a thought, he flipped on the shower and stepped into the hot spray. He snarled as he cleaned himself and wrapped a fist around his impatient shaft. He had a plan, damn it—her being seen and photographed with him tonight would remove any objection she'd have about spending the week with him because of the paparazzi. Devious. He stroked harder, the image of her branded in his mind. Yeah, he knew he was being fucking devious by claiming her that way, but better to rip the Band-Aid off than have his fame be an excuse.

Besides, she'd melted at the idea of a little exhibitionism. Not that he'd actually share the sight of her. As his thighs trembled and his spine turned rigid with the building pleasure singing along his nerve endings, he knew he'd only taken the edge off. Shannon was a fire in his blood that no amount of water would quench.

After rinsing the evidence down the drain, he shaved, slapped off the shower, and with quick efficiency, dried and dressed in a black bespoke suit with a black turtleneck that allowed him to avoid the need for a tie—a signature red-carpet look for him. Another image briefly overlaid the one in the mirror. Another version of him in unrelenting black.

Was he being too ruthless? Being unfair to Shannon by claiming and seducing her? Fist clenched, he shook off the questions, the doubt. Leaving his mental image behind, he prowled toward the kitchen. A warm glow sparked in his chest. She'd cleaned her plate, eating the full English breakfast he'd prepared for her.

As she turned from placing her dishes in the dishwasher under the island counter, she caught sight of him and gasped. Her cheeks flushed and her eyes fluttered closed as he approached. By the Nine, she was gorgeous. Stopping with a few centimetres between them, he put his finger under her chin to tilt her face up. "Open your eyes, darling."

Her lashes rose, granting him those intelligent hazel depths that so fascinated him. Her chest rose and fell, shallow, rapid breaths painting the air between them. That unruly beast between his legs raised its head and roared its approval in steely salute. How was he to resist her long enough to get her to the venue? Especially with the counter so close behind her and the perfect height for him to finally taste the nectar he craved?

Unable to hold the truth from her with the desire so clear in her gaze, he murmured, "You are deadly to my self-control, sweet Shannon. I find myself thinking such wicked thoughts that I can scarcely hold back from making reality." His thumb caressed the satin of her cheek as he took in every detail of her features, including a silvery crescent-shaped scar on her left temple that bisected her eyebrow and a tiny wedge cut from the top edge of her ear. What stories did these minor imperfections tell? "Your dilated pupils, rapid heartbeat, and flushed cheeks tell me the response is mutual, but if I've misread, I need you to speak up. This desire has taken on a life of its own, that not even the repeated assistance of my hand and imagination can seem to tamp down in your presence."

Her nostrils flared and a whimpered moan escaped as her eyelids lowered to hide her gaze. But it was the sight of her pink tongue wetting her lips and her full-body shiver that had him growling, "Bloody fucking hell, woman, you are killing me!" The ideas he had for that mouth, that tongue. She inspired no shortage of fantasies he planned to enact.

Shannon met his gaze again, retorting, "You're the one who is the walking orgasm."

Tod's eyebrow rose, lips twitching as she gestured to his body. Yeah, she'd be orgasming all right. Over and over and over. In every way he could think of.

She laughed. "Gods, talk about meltdown."

Tod snorted. "It's certainly not food I'm hungry for. We should go now so we aren't late." He held out his elbow for her, and Shannon slipped on the sexiest silver heels that immediately sparked images of those heels wrapped around his waist as he plunged into her heat. Fuck. He was going to have a permanent imprint of his zipper on his damn cock at this rate. Teeth grinding at the visceral desire, the sheer inferno of need snapping and searing at the threads of his control, Tod led her down to the car, then wove through the London streets with only a fraction of his mind. As fast as he pushed erotic fantasies out of his thoughts, they returned.

Halting at the line of cars, they inched along until he stopped at the start of the red carpet. After tossing the keys to a valet, he opened Shannon's door, waving off another valet's assistance. No way was anyone else touching her. She was his. He helped her to her feet and tucked her hand into the crook of his elbow.

Her gaze taking in the surroundings, Shannon muttered, "Well, I'm glad I wore a posh dress, considering you didn't tell me it was a red-carpet affair."

Tod smiled and met her eyes. "Darling, if you were any sexier, we would never have made it out of my flat." He patted her hand, then glanced around them. "You don't have to talk to anyone. Just stick with me, please. I don't want some fool attempting to hit on you." His voice dropped to a low growl with a muttered, "It won't go well for them." Even the idea had him fighting not to snarl at nearby men, to warn them away.

"Same, Tod. I won't appreciate it if some woman puts her hands on you."

Tod blinked and met her gaze. A fierce light lit those hazel eyes from within, and the set of her jaw told him she meant every word. Warmth curled in his chest and his lips quirked. Possessiveness wasn't something he usually tolerated in his dates, but from her... yeah, he liked Shannon claiming him. He nodded his agreement and squeezed her fingers lightly.

The red carpet had its usual chaotic demands to turn this way or that for photos. Exactly as he'd expected, a flood of questions bombarded them—who was Shannon, were they dating, where did they met—as well as requests for autographs. Tod stopped every few metres, posed with her on his arm, and then waived off the requests and questions. He had no doubt that Shannon would be linked with him on every major media site providing coverage for the event.

Yes, the damage was done. No longer would the potential of his fame or reputation be an impediment to her spending this time with him. Indeed, she'd need his assistance to shield her from the paps' relentless pursuit, and his flat was far more secure than a hotel. Perhaps he could get her to cancel her reservation entirely and stay with him. That would be ideal.

Tod greeted his fellow actors, writers, directors, and others on the carpet that he knew with a quick hello, never lingering. With the first part of his plan accomplished, he didn't need to loiter and he whisked her along through the crowd.

Until the big, red-haired behemoth blocked his path. Damn him.

Chapter 6

PANDORA'S BOX

Sweat trickled down Shannon's back, and her cheeks hurt from smiling. Like running a gauntlet, this was so much more intense than the media interviews and film crews she'd dealt with on occasion. Faces and words blurred into a cacophony until a massively built man with a chest and shoulders twice her width halted their progress. He crossed thick arms over the ice blue Henley and navy blazer covering his chest, a single eyebrow raised.

"Aren't you going to introduce me, brother?" His deep voice rumbled, almost vibrating Shannon's lungs.

He was as tall as Tod but wider and thicker compared to Tod's quarterback frame. While they shared bright auburn hair, this man's was much longer and tied back in a queue at the base of his neck. With the same pale wolf-blue eyes and narrow lips on a square jaw, his brother was undoubtedly handsome despite the slightly uneven jog to his nose that gave evidence of a past break.

"Fine," Tod sighed. Flashing Shannon a quick smile, he said, "This enormous beast is Tempest, my older brother. Tem, this is Doctor Shannon Murphy, a brilliant and beautiful scientist far too good for the likes of you."

Shannon blinked and her cheeks flushed. He thought she was beautiful and brilliant? Really? Even if Tod was only being polite, the compliments gave her a lovely glow. It had been a long time since a man complimented her on anything other than her science. She basked in the feeling as she held out her hand and searched her memory. She was sure her sister had drooled over Tempest Corvus at some point. He was famous in his own right. Some kind of... sport. "Nice to meet you, Tempest. You play professional... rugby?" The answer popped into her mind as she started to flounder.

Tempest's smile widened as his hand engulfed hers. Yet for all his huge size, he didn't try to squeeze or prove his strength. Instead, he was gentle, exerting just the right amount of pressure. How refreshing. "I did, yes. But I've since retired from the Leicester Tigers and abandoned the UK to my little brother. I own the Sydney Wreckers, a pro club in Australia. Although, of late I've been following Tod into the sexy action star business." He waggled his eyebrows at Tod with a glint in his eyes.

"Yeah, that's enough of that," Tod said, prying Tempest's fingers open to release hers. "Stop flirting with my date."

What? Shannon blinked. He hadn't been flirting with her. Why would Tod think—

Tempest laughed, a big booming sound that had others around them smiling in response. There was something very likeable about Tod's brother. But although he was attractive, she felt no hint of interest in him.

"It was a pleasure to meet you, Shannon." Demands for Tempest's attention grew louder as a slender man tried to draw him toward a set of cameras.

"Likewise," she murmured.

"Go. Do your interviews," Todd told him, waving his brother off and shaking his head when Tempest finally left. "He's filming a movie in the same universe as my assassin series." With a hand at her back, Tod led her into the building.

The escape from the shouts left Shannon's ears ringing. She exhaled a relieved breath. That kind of fame wasn't anything she'd ever sought for herself. Good gods, who could live like that?

"Let's go find seats," Tod suggested.

"Sounds good," she agreed.

Instead of one large theatre, the building was divided into numerous smaller theatres. Although they all had a big screen, each theatre was unique, with eclectic seating ranging from benches to couches, to reclining chairs, and even bar stools with high-top tables.

"What's your preference?" Tod gestured to the various doors.

After Shannon chose a theatre with couches and reclining chairs, they settled into a deep loveseat with an ottoman at the back corner of the room. Perfect for her plan to tempt him. When Tod removed her wrap to lay it on her lap and put his arm around her while they waited, she smiled and leaned against him.

But as her bruised arm pressed against a hard edge in his jacket, she flinched and bit back her pained gasp. What the fuck was that? His phone? Careful to not brush it again, she turned into his body and tucked her arm under his to keep it hidden. Godsdamned Trent. Bad enough the ugly mark was there. She did *not* want Tod asking about it. Shit. Or finding out about her embarrassing ex she couldn't seem to get rid of. Not exactly hot, sexy fling-type conversation. Who wanted to admit to being so stupid? Besides, no sexual partner ever wanted to hear about a previous one.

Fortunately, Tod was in the mood to distract.

Her negative musings scattered as his fingertips caressed her arm, elbow to shoulder and back again. Then up to her neck, or down to her inner wrist and back again. The light touch created shivers, raising gooseflesh. She loved the teasing, even as it drove her wild. When the lights dimmed, Tod's name whispered across her lips, and their eyes met. Had he already been thinking along the same lines as she had?

His mouth turned up in a little wicked smile, and he blew lightly on her neck. A wave of electricity rippled over her. Her back arched as she gasped involuntarily, nipples tightening to hard points while her fingers dug into his thigh. Holy fuck. What was it about this man? She'd never been aroused so quickly, so effortlessly.

Instead of stopping his sweet torture, Tod lifted her over his leg to sit between his now-spread thighs.

Shannon's heart thundered, and she glanced around them. "Won't someone see us?" Not that she truly cared. After all, wasn't this her chance to live in the moment, to channel her inner bad girl she'd never before let loose?

"No, it's dark enough back here. There's no one behind us, and I'll make sure no one notices."

How would he... But he distracted her from further questions by shifting her hair to the side. His lips found the nape of her neck. Pleasure spiked, her fingers flexing, and she scraped her nails on his thighs. His every touch had her complete and utter attention.

She wasn't sure what he'd planned, but whatever it was, she wanted it and she wanted it here. The eroticism of the public place, the dark, warm theatre, and the bad boy cradling her between his legs fired her desire to searing intensity. She hadn't been sure she'd have the courage to make the first move, but she needn't have worried. It was almost like he'd read her mind.

As the movie's opening theme started, his fingertips glided over her shoulders. A moment of panic had her jolting, but he missed the bruise as his touch continued to the tender flesh of her inner arms, then to her hands, which he caught in his larger ones. He nibbled along the base of her neck. Shannon's core clenched, and she bit her lip to hold back a rising moan. Gods, it was as if he knew her every erogenous zone without having to ask.

Pushing back against him revealed evidence of his own burgeoning desire, his rigid length tantalizing against her ass. Need surged—a drumbeat pulsing in her veins. Her hands flexed in his firm grip. Being unable to reach him, to touch him, increased the intensity of her craving to explore him.

"I am going to make you come, but only if you remain quiet. Can you do that for me?" he purred against her ear.

Sparking prickles shot through her as if she'd touched a live wire. "Yes," she breathed.

Without further warning, Tod eased his hand under the wrap and into the slit of her dress. He tugged the opening, pulling the fabric to her hips. Wrapping a hand around her thigh, he lifted her knee onto his and spread her legs wide using the cage of his own.

Shannon scarcely dared breathe as those long fingers teased their way up her inner thigh. Her heart pounded, anticipation rising. Lightly, he brushed over the gusset of her thong, leaving tingling in his wake.

"Someone has been thinking very naughty thoughts to have soaked her knickers right through. That is so fucking hot, darling," he murmured.

"Totally your fault," she whispered. Holy fuck, but she loved him talking dirty as he teased. Why the hell had she waited so long to do something this wild?

Moving the thong to the side, he stroked lightly over her heated flesh, before parting her to dance over the quivering nerves at her apex. A bolt of electricity shot up her spine. Her teeth clenched to muffle a gasp as her hips jerked in reaction. Impossible to deny. No way could she still the desperate movement as his intimate touch shocked her system.

Tod released her hands to pin her hips—a muscular arm wrapped low around her waist. Even so, her body writhed. But his strength held her fast, as those clever fingers stroked, tapped, and circled in a merciless rhythm. Good gods. It was like trying to ride lightning.

Frantic, her heart pounded faster, like it would leap right out of her chest. She gripped his thighs as she fought to keep her breath shallow. Muscles quivered under the onslaught. Only his firm hold kept her hips from bucking. As if she were a champagne bottle, the pressure built within her with relentless force, and she struggled to stay quiet.

"Come," he demanded as he bit her neck.

Helpless to resist, Shannon slapped a hand over her mouth to muffle her cry as the orgasm bubbled up through her, up her spine, and out her head in an explosive surge. Ripples of sensation rolled over her skin in waves.

Holy shit! Silently, she panted, trying to recover as he continued to play with her, teasing around her opening.

"Mmm, I liked that," he murmured.

A whimpered agreement slipped from behind her hand. It had been incredible. She couldn't remember the last time she'd climaxed so hard. Maybe she'd never come that hard. It was impossible to think, to remember with his fingers continuing to tantalize.

And he didn't let her rest. No, instead his strokes grew more insistent, driving her arousal up again. She wouldn't have thought it possible so fast, so soon, but he was relentless.

Still, the pulsing of her core created an empty ache, an instinctual need to be filled. As if he'd sensed it, two fingers dove inside, curling to find just the right spot, as his thumb circled and pressed against the sensitive bud.

Bloody everlasting fuck! How...

Driving her insane, the pleasure was almost too much. She fought to hold in a scream while the heat built into an inferno, searing all concept of restraint.

"More," he growled in her ear. "I want you to come again."

It was as if her body was keyed into his words, and he had all the passcodes. As she helplessly trembled in reaction, he drove her to orgasm again, and yet again, in the warm darkness of the room while the movie played. Blind to her surroundings, pulse pounding in her ears and thoughts scattered, she could scarcely recover between waves. Her body spasmed around his merciless fingers at every thrusting movement.

At some point, he removed those clever digits from her centre and pulled down her dress.

With her thoughts fuzzy and body still buzzing, it took Shannon a minute to cooperate with his attempts to lift her from the loveseat and ottoman. Trembling and limp, her legs didn't want to respond. But with his arm tight around her waist, he half-carried her out a small nondescript door behind them.

He brought her down a dimly lit back hallway that lacked the gilt opulence of the public spaces. The first few doors Tod opened had rooms filled with shelves and cardboard boxes. When a small office was revealed behind the next plain wooden door, Tod drew her inside. In the next moment, a click sounded, and a small desk lamp flickered to life, providing shadowy illumination.

"What?" she managed before he lifted her onto the cold metal desk, shoving the paperwork, pens and other clutter onto the floor with a crash.

"I'm done waiting," he growled.

Her sex clenched. *Oh my.* "Then fuck me, Tod." Even as the words left her in a husky challenge, a part of her wondered where this bold wanton had come from. Where had she gained the confidence, the strength to bluntly demand what she wanted?

His predatory expression darkened, and she shivered. Gods, wherever this boldness had come from, she liked it. She wanted him, hard and deep, pounding her into this desk.

Slowly, he raised her dress above her hips. With their eyes locked, he ripped her thong off, then stared hungrily down at her aroused flesh. She'd never felt so desirable. The sheer carnality on his face had her spreading her thighs in explicit invitation.

He licked his lips, eyes rising to hers as he lifted her knees over his shoulders. Oh wow. Would he really? Trent hadn't liked oral sex. It had been so very long since anyone wanted to taste her.

Lowering his head, cool lips met heated skin as he kissed his way up one thigh. Bypassing her core, he ran his tongue up her other inner thigh, creating a fine trembling chaos in his wake.

"You are a tease," she whined, squirming.

He lifted his head for a minute to catch her eye, and a slow, sinful smile stretched his lips. Watching her expression with the unblinking intensity of a predator, he lowered his mouth to blow cool air across her core. "Such a pretty pink flower, blooming with nectar just for me." He licked a long stroke, and her hips jerked at the flash of sparking nerves.

Oh. My. Gods.

His eyes glinted, and his lips twisted into a smirk. "Enjoy that, do you, darling? So do I. Fuck, you taste like sunshine and lemons."

"Yes, oh gods yes," she whimpered as a small corner of her mind wondered what sunshine tasted like, while the remainder screamed, *please, please more.*

When he flicked his tongue, her thoughts shredded, scattered to the winds of the erotic storm brewing. Each talented stroke sent lightning strikes flaring outward. Not able to stay quiet, she covered her mouth with one hand to muffle her screams. Oh, holy fuck. It was so much better than she ever remembered. So much more. So good. Gods, so amazing.

Not hesitating now, Tod rapidly drove her to climax, scorching pleasure straight up her spine to sear her brain.

Breath sawed in and out of her heaving lungs and a second heartbeat throbbed in her core. It took longer for her to become aware again in the aftermath. Holy hell. Had her brain leaked out her ears that time? Bad boys win. Absolutely. Why had she spent so many years being good? Fuck. She was a godsdamned idiot.

A rumbled purr vibrated against her sex. "I could eat you all day, but I can't wait. I've got to be inside you." He rose and swiftly unbuckled his pants with those long, clever, beautiful fingers.

Yes, oh yes. "Please." She tried to reach for him, but he was having none of it.

"No, not this time." He held her hand. She still tried, unable to help herself.

Growling, he took both of her hands in one of his and pinned them above her head on the desk. With his other hand, he teased his cock over her soaked folds, coating himself.

"Please." She writhed, fighting against his hand, trying to drive her hips up to impale herself, desperate to have him inside her, but unable to find enough leverage. The tip was positioned at her entrance, taunting her. She squirmed in frustration, needing him.

"Please! Oh my gods, please!" she begged.

A dark smile grew on his face as his hand came up to pin her throat to the desk, tight with warning, but not painful in any way. With her hands locked down as well, it was such a dominant hold that her instincts sat up to take notice. Not hurtful. Not like Trent's lazy forays into sex. He'd never expended the effort to dominate in bed. No, this wasn't something she was used to. Not at all. But it struck an visceral chord within her, nonetheless, and her sex clenched.

"Begging for your god, are you? Let me fulfill that desire."

Tod slowly filled her, a burning stretch despite how ready and wet she was, right on the threshold of pleasure and pain. It was exquisite. Perfect. Heat welled behind her eyes.

Once fully seated, he closed his eyes and groaned, speaking, but she couldn't understand his words.

Shannon writhed, needing him to move. "Please, please," she moaned, unable to articulate her needs.

When his lashes rose, that predatory gaze pinned her in place. Leaning over her, his face only inches from hers, he began pistoning in and out. She couldn't look away as those mesmerizing eyes changed from pale blue to brilliant deep emerald. His bright auburn hair darkened and lengthened to a thick, vibrant black cascading around them. Even his face narrowed to sharp-edged cheekbones, losing the dimples and the divot in his chin, and his skin lost its tan and took on an icy white cast, despite the flush to his cheeks.

Intensely aroused at the delicious friction of his cock with each hard thrust and the blatantly erotic hold on her neck and hands, Shannon shook her head. What? What was she seeing? Blinking, she tried to clear her vision, but still, his changed appearance remained. With her senses overloading, her thoughts fragmented as soon as they formed.

He maintained eye contact as his thrusts sped up, pounding her into the desk and inflaming her body. "You are mine, Shannon. Aren't you? Who do you belong to?" he demanded in a low rumble.

Belong to? She didn't understand and shook her head. How did he—

A tightening of his hand at her neck, hips driving into her. Each stroke searing ecstasy up her spine. She was falling into those unrelenting green eyes, eyes that wouldn't release her.

Why were they green?

"Tell me. Who do you belong to?"

The possessiveness and overwhelming dominance in his tone, his hold, and every move of his body had her instinctively tilting her chin up, giving him better access to her vulnerable throat, even as the words tumbled out of her mouth in a breathy moan. "You. I'm yours, all yours."

"*Loki*! You belong to Loki! To me!"

She writhed on the sharp spikes of intoxicating pleasure, unable to think, unable to understand.

"*Loki*! You belong to Loki! *Say it,* Shannon!" Releasing her hands, he circled her clit, driving her to the very edge of reason, to the abyss of sanity.

"Loki! I belong to you, Loki," she yelled, unable to imagine any other answer in the furious grip of passion's predacious teeth.

After removing his fingers from her throat, he grabbed the back of her neck, lifting her lips to his. "Come with me!" he demanded between fierce kisses.

Crying out into his kiss, she shattered, clenching around him. Wave after wave tore through her, the bursts of fireworks exploding from her centre and propelling her soul out into the cosmic ether. He roared something she didn't understand, then a long guttural moan escaped as he pulsed deep inside her, extending the waves of her climax.

They clung to each other, panting. He feathered kisses on her lips, cheeks, eyes, and down her neck, holding her there as their breathing finally calmed.

Until sanity returned.

Gently, he slid out of her, setting off another delayed orgasm while her body spasmed in reaction. He gathered her in his arms, turning to sit on the desk as she trembled, wrung out emotionally and physically. Staring up at him and his changed appearance, Shannon tried to get her exhausted, passion-fogged mind to work. With hesitant fingertips, she touched the dark hair tumbling around his shoulders. It was silky soft to the touch. Real. How could it be real? And he seemed taller and broader, or perhaps her limbs were just that weak. Why did she feel so small?

"I don't understand. Is this a dream? Am I asleep?" Did he sex her so good, she'd passed out? She patted his face and traced over his chin with its missing dent. Where did it go? Surely this wasn't real.

A rueful lopsided smile appeared as he stroked her face with featherlight touches. "I know. Yes, this is me, my actual appearance. Tod is me too, but he's a role I play, a character I invented to allow me to move around this world more easily. I've had many names over the years, but I was born Loki, an immortal god."

The more he talked, the more Shannon's head cleared. This was no dream. Not with the heat of his body soaking into her, his orange-and-smoky-cedar scent surrounding her, her every sense alive and awake.

A god? An actual fucking god? A walking, talking, fucking god?

No... no freaking way. Nope. Not possible. Gods were stories. They were allegories. They weren't real. No way.

Her calming heart pounded in her chest like it was preparing to take flight. A shiver rose the fine hairs on her skin. How did he change his appearance? What the hell was he? Superhuman, alien, a supernatural being? He couldn't be an actual god.

A sudden urge to laugh bubbled in her chest, and she forced it down. Who had she given herself over to so fully? He was good in the sack... no doubt about it. Bad boy to the bone, complete with hidden secrets.

Oh fuck.

She'd never been so vulnerable, never responded so quickly, so completely to another. Was this the consequence of channelling her bad girl side? This wasn't like her. How could she have just said she belonged to him? Fuck that. It was supposed to be sex. A hot fling. Not this intense connection. Just sex. Sex with... shit, was he Tod or Loki? What the hell was she supposed to call him? A god?

Nope. No—no—no. No way.

Keeping her face outwardly the same, she pushed up out of his arms.

"I need to go clean up." She tried to stand and staggered with more than post-coital weakness making her limbs tremble. She could barely look at him, at his changed features. Surely, this wasn't real?

"Are you okay to make it to the restroom?" His tone had lost its deep dominant growl and seemed almost hesitant as he added, "I'll come with you. It's my fault you can't walk."

After straightening her dress and pulling her wrap around her shoulders, he tidied his clothes with a wave of his hand and some kind of black mist, shrinking and returning his appearance to that of Tod.

Holy shit. Unnerving. She locked down her expression as all the spit dried in her mouth. Nope. No way did she want to reveal that she was freaking out. How would he react? What happened to mortals who found out about gods? There had to be some reason it stayed a secret. A cold sweat broke out on her back, and she shivered.

"Now that the cat is out of the bag, I'd like to be myself with you, but not here. I need to get you into a bath. You're going to be sore. I was..." He gave a little chuckle. "A little rough and should have restrained myself. You had me losing both my head and my control." His tone sounded apologetic, but how could she believe it when she couldn't even trust his appearance? "I can at least save you the walk. Hang onto me." He wrapped his arms around her.

In a blink, they were outside the women's restroom. Alarm shot through her, and she clenched her jaw, stifling her cry. Instead, she blurted, "How?"

"I teleported us. I can teleport a few kilometres." His lips twitched up in the corners, and he shrugged one shoulder as he pushed open the heavy metal door.

"I can manage." Shannon waved him off sharply to cover the jerkiness of her movements, fighting the fear she kept stuffing down, trying to keep it hidden.

Hands up, he backed away. "Okay, I'll be right here when you're done."

As soon as the door closed behind her, the panic she'd been denying surged like wildfire over dry prairie grass. With a metallic taste coating her tongue, she panted, eyes darting around her. Where? Where? She had to get the fuck out... away. Dashing to the far side of the long bathroom with its double row of stalls, she discovered a second exit.

Yes! Thank fuck!

After bolting out and down first one long hallway, then a short one, she located an employee side door.

Please... please... please.

Heart pounding, Shannon glanced behind her, then shoved the door open and strode down the dark street on weak, trembling legs. She flagged down a taxi. Once she'd given the driver her hotel address, she sank back into the seat, shaking. Thank gods she'd brought her little clutch purse. It had her wallet and passport. Anything else, she could replace.

Shannon was running, but whether she was running from Tod or what he'd made her feel, she wasn't yet willing to face.

All she knew was she needed to escape.

Chapter 7

DITCHED

Five minutes had become ten. Clenching and unclenching his hands, Loki paced the dimly lit hall with its dark blue carpet and gold wall sconces interspersed with current and upcoming movie posters. By fifteen minutes, he couldn't restrain the building tension within himself any longer. He pushed open the door.

"Shannon?" he called into the restroom.

No response.

"I'm coming in!"

He cautiously tapped the first metal stall door open—it was unoccupied. Loki moved to the next and gave it a light push. No one there. He slammed open the rest in rapid succession. Every stall in the long row was empty.

Totally empty.

No sign of her.

At the sight of the second entrance, his heart clenched. No! Oh Norns, please no! Running to reach it, he flung the door open and burst into another hall.

Empty.

He teleported to each end of the long, dimly lit hall that mirrored the one he'd waited in like a fool.

Nothing.

No sign of her anywhere.

Thor emerged from a nearby theatre as Loki strode back and forth across the carpeted floor, yanking at his hair like it would halt the movie reel flow of nightmare scenarios electrifying his thoughts. Another god hiding in plain sight, Thor—in his current form—was almost a foot shorter at just a few inches over six feet and less brawny in his Midgardian clothes. But unlike his brother, Thor wasn't as skilled in illusion and wore his natural colouring.

After taking in Loki's expression, Thor clapped Loki on the back. "What's the matter?"

"I've lost Shannon. She went into the bathroom and never came out." Loki's control slipped on his seidhr, letting a nimbus of black magical energy surge around him. "I don't know if she was taken, or ran, or what!"

"Whoa, calm down Loki," Thor whispered, after checking the surrounding hall. "You know I'll help you. What happened? She seemed to deal with the red carpet well enough when you introduced her. And the two of you looked pretty happy, curled up together in the back of the theatre earlier."

"We were, or are... were, I thought!" Struggling to keep his emotions in check, Loki took several deep breaths. "I lost control of my seidhr. She saw me change, saw the real me."

"What?" Thor's blue eyes widened. "How? You haven't lost control since you were a kid!"

Mind racing and unable to keep still with the driving need to find her, Loki bounced on his toes. "We left the lounge to fuck each other's brains out. Yggdrasil's roots, the woman has been driving me wild since we met on the plane." He couldn't admit to his brother that he'd plotted Shannon's seduction, that he wanted to ensure she spent the week with him, and that some part of him worried she might slip through his fingers. He ran his hands through his hair. "I couldn't wait any longer. Neither could she! We were both mad for each other, like nothing I've ever felt before. In the midst of it, I couldn't hold my Midgardian form and shifted back to myself."

Loki's gut twisted. It seemed disrespectful to talk about her that way to his brother—they didn't share those kinds of details—but he was at his wit's end. Had he scared her when he changed? Bor's balls... of course he had. He should have known she wasn't as calm as she'd appeared.

Thor raised an eyebrow. "Um, Loki. You lost control during sex with her? No seidhr, just your truest self?"

His brother's words rang alarm bells from the distant past, lessons learned as a child so long ago. Loss of seidhr and presenting your truest self were part of the Asgardian binding ceremony if you found your soulmate. Only your soulmate could cause that to happen involuntarily after the age of maturation when an Asgardian gained control over their powers.

But the blessing from the Norns was rare.

"C'mon, Thor. No way," Loki scoffed. "She's mortal, remember? There is no way she can be my soulmate." Could she? Why would the Norns bless him, of all people? After all his sins?

Thor peered at him. "How sure are you that Shannon is mortal?"

"Well, now that you have me doubting myself, not very." Uncertainty roiled inside Loki, his stomach flipping. "What am I going to do?"

Thor pursed his lips, brow furrowed. "If she left on her own... What do you know about her? Does she have a home here?"

A bolt of inspiration struck, electrifying Loki's veins like his brother had hit him with Mjolnir. Of course! Her hotel! "No, but I know where to start looking."

"Do you want help?" Thor offered.

Loki clapped him on the shoulder. "Thank you, brother. I appreciate the offer. I think I'm good at present. You should get back to that lovely Midgardian wife of yours. You were lucky Amelia and the girls were able to avoid the red carpet, but I know how rarely they join you at these events."

Thor smacked Loki on the back. "I'm envious of you, Loki. A soulmate is no small thing in this long life of ours. I love Amelia and try my best to be a good husband and father to our children, but I will mourn when she and the girls are lost to time. Go find and woo Shannon properly so I can get to know my new sister." After a last thump on Loki's back, Thor returned to the theatre.

Loki stood frozen, mouth dry, barely breathing.

He hadn't considered the implications. If Shannon *was* his soulmate, they'd be bound for eternity. He wouldn't lose her in a few tens of years—a blink of an eye to someone who'd lived thousands. Was it an illusion? A soap bubble that would pop as soon as he reached for it? How could it possibly be real?

When one lived as long as Asgardians did, one expected to go through the cycle of love and loss when having relationships with mortals. Many immortals refused because it always ended in death. At times, the weight of loss got so heavy that Loki had retreated to Asgard for hundreds of Midgardian years. He'd even attempted to marry another immortal, until she, too, was taken from him. *Murdered.* He pushed that violent memory away.

Always, he was drawn back by the vibrant life, the teeming chaos, the constant force of change that characterized this quickly evolving planet.

Loki had created different pantheons with his fellow gods, playing different roles as mortal beliefs changed, like the Egyptian god of chaos, Set. Other times, he and Thor would swap, and while Thor thundered about making war, Loki became Bastet, the Egyptian fertility goddess. He'd loved many, often... but still, the joy of his explorations became muted by the loss of too many lovers, and he'd retreated to Asgard.

The Norns, or Fates, had prompted his latest return to Midgard, telling him to try something different, that this world had moved beyond pantheons of gods. Loki licked his lips, blew out a heavy breath, and paced in circles. With his powers of hypnosis, Loki had implanted memories in those from the orphanage in Manchester who'd supposedly raised Tempest and Tod Corvus, brothers who'd built on those humble beginnings to become famous in rugby and music and were now reunited as action movie stars.

Loki tugged at his hair. Had the Norns set this up, set up his meeting with Shannon? It was impossible to know. They never explained themselves.

Yggdrasil's roots. Could it be possible? Could she really be his soulmate?

Chapter 8

RETAIL THERAPY

Seated at the hotel lobby bar, Shannon clutched a stiff drink, trying and failing to avoid thinking about Tod. No... Loki. Was he really Loki? Her mind replayed his change, his transformation in front of her. Her hands shook, and she shoved the tumbling chaotic thoughts away. She couldn't deal with that now. Not yet. She had to hold it together just a bit longer. She had to.

With a pleased smile, the concierge approached and handed her a list of appointments. Once she'd claimed she'd lost her luggage, he'd offered to call around to find stores that would stay open despite the evening hour—the benefit of staying at a high-class, full-service hotel. "Here you go, Doctor Murphy. They will take excellent care of you."

"Thank you so very much. I appreciate it," Shannon said as she shook his hand and tipped him heavily for his extra effort.

"Absolutely my pleasure, Doctor. I've taken the liberty of having one of our hotel drivers pull up front. He will take you everywhere you need to go."

The concierge held out his arm to escort her through the lobby. She'd always loved the gentlemanly behaviour of the British, but almost flinched at the reminder of Tod... Loki. Still, she took his arm and thanked him again after he opened the car door and helped her inside.

She gazed out the window as the car pulled into traffic. The dark night had her recalling shorter bright auburn hair morphing into locks of pure midnight.

Just hold it together a bit longer, Shannon told her reflection, raising a trembling hand to the glass.

True to his word, the driver ushered her from an upscale women's fashion store with beautifully tailored suits and dresses to a trendy but fashionable shop with a range of more casual clothes. The last stop was Victoria's Secret since she needed more than outer clothes. A weakness of hers, for sure. She came out with far more pink-and-white striped bags than necessary. Comfort shopping at its finest.

Yet with each stop, she couldn't help but remember getting ready that afternoon at Tod's flat. No... no, not Tod's... Loki's. Her heart pounded as her thoughts circled. How could it be Loki? A god? Really?

She couldn't think about this. She couldn't.

When the hotel driver helped her into the lobby with her purchases, the concierge waved over a bellhop to assist. "I hope you don't mind, but I took the liberty of having extra toiletries and a suitcase delivered to your room from our hotel shop. If it is not to your liking, please call down and we'll exchange them or take them back. Is there anything else I can assist you with, Doctor Murphy?" the concierge asked with a smile.

Shannon's usually organized brain was scattered, and she rubbed her temple. She hadn't even considered how she'd get her purchases home since she'd lost her backpack. "Thank you, Mister Knight," she said, reading his name badge. It took her two tries. Everything had started to distort, like reality was bending in a carnival funhouse. She gritted her teeth and forced herself to hold on as the elevator closed.

At her floor, the bellhop helped Shannon to her room and left as efficiently as he'd arrived. Flopping on her bed with the adrenaline surge now long gone, she allowed herself to consider today's revelations.

A god. Was Tod really a god?

It was unbelievable. She'd grown up with stories of gods. They surrounded her mother's First Nation Peoples, taking the form of animals, of the sun, moon, and stars, of elements of nature. Shannon had always considered them a form of allegory, or perhaps metaphorical as a way for the early people to explain their environment. To think that might not be the case... it was a boatload to process.

If Tod was the god Loki... A nervous giggle bubbled up. Even thinking it seemed ridiculous, but if he was, then being immortal would explain his absolute mastery of the sensual arts. Damn. A shiver rippled over her skin, followed by a wave of heat, and her hand slid up her torso to her neck as she remembered being in his arms, the feeling of him driving into her, hard and fast. She couldn't believe how much she'd enjoyed the way he'd held her down. So fucking hot. And that they'd done that in the back room of a movie theatre. She slapped a hand over her face. Incredible. Completely outrageous.

With her eyes closed, her mind flashed on him changing. Shit. Don't think about that.

Heart jolting in her chest, Shannon took a shaky breath and tried to release it slowly. Instead, she let her fingertips trail over her neck, remembering his lips, his touch. The sex was wildly hot. No doubt about it. She'd never orgasmed like that before. Hell, she'd lost count of the number. Way more than she'd thought possible. That intense connection between them... electric. And that dominant neck hold, or the bite thing he'd done on the plane? Sinfully erotic.

Why had she let him do that?

She'd been so willing to let him do anything, to take charge... even submitting and saying she'd belonged to him.

To Loki.

A god.

Fuck.

Being that vulnerable to someone else, to their approval, to want that kind of emotional claiming? She couldn't. She couldn't go down that path again. Nausea churned, and she pressed her hand to her stomach. Bad things happened when she allowed herself to be emotionally vulnerable.

No, she couldn't do that.

Not again.

Trent had taken her emotions and weaponized them. He'd cut at her self-esteem in thousands of tiny slashes. Shannon was never pretty enough, slender enough, or dressed well enough. She was too nerdy, too messy, or lacking in femininity. She was his favourite target, his punching bag for his need to stroke his ego.

Although she'd managed to pull herself together and mostly cut ties with him, it had been a nasty battle to entirely separate her career from his. Even three years later, Shannon still had emotional scars to match the physical ones. Her fingertips coasted over her bruised arm. No shock she hadn't trusted anyone since then. Especially when the fucking bastard showed up out of the blue to remind her.

It made it hard to date. She'd buried herself in work instead. It had become both her temporary salvation—her escape from him once he was banned from her lab—and her only source of success, of self-esteem. She'd poured herself into her career and found new collaborators, new biochemists to complement her forest ecophysiology research. Fought against the misogyny so present in the sciences. She'd made a name for herself. She'd risen to the top of the ranks. Safe. Tenured. A full professor.

The idea that she'd felt so much, so deeply, so fast with Tod... or Loki after what Trent put her through. No more. She wouldn't go back. Not even for a maybe-god who seemed to have the key to her sensuality.

Fists clenching, she thumped the bed as the physical and emotional exhaustion caught up with her.

No, she wouldn't see him again.

Chapter 9

THE STRAY

Waking up was a process. Sore muscles protested movement when Shannon tried to roll over. Groaning, she lifted a hand to push her hair off her face and blinked. She was still in her black dress with her silver and blue wrap around her, tucked under her chin like a cover. Crap. Well, at least she'd kicked her shoes off before collapsing.

The sun shone through the gap between the hotel room's curtains, but she had no idea of the actual time.

Reluctantly, she sat up, wincing at the tenderness of her inner thighs and more sensitive areas. Sitting was decidedly uncomfortable as muscles unused to *that* kind of exercise made their presence known.

"Ouch!" she yelled as she rose, hissing through the quick flash of pain before she mumbled, "Freakishly well-endowed damn sex god." Shannon couldn't really complain about the most spectacular, mind-blowingly amazing sex she'd ever had, even if she was now paying for her indulgence. Hell, the physical side of things had totally been worth it. Absolutely and completely. A day to remember and celebrate on her calendar for all time.

Undoing her dress and bra, she let them fall to the white bathroom tile then stepped into the blistering hot shower spray. Moaning, Shannon let the heat of the water soak the aches away.

The hotel soap smelled of vanilla, a favourite, and she lathered her way down her body. Still incredibly sensitive, she shivered as she gently washed off the dried evidence of last night's pleasure. Damn. Where had her head been that she didn't remember to ask him to use a condom? She paused mid-scrub and a giggle erupted. Did they make god-sized condoms? He was *not* small. At least she was on the pill, so she didn't need to worry about that end of things. Still... could gods pass on STDs? If his reputation was anything to go by, Tod... Loki... fuck, whatever the hell his name was saw a lot of action. But no, surely a being that could shapeshift and freaking *teleport* could avoid catching or passing on disease.

Reassured, Shannon ran the cloth between her legs. Light pressure sent a wave of delicious arousal flooding through her groin, but a too-vigorous stroke had her wincing—some bruises to add to the collection ringing her upper arm. At least these were from pleasure. Hell, she'd be willing to garner more if it meant she experienced *that* again. Loki forcefully thrusting, climaxing inside her—the flash of intense sensory memory created such a vivid echo, her sex spasmed in savage remembrance. And despite the vanilla odour wafting from the soap in her hand, she'd swear his orange-and-woody leather scent surrounded her even now.

Switching the detachable showerhead to a light rain, she rinsed the soap off. She was unable to stop the flood of memories, and when she reached the junction of her thighs, the water pressure had her clutching the shower wall as simmering nerves ignited and burst into blissful euphoria.

Damn.

Gasping, Shannon slapped the water off. Eyes closed, she leaned against the tile until the weakness in her knees dissipated. Gods, she was as wobbly as a newborn fawn.

When she opened her eyes again, there was no sign of Tod or Loki, despite the evidence of her other senses. Shaking, she left the dubious safety of the shower and wrapped a towel around her body.

Still not convinced, she opened the bathroom door and peeked into her hotel room.

Again, no sign of him.

Just that lingering scent.

Uncomfortably vulnerable in a towel, she headed to yesterday's purchases. She withdrew a matching royal-blue and silver bra-and-panty set. After sliding the panties up her thighs, she hissed.

Nope. No way. Too sore. Too sensitized.

Hastily tearing them off, she pondered her choice of clothes—either the dress pants where the seam might not bother her or the skirt where it absolutely wouldn't rub. Jeans were not an option. Decision made, Shannon tugged on the black pencil skirt and a royal-blue cowl-necked silk top. Once she finished getting ready, a black fitted blazer would complete the look.

Back in the bathroom, she stared at her throat in the mirror. With her hair up in a towel, the impression of teeth was clearly visible where her neck met her shoulder. A trail of hickeys ascended to her ear. Amongst her other more pressing aches, she hadn't noticed these at all.

"Damn it, Loki! I need to look professional!"

Yes, he was *definitely* Loki—trickster and God of Chaos, if she remembered her Norse mythology. The name suited him with this bloody stunt. He'd probably be pleased at seeing his marks on her, the bastard. Grumbling, she hunted through the few pieces of make-up in her small purse. She dabbed concealer on the hickeys higher up her neck but left the ones further down. Her jacket collar should hide them.

Yet, a kernel of amusement grew within her, and she couldn't help smiling as she touched a hand to the passionate marks. Clothed, showered, and rested, Shannon was far more confident this morning. Her equilibrium restored. There was no denying that dominant possessive streak of his was sexy as hell. She didn't have to be vulnerable. She was a strong, independent woman. It didn't matter what she said in the throes of passion. No, it didn't have to mean anything. Loki's dominance wasn't a threat.

Instead, she'd treat it as it was intended—an powerfully hot encounter. Exactly what she asked for from a vacation fling. She'd wanted to tangle in the sheets with a bad boy. Well, he was that. And more. Loki was different, so incredibly different from anyone she'd met before.

She snorted as she applied eyeliner and mascara. What an understatement.

The scientist in her wanted to find a different explanation, but in the bright light of morning and wearing the evidence of their passion on her skin, she trusted her observations. She knew what she'd seen, what she'd experienced. There were no special effects, drugs, or alcohol involved. It had happened.

Even if it was so far beyond anything Shannon had expected or frankly, thought possible.

She shifted her weight from foot to foot, looking away from her reflection's knowing eyes. That she'd run last night was a little embarrassing. Not usually one to panic, away from the immediacy of it, she was curious. Why hadn't she asked him questions? Was he truly immortal? How long had he lived? He didn't give off a sense of great age. What other powers did he have? Was it just experience and sexual prowess that had enabled him to hit every erotic note so perfectly? Or was he some kind of sex god?

A bolt of lust speared her as she recalled his mouth… his tongue… between her thighs, and she grabbed the edge of the counter, her knees weakening. Damn, damn, damn, he was *fine*. Hot as hell. She'd sell her soul for more of Loki's mind-blowing expertise.

Did Loki care about souls? By the gods—she halted mid-thought—which were real, apparently. Could they hear her when she said that?

She shivered and put her forehead down on the cool granite, trying to still her racing, scattered thoughts.

Every other sexual experience of her life paled in comparison. Between Loki's identity and the way he'd turned her into a being of pure sensation, it was no wonder her brain was all over the place today. And hell yes, she wanted more.

Lifting her head, she met her reflection and picked up her brush and hotel blow dryer. Now that she'd experienced his overwhelming dominance, that sheer animalistic force, she knew what to expect and could guard against being so vulnerable. She didn't need to give in or lose herself.

Not that she'd see him again. Not after the way she'd taken off. He had his choice of women throwing themselves at him. She sighed. Too bad.

Would it have been as life-altering the second time? She flicked off the dryer. The clench of low-down need answered her.

Finished with her hair and make-up, Shannon dug out her phone. She couldn't keep this to herself. She needed to share her incredible night with Lynda. But when she flicked the screen to life, the 9:18 a.m. had her squawking, "Damn. I'm going to be late!"

After putting on her fitted jacket and last night's jewellery, and sliding her feet into her heels, she dashed down to the lobby.

"Good morning, Doctor Murphy," the concierge called out.

"Good morning, Mister Knight. Don't you get to sleep, too?"

He smiled. "I'll be going off shift shortly. Mister Bainbridge will be here to assist you should you need anything. May I call you a car?"

"Thank you. Yes, please."

As she watched, he signalled to a shiny black town car that pulled up in front of the hotel. Opening the door for her, he helped her in and wished her a good day. Shannon gave the driver the address for the Natural History Museum, the location for the conference.

Upon arrival, the driver helped her out, and she made her way up the front steps. A sleek black cat passed in front of her, blocking her path. Was this one of the museum cats? At more than a century old, the museum had a mice problem at times, but she'd thought her colleague based in the museum's research division had mentioned the cats were restricted from public areas. Did this beautiful beast escape? It certainly wasn't an alley cat with such a thick, glossy ebony coat. Bending down, Shannon held out her hand, and the cat bumped against it, letting her pet its silky fur.

"You're a gorgeous creature, aren't you?" She chuckled as it pushed against her hand when she stopped petting it. "I'd love to give you more attention, but I'm afraid I really must go," she told the cat. That it cocked its head as if listening had her grinning. Yes, this was definitely an animal used to being cosseted by people.

Straightening, Shannon passed through the museum's golden stone-arched entrance and stopped at the conference registration desk. After picking up her name tag and conference bag, she headed to the opening session in the events theatre, next to Earth Hall. Once seated at the end of a row, she relaxed, relieved to see they hadn't quite started yet. As she settled into her chair, a black cat leapt onto her lap, startling her.

It was the same cat. It sniffed at her, then kneaded her lap for a few seconds before circling to sit, purring. Tentatively, she extended her hand. It butted its head against her fingers, demanding attention. Bemused, she stroked the cat's soft fur as it purred in her lap and the first talk started. The animal reminded her of Research, the cat that roamed the halls between faculty offices at her university.

A few minutes into the talk, one of her least favourite American colleagues sat in the chair beside her. Internally, she groaned. No, damn it. She didn't want to deal with him today. For fuck's sake. She'd flown all this way to get away from pushy assholes.

"Hey Shannon, I was hoping you'd be here so we'd get a chance to catch up," he said as he leaned into her personal space.

"Hi Mike, I'd really like to hear this talk, okay? Perhaps we'll have time to talk later." Or never.

"Do you have dinner plans? I hear there is going to be dancing at the reception." He laid his hand on the back of her chair, leering as if his spray-on-tan complexion and bad breath didn't make her nauseous.

Not taking a hint, as usual. Shannon sighed. Ever since Trent had spewed insults about her being a slut for grant money in front of him, this damn used car salesman of a scientist had hit on her. What would it take to get rid of Mike this time?

As he reached to pat her on the leg, the cat hissed and bit his hand before he could touch her. Yelping, he pulled his hand back.

"Yeah, my pussy bites. I'd appreciate it if you gave me some space," she said, trying not to laugh while she stroked the cat. Raising the now-purring animal to her chest, she leaned her face down to the cat and whispered, "Good kitty." She snuggled it to her neck while she watched Mike scuttle away to a new chair in another row.

Seemingly happy cuddled up to her, the cat licked Shannon's neck, tickling her with its rough tongue. Trying not to giggle, she nudged it away and back down to her lap as she focused on the remainder of the keynote talks. Or, at least tried to. Despite her best efforts to pay attention, her mind drifted to Loki instead.

Were all the pantheons of gods real? Odd that ancient people knew gods were real, but the modern world didn't. Did gods like Loki evolve on Earth, or was Asgard real? If Asgard was real, then surely there were other planets with life. Did they have ecosystems like Earth? Why were gods here if they had other realms, other planets?

Lost in her thoughts, she almost jumped out of her chair when the crowd started clapping. She hurried to join in, even though she'd not heard any of the four speakers.

Afterwards, there was a luncheon in the exhibitor's hall. Putting the cat down, she headed to the event and browsed the booths. Chatting with a few acquaintances as she moved up and down the rows, she got a few smirks and double-takes directed her way. It puzzled her until a few minutes later when Kristen, a friend from Mackenzie University in Ottawa, joined her.

"Hey! When did you get in?" Shannon asked as they hugged.

"Ugh! Just this morning. I am so damn jetlagged!" After rubbing a hand over her dark forehead and then smoothing down her ochre and black pantsuit—a style Shannon wished she could wear but didn't have Kristen's tall slender frame—Kristen dragged Shannon over to one of the catered lunch lines and smirked. "So, who's the new guy in your life? C'mon, I want details!"

"What?" Shannon asked, blinking at Kristen as they picked up plates, paper-wrapped sandwiches, and salad.

"Well, unless you've gotten waaaay more flexible than when we used to do yoga in grad school, you didn't put those hickeys on yourself," Kristen teased.

Shannon's face went up in flames, as her fingers rose to hide her neck. "Damn it. Not all of us have gorgeous black complexions that hide hickeys."

Finding open seats at a circular table, the two women sat, and Shannon pulled long strands of her hair forward to lie along the side of her throat and those damn marks. That was why she'd been getting those looks. Groaning, she covered her face with her hands.

Kristen smirked and punched Shannon in the shoulder. "Hmm... sounds like you've got a story to tell me. C'mon. Spill."

Shannon cursed and dropped her hands. "Yes, I met someone. It's... he's... well, it's complicated," she struggled to explain. "We just met, and it's intense."

She wasn't about to tell Kristen that she'd had a one-night stand with an immortal god she was pretty sure she'd never see again. Oh, holy hell. Her pulse started to thunder in her ears. She'd had sex, really, really hot sex... amazing mind-melting sex... with an immortal god.

A chill shivered down her spine and goosebumps broke out on her arms.

A brutally sexy immortal god. And... she... oh fuck, she'd totally bailed on him.

Picking up a water glass, she filled it from the pitcher on the table then drained it even as her foot began tapping under her chair. She'd ghosted an immortal god after he gave her a ridiculous number of orgasms. After she discovered the secret he went to great lengths to keep. An immortal god who had endless years to find her, to pay her back for ditching him.

Shifting in her seat, Shannon fought the urge to flee.

And holy hell. Not just any god. Loki. A trickster god. The fucking God of Mischief, if popular culture was to be believed. A jolt hit her. Oh wow. He'd probably met... probably *knew* the various actors and actresses who had portrayed him over time. What did he even think about them? They were all fine, no mysterious accidents or anything. But... did he take those portrayals personally? Presumably, they didn't know his secret. Her stomach quivered—a thousand butterflies taking flight all at once. Quickly, she ate a few bites of her sandwich as her eyes darted around. Holy crap. How much trouble was she in?

"I'll say! You don't so much as kiss a guy until after a few dates, yet here you are with love bites, and I haven't even heard of him."

"He's..." Distracted by the cat that jumped up to perch on the seat next to her, Shannon paused.

"He's what?" Kristen prompted.

It was the same black cat from before. Tail wrapped around its front paws, intensely brilliant green eyes staring at her, unblinking. Familiar brilliant green eyes. Her mind flashed on snippets of Norse mythology.

"Son of a bitch!" Shannon pushed her seat back and stood, staring at the cat that continued to calmly make eye contact.

Chapter 10

CATITUDE

Loki continued to stare into Shannon's wide, shocked eyes, smirking in that enigmatic way cats were known for, then giving her a slow blink. If a cat could laugh, he would have. He hadn't been sure whether she would figure it out or not, and he certainly hadn't expected her to do so with such speed. Especially since he'd not given her any clues yet. Such a clever mind to go with that beautiful, sensual form of hers.

Was she human? Every indication suggested she was. Her reactions didn't give any hints of falseness. But the more time he spent with her, everything he learned about her... it deepened his craving for her. How could she be mortal when he felt this soul-deep connection between them? It was almost like he could touch her mind, tempting him to reach out with his telepathy.

But if he couldn't... he wasn't sure he wanted to know. Not yet.

He couldn't stay away. Just sitting a few feet away had him aching to touch her, to cuddle up to her. Yggdrasil's roots, but he loved the feel of her petting him, the soft stroke of fingertips with the slight scrape of nails against his fur. And... yes, soothing the hurt he'd tried not to dwell on when she'd left, abandoning him last night. Without even a word. His tail lashed, hitting the back of the chair.

The curly-haired woman, Kristen, who seemed to be a friend, leaned around the table to join Shannon in admiring Loki's cat form. Of course, they were admiring him. His ebony coat gleamed in these lights, and as he shot a leg in the air, he cleaned away a spot of dust with his tongue.

"Oh, what a gorgeous cat! One of the museum cats Phillip told us about?" Rising from her chair, the woman started over to him. He preened and lifted his head. Her hand reached out—

"Stay away from him," Shannon growled to her friend, her tone caressing Loki as her fingers had earlier. Her expression, the possessive claim revealed by those narrowed eyes and clenched fist, had the tip of his tail flicking in delight. She didn't want anyone else to touch him? A shiver rippled over his fur. Did she regret running from him last night?

Not that he truly blamed her. Not once he'd had a chance to consider how shocked she must have been, discovering his true identity like that. It hadn't been the most auspicious way to reveal himself, already balls deep and ravaging her perfect curvy body with primal demand. His lips drew back in a slight snarl. Yeah, he'd been a bit of a lumbering auroch, stampeding over her senses.

"What's the matter with you?" The woman had paused and frowned at Shannon, her hand still outstretched towards Loki.

"He bites."

Loki blinked at Shannon. When had he—

"He bit Mike earlier," she added.

Oh yeah. Ears twitching with feline amusement, Loki met Shannon's narrow-eyed gaze. That slick-haired greasy ass had totally deserved it. He was lucky all Loki had done was bite him.

"Cat has good taste then. Mike's an ass," Kristen said as she pulled her hand back.

Loki swished his tail, flicking an ear and gazing around the room. This friend of Shannon's was a good woman with discerning taste.

"Speaking of assholes, any word from your ex?"

What? Shannon had an ex? Ears flattening, Loki's head whipped around to pin Shannon with his gaze, every muscle tensing. Instead of answering right away, she took a few bites of her sandwich, chewing and swallowing. Her eyes strayed to his, then away again. Was she not answering because she didn't want him to know? Whiskers quivering, he was on the cusp of sending out a telepathic probe, the need to know overriding his fear of their connection being proven false.

Seconds stretched as Shannon took a drink of water and glanced around. Bor's balls, he was just going to do it. Focusing on her, reaching out—

"Yes."

—Loki yanked his power back at Shannon's quiet word, ears pricked forward.

"He came by and threw a fit when he caught me leaving for the airport. The restraining order doesn't seem to be having any effect."

Loki's growl and Kristen's melded. He wholeheartedly approved when she said, "He's dangerous, Shannon. I was glad when he got banned from entering your campus building."

Yeah, this woman was a good friend, the kind of person Shannon needed around her. He was going to find that ex and—

"What about your asshole department head?"

What. The. Fuck? Loki's claws, already out at finding out about her ex, dug into the chair and slashed the fabric. Was Shannon surrounded by enemies? No. *No way* was he letting these puny mortals threaten her. She was his.

Shannon wrinkled her nose. "The usual bullshit, but despite Bill, my promotion came through." She grinned and pumped her fist in the air.

Loki gouged the chair's cushion as his ears twitched. If this *Bill* kept to just words, perhaps he wouldn't interfere. His clever woman had bested him already. By the Nine, but she was spectacular.

"Holy crap! That's awesome! Congratulations. No doubt Bill is fuming, but it must really burn Trent's ass that you are the youngest full professor in the faculty and he's still only an associate." Kristen raised her water glass, clinking it with Shannon's.

Shannon drank to the toast and chuckled. "Yeah, the dean pushed it through, despite Bill's objections. Trent thinks I screwed Bill to get it, of course."

Kristen snorted and rolled her eyes. "Of course, Trent thinks that. He's an asshole."

Trent. Loki rumbled his disgust, the sound deep and almost below human hearing. Was that the name of her ex? Asshole was far too polite a term for that dead man walking. He was going to rip that—

"We totally have to celebrate with the guys later. Tell me more about *your* guy, though," Kristen teased, winking and flashing a wide, toothy smile.

Loki's head whipped up, yanked from his furious thoughts to meet Shannon's gaze. She grinned at her friend, and with a sidelong glance back toward him, said, "I suspect you will get to meet him."

What was she planning? The little mischievous twist to her lips had him wanting to shift, to return to his two-legged form and kiss her, to taste the amusement gleaming in those clever hazel eyes. He arched his back. Yes, he wanted to play with his beautiful, intriguing woman. *Was* she his soulmate? Yggdrasil's roots, he was scared to dream that big.

Kristen wiggled her eyebrows, grinning. "I would hope so, but give me the dirt now."

"You are incorrigible."

"Of course. What are friends for, right?"

Shannon bit her lip, hesitating, and a bolt of lust roared through Loki, sending a shiver through his fur. Her eyes flicked to him, then back to her friend. "He currently lives here in London, although I'm sure that's not where he's originally from."

Ha. Loki cocked his head. *You got that right, darling.*

Almost like she could hear him, she snorted a laugh. "He's taller than me, a sharp dresser, and can be quite gentlemanly when he wants to be."

Loki blinked as Shannon squirmed a bit in her seat and the tip of his tail flicked as he caught a scent...

"Not too gentlemanly if he gave you those," Kristen snorted, flicking a finger at Shannon's neck. "But that's the best sort, isn't it? A gentleman who knows how to be bad?" Her brown eyes twinkled as she teased.

"Yes, he definitely has a wicked side. There is certainly more than meets the eye."

... oh fuck me. Muscles turning rigid, Loki locked his position as savage need blasted through his body, searing his senses and threatening his control. A swirl of smoky black seidhr wafted around him and with a silent snarl, he yanked it back. He wasn't ready to reveal himself, despite the delicious scent of hot, ready woman, *his* woman, filling his nose. Knowing she wanted him soothed the last of the savage hurt that remained from her panicked flight last night, regardless of how understandable it had been.

"I want to hear more, but we better get back to the talks. Will he be coming to the reception tonight?"

"I wouldn't be surprised if he shows up." Shannon met Loki's gaze as he fought to control the need to shift, to take her into his arms to sate the raging desire between them.

"Good! I want to meet him. He can help fend off the sketchy types that think conferences are a great place to cheat on their wives and hook up with female colleagues." Kristen rolled her eyes, rose, and headed back to the lecture theatre.

Fuck, yes he would be there. Loki flexed his claws. No sketchy types would be hooking up with his Shannon. Not happening. He bared his teeth. The soul stealers of Niflheim were always looking for warm bodies.

Shannon stood and picked Loki up to cuddle against her chest. Pressed against her warm body was exactly where he wanted to be. A purr escaped as her fingers stroked his fur, soothing his need to be with her. When she murmured, "I know it's you, Loki. You do make a stunning cat," he relished the attention, the touch that satisfied the ache in his chest, and rubbed his cheek on her skin, marking her with his scent as he had so many times this day.

Whether she knew it or not, she was *his*.

Chapter 11

THE BET

If the cat's limp-boned relaxation was anything to judge by, Loki didn't seem to be holding a grudge. And he'd sought her out immediately. What did that mean? Shannon's fingers paused on his silky fur. It was Loki, right? The way the cat had followed the conversation between Kristen and her... it had to be.

Ugh. She shook her head. Could her life get any weirder? How did that even work? Where did the mass go? Did he have different instincts as a cat? Or was she now a crazy cat lady, thinking this was Loki? She bit back a chuckle as the cat nudged her hand, and she resumed scratching behind his ear. It had to be him. The cat had too much presence, too much intelligence, and an almost magnetic connection when she held him.

Like a force of nature that refused to be contained.

Taking a seat beside Kristen, she almost snorted. That much personality, that much dominance packed into the tiny body of a house cat... it was bound to peek out. Hell, there was no hiding the bad-boy eroticism. He had too much charisma.

And as a man... heat curled in her abdomen as memories of last night rose. The way he'd held her down, thrusting hard and fast, every stroke sending ecstasy through her. Gods, it had been incredible. She shifted restlessly in the chair.

Yeah, who was she kidding? She definitely wanted more.

Yet a flicker of unease twisted in her gut as she gazed down at the cat purring in her lap.

Had she thought this through? No doubt there were undeniable sparks between them. But a lasting connection? So fast? No. No way. Besides, it wasn't practical to continue to see him beyond the week. They lived on different continents... hell, different worlds, most likely. And really, he was a god. It wasn't like he would want anything beyond a short fling with her. He could have anyone.

Her heart sank.

He was probably just amusing himself with her. Surely, she could protect her emotions. Wasn't it worth it? She had so many questions for him, and oh my gods, but the sex was unfuckingbelievable. Like Pandora, Shannon wanted to take the risk, to open that sinful box again. Toe-curling sex didn't come around every day, after all. Not for her, anyway.

Of course, none of that would make a difference if she didn't get Loki to reveal himself. As she considered the problem, a plan came together that had her smirking at its simplicity.

Yes, two can play this cat-and-mouse game, Loki. Either her idea would work with a few easy modifications to her current agenda, or she'd make a fool of herself. Still, that he'd sought her out gave her the confidence to at least try. She'd regret it forever if she didn't.

Bringing the cat up towards her face, she met his eyes. "Very well, don't admit it. I bet I can make you reveal yourself before I leave here tonight, but if I can't, I'll meet you at my hotel afterward. I expect you've already figured out where I'm staying?"

Again, the cat simply purred.

Kristen quirked an eyebrow at Shannon, inclining her head at the cat. "I thought it bites?"

"He does. Just not me, not unless I want him to." Shannon snickered at her joke when the cat lifted his head and slowly blinked at her. Yeah, she understood cat behaviour, and Loki gave himself away without even realizing it. Warm pleasure flowed through her at the thought of how he'd defended her. Her plan would work.

Kristen frowned but then simply shook her head, eyeing Shannon oddly.

In the hours that followed, the cat curled up on Shannon's lap or chest while she listened to the talks, trailed behind her during breaks as she chatted with colleagues, and darted away when anyone but her attempted to pet him or pick him up.

She couldn't stop smiling. His constant attention spurred her confidence, reassuring her that she'd been correct in recognizing him in this form. She was going to have fun with this trickster god. He had no idea she was about to jump on one of his buttons with both feet.

"Still have your shadow?" Kristen peered behind Shannon as they stood in line at one of the bar stations tucked amongst natural history exhibits in the large hall where a massive skeleton of a blue whale swam suspended over their heads.

Shannon smiled and gave a careless wave of her hand. "I'm sure he's around." Of course, she knew exactly where he was, and she deliberately avoided looking in his direction. Loki's fixed gaze was like a fiery warmth heating the blood in her veins. Anticipation surged, adding to the simmering arousal that had plagued her all day. Soon she'd have her answer and know whether he was only amusing himself or if he also wanted a repeat of last night's passionate storm.

The bartender swiped a cloth along the top of his station. "What would you ladies like to drink?"

Shannon pointed at the dark bottle of merlot sitting beside the hard liquor selections."Red wine, please."

"Me as well," Kristen told him.

With their wine in hand, the women mingled. Like in her mother's stories of Raven, Shannon decided it was time to create a little mischief.

"Shannon!" a deep voice said as a man wrapped his arms around her.

Turning her head, she spotted the deeply tanned face of a friend and colleague from the University of California. Perfect. "Brian! When did you get in?" She twisted to briefly return his hug.

Slower to let go of her, he kissed her on the cheek first. "This afternoon. Are we going to manage to get you on the dance floor, finally? After everyone has had a bit more social lubrication, I am pretty sure they are breaking out the music."

"Hmm... maybe." With a laugh, Shannon glanced down under the nearby cocktail table to see a pair of brilliantly glowing green eyes, narrowed, glaring at her. She turned away so Loki wouldn't see her smirk. The one thing he'd mentioned he didn't want her to do... yeah, she was going to stomp that button hard.

"Is Jay or Rick here yet?" Brian asked. "They were due to arrive before the reception as well."

"I haven't seen them yet," Kristen answered, and Shannon shook her head.

"How are you ladies for drinks? I'm going to go get us a round of tequila."

Kristen and Shannon groaned at Brian's comment. Tequila shots were a tradition when they got together, but inevitably, a hangover the next day was the result.

"I beat you to it!" a new voice said, as a hand came to rest on Shannon's waist. "Hey babe, good to see you." Jay kissed her cheek and held a tray with tequila shots.

Shannon almost snorted and rolled her eyes, barely choking back her usual retort. Every woman was *babe* to the Latino. Instead, she murmured an acknowledgement without removing his hand or snarking at his liberties. A glance under the nearby table, and she almost gave a hip wiggle in delight. The cat's eyes were narrowed and his tail thrashed back and forth. Gods, it was perfect. She couldn't have planned that better had she given Jay the line.

They each took a shot glass, clinked their toast, and downed the tequila in one burning gulp.

"Damn! I missed the first round?" Rick asked as he joined them.

"No worries, man. I'm off to get the next!" Brian said, taking the tray from Jay, who'd thankfully released Shannon's waist to do his shot.

Rick finished hugging Kristen and came over to Shannon for a hug. "Looking sexy and ravishing as ever, Shannon. When are you going to ditch that wet rainforest and come live with me on the beach in the sun?"

It had gotten noisier in the hall as more people arrived and the reception grew rowdier. Despite that, Shannon could have sworn she heard a savage snarl, followed by a low, animalistic rumble. "Funny, Rick. Very funny," Shannon told him dryly, stepping out of his arms as she gestured to his bright blue, green, and orange Hawaiian shirt. "When are you going to stop being a stereotype?" Like Jay, Rick had no real interest in her as ruggedly built swarthy island native hit on everything in skirts. His words were meaningless, except to someone who didn't know them. She glanced back. The cat was several feet away under the table. Clearly pissed, with his back arched and fur spiked up—there was nothing languid or relaxed about Loki now. Still, there was no way she'd be able to hear growling from that far away. Her ears had to be playing tricks on her. Didn't they?

As Brian returned with a second round of shots and bottles of water, Kristen held up her hand. "We need to celebrate! Shannon got promoted to full professor!"

"That's fantastic!"

"Congrats!"

"To Shannon!"

"Keep kicking ass and taking names!"

Shannon laughed, and they tossed back their shots. The DJ started the music, kicking it off with Bon Jovi's "Livin' on a Prayer" blasting out of the speakers.

"Here's to the awesome music of the eighties!" Brian toasted when Rick arrived with another round.

"Absolutely!" they agreed and started to sing along to the lyrics, dancing in place.

Coming over beside her, Brian used his shot glass as a pretend mic, and Shannon joined him. They leaning into each other, singing, and when the guitar intro of Guns N' Roses' "Sweet Child O' Mine" started, they bumped their sides together. The growling sound increased. Shannon glanced around but no one else seemed to notice. She bit her lip to hide her grin and eyed the cat. How was she the only one to hear it? Or did the others hear it and not realize what the sound was?

When the Cranberries' "Zombie" came on, Rick and Brian each came to put an arm around Shannon, and they danced as she sang. As a group, they enjoyed karaoke, but she tended to avoid dancing or more contact than a simple hug. Despite the friendly distance she kept them at, the guys frequently tried for more. Not because they wanted her or thought she was sexy... no, they just wanted a woman in their hotel bed and would settle for her if they couldn't get a woman they actually wanted. It was exactly what she'd been counting on and essential to her plan of pushing the territorial Loki into revealing himself.

As the growling increased in volume until it was almost louder than the music, elation burst through Shannon like champagne bubbles overflowing a bottle. Barely able to hold her composure with her heartbeat thundering faster than the music, she deliberately avoided glancing at the furious cat who'd moved almost to the edge of her heels. What would it take to push him over the edge?

When Def Leppard's "Pour Some Sugar on Me" started, Shannon didn't object as Jay boldly pulled her into his arms, far closer than she'd normally allow. He attempted some dirty dancing, and she hid her smile against his shoulder. Trust the Latin lover, as they teased him about his reputation and Cuban heritage, to try to take advantage of the slightest opening she'd given the guys. If this didn't get Loki, she'd have to call a halt. Shannon didn't want to lead them on.

The growling turned into a distinctive British baritone full of menace. *<If he doesn't get his bloody hands off you right fucking now, I'm going to shred your friend into oblivion, so even Hela won't be able to find his soul.>*

Shannon gasped. His voice was in her mind. Joy surged, and she bit back the giddy laughter that wanted to bubble out. Half a second later, she was tugged out of Jay's arms and back into a hard chest. The familiar scent of woodsy citrus surrounded her. Loki's arm formed a rigid band around her waist, pressing her ass tight against his aroused length, moving them to the music.

Laughter was incinerated by blistering heat as her senses caught fire.

Starting at her waist, Loki's hand slowly glided up over her breast to her throat, then tilted her head to the side. Her pulse rose to almost a taste in her mouth, and her breath hiccupped then caught as he spoke, his mouth at her ear. "You are *mine* and the next mortal to touch you will die," her furious god warned in a deep, menacing snarl.

She knew his touch, his voice, and his body against hers. Familiar in a way she couldn't explain and shouldn't know in such a short time. She couldn't deny the chord it struck within her. Like raw metallic ore put to the forge, she yielded, softened, and surrendered to his dark dominance, even as her body tightened and clenched with quivering need.

Putting one hand over his arm at her waist and reaching her other up to tangle in his short bright auburn hair, Shannon pushed her ass back against the stark, unyielding evidence of his desire.

"Yes, Loki, I am yours. Only yours." At least for now. At least like this.

He bit her neck, teeth scraping, then tongue caressing the bite mark. Electricity sparked in her veins. "Mine," he growled, lips continuing to explore her neck in a proprietary claim. They danced the rest of the song like that, oblivious to everything else around them.

When the music shifted to Third Eye Blind's "Semi-Charmed Life," Loki turned Shannon in his arms, gazing down at her and smiling as he gently brushed her cheek with his fingertips. "You are a tease, darling." Amusement filled his eyes.

"I won the bet," Shannon told him with a smirk.

Throwing his head back, he laughed. Smiling widely, he leaned down and kissed her. "Indeed you did, my gorgeous, wicked temptress. So what do you want as your reward?"

Her senses buzzing with more than the shots of tequila, she still craved a little liquid courage for diving down this rabbit hole with him, a veritable god. "I'd like to try Asgardian mead. Or is that a myth?"

"No, darling, it's not a myth. Introduce me to your friends. Promise me you will stay out of their arms, and I will go get your reward." His pale-blue eyes were serious while he waited for her answer.

"I promise." Shannon had no desire for anyone else but him.

He kissed her again before they turned to face her friends. *<Remember to introduce me as Tod,>* he reminded her with his voice in her mind again.

Seeing her friends and their varied reactions had laughter bursting from her. Kristen smirked. Brian and Jay were arguing. Rick simply stood there with his mouth gaping.

"Hey guys, this is Tod." Shannon gestured to him.

Loki shook each of their hands as she introduced them. When he got to Jay, Loki gave the shorter man a hard smile. "Sorry mate, but I really don't share well."

Jay put his hands up in surrender with a crooked grin. "Totally get it."

Rick finally got over his shock and spoke. "You're Tod Corvus. You're the Assassin, Sicarius. Wow, I'm a total fan."

Loki gave him a little nod. "Thanks. It's nice to hear you appreciate my work."

Kristen laughed as she came over to elbow Shannon. "The lead singer-songwriter of Raven's Chaos himself? Damn, Shannon. Go big or go home, right?"

<*Am I that big, darling? Are you sore? Is that why you aren't wearing knickers?*> Loki said in her head.

Shannon coughed as she almost snorted the water she was sipping out her nose.

With a lopsided smile, eyes gleaming in amusement, Loki patted Shannon's back as she caught her breath. "I believe it's my turn to go get a round of drinks," he announced. <*Remember your promise. I'll be back in a few minutes.*>

Chapter 12

Asgardian Mead

Rick shook his head, brown eyes wide and round. "Seriously, holy shit, Shannon! Where did you meet Corvus?"

"On a flight."

Shannon wasn't about to tell them it was barely forty-eight hours ago. She could hardly believe it herself. It seemed so much longer, given all that had happened. Still, if she was going to have a fling, a sexy bad boy immortal certainly was a brilliant choice. It wasn't like a god would want anything more than a few nights with her, a mortal. And if that thought made her heart pinch with a twinge of disappointment, she ignored the sensation. She couldn't afford to feel like that, to want more. A relationship was too much. Too risky. Especially with someone of his reputation—a player who had a different woman on his arm and in his bed every night. She was too plain, too boring, and too chubby to hold his interest longer. Damn it, she needed to just enjoy the fling, the fantasy of it.

"That was some of the hottest damn dancing I've seen outside of a movie. Hostia puta!" Jay burbled. "I don't know how the rest of us are still standing." Winking, he gave Shannon a playful leer.

Heat flushed Shannon's cheeks.

"Have you seen the hickeys he's left on her? Damn, so jealous!" Kristen teased as she fanned herself with a grin.

"What hickeys?" Brian asked. "Proof! We're scientists. We want proof!" He chuckled at Shannon's eye roll.

"C'mon, Shannon. Let's see!" Jay teased.

"You guys are so juvenile," Shannon huffed. "It's too warm in here." She removed her jacket, laying it on a stool under the cocktail table and trying to convince herself it was the drinks and number of bodies in the hall that had her overheating.

"Uh-huh. Sure." Kristen nudged Shannon with her elbow. "And the hot rock god has *nothing* to do with it?"

As Shannon scowled at her friend, Loki returned with an amber bottle and a stack of shot glasses. Her eyes widened and she glanced around. That was fast. Had he teleported like he did at the movie theatre? Wasn't he worried about someone seeing him appear and disappear?

"Who's juvenile?" he asked with a knowing twinkle in his eyes as he put the bottle and glasses on the white tablecloth covering the round table, standing slightly behind her.

"These idiots!" Shannon waved at her friends. "They are overly interested in my love life. You'd think they'd never seen a hickey before."

With a half smile, Loki hooked his finger in her cowl neckline, tugging it towards her shoulder. "What? These little love bites?" He kissed her neck, right on the bite mark as her friends hooted.

"You're an exhibitionist," Shannon managed to gasp, biting back a moan. Gods, but she wanted him to continue. Every time he touched her, she went up in flames.

"I have no embarrassment at others seeing how deeply you have claimed my affections. It gives me great satisfaction to see the marks of our passion on you." *<I'm not showing off the love bites on your thighs. Those are just for me.>* His telepathic voice was a possessive brand as his lips moved against her neck.

Fuck, but that erotic purr shivered over her senses and weakened her knees. He had to have felt her pulse leap at his words, the sexy bastard.

Drawing back after steadying her, he smirked. "I brought enough for your friends to have a shot as well. But, I'll warn you now, it is not to be trifled with. It's incredibly strong." After pouring a round of the golden liquid for everyone, including himself, he capped the bottle firmly and handed the drinks out.

They lifted their shot glasses.

"To Shannon and Tod, may they have many more love bites to share!" Kristen toasted.

Laughing, Shannon tossed the shot back. Unlike the tequila, it didn't burn. Instead, it tasted warm like honey. And gods, it went down smoothly, like melting butterscotch candies, heating her every inch of the way.

Within minutes, her friends were swaying on their feet. Kristen tried to talk, but her words slurred. She waved her hand, giggling as she sank onto a chair beside Rick. Jay and Brian clung to the nearby cocktail table, their voices loud as they spoke with the exaggerated enunciation of the seriously inebriated.

Shannon didn't seem drunk, though. Instead, she found it exhilarating. A tingle followed the trail of the mead down to her stomach, then outward. Nerve endings came awake all the way to the tips of her fingers and toes. Her skin prickled.

She'd never felt more alive.

"Wow! That was some shot!" Shannon told Loki.

His head tilted as his gaze narrowed slightly, glancing from her to her friends and back to her.

Jay stumbled into Brian, the two leaning against each other to stay standing. When they almost fell over, Shannon quickly helped her friends sit.

"Huh. I think they are done for the night. We should call them taxis."

"I agree. They do not have your tolerance for alcohol."

Something about Loki's tone had Shannon eying him. Was there was a hidden meaning she wasn't catching? His innocent expression wasn't convincing. Still, she needed to take care of her friends. She walked outside and flagged down a couple of taxis. Together, Loki and Shannon got the others into the vehicles and sent off to their hotels.

"Do you want to go back inside for more dancing?" Loki asked as he and Shannon stood outside on the stone steps. "Don't think I've forgotten the question you have yet to answer."

"What question?" Her body buzzed and tingled. She couldn't remember what he was referring to.

His hands slid down from her waist, over her thighs, and around to cup her ass. "Why are you not wearing knickers? I was curled up on your lap all day, and your lemon sunshine scent made me want to crawl right under that tight skirt and lick you up. You can't imagine the self-control it took to not give in."

The visual shocked Shannon, her breath catching at the same time as her core clenched. "I don't... I don't know how to respond when you say such erotic things about being in another form."

Loki laughed, a wicked, low rumble. "Regardless of the shape I inhabit, it's still always me, darling. I can no more stop lusting after your sweet self than can the moon change its orbit around your planet."

It was becoming difficult to think, everything feeling too sensitive. Hot. She was too hot. A fine film of sweat rose on her skin, and a second pulse beat between her thighs. Distracted, Shannon rubbed the hard points of her nipples against his chest, grounding the prickling sensation there, providing some focus. "Please take me back to your place, Loki. I need you."

With concern in his gaze, he said, "Hold on," and the next moment, they were in his flat.

Taking his hands from her ass, Shannon pulled them up to her breasts, kneading. "Please, Loki. Touch me. My body is on fire. Fuck, I need you to touch me." She arched into his fingers as he twisted and pulled.

Dragging down the neckline and cups of her bra, his clever digits pinched and twisted one aching nipple. His teeth tugged the other, before sucking it hard into his mouth. It drew the fiery sensation in a highly pleasurable way, sending electric sparks flaring between her nipples and her sex as if they were connected by a single nerve.

But it only partially relieved the buzzing in her body.

"Gods yes!" Shannon cried as she clung to him, trying to increase contact with his firm body.

Mouth still busy at her breast, creating glorious waves of pleasure at each nip and pull, he yanked her skirt up to her waist. Long fingers stroked over her core, and she moaned, wanting more, deeper, harder.

The sense of being on fire, body snapping with electricity, was getting stronger, but now centred on where they touched. Between each draw of his mouth and the plunge of those strong fingers, it zapped back and forth, cycling and building.

Desperate with need, Shannon yanked his hair to get him to look at her.

"Fuck me, Loki. Gods! Please fuck me!"

Shoving her back against the wall, he lifted her legs as he entered her hard and fast.

Screaming, Shannon orgasmed at the first thrust. It was overwhelmingly perfect, right on the knife's edge of too much.

He held her, not moving until she stopped convulsing. Little forks of electricity shot through her, sparking from her core. She panted, gazing into his eyes, half-lidded with dark desire.

"Hold on, darling," he purred with a small seductive smile before his mouth took hers. His tongue danced inside as his hips started to move, mouth and cock in sync.

The first few strokes were slow, and she broke her lips from his, writhing as the sparks demanded more. "Harder, please, Loki. Fuck me harder!" Shannon begged as she tightened around him.

With a low snarl, he thrust hard and fast, tilting her hips to get the angle he wanted.

Tugging his hair, she lost herself to the incredible friction. As he panted into her neck, each powerful stroke drew the buzzing, sparking electric sensation tighter, building it rapidly with the heat and intensity of a star compressing.

Moaning, it burst through her like solar flares escaping as her sex shuddered with orgasm.

"Fuck. So fucking tight," Loki growled as he rode out her climax, not slowing his thrusts.

The sparking sensation increased in strength with each masterful stroke, flaring out from her centre to reach more of her body with each shooting burst.

The coiling, burning pressure built and built… until at last, rigidly held at the crest while their hips crashed together in pounding thrusts, the supernova of energy exploded, bursting out of her body, leaving her trembling as Loki shouted his release.

Neither of them moved for a few minutes. They panted, clinging to each other until they caught their breath.

Loki was his black-haired, green-eyed self again, and Shannon ran her fingers through his silky locks. Raising his head from her neck, he smiled and kissed her tenderly.

"Not that I'm in any way complaining, but what was that?" His eyes searched hers for an answer.

"I'm not sure," Shannon said as he eased her from the wall. She lowered her legs from his waist, then turned to brace a hand on the wall. "Holy crap!" she gasped as she took in the devastation surrounding them.

Everything within a five-metre radius was destroyed. The wall appeared to have an impact crater radiating several metres, then cracks spreading further from that. Even the floor was cracked.

Loki spun her around to check her back and head with quick fingers. "You're okay? You aren't hurt?"

"No, I'm fine. Better than fine. I feel fantastic." That weird tingling, buzzing sensation was gone.

"What weird tingling, buzzing sensation?"

"The one that started after I drank the mead. It was like electrical shocks moving throughout my body, and a buzzing, like the sound of bees or maybe the hum of an unshielded high voltage wire. It just kept getting louder... Wait, how did you know about the buzzing sensation?"

"You told me." Loki's eyebrows drew together.

"No, I didn't."

"Yes, you did. You said you felt better than fine, you felt fantastic, and the weird electrical buzzing sensation was gone."

"No, Loki. I thought that. I didn't actually say it."

Tilting his head, he said, "I know you can hear me when I speak to you. Say something back to me."

<*What am I supposed to say? Ask if you can hear me?*>

Loki laughed. "I can hear the annoyance in your voice, whether it be out loud or in our minds, darling. It appears you have acquired an ability."

"What, so you can read my mind now?" <*Fuck!*>

"Only when you project it so clearly. And yes, right now you are mentally shouting." He laughed harder.

"Why can't I hear your thoughts? I'm going to smack you if you don't stop laughing at me!"

Smiling, he kissed her as he rubbed his hands up and down her arms soothingly. "I will teach you how to shield your thoughts so you only share what you want to share," he reassured her.

Bending down, he swept his arm under her knees and back, lifting her as she settled her hands around his neck. "How could I have developed this ability?"

Shannon asked as he carried her into the darkened bedroom. A tiny part of her thought she should be more worried about this sudden change, but between the post-coital bliss and her scientific curiosity, she couldn't seem to get too worked up about an exchange of telepathy.

Setting her down, he removed her clothes, and with a wave of his hand, got rid of his own. Climbing into the bed behind her, he pulled the duvet over them and tucked her into the curve of his body. Her muscles relaxed, sinking into his heat. Damn, it felt good to be held. She hadn't realized how much she'd been starved for comforting touch.

"I suspect it's a combination of your genetics and the Asgardian mead. A tiny proportion of the Midgardian population contains genes from past matings with the gods. If you have enough of those genes, the mead could have triggered their activation."

"Wait, back up. Past matings with the gods?" A bolt of alarm kicked her heart into a rapid tempo, and she jerked upright, twisting to stare at him. "You all just litter humanity with your offspring? Good thing I'm on the pill!" Fuck. Once again, she'd failed to consider birth control or whether he was safe or would give her some sexually transmitted disease. Her fingers dug into the bedding. Where was her damned head?! All he had to do was put his hands on her, and poof, there went all her rational thoughts.

Loki hadn't moved, other than to prop his head on his fist as he met her gaze with an amused twist to his lips. "I'm a god, darling, not a mortal man. I can't get those diseases, so calm those racing worries of yours." He tugged her back down and ran his hand down her back, caressing her in soothing strokes. "We have to choose to have children with mortals. It requires magic to combine the different genetic essences and doesn't happen by chance. True, sometimes it is just sex that leads to children, but other times, gods fall in love and marry their mortal beloved. They raise families with them until the mortal dies."

"Hmpft. Okay." She blew out a relieved breath and sank against him, surrounded by firm muscle and the press of his thigh between hers.

"Shhh... go to sleep now. We'll talk more in the morning." He kissed her temple and tightened his arm around her, cupping her breast. A wave of fatigue hit, her eyelids closing, and it didn't take long to drift off to sleep.

Loki woke to wet heat surrounding his hand and the decadent scent of lush arousal filling his nose. Curling his fingers to drive them deeper within her tight body, he took over pleasuring the squirming woman in his arms, stroking over the ridged spot inside that made Shannon shudder and keen her approval.

"Mmm, darling. I thought I was having an erotic dream until I realized you were broadcasting your need into my sleep," he murmured in a sleepy rumble. He wasn't sure why she was awake after he'd exhausted her earlier, but it was certainly no hardship to enjoy his soulmate again.

And she was his soulmate. He could scarcely believe his fortune. The mental connection was undeniable. Not only could they speak to each other effortlessly, but since he'd given her the mead that held the adtetraphos minerals not found here on Midgard, her thoughts had become crystal clear, as if she was in his mind with him.

Buzzing with excitement and ready to shout his joy to the stars, he hadn't found it easy relaxing enough to sleep earlier, even with the deep satiation that came from pleasuring his mate. But she had needed the rest. It was no small matter to awaken her true genetic potential. He'd expected her to sleep for many hours, not a scant two. Still, now that she was...

She whimpered. "So good. Please don't stop."

"Oh, I won't. You're mine, Shannon." He lifted her leg over his, opening her up to him, driving his fingers deeper through slick folds as his thumb brushed over the sensitive bundle that had her hips jerking.

"Oh my gods, yes," she moaned, writhing in his hold as she plucked at her nipples. "Harder, gods... Loki... please, harder!"

Wild in his arms, she seemed almost desperate and her thoughts frantic. Even as she screamed with orgasm, it didn't relent. If anything, her need intensified.

Was she still transitioning?

Before she could whimper again, the pleading sound tearing at him, Loki flipped her onto her stomach. With her head down and tugging her ass up, he entered her in a single hard thrust. Yggdrasil's trunk, branches, and many gleaming leaves. His eyes almost crossed, and his breath whooshed out as she squeezed him like a silken glove.

"Norns, Shannon. You'll have me spending like an untried youth." As he started to move, lightning burst through his body, searing nerve endings.

"Don't care... just don't stop," Shannon moaned, fisting the dark sheets and shoving back towards him eagerly.

He held her in place by her hips, and their pace turned frantic. Every stroke built the charge between them, flashing higher and higher. Muscles tensed. Breath rasping. Without warning, she screamed as an orgasm shook her and Loki paused, the rhythmic pulses surrounding him stealing his breath.

"By the Nine... so fucking perfect," he groaned as it threatened to pull him over. Yet he couldn't. Not yet. She had too much energy within her, lighting up her arteries and veins to create a glow around them. He'd heard of sex magic like this in the elves, but never had he seen anyone lit up like a summer swarm of glowflies. He had to purge more of this energy.

No sooner did her trembling ease off and he started to move again, than the lightning flared within her, building anew between them with unrelenting sparks that bit at him wherever they touched. Quickly, it reached fever pitch.

Shannon bit the sheets, hands grasping for purchase as her body writhed.

"Again, darling... now," Loki growled, needing her to release more of the transition energy, the fuel activating her hidden immortal genes. He'd never seen an adult transform. Every immortal he knew had done so as a child. Was this too much? Could her body handle this much energy? Bor's balls, but he wished he knew which immortal race had contributed her genes. Was she in danger?

Shannon screamed into the bed, spine bowing as she orgasmed and the energy wave rippled over her body. Yet the reaction demanded more, building again within her until her entire skin glowed with it.

"Loki... Please!" Shannon writhed, skin cracking with fiery sparks.

Desperate to free her from the energies' grip, Loki swore, thrusting harder and reaching a hand down to her clit. "Come now!" Loki demanded as he roared out his release, the flood of his seed and the dual orgasm between them triggering an intense blastwave from her body.

As the last of the orgasmic ripples eased between their joined bodies, Shannon's thoughts turned peaceful for the first time since Loki had awakened.

She still gasped for air, heart pounding, but that prickling transition energy within her had calmed.

Thank the Norns.

Loki's own thoughts were turbulent, and it took him a while to calm as he turned his precious bundle so he could cradle her to his chest. That had been far more intense than earlier this evening. Was she at risk because he'd given her the mead? He'd never forgive himself if the transition hurt her. The thought of losing her when he'd just found her, his soulmate... Shannon's sweat-soaked form trembled in his arms, and he kissed her neck, shoulder, and ear, then comforted them both with long strokes down her back. She fell asleep in his arms, but this time, he couldn't rest. Instead, he memorized the curve of her spine, the dimples above her ass, and those luscious hips, and found peace in the rhythmic beat of her heart against his flesh.

Until she flinched and the buzz returned to her skin.

No delay this time with him already awake. He'd purge as much energy as possible from her. He lifted her over him to allow her to sink onto his cock, to take him at her own speed. Yggdrasil's roots, she was a gorgeous sight rising above him, breasts bouncing and her hair surrounding them.

Still, the transition energy wouldn't release its grip with just her orgasm, despite Loki's best efforts to drive her over again and again. Every time he purged the building wave from her, it returned faster and stronger. Her hair floated out from her body, cracking and snapping with flicks of lightning. When she cried in frustration, he took over.

"Shhh... love, don't cry. I've got you. I will help you." He guided her hips with his hands, thrusting up into her hard and fast the way she needed.

"*Gods*, Loki!" Shannon screamed as they came together and the shockwave exploded from their joined bodies. Limp with exhaustion, she collapsed on top of him.

"I'll take care of you and get you through this, I swear," Loki growled as he stroked her back, brushing the hair away from her sweaty face.

Throughout the night and into the next day, the pattern repeated, giving Shannon about an hour of respite before the uncontrollable need and unrelenting energy built again. Every time, Loki woke her as soon as the sparks returned, drawing unforgiving energy from her with all the skill he'd learned as a fertility god over the centuries. Every inch of his gorgeous soulmate was pleasured and explored, drawing the energy from her repeatedly. Yet only a paired orgasm, the connection between them woven across space and time, released a large enough blast to temporarily sate the transition.

When she finally slept deeply, the last of the energy thankfully dissipated, Loki cradled her, stroking her hair away from her sweat-soaked face. He'd never heard of a transition lasting so long or being so intense. She couldn't be human or mortal. No way. He was certain she'd crossed the threshold to immortal. Someone with only a few genes wouldn't have generated so much energy. She had to be an immortal. But where was she from that she'd grown to adult without access to the adtetraphos minerals common on the immortal planets? Had she been born to immortals exiled or hiding on Midgard?

And that glow... if she was Sidhe, how did she end up on Midgard? Those sick fuckers were driven out two thousand Midgardian years ago, in the same war that cost him Sigyn. Surely Shannon could only have Elven genes descended from a time before the last war if that was the case. No way would the Norns have mated him with one of his enemies.

He frowned, studying her features. Except for a few like the Jotun who had distinctive flesh, skin tone wasn't a reliable indicator for many immortal races as it tended to vary with godly affinities. But her golden olive tones suggested too many possibilities. Perhaps she had Vanir parents. Many of the Vanir were fertility gods. It was where his fertility god heritage came from. And Vanir often had affinities with nature, which might explain her choice of career. Yes, she was probably Vanir. He caressed her soft cheek as anger at her parents stirred in his chest. How in Bor's beard could they have left her in this vulnerable state?

When she mumbled in her sleep, stirring restlessly and frowning, he placed a gentle kiss on her forehead. He had to remember she'd pick up on his feelings through their bond. He rubbed at his breastbone, sensing her presence as a warm glow chasing away the emptiness that had plagued him for so very long. Was she a full goddess with the ability to manipulate seidhr? Would she have additional powers? He'd have to wait and see, but either way, she was his and he was never letting her go. Not ever. Not even if she was one of the damn elves.

"My soulmate. My darling Shannon. Norns, I'm the luckiest male alive," he murmured as he conjured a cool cloth and bathed the sweat from her body. "I'll cherish you always, my love."

PART 2

Winds of Change

"The meeting of two personalities is like the contact of two chemical substances: if there is any reaction, both are transformed."

Carl Jung

Chapter 13

WE DIDN'T START THE FIRE

A sensual murmur penetrated Shannon's brain but she didn't catch the words until they came again.

<*Shannon. Wake up, darling.*>

<*Tired, go away.*> She groaned and shoved her face deeper in the soft blankets that smelled comfortingly like leather, cedar and citrus.

<*C'mon, darling. I've made you food. You burned a lot of energy over the last eighteen hours.*>

<*Pest. I don't want sex right now.*> "Let me sleep," she half mumbled, half thought, and waved a tired hand in the direction his mind seemed to come from.

"Well, that's new." Loki's tone rose in surprise.

Opening one eye, Shannon peered at him. A wall of red and yellow flames hissed and crackled in the air, midway between the end of the bed and the doorway to the bedroom where Loki was standing. His outline was barely visible through the thin, lethal barrier.

"Oh my gods!" She jolted up out of bed, heart pounding, now wide awake.

"Calm down. It's not burning anything. Do you see?"

He sounded curious and intrigued. Foolish man. God. Whatever.

"There is a *wall of fire* inside your flat and you want me to *calm down*?" She gaped at him, wringing her hands, then eyed the bathroom. Could she get past the fire to escape? Or would she be better going for a window?

"Shannon! I need you to calm down. You are making the fire, and it's growing," he said sternly.

"Me?" The shock of his words had her thoughts stuttering.

"Yes, you. Think calm thoughts. Do yoga breathing. Maybe think about water."

Calm thoughts. Calm thoughts. Water, mist, cool air like the rainforest on a spring day. Just walking in the rainforest around my house. She closed her eyes and practiced a few yoga breaths, trying to draw air in and let it out slowly. *Oh gods. Don't freak out. Don't freak out. Stay calm.* She continued the yoga breathing while she fought the thundering of her heart and the taste of panic on her tongue.

"Good. That's excellent," Loki praised in a soothing tone.

Hesitantly opening one eye, Shannon peeked at where the flames had been. A wispy cloud hovered in the air, but there was no sign of fire. She let out a loud shaky sigh and her hand shook as she shoved her hair back.

Loki chuckled as he strode toward her with a plate of food. "It's making for interesting weather in here. I'd say you've gained a few more abilities, my love. You seem to control at least three of the four natural elements."

Don't freak out. Stay calm.

Knees weak, she sank on the edge of the bed, and he handed her the plate. It was breakfast, even though it was clearly late afternoon outside based on the position of the sun visible out the large windows. Her fist clenched around the fork. Shit. She'd missed the talks. No way would she make any of today's sessions. Although, it wasn't like she'd be able to focus on her conference after making a freaking *wall of fire* appear. How the hell had that happened? Control of fire? Water? When had her life turned into Harry Potter?

A shimmer of heat formed in the air in front of her, and her pulse leapt into her throat. *Oh gods. Calm. Stay calm.*

It dissipated, and blanking her mind by reciting tree species names, she started to eat. At the first few bites of food, a rumble sounded and her stomach cramped.

Loki raised his eyebrow, a knowing grin on his face.

Shannon wrinkled her nose at him and waved the fork. Quickly, she shovelled food in and didn't pause until she'd consumed half the plate. "This is great. Thank you. You were right. I needed to eat."

His grin widened into a smirk. "Of course I'm right. I am a god, after all."

"Yeah, yeah, yeah... don't let it go to your head," she grumbled. Mornings weren't her best time of the day, and she needed some serious caffeine to deal with this ludicrous shit. Even if it wasn't really morning. How had she slept so late? A flash of heat shot through her abdomen, reminding her of last night, and she shifted her naked thighs then shoved another bite into her mouth and chewed.

At least the food was settling her growling stomach, as long as she didn't think about... She glanced toward the bedroom door where the wall of fire had been, and nerves churned in her belly. Pausing with a forkful of eggs and a hand pressed on her bare abdomen, she tried to still the sudden nausea. Maybe she shouldn't have eaten after all.

"Oh no, darling." His green eyes glinted. "Your very vocal admiration of my godly status over the last hours is what is going to my head."

The memory of her veins glowing and that prickling pressure inside her that just kept building had her swallowing hard, emotions forming a lump in her throat. *Don't freak out. Breathe.*

Hardly able to get words out above a whisper as she stared at her unmarred skin—no sign of the strange glow or cracks—she asked, "Is that going to happen again? Sex with you is... incredible, yes... but I don't want to be a mindless beast, a slave to it. That was... overwhelming." And scary. Not just the unexplainable light show. It had also been the conflicted feelings of intense connection, but loss of self she'd experienced. It was far more than she'd bargained for from this fling. The remembered intensity sent a shiver down her spine. She couldn't seem to keep her emotional distance. She felt like he was inside her somehow.

Sitting on the bed, Loki hugged her and used a finger to tilt her chin up to meet his gaze. "No, I don't think so. It hasn't reoccurred for the last four hours. I won't let you go through this alone, Shannon. I'm yours, and you are mine. Mine to care for and protect."

It was so weird. Shannon sensed he meant every word. Literally felt it inside her chest like a warmth surrounding her heart. How could he feel that way so fast? Why her? And why was she so certain he did? Yet his confidence and concern were undeniable. Despite her fears of this level of intimacy, his reassurance had tears welling and she swiped the back of her hand at them. "Thank you, Loki. Thank you for helping me through that."

He kissed her tenderly, thumb caressing her cheek, and she sank into the sensation. Damn, he was good at that.

He pulled back, mouth quirked up in a half smile.

"Wait, did you just thank me for fucking your brains out repeatedly? In every way I wanted to? Because that was my pleasure." He winked, emerald eyes gleaming. "And I do mean it was my pleasure, which I plan to repeat frequently. Albeit, not quite at as frenzied a pace as was required last night." He waggled his eyebrows at her.

A bubble of laughter surprised Shannon, lifting the weight pressing on her. His playfulness was exactly the balm she needed to soothe her scattered and frantic thoughts.

He reached for the fork. Laughing, Shannon lifted her arm away, trying to keep it. A frown then alarm crossed his features, and faster than she could blink, he'd caught her arm, cradling it gently as he moved to her other side and examined the deep purple fingermarks still visible.

A flush rose on Shannon's cheeks even as her stomach dropped. She looked away, not wanting to see the disgust on his face. He'd heard her talk about her ex yesterday, but the last thing she wanted to discuss right now was Trent. Especially after the wild night last night and... gods, she didn't even know what to think of the rest.

The light touch of fingertips to her chin turned her face back towards him, and she swallowed before meeting his eyes. Her breath caught at the pained expression, his eyes glistening with unshed tears.

"I'm so sorry, Shannon." He shook his head sharply. "I can't believe I—"

"Oh! No... no, Loki. You didn't do this. I had these bruises when I got on the plane," she interrupted, the words falling out on top of each other in her rush to correct his misunderstanding.

He blinked, then his eyes narrowed and his voice lowered into a dangerous growl. "Your ex. The one you mentioned yesterday to your friend."

"Yes, but can we please not talk about him?" Too many thoughts and feelings were swirling around in her brain. She'd already caused one fire this morning. Holy hells, she'd caused a fire. A fire! How was that even possible? Did she speed up atoms? Create friction? What was she burning to create the flames? Oxygen?

A tingling warmth on her upper arm had her opening her eyes—she hadn't realized she'd shut them. Loki met her gaze with a small, tight smile, a muscle ticking in his jaw, then he lifted his hand from her arm. The bruises were gone. What the fuck? Not even a green or yellow tinge remained. As if the bruises had never been there. How did he get rid of the inflammation? The blood cells in the tissues? Did he speed up the healing process? Or did he remove the cells and fluid entirely, repairing—

"We can leave the discussion of him for another day, darling," Loki said, his tone still a deep rumble, interrupting her racing thoughts. "But how about you finish your breakfast?" He took the fork from her and fed her the last of her food.

"Thank you," she managed as in between bites, he distracted her with kisses. Damn, he could kiss. Shannon shivered, pleasure still tickling her senses as she chewed the last forkful.

Smiling one of those wicked little grins of his, he took the plate away, and in the next moment, it disappeared in a swirl of black. She blinked. Yes, the plate was still gone as if it had never been there. Where did it go? Was there some cosmic trash pile? She took a deep breath in, held it, and let it out slowly, trying to calm herself before her mind raced off in yet another direction.

"So how are you all energetic today, not needing sleep?" *Stop freaking out, Shannon. Get it together, damn it.*

"Darling, are you *really* questioning my stamina after last night?" He raised a black eyebrow.

She snorted a laugh at the appalled affront in his expression.

"I've lived the equivalent of many human lifespans, Shannon. I don't need as much sleep as a mortal. Gods are gods not simply because of their powers and affinities, but because those things give us energy, fuel for our life forces. Besides chaos, I get energy from stories and music, but I'm also a fertility god. Sex with you recharges my energy. It certainly doesn't drain it. But by all means, if you need me to prove it to you again, I'm at your disposal." He stood and bowed with a flourish of his arm.

She held a palm out and laughed. "Stay away, sex fiend. Let me recover first." Then she frowned. "So that's why you've got a career as a musician and actor? Those things give you energy?"

"And sex... don't forget the sex." He grinned and wiggled his eyebrows before his expression turned serious. "How do you feel?"

Shannon fought down the flash of fury at the reminder of his reputation and numerous conquests and focused on Loki's question. Ignoring her mental conflict, physically she felt good. Really good. Amazing, actually. She wasn't tired, and even more surprisingly, she wasn't sore despite the numerous times her well-endowed god had bedded her.

Loki's lips twitched with amusement. Damn it. Was she broadcasting her thoughts again?

Rolling her eyes at him, she flicked a hand as she rose to go to the bathroom. A thud sounded behind her, and she turned. Loki was picking himself up off the floor.

She frowned. How'd he fall? "Are you okay?"

"Sure, darling. I always get tossed around in the bedroom by my lover's newly awakened powers after spending hours seeing to her pleasure in our bed."

Shannon's mouth dropped open, working her way through the meaning of his dryly amused words. "Oh shit! I knocked you on your ass with a flick of my hand?"

He walked over to her, capturing her fingers in his. "Yes, love. Indeed, you did. Be careful where you fling those lethal weapons now."

She gazed up into his amused eyes, yet she didn't feel like laughing. Not about this. "I didn't mean to. I'm sorry." She could have hurt him, burned him. Holy crap, how was she going to deal with all of this? Being out of control was untenable. She *hated* it. Why was she able to do this? It made no sense that she had special genes. Whatever it was, this power, she didn't want it.

He smiled down at her, releasing one hand to touch a fingertip to her nose. "I know. It's just chaos in action, my darling. Far be it from me to complain about a little chaos. Let's go shower."

She opened her mouth to tell him to take it back, take these abilities back, but his lips descended, stealing her thoughts. Sweeping her into his arms and carrying her into the bathroom, he showed her just how slow and sensuous he could be when they had nothing but time.

Chapter 14

SHATTERED

Loki's bedroom was destroyed. The bed frame listed to one side like a boat taking on water, with the headboard in pieces. Chunks of drywall were missing. Brick, timber, and wires peeked out, the guts of the building exposed in a tragic peepshow. Shattered remains of a mirror and night tables left glittering shards of glass and wood in a barefoot minefield around the bed. Fortunately, the walk-in closet and windows appeared to have been outside the zone of devastation.

Even after the wall of fire, the clouds, and the water vortex she'd accidentally created in the shower, Shannon gaped at the level of destruction she'd caused last night. That fire had seriously rattled her brain for her to have missed all of this when she'd leapt from the bed and then ate her breakfast in a fog of confusion.

Loki kissed Shannon on the neck from behind, resting his chin on her shoulder. Yet despite his attempts at comfort, fear and panic churned in a toxic stew within her stomach.

"I'm sorry..." she started, not sure what to say. How did one apologize for destroying another's home? Acid crept up her throat and she swallowed it down, trying to not feel too much, to not notice the unsteady beat of her heart and little shooting pains in her lungs. Gods. Weren't fires and water spouts enough devastation for one day?

Loki shrugged. "It's nothing I haven't done in a moment of anger or despair, darling. God of Chaos, after all."

He sounded completely nonchalant, but how could she believe that? Was this kind of destruction normal around immortals? Trent would have freaked out and thrown a screaming fit.

"Is… is there a way to get rid of these abilities?" she whispered in a quiet squeak, shoulders rising as she hunched slightly.

"No. You'll need to learn to control them."

The tiny kernel of hope that she could just ignore the issue died at the certainty in his tone.

"How…" Shannon took a shuddering breath in, then slowly exhaled and tried again. "How did you learn to control your powers?" *Focus. Calm. Breathe.* She took another breath and blew it out slowly.

Loki wrapped an arm around her, palm spread at her waist as the heat of his chest sank into her back, surrounding her. "We learn as we mature into adulthood on Asgard. I suspect you will figure it out much faster, given you are no child," he murmured as he caressed her hair with gentle fingertips.

"Where do I start?" Her throat bobbed as she swallowed, then swallowed again against the churning miasma bubbling within her.

"At this point, your powers are likely tied to your emotions and intent. You'll need to develop the sense of crafting your will to create what you want. I don't manipulate the natural elements specifically, but there are a few parallels. Without conscious thought, you speed up the friction of atoms, creating fire; change the density and movement between atoms, creating air currents; or combined with water, create clouds or that lovely water tornado in the bathroom. These are similar to forms of telekinesis, which I also have, but mine is not as strong or refined to specific types of atoms as yours likely is."

Calm, stay calm. Focus on the science. Science was logical. Surely, she could figure this out. "Okay, that makes some sense, although I don't understand how I'm doing that."

"That part is magic, darling. I can't explain it quickly in terms of your science, as you haven't developed the theory for it yet. I'll teach you more, but I don't want to overwhelm you right now."

Ha. Too late. A burble of hysterical laughter rose within her, and she choked it down.

"Suffice it to say," Loki continued, "magic, or seidhr, is a form of energy we have differing abilities to draw on and manipulate." He gestured to the shattered mirror. "Imagine drawing the pieces back together, picturing in your mind what the mirror looked like before."

Closing her eyes, Shannon took another deep breath in, then out, and tried to relax and concentrate on the idea of pulling it back together, of pieces joining, cracks filling into a seamless whole.

"Open your eyes."

She did and found the mirror as it had been before last night, a single smooth pane of glass, but the back was a fine spiderweb of cracks.

"Wow! That's incredible." She couldn't help her little squeak. Had she melted the glass fragments by adding heat or did she briefly change their matter state? How did it work? For the first time, the possibilities seemed amazing. Maybe this wasn't so bad after all.

"Yes. Keep in mind you can shatter it again just as easily."

"It's easier to destroy than restore it, isn't it?"

"Yes. Often only a single power or affinity will allow you to remake something, but destruction can always be caused in multiple ways. Chaos wants to happen." He smirked.

Taking her hand, he pulled her out of the bedroom. "Come, Shannon. Let's go outside and see how you do in the wider world."

She halted, pulse pounding. "Um... I'm not sure I'm ready for that, Loki. What if I damage something? Accidentally hurt someone? Won't people see?"

He chuckled and coaxed her forward. "I promise I will make sure no one sees, and I will prevent you from hurting anyone. If you damage something, I'll fix it."

"You can do that?" She held his gaze, waiting for his answer.

His smile widened, and he waved a hand at the mirror. The spiderweb of cracks disappeared, smoothing out. "Yes, love. I can. You and everyone around you will be safe."

"Okay." She pulled on the comfortable shoes she'd worn on the plane, and they headed out of the flat, walking past multi-story brick and stonework buildings along a tree-lined street to the nearby Hyde Park. The sun had already set, with streetlamps casting shadows on the sidewalk. As they got closer to the park, a low murmur became a deafening roar.

"Why is it so loud?" Shannon shouted to be heard over the din, slapping her hands over her ears.

Loki cocked his head and his mouth moved, but she couldn't hear him. There were too many voices overlapping. Was there some event in the park? How did the noise not bother him?

<*Focus on just my voice,*> she heard over the cacophony. <*Imagine a wall between you and the voices, and the only one you hear is me*> With his hands on her cheeks, Loki stared into Shannon's eyes.

As she gazed back at him, she pictured the two of them inside a large bubble. The voices gradually receded until they were background sounds, muffled by the bubble.

"Is that better?" he asked.

"Yes!"

"You can do the same thing to keep your thoughts to yourself. Develop the practice of keeping a mental wall up as a shield. You can make it thin or thick and create separate areas for different thoughts. Once you practice enough, it will be unconscious, like breathing, and you won't have to think about it to maintain it."

"Where are all the voices coming from?" Shannon looked around the wide-open green space and surrounding trees of the path they'd chosen. Late in the evening and with no events occurring tonight, there were few people about. What was she hearing?

"Imagine thinning the wall in one spot to pick a few voices out of the crowd. What are they saying?"

Closing her eyes, she visualized the bubble and chose one small area to draw those voices in.

<*Hey, over here. Over here, ladies. Look at the magnificent spot I have picked out! Over here, ladies.*>

<*Those are my nuts! Get away! Mine, my nuts!*>

<*Puh-leese. As if I'd pick him to watch my eggs. Look at how droopy his tail is. I can do better.*>

Loki laughed. Shannon's bubble wavered before she firmed it up again.

"I can hear the voices through your mind. It's the animals. You are hearing the animals," he said with a smile. "You should also be able to talk to them, as I can. It's handy when I'm shifted into a different form."

Her mouth dropped open as she blinked at him for a few seconds. "Wow… that's… wow. As a scientist who studies the environment, we often talk about wondering what animals think, but now I can actually find out!"

Shannon's pulse leapt as her mind spun with the ramifications. Holy cow. This would spark so many new avenues of research. It would revolutionize their understanding of ecology and behaviour, species interactions, and community dynamics. It was ground-breaking. There were so many questions—

Loki shook his head, interrupting her train of thought. "You can't reveal the existence of the gods, Shannon." He took her hand as he held her gaze. "Particularly now with the current culture of Midgard. You'd either be labelled as a crackpot and they'd want to lock you up in a psych ward, or they'd believe you faked it with some sort of special effect, thereby losing all your scientific credibility. This world has forgotten gods and magic are real."

"What? No." Frowning, Shannon yanked her hand free and stepped back. The brief pillar of calm she'd created to bolster herself by focusing on her curiosity, logic, and science crumbled under her feet. Her fists clenched, and she took another step back. "No, I don't accept that. I'm sure there are ways of using science to support my findings. My friends would believe me."

His eyes refused to release her as he winced, lines forming on his forehead. "They will turn on you, Shannon."

A panicked rhythm pounded in her veins, creating a thundering drumbeat. She couldn't get enough air as she desperately tried to suck in a breath. When he moved towards her, she held out a hand to ward him off, even as she put more distance between them. No. No way. How was she supposed to hide these abilities? What if she made a mistake? The acidic churning in her stomach burned her throat. All the feelings she'd been trying to stuff down all day swirled up in a toxic brew of volcanic uncertainty.

"No, they won't, Loki! They wouldn't do that!" she rasped out, trying to convince herself as much as him. Nightmarish images of her being locked up in a straitjacket or strapped to a bed created a cold sweat on her back.

Sympathy etched his face. "You can't tell your friends. We will need to look into your family to see where the god genes came from. If it was your grandparents or further back, you may not be able to tell your parents or siblings. It could destroy your relationship with them."

"No!" The chill of fear competed with the swirling heat of denial. Hide this from *everyone*? It wasn't possible. Not if the powers were linked to her emotions. She wasn't a robot, damn it. What the hell was she supposed to do? Become a hermit? Fuck that. She was *not* losing her career.

He held a hand out to her. "I'll help you and be here for you. But please, Shannon, don't do this to yourself. Please, I'm trying to save you this pain."

"I *don't* believe you!"

Wind whipped around her, and Shannon's feet lifted off the ground. Her body burned, thoughts raging like firecrackers, seeking an outlet, a crack in his logic. Anything that would let her deny it. She couldn't accept his words.

Why would he say such hurtful things? It wasn't true. It couldn't be true. How *dare* he attack her career, her one source of success? *He's like Trent, stalking me, tearing me down, trying to take away anyone that would stop him,* a voice inside insisted. Just like Trent had insisted he was the only one who could help her, guide her. That she'd be nothing without him. She'd proved him wrong. She'd prove Loki wrong, too!

"Please, Shannon..." Loki fought against the wind shoving him back. "I'm trying to protect you. They can't know about you or they will reject who you are."

Protect her? Trent had said that, too. That he was just telling her the truth, so she didn't delude herself, didn't overreach her place, didn't embarrass herself. But it had all been lies. Lies to control her. No, this couldn't be true. It couldn't.

"This is my *entire life* you are talking about!" She was unable to draw a full breath. Her head spun, eyes blurring. Spots filled her vision at the thought of losing everything. Her career. Her family. Her friends. Fuck, even her very genetics. It had to be a lie. It had to be.

A hand reached for her and she shoved it away, jerking in clumsy lurches as the raging winds buffeted her.

"*NO!*"

Godsdamn it, she'd fought too hard for her life. Dedicated her entire adult existence to science. Barely escaped Trent's clutches, finally earned success on her own, and created her place in life. She couldn't do this again.

No, she didn't *want* this.

None of it.

She couldn't breathe. He was suffocating her, trapping her. Gods, she couldn't breathe. Flailing her arms and legs, Shannon punched and kicked at him. She had to get away.

The burning winds swirled her higher off the ground, out of his reach, where he couldn't hold her down or try to cage her.

"I don't want you to experience the pain of their jealousy, or worse, their fear of you," he shouted over the howling wind, reaching up for her. "You aren't safe, Shannon. Please."

Snarling, Shannon flew higher into the air, lightning cracking around her shaking limbs and hitting the surrounding ground. Each boom of thunder echoed in her mind, her pulse pounded in her veins, rain falling with hot tears streaking down her cheeks.

Who was he to change it all? Another man telling her what she could and couldn't do, trying to control her! Just like her ex. Another trying to destroy her life and take everything from her? No! She wouldn't let him!

<Don't leave me! Shannon! Please!>

Blocking Loki's mental cry, Shannon screamed in a wordless fear-fuelled rage that tore the sound from her ravaged throat. She couldn't lose it all. She couldn't! The wind carried her into the sky away from him, far below on the ground.

Chapter 15

LEFT BEHIND

Loki had never envied Thor's ability to fly in storms until now. As the wind died down, he stood on the torn ground, staring until Shannon disappeared from his sight. Even as a bird, Loki wouldn't have been able to fight those winds to follow her.

Collapsing to his knees, he fisted his hands in his hair as conflicting emotions tore through him.

That he couldn't go after her had tension transforming his muscles to Dwarven iron. His supposed silver tongue had failed to find the right way to protect her, to convince her. Bor's balls, he'd felt her fear and confusion cutting into her mind like shards of that broken mirror.

Damn it. He knew what it was like to find out you weren't who you thought you were, that your life had been a lie, and to have your sense of identity torn from you. It had taken him decades to deal with his anger and pain after discovering Odin and Frigga had lied to him about being adopted, furious they hadn't told him the truth before Frigga's twin sister, his birth mother, had died. They'd robbed him of the chance to get to know Revna.

And if he hadn't been acting out in childish jealousy and resentment, he never would have set up the situation that resulted in his oldest brother's death. A mistake, a stupid childish prank he could never take back. It would haunt him for eternity. Of anyone, he should have been able to reach Shannon, to spare her some of that pain.

Why hadn't he found a better way to introduce her to her new reality?

His pulse pounded a guilty refrain over and over with every beat in his head. This was his fault. His damn fault. How did he screw it all up? Tears streamed unchecked down his cheeks.

And now he'd lost her.

His soulmate. The one person in the entire universe he should have been able to reach, to help, to protect. The bitterness of failure coated his tongue.

Most mortals likely couldn't hurt her physically now, which was only a little reassuring. She should be stronger, faster, and have advanced healing... he hoped. She *had* to be an immortal. Didn't she? It had been so long since a demigod had transitioned that he couldn't remember the limits to a mortal's power when they didn't fully crossover.

No, she was a goddess, a powerful immortal. No way could she have channelled so much energy if she wasn't. But still, she was on her own, a fledgling with powers she barely understood, in a world that was not kind to anyone different, to those that didn't fit into a social construct mortals accepted.

Damn it to Helheim! He yanked his hair.

Horror grew within him, icing his veins as he realized how much she didn't yet know. There were other dangers, predators of the immortal world that could and would kill her... or worse, keep her alive to torment for eons.

And his enemies.

By the Nine, Loki had so many enemies after two wars against the elves, skirmishes with the giants and the Shen. Conflicts with demons and the soul-stealers cropped up occasionally, although not in the last few hundred years here on Midgard. Let alone dwarves and other gods he'd pissed off.

He'd failed to warn her or prepare her at all. She had no idea. None.

Yggdrasil's roots—his chest tightened, heart clenching—he might lose his soulmate before they ever got a chance to really know each other. After losing his wife Sigyn, a fully trained Asgardian warrior, to the Unseelie—the dark elves—the terror of Shannon's vulnerability stole the breath from his lungs.

He couldn't do it, couldn't go through that again. Not his soulmate. His one perfect match.

Black spots grew in his vision as his body arched, muscles rigid, seidhr swirling and escaping his control as the pressure built, coiled, and strained his every cell. Screaming with eyes turned blind, he released an explosive burst of telekinesis that shattered every carefully trimmed hedge, rosebush, and tree in a twenty-metre radius. Grass tore from the soil, leaving a blackened blast crater around him.

He didn't know how long he sat there on his knees, panting, seidhr flaring in black waves around his body, but he glanced up when Thor thumped down in the dark nearby. He'd recognize his brother's heavy tread anywhere.

Wiping away the tears he hadn't realized were still flowing, Loki stood to meet him. His limbs still shook, muscles flexing as he fought the desperate need to follow Shannon even as he knew he couldn't catch up.

"What's happened, brother? I came out to investigate an unusual storm that disappeared before I could track it down, and instead, I find you in a circle of devastation. What did the flora and fauna do to deserve your enmity?" Thor called out in his booming voice before he reached Loki.

"I failed her, Thor," Loki told him in a subdued tone, voice raspy after his screams.

"Who?" Thor put his hand on Loki's shoulder, then glanced around. "Your mortal?"

"You were right. Shannon isn't mortal. She's my soulmate." Loki swallowed, voice cracking. "I awakened goddess genes in her when I gave her Asgardian mead. She's strong, powerful. We hadn't figured out her lineage yet, or even all of her powers, but she's an elemental and can communicate with animals."

"That's great! I'm so happy for you, Loki. But... where is she?" Thor glanced around him again, frowning.

"That's just it. I fucked up. She was already confused and afraid from the transition. It was... it was intense." Loki closed his eyes, fists clenched as he pounded his thighs. "Fuck. I was so stupid. Instead of easing her into it, I pushed too hard. She freaked when I tried to tell her she couldn't use her powers to change the mortal world's understanding of science. She's a scientist, a professor, that's who she is. It's everything she's worked towards her entire life."

Thor's eyes widened, and he opened his mouth to reply, but Loki forestalled him with a hand as he continued, "If that wasn't bad enough, I was stupid. I told her she couldn't tell her friends or her family. I was trying to tell her the dangers, to protect her, but instead, I ripped her entire sense of identity from her."

Eyes stinging, unable to hold his tears back, Loki swiped impatiently at them. "I was such a git, wrapped up in how happy I was at finding her. I wasn't paying enough attention to her feelings until it was too late."

Thor winced. "That does not sound like your usual eloquent self. Where is she?"

Loki waved a hand toward the sky. "She was that storm you spoke of, the one that disappeared before you found it. I don't have your ability to fly in winds like that. I couldn't follow her."

"What?" Thor choked out, his voice rising. "She's already able to fly using storms? When did you unlock her powers?"

"Last night." Self-consciously, Loki wiped his cheeks, then crossed his arms over his chest.

Thor stared at him.

"I know, Thor. Don't look at me like that."

His brother continued to stare at him.

"Yes, she's a fucking fledgling with enough power to do serious damage if she has a mind to!" And a prime target for everyone who hated him. It was a nightmare.

"Loki, we need to find her quickly, before the giants, dark elves, or any of our many enemies find her to take advantage of her lack of knowledge and training! They'd cage her to plunder her power resources." Horror crept into Thor's tone. "But Bor's hairy balls, if they find out she's your soulmate, they'll torture her to pay you back."

Loki's heart gave a panicked beat, and he locked muscles that didn't want to hold him upright. "I know, Thor! Stop adding to my fears. I already feel guilty. I handled this entirely wrong. Fly, see if you can find where she touched down. I'll try her friends, places familiar to her." Norns, please let them find her quickly.

Thor rose from the ground, wind swirling around him. "I'll let you know when I locate her." At Loki's nod, Thor sped into the sky.

Meanwhile, Loki blew out another couple of breaths to calm his frantic pulse, then teleported back to his flat to get addresses of where she might go, starting with her hotel, conference, and friends.

Surely they'd find her first. They had to.

Chapter 16

ANYTHING BUT EARTHQUAKES

Shaking, vision narrowed, and heart circulating despair with every frantic beat, Shannon was swept far into the night sky. In bursts of lightning, she screamed her denial until her voice turned hoarse, and eventually, when the worst of the furious tempest passed, she cried. The winds slowed, carrying her shattered shell with a flood of tears and rain to the ground.

As dawn crept above the horizon, she found herself on a steep mountainside staring down at brilliantly blue waters that stretched as far as she could see. A light breeze caressed her face with the scent of salt and spicy sage. Wiping still overflowing tears and sinking to sit, she watched waves crash on the rocky shoreline far below until she calmed enough to consider Loki's words.

Her chest ached, but the rational, logical part of her acknowledged the painful truth. The modern world wasn't ready to accept the existence of gods. Science wasn't ready for this kind of knowledge.

It was why she'd reacted so badly. Despite knowing he was right, she hated that he'd forced her to face it immediately, practically shoving the truth at her. Even if some of her friends believed her, believed her findings, she risked them resenting her over something out of her control. Jealousy was ugly and destructive. The pain of being stabbed in the back by a trusted friend never fully healed.

Hell, Trent had been jealous of her career success and look how that had turned out. And Lynda, her best friend... no, out of the question. But maybe... maybe Kristen?

She pounded a fist on her thigh. How could she burden her friend with this? Restless energy gripped Shannon, and she rose, climbing the small distance to reach the peak. Yet the feeling didn't abate, and a sinking weight, leaden in her gut, answered her. She couldn't. To force Kristen to acknowledge Shannon's new truth and then keep silent about it? Something of this magnitude and its potential impact on the scientific community? No, that'd be no better than what Loki had done. Just thinking it was selfish. It would tear their friendship apart.

Shannon paced circles into the hilltop, dodging low-hanging olive tree branches, the occasional fig tree, and sagebrush, rubbing her arms as she wandered.

Would people fear her if this got out? Absolutely. If they didn't understand or couldn't control it, people would be afraid. Just the nature of humanity. Rationally, she saw the point Loki had been trying to make. She didn't like it, damn it, but it made sense.

Still, it didn't mean she couldn't be selective with who knew... like maybe her family. Were they like her? They had to be, didn't they? Her dad had passed away ten years back—a storm took his life and destroyed his boat while salmon fishing—but her mom and two siblings still lived in British Columbia. Mom told her that their background was Irish and First Nations, tracing their lineage back through the Fraser River tribes.

But if that was true, where did the god genes come from?

Staring up at the sky, Shannon sat on a nearby rocky ledge and considered the childhood stories her mom had told her. Stories of Raven creating the sun, moon, and stars, or teaching humans to make nets and fish for salmon, Sasquatch protecting the forests, and the Orca people, Lords of the Ocean, stealing women for their underwater villages. Were these First Nation legends based on actual gods? Knowing gods existed, that actual magic existed, how was Shannon to know what was real and what wasn't? Everything she thought she knew could be wrong. It was a lot to accept. Shaking her head, she rocked in place. Damn it, too much.

How would her family react if they didn't have enough god genes to get powers like her? Shannon shivered, a chill climbing her spine. She loved her family, but they weren't always very nice. Her mom had Shannon's older brother while still in her teens and wasn't the most mature of individuals. Rose was prone to passive-aggressive attacks, as Shannon had seen during arguments with her uncle, their only other living relative, aside from her immediate family. He was even worse. Shannon tried to avoid Uncle Colin for the most part. Both her mom and uncle were champion grudge-keepers. Growing up with them was probably why she'd tolerated Trent's abuse for so long.

No, she couldn't do it. Telling her mom or uncle about what had happened or offering them Asgardian mead would be like throwing a hand grenade into a box of fireworks. A shudder wracked Shannon's torso. There was no way it would end well.

Her older brother was different and more like Shannon. Liam was a bookworm. He loved his music, stories, and talking about the past. He was an English and music teacher in the town they'd grown up in, living just down the road from her mom. Despite the seven-year difference in ages, Shannon was closest to him. She spent most of her time with him and his wife when she visited. She didn't think he'd resent her, but on the other hand, he and Sarah were happy with their life the way it was. Her brother didn't do well with change, with chaos or disruption. He liked things predictable.

He wouldn't reject her. It'd be difficult, but he'd believe her. Still... she couldn't do it. She loved him too much to shatter his beliefs. This wasn't a weight he needed to carry. Not on her behalf.

Shannon loved her older sister too, but she was not oblivious to Heather's faults. Her sister was selfish and vain. Shannon had grown up with her sister's catty remarks. Heather would fluctuate between wanting to treat Shannon like a doll, as Heather was six years older than Shannon, to cutting her down when Heather decided her little sister was getting too much attention. Shannon snorted and shook her head. There was no way she could share anything like this with her sister. It would annihilate any possibility of a relationship between them.

Her chest hollow, aching with loss, Shannon rocked in place, her arms wrapped around her middle.

Loki was right. She hated it, but he was.

She couldn't tell her family. She couldn't tell her friends. These godsdamned abilities had isolated her from everyone she cared about, ripped them from her.

What did she have left?

Nothing. No one.

She keened, and her trembling shook her down to her bones.

Her career... Where did she even stand with that now? With gods being real, how could she trust what she understood of science? Everything she'd worked for, all her degrees, getting tenure, her promotions, and fighting for equality against a system that seemed to reward misogyny. Hell, all her years of research and struggle to have her findings and opinions heard before Trent, then after with him trying to damage her reputation... a full seventeen years, half of her entire frigging life. She'd clung to it as the only great thing left in the wake of Trent's destruction. She'd been successful despite him.

For fuck's sake, she'd spent all her adulthood striving for this career, to be a scientist. Was it all inconsequential now? Tears welled, overflowed, and coursed down her cheeks. Who was she without that? Without her family? Without her friends? Head in her hands, she sobbed as her heart broke.

"Do you mind shutting off the waterworks?" an annoyed voice snapped. "You are ruining my hair and make-up!"

Adrenaline speared Shannon's spine. She snapped her gaze up to spot a tall woman in a beautiful white empire-waisted gown covering one shoulder strolling around the trunk of a nearby fig tree. The woman stopped within a metre of Shannon's rocky ledge. Long straight raven-black hair framed a bronze face with dark kohl-rimmed eyes and a mouth pressed tightly together in irritation.

"Oh! Umm... I'm sorry!" Shannon blurted, then searched her sparse surroundings. Where the hell had the woman come from?

The woman waved her hand imperiously, gesturing to the overhead rain cloud. The only rain was here, near Shannon, with no other clouds in sight.

Lovely. On top of everything else, she'd turned into Eeyore.

Squeezing her eyes shut, Shannon imagined warmth and gentle breezes. The last few drops of rain hit and then silence. When she opened her eyes, the cloud had dissipated.

"That's better. Now, who are you? I don't recognize you," the woman demanded as she reached up to pluck figs from a nearby branch.

Shannon blinked. Why would this stranger think she'd recognize her? "I'm Shannon, Shannon Murphy."

"I've never heard of a goddess Shannon, let alone one with two names at the same time." The woman wrinkled her nose. "With a weird name like that, you almost sound like a mortal. Clearly, you aren't, though. What pantheon? Where are you from?" Popping another fig into her mouth, she chewed, ebony eyebrow raised as she waited.

Shannon's cheeks flushed at the woman's condescending tone. Was this stranger another immortal? And thought Shannon was as well? Was she? "I don't know. I'm from Canada. British Columbia."

The woman frowned at her. "How can you not know what pantheon? What realm are you from?"

Her imperious tone had Shannon straightening with fists clenched. Damn it, she hated being treated like she was stupid. "Here," Shannon snapped through clenched teeth.

The woman laughed. "What, are you *new*?"

Shannon scowled.

The woman paused, taking in Shannon's expression. "Oh, for the love of Ra! You *are* new! What... did someone slip you some food of the gods?"

Shannon pressed her lips together, crossing her arms. If this bitchy stranger was just going to fucking mock her, Shannon didn't care to continue this conversation. "Yes, actually," she snarled. Could she make it rain again and chase the damn harpy away?

The woman laughed harder, then stopped suddenly and cocked an eyebrow. "Hilarious! Do you want to talk about it?"

"No, not really." As if Shannon wanted anything to do with this horrible woman.

The woman held a hand out, palm towards Shannon. "Okay, that's your business. I'm a firm believer in not forcing someone to talk about things they don't want to." She shook her head. "Too many nosy gods anyway that need to just mind their own damn business. Come on, then." She turned her hand, extending it.

Shannon looked at it like it was a venomous snake, and raised her eyebrow. Why the hell would she take the hand of some nasty, rude stranger? She might be *new*, but she wasn't a fool, thank you very much.

The woman's lips twitched, and she shrugged one shoulder. "I'm sorry I teased you a little. But we can't have you wandering around causing havoc or falling victim to unsavoury types." She wiggled her fingers, hand still outstretched. "Let's figure out what you can do, shall we? You don't have to come with me, but I assume you want to learn about your powers?"

Okay, well that was true. And Shannon wasn't sure she trusted Loki. Not when he'd caused all of this without warning her in the first place. If this woman was dangerous, then Shannon would just fly away in another storm... if she could figure out how she did that in the first place. Damn. Maybe she did need this woman... or goddess, presumably.

Their palms met, and the woman helped her up.

"Yes, I do. Who are you?"

The goddess rolled her eyes and shook her head again with a little frown creasing her forehead. "Oh! Did I forget to introduce myself? I'm Isis. I go by other names, of course, as all of us gods do over time, but mostly, I prefer Isis."

Wait... Unsavoury types? Who did gods have to worry about? "What did you mean by unsavoury types?"

Isis wrinkled her nose. "There are some gods and immortals that you are better off avoiding. Not all are nice, Shannon."

Huh. Not much of an answer. Still... Shannon looked around at the brown hills with only hints of green, scrubby vegetation interspersed with trees, the white town with bright blue roofs in the distance, and the deep blue waters. "Where are we, exactly? It was night when I got here."

Isis smiled and patted Shannon with her other hand. "We're on the Greek island Kasos, but I'll take us to my estate outside Alexandria in Egypt. We can have breakfast and get to know one another." As she spoke, she pulled Shannon into the sky with a shocking strength.

Shannon stared down at what must be the Mediterranean Sea. Good thing she wasn't afraid of heights. A sudden thought had Shannon jerking her gaze back to Isis, eyes wide. "Won't mortals be able to see us?"

Isis grinned, dark eyes twinkling. "No, I've cloaked us with my magic. Neither their satellites nor their eyes will see us. Any eyes. Don't worry."

They sped through the sky faster than Shannon would have expected, landing a short time later in a large courtyard with date palms, olive, pomegranate, and fig trees, and blooming hedges of oleander. Water trickled in fountains and brightly coloured clay tiles created intricate patterns on the walls where grape vines were trellised. Single-story tan buildings with red clay tile roofs had interconnected walkways between them and shaded alcoves.

"How did you find me?" Shannon asked as Isis led her to a table covered with a white linen cloth and one place setting in a shaded area between the buildings and under a large date palm.

"I take a spin around the Mediterranean every few days to see what's going on. This has always been a somewhat volatile region, and it's important to pay attention. A single storm cloud raining on an individual mountaintop is not a normal occurrence." She smiled as she waved Shannon into a seat.

Her staff, dressed in flowing fabric the same tan colour as the buildings, brought out a second place setting, and soon, fruit, breads, and yogurt were set out on the table.

"Please let me know if you'd like something else. As my guest, I want you to feel comfortable."

Wow. This goddess's mood sure bounced between extremes. "Thank you, Isis. I appreciate your hospitality." Shannon's stomach growled and she blushed, but Isis just smiled and passed her the various dishes, encouraging her to take more. Glancing around, Shannon noticed several women tending the gardens and cleaning the water features. All appeared human. "Does your staff know you are a goddess? Or are they not human?"

Isis's eyes glinted. "They're human and yes, they know, but they also worship me. Not that I ask them to, but I've protected them and their families for generations. Most are women I've rescued from bad situations."

"Do you worry about them telling anyone?"

"As long as they keep my secrets, they don't have to worry about the changing politics, warlords, or terrorists. They view it as an honour to live and work on my estate."

Shannon could see how that kind of mutual loyalty would benefit both.

Isis's expression turned lethally sharp. "And if they ever betrayed me, I'd kill them and every single one of their family members back three generations, wiping out their entire genetic line."

Shannon froze, halted by the vicious words and predatory smile. Holy hell. *Note to self, don't piss this goddess off.* The unpredictable mood shifts were giving her whiplash. Maybe she wouldn't stay too long with Isis. She clearly took revenge to the extreme. Not someone Shannon wanted to get on the bad side of. Ever.

They ate in uncomfortable silence for a few minutes before Isis started quizzing her on what she knew of her powers.

"So we know you can manipulate air, water, and fire. That's three out of the four elements, so you probably have some affinity for earth as well."

Shannon frowned, thinking of the mirror in Loki's bedroom. "What would an affinity for earth look like?"

Isis tilted her head back and forth, lips pursed. "It depends on how strong and specific your powers are. It could be as small as moving grains of sand or causing earthquakes. Or it could be the ability to influence growing things, plants in particular."

Earthquakes? Shannon gulped the bite in her mouth in a painful lump and a panicked fluttering twisted her belly. Holy shit. Nope. Hell no. Fire was bad enough. "I melded shards of a mirror back together, so that's like manipulating sand, right?" Kind of. She'd only been partially successful.

"Yes, very true." Pointing at the date palm tree over their table, Isis said, "Focus on the tree above us. See if you can sense it, feel its energy, the movement of water and nutrients through its structures. Think about it flowering."

Yes, please. That would be so much better than frigging earthquakes. Shannon shivered, crossed her fingers, and closed her eyes, picturing the tree. Excitement leapt in her breast, heart beating a rapid tattoo. She *could* see it, see the movement of air on the trunk and fronds. In her mind, a visual appeared of water flowing into the roots and up the trunk. She sensed the sugars moving to the top, flowers bursting open.

Clapping her hands, Isis cheered. "Well done, Shannon!"

When Shannon opened her eyes, the tree was flowering. It looked exactly as it had in her mind's eye. She grinned, wiggling in her seat. Definitely better than scary ass earthquakes.

Chapter 17

LIES & MISDEMEANERS

Seated at the same table the next morning, after a sleepless night spent tossing and turning on the colourful silken sheets and soft bed of her otherwise sparsely furnished bedroom, Shannon eyed her mercurial hostess. What mood was Isis in this morning? Did Shannon dare ask more questions? There was so much she didn't yet know.

When the goddess smiled at the woman who brought platters of food to their table, the tension seeped out of Shannon's shoulders and she asked, "Why are you so sure I'm a goddess?"

Isis handed Shannon a basket of freshly baked flatbread. "Because your powers are far too strong for you to still be a mortal demigod. If you had one weak ability, perhaps, but you don't. You're an immortal goddess now."

Shannon took a piece of bread then spooned out mint from a clay jar, and selected tomato, and a fresh white cheese that reminded her of feta from a platter on the round table between them. As she chewed her open-faced sandwich, she considered the truth of Isis's words. Yesterday, they'd experimented to get an idea of the range of her powers... and Isis wasn't wrong.

When she'd gotten frustrated at manipulating air, Shannon had accidentally set fire to one of the hedges, then somehow sent a lightning bolt streaking across the pavilion to barely miss one of the women tending fish in a small pond. Upset at the near miss, Shannon created localized pouring rain that flooded out that same pond, and she ended the day the same way she'd started it—in tears.

She was a menace. No way could she be around anyone until she got these impossible abilities under control.

Despite the rocky start, over the next few days, Shannon fell into a comfortable routine. In the morning, Isis taught Shannon different aspects of her powers, and Shannon practiced as Isis monitored the region in the afternoons. Occasionally, Isis brought Shannon when she resettled children who'd lost their parents to conflict or helped women who'd been hurt and abused. Shannon admired Isis's work but wasn't confident enough to attempt healing anyone.

After one of those trips, Isis brought back a phone for Shannon. Despite the remote location outside the city, Isis's estate had all the modern amenities, including internet and cell service. Two days remained of Shannon's conference, but she couldn't return to London. Not when every emotion set off her powers. She was a disaster powder keg, blowing at random intervals. Instead, Shannon had the hotel ship her things to her Vancouver home and emailled Kristen.

FROM: Shannon<smurphy@uvc.ca>
TO: Kristen<kparker@umackenzie.ca>
DATE: August 7, 2021 7:59 PM
SUBJECT: Sorry for not catching up more
Hey Kristen. It was great to see you. I know we planned to talk about some collaboration ideas but something came up. I'm tied up and can't make the rest of the conference.

FROM: Kristen<kparker@umackenzie.ca>
TO: Shannon<smurphy@uvc.ca>
DATE: August 7, 2021 8:26 PM
SUBJECT: re: Sorry for not catching up more
Yeah, I'm sure "something" came up all right. Are you literally tied up? Somehow, it doesn't surprise me that Tod has a kinky side. LOL! I'd skip the rest of the conference too if I had a hottie like that in my bed. Have fun and do everything I wouldn't do :)

FROM: Shannon<smurphy@uvc.ca>
TO: Kristen<kparker@umackenzie.ca>
DATE: August 7, 2021 9:03 PM
SUBJECT: re: Sorry for not catching up more
My lips are sealed :)

FROM: Kristen<kparker@umackenzie.ca>
TO: Shannon<smurphy@uvc.ca>
DATE: August 7, 2021 9:34 PM
SUBJECT: re: Sorry for not catching up more
Ha! They better not be! ;) Not as much fun if you don't use your mouth!

Shannon chuckled, her heart lightened by the exchange. She hated misleading Kristen, but there was no way she'd burden her with the mess her life had turned into. Her next few to-do list items went smoothly as well—she put in for two months of vacation time and applied for a year of sabbatical leave from her university. Whether she stayed with Isis or not, Shannon needed to figure out her future path and how to control her powers before she'd risk spending time around anyone who couldn't defend themselves. It was bad enough that Isis's staff avoided her now, scampering away whenever they saw her coming. Not that Shannon blamed them.

Of course, not all her friends were so understanding.

FROM: Lynda<lynda@wardenmarketing.com>
TO: Shannon<smurphy@uvc.ca>
DATE: August 3, 2021 0:34 AM
SUBJECT: TOD CORVUS?!
What the hell, Shannon? When did you hook up with TOD CORVUS? Do you have any idea how famous he is? Why did I have to hear about you being on a red-carpet event with him from the gossip rags? It was so embarrassing that Silvie saw them and told me, before you, my best friend! How was it? Who else famous did you meet?
Does he need a marketing company? Tell me you gave him my name!

FROM: Lynda<lynda@wardenmarketing.com>
TO: Shannon<smurphy@uvc.ca>
DATE: August 5, 2021 2:34 PM
SUBJECT: FW: TOD CORVUS?!
Did you miss my earlier email? Details!! I need details... and contact information!

FROM: Lynda<lynda@wardenmarketing.com>
TO: Shannon<smurphy@uvc.ca>
DATE: August 7, 2021 5:34 PM
SUBJECT: FW: TOD CORVUS?!
Are you dodging my emails? I know you have internet at that fancy ass hotel!

FROM: Shannon<smurphy@uvc.ca>
TO: Lynda<lynda@wardenmarketing.com>
DATE: August 7, 2021 9:27 PM
SUBJECT: re: FW: TOD CORVUS?!
Hey Lynda. No, I'm not actually at my hotel any longer. I got a chance to do some fieldwork in Greece and Montenegro so I left the conference early to get set up. Meeting Tod was just a random luck thing. I haven't seen or heard from him since I left London earlier this week.

FROM: Lynda<lynda@wardenmarketing.com>
TO: Shannon<smurphy@uvc.ca>
DATE: August 9, 2021 3:42 AM
SUBJECT: re: FW: TOD CORVUS?!
I can't believe you didn't tell me. I could have flown out to join you on your red carpet, you know. Why the hell would you ditch a rich, famous musician like Tod Corvus to go tromp around in dry, boring forests? Did you at least tell him about my company? Give him my name?

Shannon sighed at the latest message and set it aside to reply to an email from her brother and his wife, cancelling their planned movie night. She hated lying to her family about where she was, but she wasn't prepared to tell them what had happened, nor could she say she was studying forests in the Saharan desert. As far as they knew, Shannon was doing fieldwork in Europe. At least that way she didn't have to lie about the time change.

After shifting his appearance to a rounder face with a square jaw, light-brown hair, and wearing the hoodie of a local snowboarding company with slouchy shorts, and sandals, Loki pushed open the office door for the Department of Environmental Management at Victoria Charles University in Vancouver. A short-haired Asian woman sat in front of a computer at a desk overflowing with stacks of paperwork set back behind a tall counter with several plastic bins and forms. A black sign with white lettering read "Christine" on a little placard by the monitor.

"Need some help?" she asked, without looking away from her screen.

"Yeah, I'm looking for Doctor Murphy. I'd hoped to take her forest ecology class," Loki said.

The woman continued typing without pause. "Doctor Murphy is on sabbatical leave for the next year. She won't be teaching any classes, but you can swing by her lab and talk to her doctoral student, Mark. He's filling in as a sessional for that course this September. Room 102."

"Thank you. If I email Doctor Murphy, will she get it?"

Finally, the woman glanced away from her computer to narrow dark, suspicious eyes at him. "Yes, she's checking email periodically from her field sites, but you might be waiting a while. Or you could leave your name with me, and I'll see she gets the message."

Loki gritted his teeth, tempted to walk around the counter and use his telepathy to force the woman to tell him where Shannon was. Damn it. How could Shannon hide so well? He'd searched her hotel and her home. No one seemed to know her location.

Giving in to the impulse, he swiftly circled the counter and desk. Ignoring the woman's loud squawk of protest, he pressed his fingers to her forehead as she attempted to lean away, batting at his hand.

The information wasn't hard to find. The woman was already thinking about Shannon. Bloody everlasting fucking hell. Shannon hadn't left a forwarding address. Her sabbatical plan stated fieldwork in the dry forests of British Columbia, southern California, Australia, Greece, Spain, and Montenegro. Bor's balls, he might as well search every dry forest on the fucking planet. If she even was in a dry forest somewhere.

After wiping the receptionist's mind of his intrusion and planting a memory that a nondescript student had stopped by to ask for information, Loki left the office, turned a corner, then teleported outside.

"Heimdall, open the Bifrost." The swirl of the rainbow-hued wormhole wrapped around him and deposited him on the white stone platform of the Bifrost chamber on Asgard. "Any luck spotting her?"

"No, Prince Loki," Heimdall's deep baritone replied from his position against the wall as the god lifted his palm from the hovering control panel. "I have been unable to track your soulmate. She doesn't register anywhere within my sight on Midgard or those areas I can see across the Nine Realms."

Loki cursed and thumped his forehead against one of the pillars that formed the base for the arched ceiling before turning to face the massive God of Roads, Boundaries, and Sight that acted as guardian and gatekeeper of Asgard. Frustration lined Heimdall's dark marble face shot through with golden striations, evidence of his half-Jotun heritage. In a rare move, the eight-foot-tall god approached Loki and put a wide hand on his shoulder.

"I won't stop until we find her, my prince," Heimdall vowed.

Loki rolled his head, attempting to relieve some of the tension as he blew out a heavy breath, then patted Heimdall's hand and acknowledged the attempt at comfort. "I know. Thank you." He didn't doubt the guardian's efforts on his behalf. Heimdall was fiercely loyal. With Shannon being Loki's soulmate and future royal consort, Heimdall would continue to spend every available moment searching for any sign of her.

How had they not found her yet? Loki refused to believe Shannon no longer lived. No, the warmth in his chest, that deep sense of connection said she lived, even if she wouldn't answer his mental call. She had to be okay. Anything else wasn't possible.

Unable to stop his spiralling thoughts, Loki asked, "Where's Thor?"

"Greece."

"Please drop me there." In the next moments, the wormhole swirled Loki off the Aesir homeworld and back to Midgard, to Earth. As the lights dissipated, he found himself on a craggy mountaintop of windswept olive trees and scrubby salvia plants with Thor scowling at him.

"This is where her initial storm stopped." Thor waved a thickly muscled arm. "But as you can see, there is no sign of her. I've searched all the nearby areas and have been unable to find a trail. If I didn't know better, I'd say she'd been swept up by the Bifrost... but we both know that's not true."

"Damn it! How can she have disappeared so effectively?" Loki growled, wrenching at the roots of his hair and stomping in a circle. "She is somewhere on this damned planet because, according to the departmental secretary, Shannon occasionally checks her email! Email, for fuck's sake. Electrons bouncing around as ones and zeros can find her, but we can't?"

"Have you considered asking Hermod for help?" Thor asked, wincing as his brother cursed loud and long.

"You know that fucker hates me," Loki growled. "He's never forgiven me for stealing his Hermes persona for a while, although I don't see *why* he's still so angry that he's associated with snakes or tricksters. It's not like it hurt his image." He rolled his eyes, then muttered, "Not like there are stories of him getting knocked up and birthing monsters."

Thor smirked. "Ah... the classics. Still, if she is checking email, you know he'd be able to track it to the source."

"I'll try anything, even apologizing again to that self-absorbed prick," Loki admitted. "There isn't anything I wouldn't do to get Shannon back."

Thor thumped him on the back and nodded.

"And stop your damn smirking or I'll restart those rumours about you in a wedding dress," Loki growled. "I'll even buy you a new veil."

Thor's smirk reverted to a scowl, and he shoved his brother. "Don't you dare."

Loki grinned. Perhaps an illusion was in order during the next big palace banquet.

Chapter 18

Up to Her Neck

Arms crossed over her chest, Isis loomed over Shannon's raincloud-soaked form two weeks later. "Enough moping, Shannon," Isis scolded. "You need to stop bouncing your emotions around like that child's toy on a string."

Shannon looked up from where she sat on a mat on the ground, her head in her hands. Rain drizzled over her, creating a spreading puddle. She shoved wet strands of hair from her face.

"Your staff are avoiding me. Not that I blame them. Look at this disaster." Shannon's voice rose to a frustrated shout as she gestured to the still-smouldering stumps sticking out of the sandy soil, all that remained of a once-lovely set of rosemary bushes. Steam started rising from Shannon's body as the cloud disappeared and moisture evaporated from her loose tan tunic and cotton pants.

Isis scowled. "I see, but are you paying attention to what you are doing now? Don't go setting yourself on fire as you dry yourself off."

"Yes, I'm paying attention, damn it!" Shannon rose to her feet, tossing back hair crackling and sparking with static in the evening air. After dusting the sand from her pants, she mirrored Isis's annoyed stance. It wasn't like she didn't know she had the emotional control of a two-year-old right now. Every feeling seemed to set off some godsdamned disaster around her. It was completely maddening.

Isis narrowed her eyes. "*Don't* curse or raise your voice to me, baby goddess. I never forget insults and you are *pushing my patience.*" She stepped closer, flicking a nail against Shannon's shoulder. "I'll take you out into the desert and bury you up to your neck to let the scarab beetles slowly eat you, bite by bite," she snarled in a vicious tone. "Your immortal healing will keep you alive for a long, long time."

The blanket of heat surrounding Shannon cooled as a shiver traced icy fingers down her spine. Something told her Isis hadn't just invented that punishment on the spot. Spit dried in Shannon's mouth as she murmured, "I'm sorry."

"I've had enough of your destruction around my home. Now that you know how to keep yourself warm, we'll head out into the dunes while you learn to control yourself." Not giving Shannon a choice, Isis grabbed her by the shoulders and they rose into the air. They flew over the thick outer sandstone wall of the main estate, past the mud-brick homes of her staff, beyond groves of citrus, mango, and figs, rows of grapes, then surrounding fields of maize, wheat, and rice.

When the last of the fields gave way to scrub brush then sand, all the fine hairs on Shannon's skin rose in prickling alarm. Was Isis going to follow through on her threat? Perhaps Shannon shouldn't stay with the temperamental goddess any longer to learn her powers. But where could Shannon go? It's not like she knew other immortals, except for Loki. Shannon's heartbeat picked up, beginning to race. Was she being foolish by trusting this goddess who helped so many human women almost daily? Had it skewed her perception of Isis as being benevolent?

Before Shannon could decide if she needed to try to run, to use the fledgling skills she was developing for flight, they landed in a mix of tan and white sands, almost like snow had fallen on this moonlit desolate landscape. As far as she could see, it was a sea of sand, with wind-carved pillars rising to provide topography, like shadowed sentinels to her impending demise.

"Now." Isis released Shannon and waved a hand at a nearby pillar that looked like a chunk of fan coral rising from the desert floor. "Use that anger and fear to practice throwing lightning bolts."

Shannon gaped, speechless to respond. Had Isis scared her on purpose, just to teach her? As much as she wanted that to be true, something—some sense deep inside—knew that wasn't the case, that Isis was absolutely, and unquestionably, capable of torturing Shannon. That she had tormented others. Oh gods. Did Isis have someone buried out in the desert right now? The horror of that thought had Shannon eyeing her surroundings, arms wrapped around her middle.

"Enough staring. Get to it. I don't have all night," snapped Isis.

Jolting at the angry words, Shannon flung out an arm and snapped her fingers. A bolt shot from her hand, hitting the sand only a few metres away.

Isis snorted and rolled her eyes. "You need to do better than that if you are going to fend off other immortals."

Shannon flinched and, after swallowing against the nerves churning in her belly, she tried again. This time the bolt made it only a metre short of the target. As she repeated her attempt, she cautiously asked, "Why do I need to fend off other immortals? Are they hostile?"

Were there other dangers she needed to worry about beyond pissing off her host? Were there different warring factions? Political differences? She knew so little about the new world she'd been thrust into, yet every time she tried to ask Isis for information, the goddess refused to give her any solid clues. Hell, Shannon didn't even know if there were different types of immortals. There had to be different realms or worlds, didn't there? Surely all immortals weren't hidden from human sight here on Earth? For a scientist who was used to knowing how the world worked, Shannon's lack of knowledge and Isis's unwillingness to give her answers frustrated her almost to the point of violence. Part of her wanted to shake Isis, to force her to tell her, yet those glimpses of the vicious side of Isis stayed Shannon's anger.

Isis laughed, a bitter, jagged sound that cut at Shannon's senses. "Of course, there are hostile gods. Just like humans aren't all the same, neither are immortals. A goddess should always be capable of defending herself."

Shannon gave a silent cheer as she finally hit the target even as she fought frustration at Isis's non-answer. Trying again, she asked, "Where are immortals from?"

"If you learn to defend yourself, you'll have endless years to find those answers," Isis said, lips pressed together.

Why wouldn't Isis answer her questions? She considered asking a different way, but the glare Isis shot her had her closing her mouth again. Shannon glanced around at the seemingly empty desert, silent except for the whisper of breeze as it shifted glittering silica particles in the moonlight, a slithering, almost skittering sound. A shiver on her nape, a warning within the deepest hindbrain. Yeah, perhaps she wouldn't ask again. No way did she want to get buried up to her neck or eaten by bugs. If she really was immortal now, she could afford to be patient.

Chapter 19

UNSPOKEN DESIRES

What the fuck did Loki care about fashion with his soulmate still missing? He and his brother posed with arms slung around each other's shoulders on the red carpet. "Any news, brother? Tell me you have something, anything. Please," Loki murmured out the side of his mouth, voice pitched for sensitive immortal ears. Dressed similarly in black blazers and slacks, Thor wore an ice-blue high-collared shirt in contrast with Loki's all-black attire that perfectly suited his mood. Unable to completely keep his scowl off his face, Loki appeared every bit as lethal as his true reputation, had the mortals been privy to it.

As the media shouted questions and the camera flashes blinded, Loki barely kept from snarling at them—the best he could do under the circumstances. Yggdrasil's fucking branches, it was harder than it should have been to keep from obliterating all the demanding Midgardians with an unruly burst of chaos. He couldn't work up any enthusiasm for the event, despite the turbulent energy swirling in the surrounding air, feeding his reserves.

"No, I'm sorry, Loki." Thor squeezed Loki on the back. "Did Hermod trace her email address for you?"

"That poncy bastard—"

"Tod! Tempest! Chuffed you came!" interrupted an enthusiastic Basil O'Keefe. "Tod, your song on the soundtrack is bloody brilliant." He punched

Loki in the shoulder. "How's your recording going? Are you going to create something for my next movie? They're already talking about a sequel. You have more clout than I. Use that magical voice of yours to convince the producers."

Loki mock scowled, fighting his first real smile of the evening. "I'm an assassin and rock god, not a siren. Get your facts right, relic raider."

"Sicarius, Raven, yadda yadda yadda. Whatever, mate. Get it done, your dark deadliness!"

"We'll see. Glad you enjoyed this one. Looking forward to seeing the film," Loki said, slapping him on the back. "Better get back to all your interviews. Your night, after all." Despite Loki's spiralling distress, it was impossible not to be amused at O'Keefe's puppy-like cheerfulness as the young actor bounded along the carpet to the next set of media. Meeting Thor's eyes, Loki nodded towards the entrance to the theatre.

It was a fantastic turn-out for the UK movie premiere of the popular video game adaptation, but Loki was there only to support his fellow actors, musicians and friends. Ignoring his media manager, he refused any red-carpet interviews. His real goal was to catch up with Thor.

After heading past security and getting a drink at the lobby bar, they found a relatively quiet spot in a dark corner farthest from the entrance. An impatient flick of Loki's hand sent an invisible bubble of seidhr surrounding them, creating a simple sound barrier that prevented anyone from overhearing. Still, they wouldn't be able to talk for long before someone wanted to join them.

He didn't hold back as he bit out the words clawing his throat like razored shards. "I *apologized* to Hermod, but the fucker said he'd *think* about helping me. He fucking smirked at me." His highball glass shattered, sending scotch, ice, and glittering fragments flying before his seidhr caught the mess. He curled his lip, eyes narrowed, as the drink reformed in his hand but he didn't bother to heal the cuts on his hand. They'd repair themselves soon enough, and the physical pain was a welcome distraction. A reminder of his damned failure. "I want to haul his ass to Asgard and drop him in the dungeons since I can't obliterate him into stardust."

Thor's blue eyes darkened and flashed, lightning revealed in their stormy depths. "That arrogant asshole. Just because he's sitting pretty with his social media conglomerate right now..." He glanced around, lips pressed together, then met Loki's gaze again. "I'll see if I can get him to cooperate. You didn't tell him she was your soulmate, right?"

Loki snorted. Did his brother think him entirely a fool? "No way. I'm not painting a target on Shannon's back like that." He winced, then muttered, "At least, not until I can protect her. It's not like we'll be able to hide our relationship forever." Bor's balls, he *was* a damn fool. This entire situation was chaos of his own making. He lifted his glass, using the smokey burn of single malt to give his suddenly dry mouth the spit to ask, "Has Heimdall spotted her? If she was taken, she might not be on Midgard."

His next swallow went down hard.

As much as he tried not to torture himself with visions of Shannon being held by one of his enemies, in pain and torment, he'd seen too much in the wars. He knew what horrors could be visited on an immortal body, had been done to Sigyn before her death. Nightmares plagued the few nights per week he attempted to get any rest.

And when the nightmares left him alone, erotic dreams of Shannon tortured him.

Frustrated and exhausted, he couldn't find any respite. Not that he deserved it when it was his fault she didn't know the world she now inhabited. Fuck, he'd already put a bloody great target on her back.

It was a fortunate he was immortal. These last months had been brutal. Despite being rejuvenated by his music, leaving a copy of himself with the band at Abby Road Studios while he searched for Shannon meant he constantly sapped his strength. He couldn't keep up. The energetic demands were too much. He'd lost weight, and he'd little to spare in the first place. But he couldn't stop. Not until he found her.

His brother put a hand on Loki's shoulder, grounding him. "Yes, he's looking and won't stop, but he can't see everywhere. I'm still tracking any weather anomalies that come up. There hasn't been anything like that first storm"—Thor's fingers tightened reassuringly—"but I'm pursuing even small anomalies now to uncover any trace of her."

Loki exhaled and nodded as Thor released him. "There's nothing to indicate she's missing in the mortal world. Neither her family nor friends act like she is gone. They must be in contact with her." He dragged a hand through his hair.

"Are you sure they don't know where she is?" Thor asked, expression tightening.

Loki's gut twisted. Norns only knew, but by Yggdrasil's mighty branches, he was going to fucking find out. "I'm heading back to Vancouver again to stake out her family and closest friends. If she's given them any information I can use to find her, I'm not leaving until I discover it." No matter what he had to do.

Thor's frown deepened. "With her being your soulmate, wouldn't you know if she's in trouble? Maybe she just doesn't want to be found yet?"

"I don't know. Maybe it's all my own worrying and she's actually fine, but I just don't know. I've tried to reach out. I get nothing back. Nothing!" Loki fought back tears flooding his suddenly hot eyes. "Sometimes I sense I'm almost reaching her. But mostly, it's like hitting a wall!" His voice rose, but it didn't escape his sound barrier.

Thor glanced around and shifted his broad shoulders to block Loki from the rest of the lobby. "If you haven't felt anything, you have to believe she's alright. Mother said you would know, right?"

"Yes, she said I would feel if Shannon was hurting. But..." The words stuck, emotion a swollen lump in his throat as he forced his admission loose. "But I'm scared, Thor. I'm fucking terrified she'll be taken from me before I even get to really be with her. I can't go through that again. It was hard enough with Sigyn, and she wasn't my soulmate."

Thor tugged Loki in for a hug, giving him a chance to swipe at his eyes with no one seeing. "Brother, I swear we will continue to do everything we can to find her. We won't rest until we do."

"Thank you. I... shit, Harry is on his way over to join us." Loki tore the sound barrier, and the room noise surrounded them again.

"You might want an illusion to cover those manly tears," Thor teased lightly.

"Shut it. Seriously. Fuck off." Loki rolled his eyes at his brother as he did, indeed, cast an illusion so no one would realize his current state of distress.

"Hey, you two! Thanks for coming!" Harry Chapelsworth said with a back slap for each of them. "Are you around for the holidays? It's been too long."

"No, I'm back to Australia tomorrow to support my team's upcoming charity game. We'll enjoy the after-party tonight. I'll pop over for the premiere when you're in Sydney," Thor told him.

"That would be great. It'll be nice to have you there, and we can torture young Basil together. Perhaps get him out on the rugby field to break up the usual media scrum. What about you, Tod? Are you around for the rest of the month?"

"No, I've got to head back over the pond again. Are you done reshoots, or are you heading back to Atlanta?" Loki asked.

"We wrapped last week, before the red carpet in LA. I'm off to Australia and China with O'Keefe after this, for premieres and press junkets, but I'll be back for Christmas." Harry chuckled. "Good thing too, or Elise and the kids would disown me."

Although Harry joked, the travel required for top-tier musicians and actors these days had to be hard on relationships and families. Bor's beard, even Thor found it difficult at times, despite his ability to fly and access the Bifrost. More than once, he'd mentioned his concern about balancing his various immortal duties with his mortal family and his need to be a good husband and father. For a glittering moment, the idea of a child, a family with Shannon, stole Loki's breath, spearing him with a desire he scarcely dared to think, let alone hope for—the ache so deep, so strong, he rubbed at his chest with the heel of one hand.

"Where is that beautiful doctor I met in August? I haven't seen pictures of the two of you from the paps, and you haven't been spotted with any other women since then. *Very* unlike you. Don't tell me she dumped your sorry ass. Is the bad boy Raven actually heartbroken?" Harry teased, brown eyes alight as he nudged Loki with an elbow.

Loki's heart constricted, and the fragile fantasy of a family shattered into razor-edged shards, each shaped in the horrific memory of Sigyn and his unborn daughter's death. Loki laughed, a brittle sound as anguish choked his voice. With iron willpower, he firmed up his illusion. "She's fantastic. She's busy with her career, back home in Canada. I'll be joining her when I fly back over." *Please, Norns. Please help me find her.*

Harry's mouth dropped open, gaze wide. "Holy fuck. You aren't taking the piss?" He glanced at Thor's smile and Loki's raised eyebrow. "That's great! I hope I get to meet this paragon that changed your mind about women properly soon, instead of that dodgy intro you scammed me with in August." Harry chuckled and shook his head. "You whisked her by so fast, I didn't even get to shake her hand. Who knew you could turn into such a jealous bastard?"

Loki rolled his eyes and punched Harry in the shoulder but didn't say anything. Harry wasn't wrong. By the Nine, Loki would give anything to have Shannon in his arms right now, to redo the way he introduced her to the immortal worlds and her powers, to have jealousy of his friend's attention be his only worry as Loki escorted her and showed off his beautiful goddess.

Thor frowned at him, concern etched in his expression, but while his brother suspected Loki's emotional state, even he couldn't see through Loki's illusions when Loki didn't want him to. No, instead they would only see him smile, his voice even and natural sounding, despite the tears flowing down his cheeks and the gaping hole carved out of his chest only he knew was there. It was silent in his head where she should be. His soulmate, his other half. Despite the presence of his brother and his mortal best friend, Loki had never felt so completely and utterly alone.

As the weeks of Shannon's absence grew longer, her relationship with her best friend grew rockier.

"Met any new handsome celebrities?" The snide edge to Lynda's voice came through clearly despite the staticky cell reception.

Shannon sighed and rubbed her forehead. Lynda had been her friend for twenty years, since high school, but Shannon wasn't unaware of her friend's petty jealousy issues. It had gotten progressively worse over the last five years as Shannon had achieved success with her career despite her troubles with Trent. The resentment had grown when Shannon paid off the mortgage of her waterfront home while Lynda still struggled to establish her marketing career. And after seeing photographs of Loki and Shannon on the red carpet, it had been one long guilt trip every time they talked.

"No, I haven't. I don't expect to run into any in the middle of the forest." Focusing on a nearby fig tree, Shannon used her frustration to send energy into the branches, creating first flowers, then fruit. After weeks of practice, she no longer needed to close her eyes and imagine what she wanted. Instead, she thought it and it happened. Isis had some Dr. Seussian but highly productive gardens in her courtyard from Shannon's experiments.

Even if some plants now grew in odd shapes, Shannon was thankful to *not* have an ability that could cause widespread devastation. She could move soil and occasionally small pebbles, but nothing larger. She couldn't cause an earthquake, and boy, did that take a weight off her shoulders when she'd figured out her limit.

"You'd introduce me if you were rubbing elbows with the rich and famous, right? Or have you moved too far up the social ladder for me now?"

With a finger and thumb, Shannon pinched the bridge of her nose and closed her eyes. "You know that's not the case, Lynda. I'm covered in dirt and grime, not sashaying about ballrooms or yachts. How's that investment banker you started dating? Dave?"

Successfully diverted, Lynda updated Shannon on the weekend trip they'd taken to the Gulf Islands on his yacht. Murmuring encouragement as Lynda gushed enthusiastically, Shannon picked a fig and bit into it while her mind wandered to Loki.

Whether he was trying to find her or if he cared she'd left was not a question Shannon was prepared to ask. It wasn't like they'd discussed the future in the short, intense two days they'd been together. And he had his pick of women. So many women. Surely she wasn't memorable. Either way, she wasn't ready to face him again. With her newfound immortality, she could afford to take the time to figure out who she was with her new reality first. Before seeking him out again. If she did decide to seek him again.

Still, it was almost like she sensed him, almost heard his voice at times. That odd connection they'd forged seemed to persist. Her first instinct was to shove as many mental walls between them as she could. She wasn't comfortable with him knowing her emotions or listening to her thoughts. The sexy bastard was far too overwhelming. She'd lost herself, becoming a being of sensation, not logic, when she was with him. In hindsight, she was a teensy bit uncomfortable that he'd stalked her at her conference. It was too reminiscent of Trent's actions.

Other times, Shannon almost reached out, almost brought the barriers down. Part of her longed to share what she was learning, funny things she'd seen, or even just new experiences. She'd never been to this area of the world before. These conflicting desires made no sense. They hadn't spent that much time together.

Yet as Lynda expounded on Dave's virtues, Shannon missed not being able to tell her about Loki. The two friends usually dished about any new man in their lives, so she understood why Lynda had been hurt that Shannon hadn't been the one to tell her. And gods, she'd meant to... before it had all gone completely tits up. Lynda had gotten Shannon through her break-up with Trent and, more than once, she'd come over to help get rid of him.

But damn it, she couldn't talk to Lynda about Loki. Not now. And she couldn't talk to Lynda about being in Egypt with Isis, or what she was learning.

Maybe that was why Shannon wanted to share it with Loki. Other than Isis, she had no one she could talk to about immortality, gods, and powers. Not that Isis was very forthcoming.

As Lynda's tale wound down, Shannon said her goodbyes and rolled her eyes when Lynda once again reminded her to introduce Lynda to any celebrities Shannon might meet to help her friend's marketing company. It wasn't that Shannon minded helping, but the obligation rubbed her wrong.

After tucking her phone in her back pocket, Shannon strolled through the courtyard towards a blue and white mosaic fountain. The piercing wail of a black kite drew her eyes up to spot the black raptor that was Isis's most common familiar—the only dark spot in an endlessly blue sky.

Under the prickly goddess's tutelage, Shannon had learned to communicate with all kinds of animals. The purity of their thoughts, often centred around basic needs, was a respite after tangling with her best friend. Animals didn't play mind games or attempt to guilt her. Instead, they were upfront about their desires. Even the smallest of them had thoughts, instincts really, that they projected in a way Shannon could understand and communicate with, and it opened an entirely new world. She basked in it, letting the overlapping hum sink into her mind to create a relaxing white noise when she was worn out.

And fuck, every day of attempting to learn her powers seemed to get harder, to ask more from her. She'd never known such bone-deep exhaustion as what had plagued her these days, like her body still hadn't adjusted to the new demands on it. Gods, what she'd give to have life be simple again. No immortals. No powers. No life-altering identity crisis. Some days, she was just too tired to eat. Okay, so she didn't mind that she'd lost some of the baby fat from her face and that extra padding she'd carried, but damn, it wasn't a weight-loss plan she'd recommend.

"Why can I talk with animals, hearing what they think and getting them to understand me, when I can't communicate with you telepathically?" Shannon asked Isis later that evening as they relaxed in the courtyard and sipped mint tea.

"Animals have no mental barriers. Their minds are completely open. Minds like ours have inherent barriers to telepathy. It takes a lot of energy to push thoughts to another immortal, and then it depends on whether they have further defences to prevent mental attacks. If we seriously tried, and both of us allowed the connection, we could communicate telepathically. The exception is soulmates. When the soulmate bond forms, an unbreakable physical and mental connection forms that allows effortless communication between them." Her expression turned sad, eyes unfocused as she finished explaining.

Shannon sat up in her seat as her heart started to race. "Soulmates? You've never mentioned that as a thing before."

Isis's eyes narrowed and snapped to Shannon. The goddess chopped one hand in the air, answering in a short, clipped tone. "I don't like to talk about it. My soulmate was murdered." She crossed her arms and looked away again, mouth pressed into a tight line.

"I'm sorry."

She didn't acknowledge Shannon and glared off in the distance. Knowing better than to ask any further questions and risk Isis's volatile temper—she still wasn't sure whether the goddess was currently torturing some poor immortal in the desert—Shannon sat in silence as she considered Isis's revelation.

Shannon recalled her time with Loki in vivid detail. They'd spoken to each other effortlessly. Was he just a powerful telepath, or was it something more? Were they soulmates? What did that even mean? Was that why she was still so drawn to him, even now? Part of her craved him, wanted desperately to reach out to him, to touch him. She couldn't deny that the connection, whatever it was, was strong and enduring despite the short two days she'd spent with him months ago.

That night, alone in her bed, her questions returned. Even when bone-deep exhaustion plagued her, she couldn't help but remember his voice, his body moving against her, captivated and held by the depths of his eyes. Like so many other nights, her dreams haunted her, leaving her sweaty and unfulfilled.

After tossing and turning, and with limbs lethargic with a frustrating, unrelenting need from her broken sleep and the memory of Loki's touch, Shannon gave up on further sleep and headed to the underwater ruins she'd discovered a few days ago. The numerous restless nights and unyielding desire for Loki had provided fuel she'd channeled to push herself to learn more, to find out everything she could about her abilities. After discovering water effortless to control in all its forms, she'd begun to explore the depths of the Mediterranean Sea. It became her favourite place to escape, a respite that didn't leave her so exhausted.

Since she'd learned to create a pocket of air around her head to breathe underwater, she carefully sank into the soothing blue realm close to shore. The far-off hum of boats provided a background buzz as she bobbed her way along the bottom until she reached the ancient lighthouse and the underwater fields of seagrasses. As the sun rose higher and visibility increased, the occasional ray gracefully danced through the water. Following them, she headed deeper until rows of broken columns came into view. Colourful fish swam darted through in flashes of sleek bodies.

So much of the ancient world was hidden under the water. She felt like an explorer. What had this place been in its glory? Excitement rising, she moved closer. Intact urns, some tipped on their sides, were covered in barnacles. Long strands of kelp rose and swayed in the light current. Shannon slid a hand through her bubble into the surrounding water to touch the greyish-white marble, slick with a fine layer of algae.

Something brushed her leg, then tugged her ankle.

With a shriek, Shannon jerked her foot away. The bubble around her head collapsed. Thrashing, heart pounding, she inhaled water and panicked. Oh gods. Coughs wracked her and she sucked in more water. She couldn't reform the bubble. Fuck. Oh fuck. She kicked frantically and clawed upward for the surface's faint glow far above. There was no way she'd make it. No way—

Yet her lungs didn't burn, didn't seize.

Trembling and fighting the screaming need to continue to the surface, she stopped and hung suspended in the water, patting at her chest, her mouth, and her nose. She was fine. Fine? How the ever-loving fuck was she *fine*?! Experimentally, she took another breath. She was breathing the water.

She could breathe underwater? *Holy shit!* She could breathe underwater!

Deliberately, she blew out a series of bubbles, then took a deep breath. Stunned, she swam around for a while until she returned to sit on one of the broken pillars. She stared at the brightly coloured fish of various sizes swimming in schools around the columns. Below her, a white spotted octopus moved over one of the large urns. She chuckled and floated closer. So that was the culprit that had scared her.

From then on, she spent part of each day exploring the underwater depths, basking in the rejuvenating waters that seemed to cure her lingering tiredness. When she described the ruins, Isis insisted on joining her. She'd never seen the goddess so happy, floating in the pocket of air Shannon created around her. Shannon was stunned when Isis clapped in delight, telling her stories about what the ruins had looked like in the past, which broken statues were icons of her, and of ancient life in Egypt. After being so unwilling to talk about immortal life, it shocked Shannon that Isis shared so much detail with her.

But by far Shannon's favourite pastime underwater, especially when she was feeling particularly restless from her disturbed dreams, was swimming with the bottlenose dolphins. They roamed far and wide but frequently came to find her if she was in the water. Depending on their mood, they would nudge her with a dorsal fin, letting her hold on as they sped through the depths. They were the race cars of the sea, diving, spinning, swerving, and leaping. When she lost her grip on one due to a fast maneuver, another raced to put their fin in her hand to tug her along. At times, they fought to see who got to swim with her, and she'd have to reassure them she had no favourites. For all the crappy things that had happened to her since discovering she was a goddess, spending hours with the dolphins never failed to brighten her day. Never could she have imagined getting to do this as a mortal scientist, even using scuba gear, with the dolphins constantly chattering in her ear. If only immortal life could all be like this, so free, so incandescently joyful.

Still, the way the dolphins loved to play, so mischievously, reminded Shannon of Loki. With each day that passed, she missed him more. Gods, did she want him, but at the same time, she wasn't sure she was ready to see him or even if it was wise to do so.

Her thoughts were a churning cauldron of mixed feelings and concerns. Was she asking for more trouble? Would he turn controlling and abusive like Trent? He was already so dominant in bed. Was he like that outside of it?

What if he didn't want her?

And what if he'd forgotten her? Just because he'd caused her awakening didn't mean he'd want to see her again. It had only been two days, after all, and he was a player with no shortage of women constantly throwing themselves at him. She refused to be another in an endlessly long list of notches on his bedpost.

But... were they soulmates? Other than telepathy, what did that even mean? Shannon didn't know, and she was afraid to open the persistent connection deep inside her to find out whether he'd be the best thing to happen to her or the cause of her utter destruction.

Chapter 20

DESPERATE TIMES, DESPERATE MEASURES

Dark, cold, and empty, just like his soul. Loki crept around and peeked in another window of the stone-and-slate-sided residence with its ocean blue trim and shutters. Damn it. No sign of Shannon. Still, he shifted into a large raven and flew to perch outside the second-story windows.

Nothing. No evidence that she'd been home.

He considered entering to search for clues, but just as he'd fought to not read her mind before they forged the soulmate bond, he respected her personal space now. His feathers ruffled and he resettled them. Yggdrasil's roots... he needed *her* to show him her home. Because she wanted to. Because it was her choice.

A battered silver Chevy truck with rust spots pulled up into the grey brick driveway. A young Midgardian barely out of his teens hopped out and slammed the vehicle door. Reaching into the open box, he pulled out bags, clippers, and gloves.

Now others... They were fair game.

Loki flew down to land silently behind him, shifting back to humanoid. With a quick touch to the boy's head, he probed the mind of the gardener who mowed the small lawn and weeded the extensive beds around the porch and back deck leading down to the water and a dock twice a month. He was enrolled in a local community college, taking landscape design, and hadn't seen Shannon since August. But she paid him by e-transfer each month. And fuck... He had no idea where she was or when she'd be back.

After fuzzing the memory of his presence, Loki shifted back to a raven and took flight, cawing his frustration to the sky. Earlier, he'd caught the blond teenager who collected Shannon's mail and watered the house plants once a week. She also didn't know where Shannon was.

Loki had already been through Shannon's office at the university, read the minds of her grad students, and broke into both the dean's and department head's files to find some trace of her. Still, he couldn't find any additional clues.

She was in contact, particularly with her grad students, but none of her messages revealed anything beyond Europe.

Teleporting in bursts and flying in between, Loki made his way across the mouth of Indian Arm and along the base of the mountains bordering the Fraser Valley until he located the little farmhouse in Laidlaw, just a few wingbeats off the southern side of the river. Night had fallen and the moon rose, reflecting off the muddy, churning water as he glided across Highway 1. With a creek on one side and the mountain rising on the other, the home of Shannon's brother and his wife wasn't large but it had a good fifteen acres of fields for crops. Loki landed high on a bare branch of a cottonwood tree and peered down at the dark shingles.

He'd been here before. Several times. The only clue he'd found was that there was a ten-hour difference in time between here and wherever Shannon was, but the damned Eastern European time zone spanned Finland and Russia to Madagascar. It made him want to pull his feathers out.

Not that his feathers looked all that hot to begin with, lacking their usual blue-black lustre. Splitting himself in two had become too exhausting. He'd given up recording with the band and gave everyone a two-month hiatus after Healer Moja read him the riot act the last time he'd been home. It had been years, not since the dark days after the war with the Sidhe, that she'd given him a tongue-lashing like that. She hadn't let him leave the healer hall until he ate one of Idun's apples, replenished his liquids, and recharged by reading stories to the kids in the palace nursery.

And every minute he'd spent on Asgard, he worried at the time slipping away so much faster on Midgard. But now, staring at the light that came on in the master bedroom on the second story, his mind raced to find some way to find Shannon, something he hadn't yet tried.

As shadows moved behind lace curtains, he flew down, landing on the edge of the roof above the porch, then hopping over to the partially open window and shifting to a cat.

"Mom and Heather will be here by ten for brunch," a melodious tenor said near the window. It had to be Shannon's brother, Liam. Loki hadn't spoken to him, but he'd snuck close and scanned his mind last month when the man was outside harvesting tomatoes from their garden. "Mom was joking about mimosas again."

A heavy sigh before a higher pitched voice—the wife Sarah, presumably—murmured, "Is she drinking too much again? Or is it your uncle?"

Loki's eyes slitted and he put his paws up on the window ledge. Had Shannon grown up surrounded by alcoholics? With violence that so often accompanied substance abuse? Loki hadn't scoured Liam's mind, not wanting to damage him or cause Shannon's brother any pain, and he hadn't caught any childhood memories in his brief surface scan. What he had learned was that she was closer to Liam than anyone else in the family, so he hadn't attempted to read Shannon's mother or sister. Loki's claws dug into the ledge, scoring curls of paint and wood. Maybe that had been a mistake. Family or not, her mom and uncle would *not* be subjecting Shannon to that anymore. Not if he had anything to say about it.

"A bit of both, I think. You know how she gets around this time of year. It's just hard for her with the anniversary of Dad's death last month and what would have been his birthday a few days ago."

Damn. Loki's ears flicked. It had been traumatic losing Sigyn, and he wasn't enough of a hypocrite to blame Shannon's mom for needing liquid courage to get past the memories that tormented after a loss that deep. Hell, maybe he'd toss some Asgardian mead in her drink to really knock her out.

His muscles stiffened, the hair on his back rising as a bad idea, a truly terrible idea, took hold.

One of the lamps in the room clicked off. In the remaining light, the shadows joined and the susurration of clothing falling to the floor followed, with the creak of bed springs shifting.

"So should I not make the mimosas?"

Did he dare risk it? Shannon's transition had been so strong. If they were going to have drinks anyway... he'd know for sure whether the genes came from her mom's or dad's line. And she wouldn't be alone. She wouldn't have to keep it a secret from her family. She wouldn't be cut off from everything she knew. Perhaps she'd even forgive him for his clumsy attempt to explain.

Was there a downside? Even if the genes came from her dad, Liam and Heather should both transition. Surely they'd help him find her if they were also immortals, wouldn't they?

"Yes, let's have them. We only have a single bottle of champagne between the four of us. It's not like Mom is going to get drunk on that."

Loki grinned, lips pulled back from his canines in an expression not usually seen on a cat.

Chapter 21

SURPRISE

Shannon was throwing lightning bolts at a pyramid of rocks when a large man dropped from the sky to land near her with a loud boom, shaking the ground. It threw off her aim, and she shrieked, falling on her ass.

"What the hell, man!" She picked herself up, dusted off her cargo pants, and turned to face him. Her chest tightened, lungs freezing for several heartbeats. A whispered, "Oh shit" escaped when she finally sucked in a breath. Even though he had a foot more height and a longer mane of that same fiery-red hair in warrior braids, she knew his strong, square-jawed face—Tempest Corvus... or no... given who his brother was and the massive silvery black hammer with glowing silver runes on its black shaft held in one thickly muscular arm... holy fuck, he had to be Thor.

And *oh my gods*, he was built. Already impressively fit in the mortal form when she'd met him as Tempest, now, he was, well... more. With black leather boots surrounding strong calves, leather pants encasing tree-trunk thighs, and some kind of silver and gold scale armour clinging to his chest and shoulders that any professional football defensive lineman would envy, he gave off distinct don't-fuck-with-me vibes. Not that she had any intention of doing so, especially with the almost sentient way wispy white smoke curled around the double-headed hammer and the occasional crackle of lethal-looking electricity that raced over the metal and up his arm.

Of course, Tempest was a god. Who else would pose as Loki's mortal brother but another god. But... was he Loki's brother? Or his nephew? Norse mythology was a little confusing as some sources had Loki and Odin as blood-oathed brothers. She blinked, and her thoughts froze for a second. Damn. Just how many gods were running around the planet? Was humanity that oblivious?

"Shannon!" his voice boomed, and she flinched, her heart leaping into her throat to flutter like a panicked bird.

He remembered her? What was he doing here? No other immortals had visited Isis since Shannon had arrived.

"Uh... Hi, Thor. Or do you want me to call you Tempest?" She stepped back when he moved towards her. A metallic taste coated her tongue. Should she be running? She glanced around. No way could she outrun or outfly the over seven-foot massive God of Thunder.

Those gigantic shoulders shrugged, and he waved a large hand—fortunately, *not* the one with the still-crackling hammer. "Thor is fine unless there are mortals around." One eyebrow rose as his gaze travelled over her, then pinned her in place. "You have led my brother and I on a merry chase all over Midgard, trying to find you."

So Loki's brother then. Wait... *what*? Muscles still vibrating with the need to flee, she halted mid-step, then put her foot down. Loki was looking for her? Really? Her hand rose to her throat, and she fidgeted, staring at Thor. Why? Why was Loki searching for her? Oh gods... did she—did she want him to?

It took her a minute to rein in her spiralling thoughts, but then, with her arms wrapped around her body, she forced her answer out in a harsh whisper. "I wasn't hiding, Thor. I've simply been learning my powers and adjusting to being a goddess. This is all completely new to me. I wasn't aware Loki cared where I was or was seeking me. We only knew each other for two days, after all."

Pale-blue eyes darkened to thunderstorms as Thor's brows lowered and he shook his head. "I don't understand, Shannon. You are his soulmate. It's destroying him not knowing where you are and if you are okay. He's terrified for your safety. How can you do this to him?"

Soulmate.

A deep sense of rightness, almost a relief, echoed his word. She'd suspected the connection, but hearing Thor say it, discovering she wasn't imagining that feeling inside her, eased the tension wrapped around her heart. Still, Shannon's shoulders rounded as she crossed her arms and shifted her feet. "Loki never said anything to me about being his soulmate. I don't even know for sure what that is or what it means." She wasn't responsible for his emotional state, damn it. Why the hell hadn't he told her?

Blurring talons appeared in Shannon's peripheral vision. She ducked, throwing up an arm and an instinctive shield of air. The black kite bounced off the invisible barrier and shrieked its fury. The large raptor landed, shifting into Isis clad in her usual white dress and perfectly groomed black hair with kohl ringing her eyes.

"She is *what?*" Isis snarled, eyes narrowed to slits as she darted towards Shannon.

"Been a long time, Isis," said Thor, his frown turning to a slight smile as he shifted to face her.

Fury twisted her features. "Did you say Shannon is Loki's soulmate? Are you fucking kidding me? That conniving, worthless, husband-killing bastard has a *soulmate*?" Isis screeched, coming at Shannon with hands transformed into black razor-tipped talons.

Shannon's eyes widened, and a sudden wave of dread, of loss, hit her. This was the side of Isis she'd feared from the start. But no, Isis was her friend. Why would she attack her? Surely, she wouldn't actually—

Frozen by Isis's unexpected rage, Shannon couldn't move as those claws slashed towards her raised arms.

"I'll kill her! He doesn't deserve a soulmate! He can experience my pain!"

Fiery agony struck Shannon's forearms, but then Thor was there, stepping between them. His broad shoulders and back hid Isis from Shannon's shocked view.

"Isis! I will not let you hurt Shannon to get revenge on Loki. She is innocent, and it wouldn't bring Osiris back!" Thor boomed, shoving Isis away.

"Get out of the way, you overgrown lightning rod. I'm going to kill her."

The venom in Isis's tone had tears filling Shannon's eyes as she clutched at her bleeding arms, blazing pain flaring up her limbs. This was the same woman, the same friend, mentor, who'd helped her these past four months? She'd known... suspected... that Isis was capable of atrocities, but she hadn't thought the temperamental goddess would turn on her so easily. Gods. And for something Shannon had no control over.

"Sorry Isis, but you know that's not going to happen." In the next moment, Thor swung his hammer and knocked Isis flying toward a garden wall. Before she hit the tiled surface, Isis halted her flight and charged back.

"Heimdall!" Thor shouted as he encircled Shannon's waist with one powerful arm.

A rainbow of lights surrounded them and swept them away while Isis shrieked in rage, slashing as they disappeared.

Stumbling slightly when Thor released her, Shannon found herself in a massive grey stone chamber staring up at the largest man she'd ever seen. Clothed in silver armour with a gold tree emblem on his enormous, muscled chest, he was easily a foot taller than Thor, perhaps more. Holy hell, he almost made two of her.

"Wow, you are huge!" she blurted, her brain still stuck on Isis's unexpected attack. She swallowed against the emotion choking her throat, stabbing pain flaring up her arms.

The giant laughed in a deep rumble, and a friendly smile stretched his darkly marbled face. It was like he was formed from portoro marble, the intense jet-black colour interspersed with gold and white effervescences that seemed in motion, particularly in his unique striated eyes. With numerous midnight locks braided back from his distinctive features and falling to his broad shoulders, he was stunning, like a statue come to life.

"I am Heimdall, little Shannon. I am the guardian and gatekeeper. Welcome to the realm of Asgard." He lifted his hand from a hovering holographic control pad and gestured toward an open archway leading out of the chamber.

She blinked and burbled, "Yeah, I uh... I watched the movies." Heat crept up her cheeks. Gods. Why did she say something so foolish? She could have at least chosen something from mythology, instead of referencing pop culture like a first-year undergraduate.

Unable to hold his gaze, she surveyed the alien planet revealed through the archway—a gleaming white city nestled against the deep emerald of forested mountains with sheer silvery craggy tops and a turbulent dark-blue lake, or sea perhaps, crashing waves on the far shoreline. It looked almost like home, like coastal British Columbia, if she ignored the two moons in the sky and the city architecture that blended ancient stone and futuristic gleaming metal and misty... were those force fields or some kind of holographic structures? She couldn't tell from here.

Holy shit. She was really standing on an alien planet. Breathing tangy alien air. Bleeding on alien stone. The raw pain in her arms and blood escaping past her fingers was a sharp reminder... this was no fucking dream. And a chill climbed her spine at the seamless integration of massive ancient-looking stone city walls and advanced defensive guard turrets interspersed along the wall's top at regular intervals. This was no fairy tale. There were real dangers out there. Who were the Asgardians defending against? Was she free to come and go? Would she be trapped here? Was she safe here? The shock of just how little she knew had her stepping back, away from the archway.

Heimdall's deep, rich chuckle drew her eye again as the sound echoed off the stone. "Those Midgardian movies are amusing, but do keep in mind they are fiction, little one. There is far more to this vast universe than depicted in modern stories or Midgardian mythology." His tone turned serious, his gaze holding hers. "You need to learn quickly, little goddess. I couldn't see you when Isis kept you cloaked from my sight. It is a dangerous universe."

Shannon's gaze dropped to her forearms. Yeah, no shit. Her trembling fingers tightened on the bloody gashes, trying to hold them closed. "I wasn't aware she was doing that. Until Thor showed up, Isis had been great." She swallowed, voice cracking on the last word, before adding in a hoarse whisper, "She helped me learn my powers, how to use them and defend myself." Even with the hints that Isis had a dark side, Shannon had trusted the quirky goddess. The sudden betrayal had shocked and hurt, leaving Shannon's heart fluttering unevenly after the unexpectedly violent confrontation.

Thor knelt, drew her hands away from the dripping wounds, and wrapped soft bandages around the slashes from a green kit open at his feet. "Isis is great with mortal women and children. She is a fierce defender of the weak and vulnerable. She's a little more unpredictable with fellow immortals. I'm glad she took you under her wing for a while, but her rage at Loki has endured for many years. She won't forgive him for his youthful mistake, and she will kill you to hurt him," Thor told her gently. "I am sorry, Shannon."

Shannon gave a jerky nod, fighting tears. Godsdamn it. She was *not* going to cry. "Thank you for getting me out of there, but I'm not ready to see Loki yet. I need more time to figure out who I am now and what it means to be a goddess."

Her stomach churned as Thor tied off the bandages. This day had gone from her new normal to shit so fast. There was no way she'd be pushed into anything she wasn't ready for. No way. For fuck's sake, hadn't she dealt with enough already?

A tremor rocked her.

Okay, so maybe she was afraid to see Loki again. She hunched her shoulders. What if he rejected her? What if he didn't want a soulmate? Oh fuck… what if he was like Trent? Could she even trust her judgement? Two short days with Loki had blown up her life, yet the craving for him, to be with him, was powerful. How could she resist once she saw him again?

Thor inclined his head, wiping the blood from her arms and her fingers with some kind of damp cloth. "I'm not happy about it, but I won't force you, little sister. How about we take you to the healers to properly take care of these wounds, instead of my little patch job, and figure out where your goddess genes come from? I know I'm curious. Are you?"

Little sister—his words sparked a warmth inside her. Kind of nice after feeling so adrift from her family and unable to share all the changes in her life.

"Yes." Maybe getting some answers would help her feel more in control again. Gods. Every damn time she thought she might have a handle on things, her life spun out of her grip.

After returning the kit to a hidden stone cubby, Thor offered his elbow. Shannon flashed on Loki doing the same as they disembarked the plane so many months ago. Before she knew he was a god. Before her life turned upside down.

She hesitated, staring out the archway at the world that wasn't her own.

Would she regret taking Thor's arm and diving further down the rabbit hole? What other options did she have at this point? It wasn't like she could take the blue pill and wake up back in her bed without her powers. The aliens were real, and she might be one of them. Resting her hand on Thor's muscular forearm, she fought off the tightness in her chest and looked back at Heimdall. "Thank you."

He bowed his head and smiled.

Leading her out through the open archway and along a silvery stone and metal bridge surging with the same rainbow energy as the Bifrost had—a distinct hum beneath her feet—Thor guided Shannon toward the city. As they walked, he told her about his lovely Australian wife and twin daughters who weren't aware he was a god, or that gods existed.

"Isn't it hard, lying to them?" How did he manage? Didn't it eat at him? Just thinking about trying to remember the constant lies had butterflies fluttering in her stomach. She'd had a hard enough time over the last months in her conversations with her family and friends, but to always live that way? She shuddered.

He shook his head, patting her hand where it lay on his arm. "Not when I'm protecting them. I've seen how badly it can turn out. I love them too much to do that to them. There is no way I want to drag them into the world of immortals. Amelia wouldn't be safe. She's too fragile."

The churning in Shannon's stomach worsened, waves of nausea pulsing with the energy of the bridge and joining the hot throbbing of her wounds. She'd known there had to be dangers Isis wasn't telling her about—the obvious defensive structures around the city ahead were a stark reminder—but with Heimdall and now Thor also warning her, her fears rose. "Immortals won't use your mortal family to get at you?" Was that yet another reason she needed to keep her friends and family in the dark? Gods, how did anyone live like this, in constant danger and alone? Why the hell had Loki done this to her?

"No. It's one of the few rules immortals abide by. Mortal lives are too short and too fragile to be used that way. I'd rather they live a life as happy mortals, fleeting though it may be compared to mine."

She released a shaky breath. "So you won't give your kids Asgardian food or drink?" She fucking wished Loki hadn't given her any, damn it.

"Certainly not at this point. I can't see doing it at all while their mother still lives."

She met his gaze as they stepped off the bridge. The massive white stone city wall rose high above them, easily as tall as a city skyscraper, and as they entered a large black metal gate with the doors wide open, golden armoured sentries with the tree design on their chest inclined their heads to Thor and gave her a curious glance. "Both you and Heimdall have alluded to how dangerous the universe is for immortals or gods. Isis had me learning to defend myself with lightning bolts." Not that it'd been effective. It hadn't even crossed her mind to zap Isis when she attacked her. Still... "Is it really so bad?" Enough was enough. She wanted the truth this time. No more deflections.

Thor held her stare with his own direct gaze. "I'm glad she was teaching you defence. To answer your question, yes, little sister, it is. There are many races of immortals, although none of us are truly immortal. Compared to humans, we live many thousands of years, but we can, and do, die. Since it's hard to kill an immortal, we can suffer innumerable torture and torment for long periods without dying. It can break a mind. An unhinged immortal is a very dangerous beast."

The hair stood on her nape as she considered his answer. "Yeah, an immortal Hitler or Jeffrey Dahmer... that'd be bad. But surely there can't be that many?"

He scowled. "We try to kill those that are truly depraved and beyond any hope, but each race has its horrors."

Multiple races of immortals? How could humanity have no idea they exist? "You've mentioned races several times. What do you mean?" As they left the open square behind the wall and she got her first true glimpse of the city, her eyes widened.

Smooth cobblestone streets were filled with people. They were diversely dressed, wearing everything from the intricate armour like Thor's that moved in unexpectedly fluid ways for metal, a lot of leather with toned muscles on display, and colourful flowing fabrics that wouldn't be out of line at a Renaissance fair. Weapons hung on belts, sheathed on back harnesses, or—holy crap... Shannon blinked at the tall lethal man in shimmering brown with daggers strapped to forearms and thighs as he nodded to Thor, then winked at her with a glint in his golden eyes and continued his prowl past them. It was an odd mix of advanced and old-world that had Shannon not sure where to look, trying to take it all in at once while still listening to Thor. She could easily spend weeks exploring the culture here and almost missed a step when she realized no one spoke English, yet she understood snatches of conversation as they passed.

How? Was this some kind of ability she'd gained with the ability to talk to animals?

Thor's tone lightened, losing the serious note as he drew her attention. "It's our genetic origin. I'm Aesir, the original race from the realm of Asgard. Loki is half Vanir, the original race from the realm of Vanaheim, and half Jotun, from the realm of Jotunheim. Heimdall is half Aesir, half Jotun. Isis is also Vanir. The Aos Sí, which you may know as the Sidhe and includes the elves and other fae creatures, are from the realm of Alfheim. The Shen, which you would think of in terms of the far eastern Midgardian god pantheons, are from the realm of

Kunlun. There are many more, but these are some of the major ones that have had a presence on Midgard."

Her mouth dropped open. Wow. How many known worlds or realms were out there? And there were still more races? Did they all look different? As people passed, many were no taller than her five-and-a-half feet, but others were as tall as Thor, with skin tones ranging from the dark marbled or granite tones she'd only ever seen on rock strata before meeting Heimdall, to a pure white that almost glowed under the Asgardian sun. Some had hues of green, blue, or red in pale hints of colour. She'd never seen such diversity in humanoids.

Damn. And Loki was half Jotun? What did that mean? Surely it wasn't... well... she had to ask. "Okay, so is Jotunheim actually the realm of the frost giants?" She almost rolled her eyes at herself for asking a question based on pop culture, but hell, there were *other worlds*. Planets with intelligent life aside from Earth. She was freaking standing on one with dual pale-lavender moons on the horizon and a reddish-yellow star—their sun—in the sky above. And unlike Isis, Thor was answering her questions.

He laughed, eyes glinting with crackles of lightning in their blue depths. "It's the realm of the giants, including frost giants. They aren't like in those movies or comics, although yes, the frost giants can sometimes be blue." He gestured to a woman passing with pale-blue skin with a fine tracing of white lines, almost like snowflake patterns. "The Jotuns are a race of magic-using shapeshifters. Their natural state is a large humanoid, as you saw from Heimdall's size, but they take many forms. They don't have strict genders or forms the way other races do as they tend to change periodically. It's a chaotic realm with a preponderance of massive dangerous creatures."

"Huh." What did that mean for Loki? Was he dangerous too? "Is that where Loki gets his abilities to shapeshift?"

"You've seen that, have you? Or are you referring to mythology?" Thor gave her a sidelong glance, lips twitching as he guided Shannon between enormous white stone pillars and into a hallway with another pair of armoured sentries standing watch who inclined their heads to him as he passed. "Or perhaps the recent popular stories?" His blue eyes gleamed and he winked. "That's not him. Or me, frankly." His laugh echoed off the gleaming white corridor with ornate veins of silver and gold threaded through the walls and floor around them. "Loki is only a quarter frost giant, with the other quarter fire giant, so he's not a blue popsicle. Although, that doesn't stop me from making fun of him about the Midgardian misconceptions. They do have the funniest myths and tales about him."

Shannon chuckled at the wicked gleam in Thor's eyes. Yeah, Loki and Thor were definitely siblings. "No, he turned himself into a cat to stalk me at my conference." Still of two minds about that, she couldn't help but grin as she recalled how she'd gotten him to reveal himself.

Thor snorted. "Yes, he prefers cats, large or small, but he can be other animals as well. He spent many years as the trickster gods Coyote and Raven in North America."

What? Shannon halted in place, mouth open and blinking at Thor. He raised an eyebrow in silent query.

Some of the favourite stories her mother told her were about Raven, like how he taught the First Nations to make nets and to fish when the salmon were running. That was *Loki*? She shook her head, breath quickening. He had to be hundreds... maybe *thousands* of years old. Holy cow. She couldn't conceive of living that long. But—she pressed her hand to her stomach and the sudden churning within—wasn't she going to live that long now? Wasn't that one outcome of her goddess transformation?

"That's... that's a lot for me to wrap my head around. What were you doing while he scampered across North America?" Shannon slowly started walking again, trying to not dwell on a timescale that meant she'd outlive every person in her life. Acid crept up her throat and she swallowed it down. Fuck. How had she not realized that before? Or had she just not been willing to think that far ahead?

"Loki gave me a spell to make me appear as an enormous bird for mortals, the god Thunderbird, so I could join him for a while. I enjoyed that immensely. The Aesir and Vanir tend to form most of the major Midgardian pantheons like the Egyptians, Greeks, Romans, Norse, and a portion of the gods of the Americas. We change our names on Midgard as the pantheons and beliefs of the mortals evolve. Many of the Aesir have abilities relating to hunting, war, building, and inventing, whereas the Vanir tend to be skilled in growing things, healing, fertility, songs, dance, and brewing. Our two races have mixed for a long time."

Shannon's breath hiccupped at the further weight of time pressing on her chest, an anvil making every inhale a struggle. Isis had mentioned other names, but the implications hadn't clicked. Holy shit. Shannon was a child, a bare infant in experience by comparison. How was she supposed to deal with, or have any kind of connection with a being thousands or even tens of thousands of years old? She stared down at her hand, clenching it into a fist. What she knew in comparison wouldn't even be a drop of water in Loki's palm. "You mentioned two other races?" she rasped, voice rough with desperation and lack of air, trying to distract her panicked thoughts as Thor directed her through an archway and into a room with several people in green smocks.

"I will happily tell you more, but first, let's have the healers give you a scan, okay?"

Shannon sucked in a shaky breath, held it for a second, and then blew it out, chills racing over her skin. *Get it together, damn it.* Two of the green-garbed individuals helped her up onto a bed, and a green energy beam surrounded her as soon as she laid back.

"In addition to the talon wounds on her forearms, we'd like a complete health scan and a genetic race profile, Healer Moja," Thor told a dark-haired, round-faced woman who eyed them with a raised eyebrow.

The woman's chin-length hair swung, sweeping luminous silver skin as she nodded, and her deft fingers played over what appeared to be a set of controls or readouts on the side of the beam. Warmth bloomed on Shannon's arms under the white bandages and she fought to not squirm as the pain disappeared and instead, her forearms itched.

With quick tugs, the healer snipped the cloth wrappings and removed them. Only faint red lines remained of the ragged slashes that had torn diagonally through her flesh from almost wrist to elbow, fortunately missing the two major arteries. Shannon flexed her wrists. Yeah, the pain was completely gone. Wow. Asgardian medicine was way more advanced.

"Eat this." The healer handed her a golden... was it an apple? Shannon took a bite and the flavour burst on her tongue. A mix of cherry and apple. She took another bite as the healer continued, "She is Tuatha Dé Danann, Aos Sí, my prince. Her energies are new but stable. Did she transition recently?"

Thor's eyes widened, mouth dropping open as he gaped at Shannon.

Shannon was distracted from marvelling over the unusual apple and her healed wounds. Her pulse spiked, adrenaline flooding her system. "What's wrong?" Shannon asked, wrapping her arms around herself as she started to shiver. Breath quick and shallow, her gaze darted between Thor and the healer, who looked on with calm efficiency. Was there something bad with being Aos Sí? Wait... didn't he say they were the elves? She was an elf? Her hand rose to touch her rounded ear. Didn't elves have pointed ears?

He regained his composure, giving her a fleeting smile, and patted her on the shoulder. "Nothing is wrong, little sister. I'm just surprised." He turned back to the healer. "No Midgardian? Pure Sidhe?"

"Yes, my prince." Her voice was calm as she continued to monitor the readout.

"And everything else is good? Yes, she transitioned a month ago, almost five months ago on Midgard."

The healer smiled and inclined her head, then met Shannon's eyes with her kind brown gaze. "Yes, my prince. Her energy levels are strong and stable. Both she and the baby are very healthy."

Chapter 22

A Dose of Wisdom

Shannon blinked, then blurted, "*Baby!* What baby?" with Thor echoing her.

The healer shifted uncomfortably, eyes darting between them. "Umm... this is a surprise?"

As Shannon lunged from the bed, the green energy beam shut off. She swayed on her feet. She couldn't breathe. *Oh gods.* She couldn't breathe. *This can't be happening.* Her chest tightened and her vision spotted as heat suffused her insides and cold chills rippled over her skin.

Thor laughed, smiling hugely. "I'm going to be an uncle!"

The sound thundered in Shannon's ears and her limbs trembled, the heat within flashing to a fiery inferno, even as her eyes stung. "I am going to *kill* your brother!" Wind picked up in the room, stirring clothes.

Thor's smile dropped. "Now Shannon, calm down. The healers will never forgive us if we destroy their workspace." He held his hands out to her, palms out, entreating her to stop.

With a half-whimpered cry, she snatched back control of the wind, drawing it with her as she stormed out of the room and burst into the hallway.

Blinded by tears, she almost mowed down the approaching tall, elegant raven-haired woman. In the nick of time, Shannon halted, expending effort to tamp the swirling wind down. Even so, it whipped the woman's beautiful silver brocade dress around her feet. Clenching her teeth, Shannon yanked at her control further. With one shaking hand, she shoved her hair back from her face and scrubbed at her watery vision.

The woman stopped as well, peering behind Shannon with one dark eyebrow raised.

"Mother, this is Loki's Shannon."

A burst of energy surged from Shannon at Thor's introduction, along with an inarticulate screech. "I am *not* Loki's Shannon. Damn it, I am my own person. I'm going to kick Loki's ass from here through all the realms until he is a pathetic whimpering heap at my feet!" A sob cracked her voice. "He lied to me!" Gods. How could she be pregnant? A child? With the mess her life was in?

The woman's lips quirked up, and she drew Shannon in for a hug, startling her into a gasp. Loki's mother smelled of cinnamon and apples, immediately comforting. Shannon inhaled the familiar scent as her body shook.

"I'm Frigga. I'm very glad to meet you, Shannon. Go away, Thor." She waved him off, and through the pulse pounding in Shannon's ears, she heard his reply that he'd see them later.

With an arm around her, Frigga steered Shannon's unsteady legs through a nearby arch and outside to a beautiful garden courtyard. They strolled arm-in-arm as Shannon slowly caught her breath and the lightheadedness dissipated. Frigga guided them along a meandering stone pathway filled with climbing vines, clipped hedges, and towers of brilliant flowers.

"Now, take a bite of your apple, then tell me what my infuriating, mischievous son has done to drive you to this state. Perhaps I'll help you kick his ass."

Shannon blinked, wiping her eyes again. Hearing their elegant mother speak like that drew an involuntary smile. The story spilled out in a torrent of words, the apple left forgotten in her hand.

Shannon told Frigga about meeting Tod on a flight and how he invited her to join him for the movie. That he'd revealed himself as Loki, and she'd panicked and fled. How he'd stalked her as a cat at her conference until she made a bet to get him to show himself, not knowing what her reward of Asgardian mead would do to her.

With a bowed head, she confessed her anger, fear, and denial, not wanting to listen when Loki told her she couldn't tell anyone. How hard she'd worked to become a professor, and how everything she'd thought she'd known was now worthless. She poured out her fears about how her ex had treated her. Then she quietly confessed she'd again fled and ended up with Isis, who'd taught Shannon how to use her powers.

Finally, she spoke of Thor finding and saving her when Isis discovered Shannon was Loki's soulmate, which she wasn't sure she believed. Her voice cracked as she told Frigga the healers had revealed she was Aos Sí, and also almost five months pregnant, her mind a seething tempest of shocked anger and fear.

Through it all, Loki's mother listened patiently with an affectionate, kind smile, not interrupting but letting Shannon get it all out. As Shannon neared the end of her tale, Frigga steered her to a carved wooden bench under an arbour of fragrant, multi-coloured roses. They sat, and Frigga took Shannon's quivering hands in both of hers.

"First, everything will be fine."

She waited until Shannon peeked up into her brilliant green eyes, her gaze understanding and kind, but with a comforting inner strength. Shannon let out a shaking breath and swiped at her tears again.

"Second, I will help you kick my son's ass, but I don't think you'll need it. I expect you are more than strong enough to handle him on your own."

Shannon smiled a bit at that, appreciating the glowing ember of confidence it gave her. The embarrassment tightening her chest at her breakdown eased. Gods, Frigga was so easy to talk to, to be with. Wait... the healer had called Thor a prince. She was the *queen*? But she was so normal, the epitome of warmth and understanding Shannon wished her own mother had been more often.

"Third, I expect you have some questions, so eat your apple and let me see if I can shed a little light, okay?"

Butterflies took flight within Shannon, and she nodded. "Yes, please." Obediently, she took a bite from the odd fruit still in her hand.

"You said he revealed himself. What were the circumstances?"

Shannon flinched, dropping her eyes. Heat crept up her face as she tried to think of an answer. Talking to Loki's mom about sex with her son? Nope. Not happening!

Frigga laughed, a delighted bubbly sound that made Shannon squirm. Seriously, where was the nearest black hole to swallow her? Had she thought Frigga was easy to talk to? Damn. She'd changed her mind.

"Your blush is all the answer I need," Frigga said with a smile. "I'm going to assume the two of you were having sex."

Uncomfortable and fidgeting in her seat like an errant toddler, Shannon silently nodded.

"Sweet child." Frigga put her hand on Shannon's flushed face, tipping her chin up to look at her. "There is only one set of circumstances that will cause an Asgardian master mage like Loki to lose control of his seidhr, his magic, after his age of mastery."

"What is it?" Despite her embarrassment, Shannon ached to know, to have answers.

"The Asgardian binding ceremony when two soulmates meet and are intimate for the first time. When both orgasm simultaneously, it releases energy that intertwines them across dimensional matrices."

Shannon's jaw dropped. She didn't know what to say. Hamster-like, her mind spun on its wheel.

The queen smiled, affection and delight in her expression, as she waited for Shannon to speak.

"So... so we really are soulmates?" What did that even mean? Was he supposed to be her perfect match? Did she get a choice? Did he even want this, to be stuck with her fat, pregnant ass when he had so many vying for his attention? Pregnant. Her chest tightened and she ate another bite of her apple, trying to ignore her trembling fingers. Holy shit.

"Absolutely, my darling. There is no question. I expect afterwards he could read some of your thoughts and you his? To communicate with each other through your minds?"

"Yes." Shannon recalled how intimate it felt to talk to him mind-to-mind. She missed it, despite how she'd tried to deny the feeling. "But why didn't he tell me?" He probably didn't want this. Why would he?

"Not to excuse him, but did you give him a chance to?" Frigga asked with a gentle smile.

Shannon winced, guilt squirming in her stomach. Frigga wasn't wrong. "Not really. I kinda took off within an hour or so of waking up." Another thought occurred, darker, and with a return of her earlier fury as she waited, braced for Frigga's answer. "Is that how he was able to get me preg—pregnant?"

Her heart raced, spots appearing in her vision. "Loki said it took conscious magic for that to happen between a mortal and a god. Did he lie to me?"

Frigga smiled and pulled Shannon in for a hug again. "No child. Loki didn't lie." Shannon's breath whooshed in a shaky exhale, and Frigga released her. "Loki told you the absolute truth, but it isn't the whole situation for you, is it? You are *not* mortal. You are Tuatha Dé Danann, Aos Sí. Do you know what that means?"

"Thor said something about the Sidhe—elves and other fae creatures." Shannon's hand rose to touch her ear.

"Yes, we are usually referring to the elves, but the Aos Sí come in many more forms than the pointy-eared humanoids of Midgardian folklore." Frigga smiled and took Shannon's hand, pulling it down. "In their realm, the light elves, or Ljosalfar in our tongue, Seelie in theirs, live on the parts of the planet Alfheim that are eternally summer. The dark elves, the Svartalfar, or Unseelie as they call themselves, live partially or fully underground on the parts of the planet that are eternally winter. Both are descendants of the Tuatha Dé Danann, the most human-like branch of the Aos Sí. Some of the greatest weaponsmiths across all the Nine Realms are the Dvergr, another branch of the Aos Sí different enough to be called dwarves. They live entirely underground in their own realm, Nidavellir. Then many other branches of the Aos Sí are extremely different. These are the fae you'd consider creatures of legend."

"Wow, that must be an interesting evolutionary tree," Shannon murmured, taking another bite of the apple. Had the same Darwinian forces acted on the Aos Sí like evolution worked on Earth?

"Indeed," Frigga agreed. "Just as the Vanir and Aesir tend to have different aptitudes and abilities, the same is true between the light and dark elves. However, the one thing uniting the most human-like Sidhe, those elves like you, is that sex is often a catalyst for their magic. We have to assume the same is likely true for you."

"Is that why... this is so embarrassing." Shannon cringed, trying to force herself to talk past the lump closing her throat.

Frigga's green eyes glinted—so familiar in shade to Loki's that the family resemblance was obvious. "It's okay, Shannon. I'm a fertility goddess myself. I won't faint discussing sex, even if you are talking about my son." With a smile on her lips, she squeezed Shannon's fingers. "Just ask your question, please."

Shannon glanced away, unable to meet Frigga's knowing gaze. "Is that why, after I drank the mead, it felt like I kept building up energy I couldn't get rid of without Loki... um, without him... ah, damn it... without him finishing with me?" she finally blurted in an embarrassed rush, her voice squeaking at the end.

When Shannon could finally drag her eyes back up, Frigga's lips twitched with humour, and her eyes twinkled with mischief.

"Knowing what I do about how those transitions go, how much magic and time it takes for a full adult conversion, given you were activating not just a few genes, but your entire genetic make-up, I take it this was a particularly eventful transition. How long did the transition take?"

"At least eighteen hours, I think... give or take a few," Shannon whispered in another small, embarrassed squeak.

"How many waves of magic were required?" Frigga asked in a soothing voice.

"I don't—I don't know. At least every hour," Shannon mumbled, barely able to get the words out.

Frigga chuckled, then laughed, and didn't stop until she was almost crying. After a few minutes, Shannon lost some of her embarrassment and joined her.

Frigga pulled Shannon into her arms, hugging her tightly. "Oh, my wonderful, blessed daughter. I'm so sorry for laughing, but that was quite the introduction to goddesshood. It must have been an intensely memorable experience," she teased with an amused smile as she rubbed Shannon's back.

Shannon blushed but nodded in agreement, unable to disagree. That night had replayed in her dreams many times over the past four-and-a-half months, haunting her with the feel, taste, and smell of Loki surrounding her.

"There is no doubt in my mind that at least one of your parents must be a fertility god."

Shannon blinked, picturing her dad and then her mom. No. No way. Maybe a grandparent?

"Loki is a fertility god on his Vanir side," Frigga continued. "It also explains why you are pregnant. Frankly, after that transition and the amount of magic involved, if you weren't pregnant, I'd be thinking something was wrong." She kissed Shannon on the cheek while rubbing her back. "Loki has never participated in an adult's transition before, so he wouldn't have known.

Without awareness of your parentage ahead of time, he couldn't have predicted the outcome."

Still distracted thinking about her family, Shannon murmured, "Okay, so maybe I won't kick his ass for lying to me then."

Frigga drew back, releasing Shannon to meet her gaze. "True, he didn't lie in this instance. However, given all the facts, I suspect he would have gone ahead and given you the mead, even if he foresaw the outcome. I'm sure it didn't take any convincing to get him to participate, now did it?" Her green eyes twinkled.

Shannon shook her head.

"Right. You go ahead and kick his ass," Loki's mother said, lips twitching up at the corners.

Shannon's eyes widened.

Frigga's smile broadened, and she patted Shannon's leg. "Keep him on his toes. It's good for him to not always get his way." Rising, she led them out of the palace and accompanied Shannon to the start of the rainbow bridge at the edge of the city.

It wasn't a long walk, but far enough for her to tell Shannon a few amusing tales of raising Loki and Thor while Shannon finished her apple.

"So Loki couldn't shift them back into their own bodies?" Shannon asked, imagining the two boys running around as wolf pups.

Frigga smiled. "No, he hadn't mastered that yet, and he'd used a spell on both Thor and himself, instead of his innate shapeshifting abilities. It meant he couldn't turn back, and he hadn't looked up the counter-spell before the two of them decided to go romping around what is now Italy. Apparently, Thor wanted to play with the Midgardians."

Shannon laughed. "That must have been quite the sight."

"I think Heimdall got considerable amusement out of it before he let me know what the boys were up to. Both pups were exhausted, covered in honey, dirt, and olive leaves, asleep in some goat shepherd's paddock when I went to retrieve them." With a wave of her arm, Frigga projected an image into the air of two wolf pups, one black and grey, the other red and brown, curled up together in a pile of straw while goats tugged at the straw, eating. Sure enough, Shannon saw sticky patches of fur with straw, dirt, and leaves stuck to them, especially around their muzzles and paws.

"Aww... they were adorable!"

"Too adorable! I had a hard time not laughing at their mischief when I needed to be firm with them. Just you wait and see." Wrapping her arms around Shannon, Frigga hugged her tight. "I'm so glad to have met you, Shannon. It makes me unbelievably happy to have you in our family. At the same time, I get a daughter and a grandchild."

A chill raced over Shannon's spine as her stomach twisted. Her mouth opened to reply, but she wasn't sure what to say. Her mind had blanked, and she had the completely inappropriate urge to giggle hysterically. Here, she'd thought her biggest concern was figuring out what it meant to be a goddess.

Now, she was going to be a mother. Oh gods. A mom! After the disaster of her relationship with Trent, she'd given up the idea. Thirty-five wasn't too old, but she'd assumed by the time she found someone she wanted to have kids with, it would be too late. Now... holy crap... she was a baby immortal, herself. A weight pressed on her chest. How the hell would she take care of a vulnerable child when she could barely control these new powers?

She didn't want to be a single parent, tackling this on her own. Fuck.

"Don't worry, child. Go deal with that wayward son of mine. Odin and I would love to have you join us for a meal when you are free to come back. Heimdall will open the Bifrost whenever you ask." Frigga smiled as she released Shannon and stepped back.

"Oh... umm... Thank you. Yes, I'd like to meet... Odin." Shannon swallowed the bile climbing her throat. The All-Father? *Shiiit.* Yet another overwhelming item on her rapidly expanding to-do list. A hysterical laugh burbled and she bit it back, placing a hand on her belly. Her list wasn't the only thing expanding.

Surely, if Frigga was there, meeting Odin couldn't be *that* bad. Not like in mythology. But still, he was the All-Father. Another chill wracked Shannon's spine and she swallowed, watching Frigga leave. As long as no one ended up tied to a rock with venom dripping onto them, Shannon could probably survive a family meal.

Probably.

A wave of lightheadedness washed over Shannon as she turned to cross the bridge. She stumbled and caught her balance. The bridge's energy thrummed beneath her feet, different from the feel of the natural elements. Different and distracting, but with a fluttering in her stomach, there was still something about it she recognized. She just couldn't pin it down.

She gasped. Pregnancy. Oh fucking hell. Of course. It was the baby. Oh, wow. And the nausea... fuck. It wasn't just her nerves. Damn. She should have asked the healer about the exhaustion that had plagued her these last few months, too. Was that normal? Lost in thought, it didn't take her long to reach the impressive stone-arched structure and Heimdall.

"Greetings, Princess Shannon. What do you seek?"

"Princess?" Her heart lurched at the unexpected title.

"You are Prince Loki's soulmate, bound for eternity. You are carrying a royal heir to the throne of Asgard. As a member of the royal family, your title is princess." Understanding gleamed in his gold-, white-, and black-striated eyes.

Her breath rasped as she blinked at him. Oh, holy hell. *Royalty?* How could she be royalty? And fuck, did he say bound for eternity? What, no parole for good behaviour?

Gods, did she even get a choice about all this?

What happened when Loki got bored with her? Her shoulders hunched and she put a hand on her belly. When he decided she was fat and unattractive with their child in a few months... when he wanted to continue screwing his way through the female population?

The ramifications had her stomach twisting, and definitely not from the baby this time. Fuck, she almost needed to put her head between her knees, but something told her if she attempted it, she'd be painting the chamber with vomit. Her ears rang. "Wow, you really see everything when you want to, don't you?" Her voice sounded unnatural, high-pitched and cracking.

His deep rumble vibrated in the space. "Not as much as I'd like to at times. It's a big universe. I need to be looking in the right direction to see events unfolding in a particular area. Despite my vigilance in watching for threats to Asgard from across the Nine Realms, there are places I cannot see. Something must alert my senses in time for me to focus on it."

Staring off into space, she blinked, swallowed against the acid, and blinked again. "I can't imagine. That must be an immense challenge," she managed, distracting herself from incipient hyperventilation as she considered the complexities of seeing so far, in such detail, but also how much information must be out there. It had to be overwhelming without a focus. Kind of like her situation. Her pulse pounded. *Fuck, don't think about that.* "How do you know where to look?"

"My first priority is to monitor off-planet Asgardians, in case they need help. I keep my senses open to the voices of all Asgardians, but I am always aware of members of the royal family, Princess."

A wave of cold washed over Shannon. *Royalty*. Pressing a hand to her churning belly, she had to change the topic before she lost control. "What is Loki doing right now?" Her voice was a bare wheeze as she panted.

"Should I call a healer, Princess?"

She shook her head, unable to answer in words.

Heimdall's tone turned cautious. "He is on Midgard, the Canadian west coast. He's given Asgardian mead to several individuals."

A jolt shook her as her fists clenched in suspicion. "What the hell is he up to?" she hissed. Adrenaline flashed through her blood, heightening her senses, and she drew a full breath, the weight on her chest receding slightly. "Please drop me near him, Heimdall."

Chapter 23

PRINCE'S GAMBIT

It was ridiculously easy for Loki to pour a small splash of Asgardian mead into the mimosa pitcher. Even if he hadn't been able to maintain his cloaking illusion, Shannon's sister-in-law, Sarah, had her back to the table as she removed two casserole dishes from the oven. Task done, Loki retreated from the heavy circular oak table set with its distinctive red-and-yellow china pattern of Old Country Roses. Gleaming silverware, tea cups, and champagne flutes were laid out for four on the lace-edged white tablecloth. No evidence of the extra ingredient was revealed by the crystal pitcher of frothy orange juice and champagne.

As Shannon's mother and sister arrived and were greeted by Liam at the front porch, Loki tucked himself into the corner of the kitchen, out of the way and close to the back door. His palms began to sweat, and he rubbed at the ache in his chest, at the blocked bond that prevented him from sensing his mate. Bor's balls, he needed this to work. He had to find her. It was only his hundreds of years of martial discipline that kept him from fidgeting as Liam finally poured the mimosas.

"To Dad. May he smile down on us," Liam said with his glass raised. His wife joined him, then Shannon's sister, and finally, after spinning the fluted glass by its stem, Rose, Shannon's mother, raised her glass.

Drink, Loki silently urged, leaning toward them.

"To Thomas," Rose murmured before downing the entire glass.

Liam blinked but followed suit. Sarah and Heather looked at each other, shrugged, then drank the contents. Sarah reached for the pitcher and refilled the glasses.

As they started to dish food onto their plates, Loki peered intently, waiting. Every heartbeat seemed to take a lifetime.

"Sho..." Liam cleared his throat, frowned and tried again. "Sho, Mom..." His fork fell from his fingers, and he stared at it.

Sarah shoved her plate away as her head drooped towards the table. Her eyes were closed before the thunk of impact.

Liam went to reach for her face and missed by inches. Heather laughed even as she slumped, head lolling to one side. She blinked once, then again, and the third time, her eyes stayed closed.

Loki crept closer, a sinking sensation taking root in his gut as Rose laid her head against her daughter's and passed out. Surely one of them... but no, Liam's head hit the table beside his wife's. Loki checked each of them. All four were unconscious. None of Shannon's family were transitioning.

Yet, Shannon's conversion had been powerful, far more than just a few genes.

Loki stared at her brother, her sister, and her mother. Acidic betrayal climbed his throat as the truth struck. Did Shannon know? Or had they hidden it from her? How could they? Damn them to Helheim, how could they do that to her? Unable to look at them, fury shaking his limbs, he stormed out the back door, letting it slam behind him.

Nothing. He'd gained *nothing* by this gambit. They couldn't help him find her. Shifting into a coyote, he howled his rage and anguish as he ran down the covered porch steps and out into the surrounding field of tall grasses.

A familiar swirl of rainbow lights halted him in his tracks.

"*Damn it, Loki!* What the *hell* are you up to?"

That voice. It couldn't be. Could it? Frozen, Loki scarcely breathed, so afraid to be wrong, to have the vision in front of him disappear as a tornado of feminine fury appeared over the rise. Norns, please... please. Every cell in his body vibrated as she stomped closer and the most adorable growl rumbled from her throat.

With her hands on her hips and the sun behind her, he couldn't see her face. But by Yggdrasil's mighty trunk, he didn't need to. The joy in his soul told him it was *her*.

Eddies of wind circled her gorgeous form. She wore tan cargo pants and a short-sleeved, linen shirt whose ivory colour highlighted her darkly tanned olive skin and brown ponytail with sun-kissed streaks of red-gold. Light clothing and no jacket—she'd been somewhere warm.

<*What the hell are you doing giving my family Asgardian mead, Loki?*> she snarled.

Loki almost yipped with delight at hearing her telepathy, the warm glow of her presence within the bond and his mind. In a swirl of black seidhr, he shifted from coyote to man, palms outstretched. "Now Shannon, don't be angry. Please. I was desperate. Heimdall couldn't see you. I thought if one of them had enough immortal genes, the family connection would be enough to find you." And they should have, damn it, but he clenched his jaw on adding that.

"And destroy their fucking life!" She glared at him and stepped closer.

Bor's beard, she was magnificent with her cheeks flushed, her bright green-gold hazel eyes sparkling. "I'm sorry. It was wrong not to give them a choice, but I was terrified something had happened to you," he pleaded. "It's been months. I didn't know if you were alive or..." He couldn't finish the thought, couldn't voice the fear. His hungry eyes roved over her. She'd lost some of her curves, gotten leaner. Had she been ill? In trouble? Fuck, it was hard not to reach for her, to feel with his hands that she was real, healthy, and whole. His fingertips ached with the need to touch her.

She screeched and shoved past him.

Bloody fucking Helheim, he had to warn her. Loki grabbed her fingers before she got out of reach. "Wait, Shannon! It didn't work. They passed out like your friends."

"What? What do you mean?" She yanked her hand out of his grasp and glared. "Of course, it had to work. Apparently"—she snorted and rolled her eyes—"I'm one hundred percent Aos Sí with no Midgardian genes."

"You're... oh damn. Damn, damn, damn." The small hope that there'd been a mistake died, and he stiffened, fighting the furious snarl he wanted to roar on her behalf. That wasn't what she needed right now. He'd suspected she might have some Elven genes, but full Sidhe... no, he hadn't expected that. Yet after months without her, scared for her, he didn't care if her birth parents were even the hated Unseelie. He'd fucking protect her from the dark elves and their sick practices.

He moved to try to hug her, to give her some kind of comfort.

But his heart sank when she stepped out of reach.

Not that he blamed her. He'd fucked up. Again. He shouldn't have dosed her family. Still, it didn't change the outcome or that the cursed bastards had kept a fucking massive secret she'd had a right to know. He dropped his hand, then shoved frustrated fingers through his hair. "Bloody hell. I'm so sorry. Norns, I'm so very sorry."

She scowled, jaw clenched as she kicked at the grass. Finally, she muttered, "I'm going to check on them." Leaving Loki there, she strode to the farmhouse, stomped up the white steps with their peeling paint, and disappeared inside.

Loki tugged at his hair, torn between the need to comfort her and her refusal to let him touch her. Anguish and confusion pummelled him through the bond, Shannon's emotions a raging current within him now that she'd reopened it. She hadn't realized the implications of her family not transitioning yet. But she would. Norns-curse-them, she would.

Fuck. Why? Why hadn't they told her? Slowly following her, Loki climbed the steps and leaned against the white railing of the covered porch. It wasn't like these kinds of secrets stayed hidden. Her fucking mother should have told Shannon when she was old enough to understand. He scrubbed a hand over his face. Damn them. Damn them all.

Shannon stumbled out the front door, shaking and pale. Loki's fingers clenched on the wood railing, fury swirling in his blood, trying to resist the need to hold her. How could they have kept this from her? When she staggered, knees weakening, his restraint vanished. He teleported to catch her, lifting her into his arms as he strode to the wide wooden porch swing. With her cuddled to his chest, he sat, rocking in place as the silver suspension chains creaked.

"I don't understand. How can they not be affected? They have to have the same genes as me." Thready with pain, Shannon's voice barely reached even his immortal hearing.

He drew her vanilla-lemon scent in, feeling it sink all the way down into his bones, filling the missing pieces of his parched soul. But as much as he revelled in her presence, in the bond open between them, he couldn't relax into the sensation. Not now. Not when it felt wrong to take solace in holding her after he'd yet again played a part in upending her life. Fuck. Forcing her to see another truth, tearing away yet more of her foundation was *not* how he'd wanted to be reunited with her. He stifled his growl. Bor's balls, he hated, *hated* that he had to be the one to reveal this to her. Fuckers.

His hand caressed her soft hair and down her back, trying to soothe her trembling as he shoved the words past the anger gripping him, wrestled his voice into a low, calming murmur. "You know the answer. There is only one answer."

Chapter 24

FAMILIES DON'T HAVE TO MEAN BLOOD

Shannon met Loki's, his gaze as powerful as she'd remembered. And as unflinching. But there was no pity, just a deep sense of understanding, of compassion in his expression. What did he—Realization dawned and jagged pain speared her chest, sucking a gasp from her as emotion choked her throat. "I'm adopted." The broken words cut like shards of glass as she forced them out.

He kissed her forehead. "Yes, love. They aren't your genetic relatives."

Oh gods. Why had no one told her? The ever-present nausea churned in her belly and a burning heat intensified behind her eyes. Who was she? Did she know anymore? A sob escaped, even as she tried to bite it back. Her family wasn't her family? Where did she come from? Who were her parents? How did she end up here? Unable to hold the tears at bay, they overflowed her cheeks to soak her shirt. She burrowed her head into his warm chest, and his arms tightened, his hands stroking her hair and down her spine. The sorrow in her heart was a pulsing, gaping hole.

She didn't belong anywhere. Not now. Not then. Why hadn't her birth family wanted her. Oh gods, they hadn't wanted her. They threw her away. A tremor shuddered through her. Why? And what about her adopted family? Was this why her sister hated her sometimes?

"Sweetheart, don't do this to yourself." Loki tipped her chin up with a finger so their eyes met. "Don't think about your birth parents and why they gave you up. Think about the positive. Remember your mother and father chose you to be part of their family. They wanted you and *chose* you. There is so much more to the making of a family. It's all the little things, all the shared experiences, care, and love over the years."

Peering up into his brilliant green eyes, which yes, she had desperately missed even when she didn't want to admit it, she nodded. "I know you are right. It hurts though, Loki. Gods, it hurts. In thirty-five years, they couldn't find a time to tell me?" She swiped at her watery eyes.

His mouth twisted wryly. "I know, darling. Mine didn't tell me in the hundred and fifty they could have. It was an accident I found out I'd been Frigga's sister's child, not her own."

Shannon blinked as his meaning penetrated, then reached to cup his cheek, and he turned to place a gentle kiss on her palm, the contact tingling up her arm. He understood. Maybe she wasn't sure about them together, but this... yeah, she'd take this. Her hiccupping breaths calmed. She closed her eyes and relaxed into him, listening to his heartbeat and breathing in his woody-leather-and-citrus scent as he slowly rocked the swing back and forth. The rhythm soothed the heavy weight on her soul.

Her voice was quiet when she finally broke the peaceful silence. "I like your mom. She's pretty great. You look just like her."

"You met my mother?" Loki's voice held notes of delight before the melodious accent returned to a calm baritone. "Yeah, she is, isn't she? Revna and Frigga were twins, so I suppose it isn't surprising that I take after her." He kissed Shannon's palm again, playing with her fingers. "Just remember, like in that demon-hunting show filmed around here, families don't have to mean blood. Some are just chance genetic relations, others are choices about who we include. Don't underestimate the importance of being picked as part of a family. Don't throw that away or dismiss it. It took me years to deal with the news myself. I didn't react very well when I first found out I was adopted. But to be honest, Frigga is everything I would have ever asked for in a mother."

"Do you think my mom knows who my birth parents are?" Shannon couldn't help but wonder, questions pressing in against her consciousness.

“I don’t know, but we’ll ask when she wakes from the mead. You said Aos Sí?”

She nodded, opening her eyes to meet his gaze. “That’s what the healer on Asgard told me.”

Curiosity lit in the emerald depths, and his lips curled at the edges. “I’d like to hear that story, as well as how you met my mother.”

He nuzzled her palm, holding her hand to his face. She found her fingers tracing over his soft lips. He nipped one fingertip, and she couldn’t help but smile, despite her distress. That playful side of him could never be repressed for long.

<*I missed you,*> she admitted. With the mental connection open between them after months without, she finally acknowledged the warmth of it, allowing it to fully flood her aching chest, to fill her with his presence and soothe her broken edges.

He gave her a wicked smirk. <*I know.*>

A laugh bubbled out, surprising her as she recalled their discussion of favourite movies on the plane and that famous scene. <*I’m not your Princess Leia.*>

His smile widened. <*No, you’re my goddess. My soulmate.*>

With the bond open between them, she sensed his joy, acceptance, and even... more she wasn’t quite ready to label. Did he feel her confusion and uncertainty mixed in with the desire she couldn’t hide? Gods, her emotions were all over the place, twisting around like a rudderless boat.

Even now, overwhelming panic bubbled beneath the surface, waiting to suck her down into its hysterical depths. She had a child growing inside her, a helpless being who would need Shannon to get her fucking shit together. And the godsdamned clock was ticking—only twenty of forty weeks remaining. How the hell would she tell Loki? Who knew if he wanted to be a father?

How could she even think of trying to forge a family with him?

Her own had just imploded, shattering what she thought she’d known.

Again.

Fuck.

With frantic flailing, she was treading water to keep her head above the surface as the weight of all she’d learned today threatened to drag her down, clinging like cement-clad chains to her ankles.

Loki tilted his head to lightly brush her lips with his before he drew back, their gaze connecting.

She couldn't look away. Maybe she could escape it all, escape the crushing depths for just a little while. Surely, she could take a little time... to process, to think about things? Gods, to just catch her fucking breath.

Slowly lowering his head again, he caressed her lips with another featherlight kiss.

Shannon's lashes closed and she floated in the tenderness of his touch. He kissed both sides of her mouth before running his tongue lightly over her bottom lip.

Reaching her hand up into his silky hair, she scraped her nails along his scalp, smiling into his light kisses as he groaned. Such a quiet sound, but with deep emotion to it. A warmth spread through her body at the knowledge of how much she affected him, that this intense attraction was not one-sided.

More insistence in his kisses now, and at the slight tug of his teeth on her lower lip, she opened to him, his tongue sweeping in. She was tired of trying to deal, trying to be strong. When possession and dominance coloured his still-tender touch, seeking her surrender, she gave in. Breathless from his kisses, she tipped her head, giving him her neck as he licked his way down to her pulse, delicately biting.

"Gods, Loki," she moaned. Despite their time apart, there was no shortage of desire between them. If anything, it was hotter, burning brighter. Her dreams and memory hadn't done it justice.

His hand rose to her throat, stroking, squeezing slightly as he gazed down at her with half-lidded glowing eyes. "We are going to have a discussion, you and I, about you running off and leaving me with no word for four-and-a-half very long months." His voice was a quiet, low growl.

A spike of tension clutched at her chest. Not now. She couldn't do this now. Loki's hand squeezed in warning when she opened her mouth to object.

"No, not now... this is neither the time nor the place," he warned. Relief weakened her muscles, and she sagged against him. "We are going to need privacy. I expect a lot of screaming, moaning, and begging." His eyes glittered with dark promise, and she couldn't deny the heated shiver it sent through her body.

If he wanted to play, she was willing.

Just as long as they could avoid all the weightier topics drowning her. Fuck, how was he going to react to becoming a father? Her pulse thudded, tension chasing away desire. If he hated the idea, was she going to keep the child? Raise it herself? She couldn't imagine giving her child away the way she'd been, but raising an immortal... shit, she barely understood her own powers.

As her chest tightened, Shannon shoved the thoughts down, trying to focus on Loki, on the carnality in his gaze, the slight flush to his pale cheeks, and the messy flow of his dark locks.

His hand caressed her throat again, fingertips against her pulse. She considered his threat of screaming, moaning, and begging, and let the idea sink into her mind. Despite her position cradled against his chest, she raised an eyebrow in mock disdain. Shannon wanted to tease him, challenge him... to have a chance for play before responsibility overwhelmed her. She peered at him through her lashes, cramming the desperation down and bringing a taunting half-smile to her lips.

"We'll see."

Sounds from inside the house caught her attention. Keeping eye contact with him, she slowly removed his hand from her throat and pushed away from his chest, rising from the swing. She took a few steps towards the front door, a little extra sway in her hips.

"I hear them stirring inside. You coming?" She kept the grin on her face as she glanced back.

"Not yet, darling, but you can be sure you'll feel it when I am," Loki purred as he caught up with her, hand sliding over her ass before moving up to the small of her back.

She managed a laugh, trying to feel that carefree, to ignore the weight squeezing her lungs.

Like the gentleman he purported to be when he wasn't epitomizing a bad boy, he opened the door for her. As they went through, she caught the flash of black mist from the corner of her eye. His black hair lost its length and shifted to bright auburn, while his skin took on a more tanned complexion and his face filled out from razor-edged sharpness. That little dent in his chin returned. Black leather pants, knee-high boots, tunic, and long black leather coat were replaced by black combat boots, black jeans with a tear at the knee, a white Henley shirt with the first couple buttons undone, and a waist-length black leather jacket.

He shrank from just over seven feet tall to a few inches over six. He really was a wolf in a rebellious sheep's clothing.

Seriously, he was ridiculously sexy in both forms.

A shiver of desire brought gooseflesh to Shannon's skin. She barely resisted the impulse to drag him back out the door for more kisses. Part of her needed answers from those inside the house, to find some resolution for the many weights pulling her down. What would she find? Answers? Or more questions? Yet, this battled for supremacy with the intense surge of lust too long denied. She'd missed his touch keenly. Her skin ached with need, and the lure of escaping her troubles into the passion between them was strong.

Torn, she hesitated at the doorway.

He gave her a knowing smirk. Despite the desire he let her sense through the bond, his eyes were serious, waiting for her decision.

The need for answers, for resolution to even a few of her many unanswered questions, won as she focused on the sounds of her family. At the same time, she glanced down at her attire. Her family would wonder if she showed up wearing summer clothes on a cool winter day. "Would you please change my clothes to something more weather-appropriate?"

"Of course, darling. Your wish is my command," he teased, with a glint in his now pale-blue eyes. With the bond open between them, had he caught her conflicted emotions? She wasn't hiding her desire for him, even if she wasn't acting on it. It was the one entirely truthful response she could give him while she wrestled with the rest.

In a rolling flash of black, her sandals were replaced by knee-high leather boots overtop now jean-clad legs, and a gorgeously soft calf-length royal-blue cashmere coat wrapped itself over her body. Loki certainly had style and taste when it came to clothes.

<My favourite colours. Thank you. Ready to meet my family?> Gods, was she ready for him to meet her family? She bit her lip.

<Absolutely. Can't wait.>

His calm smile and reply settled her unease, and she took his hand to lead him into her brother's home. When they joined her family in the kitchen, her mom rubbed her forehead, pushing short black locks shot with silver back behind her ear, while Liam and Sarah cleared the food from the table.

Her mom glanced up. Dark brown eyes with familiar crows-feet lines creasing her deep brown skin met Shannon's, blinked, and gave her a small, tired smile. "Hi, honey. I didn't know you were joining us for brunch today."

"It looks like it's a good thing I didn't. Are you okay?" Shannon's fingers tightened on Loki's. <*They better not have any side-effects, damn you.*>

A hidden caress stroked down Shannon's back, Loki a heated presence behind her. <*Nothing more than a mild-hangover, I promise. It's just alcohol to mortals without the genes.*>

"Something must have gone off," her sister-in-law Sarah replied, tugging her long, dark braid through anxious fingers as she looked between the table, sink, and fridge. "I'm so sorry I didn't notice!"

"Neither did I, so don't feel bad." Liam tucked his wife against his worn Aerosmith T-shirt, rubbing her back in comfort before she pushed out of his arms to collect the remaining dishes from the table.

Shannon grit her teeth. Gods, she hated to see them upset, especially her brother and his wife who were only ever kind. <*Never again, Loki. Don't you dare ever pull something like this on them again.*>

A wave of complicated emotion rippled through the bond from him. <*I won't. I'm sorry, darling.*>

"It's not your fault, dear." Mom patted Sarah's hand as Sarah took her plate. "Could I have some water, Liam? I'm sure we'll be right as rain in a bit."

He nodded and moved to fill a glass.

"So, who's the handsome gentleman you've brought with you?" Mom waved a finger to indicate behind Shannon.

Shannon sucked in a breath, nerves squirming in her belly, and drew Loki beside her. "This is my boyfriend, Tod. Tod, this is my mom, Rose; my brother, Liam; and his wife, Sarah."

Loki kissed her mom's hand when she offered it, as well as Sarah's, and then shook Liam's hand. "It's a pleasure to meet all of you. I've been looking forward to meeting Shannon's family."

"Holy shit! *Tod Corvus?*"

Shannon winced at the ear-drum-shattering shriek from her sister. Like a heat-seeking missile, Heather erupted from the hallway leading to the bathroom.

"Hey sis, yeah—" Shannon got no further before her sister launched herself at Loki.

Chapter 25

SEX, CHAINS & ROCK 'N' ROLL

Despite Heather hitting him full-on with all the grace of a runaway freight train, Loki didn't stagger. To his credit, he gave her a quick, polite hug with a pat on the back, and then managed to extract himself from her octopus-like embrace. If Shannon hadn't been grinding her teeth, she'd have laughed at Heather's attempt to grab him while his longer reach kept her at bay. Her sister was barely five feet tall, the same as their mom.

"It's nice to meet you..." Loki looked to Shannon for a name.

"Heather!" her sister said, still trying to put her hands on him.

"Oh, for fuck's sake." Shannon rolled her eyes. <*Still glad you met my family?*>

"Heather! Give your sister's boyfriend some space. Act your age!" Mom scolded.

"Wow, it's so great to meet you! I'm such a huge fan. You were amazing in *Assassin*! When does the next movie come out?" Heather gushed, running her hand down his arm, and petting him.

<*Yes... but a little help, darling?*> he asked as he replied politely, thanking Heather for enjoying his work.

Shannon stepped between them, letting Loki duck behind her and to her other side, wrapping his arm around her waist.

"Knock it off, Heather, or we're leaving right now," Shannon told her with a scowl. "He didn't come here to get mobbed by a deranged fangirl."

Her sister glared at Shannon, flicking jeweled fingers through long bleached blond hair as she thrust her chest out to emphasize her prodigious assets and cocked a jean-clad hip.

Shannon's eyebrow rose as she curled her lip, crossed her arms, and glared back. Heather couldn't stand to not be the centre of attention, or not get whatever she wanted. It wouldn't be the first time she'd attempted to steal a boyfriend, but godsdamned it, she wasn't going to be successful this time even with her wasp-like waist, bee-stung lips, and overly flirty demeanor.

"How about we all enjoy a cup of tea in the living room," Liam broke in. Mom added her agreement, leading the way. She took Heather's hand as she went by, tugging her along.

Shannon and Loki followed, and she hid her grin when he wisely chose a small loveseat with just enough room for the two of them. With her usual graceful elegance, Sarah poured the tea, while Liam brought everyone a cup. It was Shannon's favourite—Earl Grey, with a slice of lemon. Not Sarah's favourite, but her sister-in-law always kept it on hand for when Shannon visited, and Shannon loved her all the more for it.

"I take it you are an actor?" Mom asked politely before directing a disapproving scowl at Heather when she snorted.

Loki glanced at Shannon before answering. <*You don't want your family to know the truth about us? You want me to give my mortal identity?*>

She smiled into his concerned gaze. Was he worried she'd still reveal secrets of the immortal world? <*It's better if they don't know. It won't improve my relationship with them.*>

<*I agree, darling. We should protect them from the knowledge of gods.*> A swell of warmth filled the bond as he took her hand and answered her mom. "Yes, I've recently delved into film. I enjoy it."

"Are you any good? Are you successful?" Mom leaned forward to pin him in place with her eyes.

Shannon groaned, one hand over her heated face. Her mom had no tact whatsoever. <*Oh my gods, I am so, so, so very sorry about my family.*> Between her sister and her mom, Shannon wanted a hole to open in the ground to swallow her. Why did she introduce Loki to them? He'd think she was out of her mind.

He laughed and squeezed her hand reassuringly. Shit. Had he caught her thoughts?

"I'll let my audience be the judge of that," he replied.

Heather snorted again. "C'mon, Mom. He's an A-list actor and musician worth millions. Remember the Assassin movies? That's him." She waved a hand towards him as she sulked in her chair, a petulant look pinching her dark face. You'd think a woman of forty-one would be more mature, but this was typical behaviour when she didn't get her way.

"Actually, I prefer your music. My students love attempting the melodies," her brother interjected.

"Thank you." Loki perked up, inclining his head and smiling at Liam.

"Not that I don't think your portrayal of Sicarius isn't brilliant. It absolutely is. I'm just a fan of Raven's Chaos," he told Loki, warming to his topic as he adjusted his black-framed glasses, then ran a hand through his short, dark-brown hair.

"Liam is an English and music teacher at the high school," Shannon told Loki.

Loki sent her brother a wide smile. "A fellow fan of the lyrical line. What's your favourite song?" *<I like him,>* he told her as he continued his conversation with her brother. *<But I have to admit, I don't particularly care for your sister.>*

<Yeah, Heather and I don't get along very well, as you can see, but my brother is great. Really great. It's Liam and Sarah who I tend to spend time with when I visit.>

As Loki and her brother bonded over music, Shannon asked her mom to join her in the kitchen. She waved off Sarah's inquisitive look. No surprise when Heather ignored Shannon, pretending to play with her phone while she took photos of Loki. Shannon winced and warned him, but he'd already noticed and wasn't worried.

<Go talk with your mum. I'm good here, chatting with Liam,> he reassured her.

Shutting the French doors between the two rooms for a little privacy, Shannon turned to her mom.

"I like Tod. He seems more comfortable and confident in himself, unlike that loser you dated previously."

Shannon winced at the reminder of Trent. “Thanks, Mom. Yes, Tod is fantastic. I like him a lot.” And she really, really hoped he was nothing like her ex. If he was, and she was stuck in this soulmate bond with him forever, it would be a nightmare. Bringing a kid into that? She shuddered. No. No way. Maybe she *would* give her child to another to raise if that was the only option to keep the baby safe. Was something like that the reason her birth mother had given her away?

“So what is it? What did you need help with, honey?” Mom asked, distracting Shannon from the dark path her thoughts had taken.

Shannon blew out a breath and fidgeted. No easy way to say it, so she bit the bullet and blurted, “Am I adopted?”

Rose appeared startled, blinking a few times. “Well, *that* wasn’t what I was expecting.” She took Shannon’s hands in hers, meeting her gaze. “Yes, honey, you are. Your dad and I never intended to keep it a secret. We just never seemed to get around to telling you. It didn’t seem to be important, as you were ours in every way but blood.”

Not—not important? *Seriously?* Shannon’s eyes heated, filling with tears, as her chest tightened.

<*Darling, do you need me?*> A whisper of sensation, like the stroke of fingertips, caressed her cheek.

She shuddered. <*No, I’m okay. Keep my family busy while I talk with my mom, please.*> A phantom kiss on her forehead and his hand gently stroking her hair comforted her.

Rose wrapped Shannon in her arms, and Loki’s touch disappeared. “Honey, I’m so sorry I never told you. I am. It’s just, well, I kind of forgot. Because it’s never been important to me, it’s not something I think about. You know we love you, right?”

She… *forgot*. Shannon swallowed the acid, trying to see her mom’s perspective. “Yes, Mom. I love you, too.” Her voice choked. She hugged Rose tight, her mom’s much shorter frame tucking into Shannon’s shoulder and chin.

“How did you find out?” Mom asked when she released Shannon, stepping back to look up at her.

“I had some genetic testing done. The results weren’t consistent with what you’d told me of our background.” Shannon fought the urge to fidget and look away. Her ability to lie on the spot was atrociously bad, and her cheeks flushed as she redirected her mom's attention. "What do you know about my birth parents?"

Her mom stared off into the kitchen, gaze unfocused as a little frown creased her brow. "Only a little. Your birth father's name is Dylan Connolly. He was a deep-sea fisherman and needed to return to the sea. There was no woman in the picture. He indicated she'd left you with him, but he couldn't take care of you out on the sea." Rose wrinkled her nose as her eyes met Shannon's. "Honestly, honey... he was an odd one."

Shannon's heart clenched, the jagged tear within a stabbing, cutting pain, and she bit back the instinctive need to curl into herself. Gods, it was true. Her birth parents hadn't wanted her. She'd been discarded. Fishing was more important than her? Really? For fuck's sake, she could breathe underwater and the bastard hadn't wanted her with him?

Mom patted her on the arm. "You were such a blessing to us, honey. I'd had a few miscarriages after Heather, but your father and I wanted more kids. We were overjoyed to bring you into our family."

Shannon couldn't deny the kernel of warmth that bloomed within her at her mom's words. It was a small balm against the bleeding tear, the sense of betrayal and loss inside her. But Loki was right. Her adoptive parents had wanted her. Unlike those who had tossed her away, they'd *chosen* her to be part of their family.

"Thanks, Mom. I'm so glad you and Dad raised me. I miss him." Shannon rubbed at her breastbone and the sharp anguish within her. But in contrast to her current emotional chaos, the loss of her father was a well-aged ache after so many years. He'd been the one to encourage her to pursue her career in science, to tell her she could achieve whatever she set out to, and to help her believe in herself. It had gutted her when he died so suddenly.

"I miss him, too. He loved you so very much." Mom wiped the moisture from Shannon's cheeks. "I'm so glad to have you here. It's been too many months, although I'm aware of how busy you get. I hope the two of you are staying to have Christmas with us?"

Shannon blinked, taken aback. She'd noticed the fresh snow on the Cascade mountains, as well as the chill in the air outside, and she'd automatically adjusted the air temperature around her—a skill she'd mastered in her first few weeks with Isis. Was it *that* close to Christmas already? Surely it was still a week away, wasn't it? How long had she been on Asgard?

<*What's the date?*> She glanced around her brother's kitchen, searching for a calendar. <*I seem to have lost track, and Mom is asking if we can stay for Christmas.*>

<*It's December twenty-third. I'm clear. I don't start recording the next album with my band until February. We can stay if you want, as long as it's not with your sister.*> The distaste in his mental tone had Shannon wanting to smile.

<*Yeah, that would never happen. We'll head to my house and come back Christmas Eve.*>

< *Good with me, darling.*>

"Of course, Mom. Tod and I are free. We'll come back tomorrow evening to spend Christmas Eve and Christmas Day here. But first, I have some things I need to take care of at home. We should head back to the city."

"Great! It'll be so nice to have us all together this holiday." Mom smiled happily, and Shannon tried to take comfort in the hug she gave her.

They returned to the living room, and Loki stood. "It was a real pleasure meeting you," he said as he shook Liam's hand.

"Likewise!"

"You aren't staying for Christmas?" Sarah asked, looking between Loki and Shannon.

"We'll be back tomorrow night if your guest room is available?" Shannon asked, already knowing the answer.

"Of course! You are always welcome." Sarah hugged her and whispered, "I like Tod. He seems like an intelligent, confident, and fun guy. A much better fit for you."

"Thanks, Sarah. I agree." Shannon hugged her back.

After a quick hug from her brother, who also whispered, "I like him," Shannon briefly hugged Heather. As usual, it was stilted and awkward.

Heading outside, Shannon and Loki waved to her family, then walked down the pathway to the curved tree-lined driveway.

"How did you get here?" she asked Loki once they were far enough away to be out of sight of the front porch.

"I flew as a raven."

"Do you trust me?" she asked, smiling up at him.

"Implicitly, my love."

A lightness filled her, an acceptance she hadn't realized she needed. She tugged him behind a large cedar—it wouldn't do to have one of her family look out a window and see them—and twined her hands around his neck, pressing her body to his.

"Hold on to me." A mischievous smile teased her lips.

Loki hugged her close, eyes alight with curiosity. Quickly, she wrapped a thick cloud around them and lifted them on a cushion of air.

His smile widened, and he laughed as they shot up into the sky. "Oh, I like this. I'll let you do all the heavy lifting," he joked as he let his natural appearance take prominence again.

In short order, Shannon set them down on the driveway of her house in Deep Cove, just outside Vancouver. Gods, it was hard to believe it'd been almost five months since she'd been home. Nothing seemed to have changed with the towering hemlocks, western red cedars, and undergrowth of rhododendrons and ferns surrounding her house, giving her privacy from both the street and neighbours. But then, that was what she paid the gardener for.

Loki cupped her cheeks. "I'm so proud of how you've mastered your abilities. I can't wait for you to show me more. For now, though, show me your beautiful home." Her heart leapt, and he kissed her, smiled, and then took her hand as she tugged him forward, almost bouncing on her toes.

They walked up to her two-story residence with its grey exterior that so often matched the winter skies and contrasted with the trim and shutters that reminded her of the ocean depths from her dock. At the frosted glass of the front door, she keyed in the four-digit O-R-C-A code to unlock the house, telling Loki as she entered each letter, even though he could teleport inside. Would he understand what it meant for her to give him this access? That she was welcoming him into her home? That she wanted him there?

As they stepped onto the hardwood floors of the front foyer, she watched him take in the sights. An open central staircase curved upward to the three bedrooms and office on the second floor. To the left, a bathroom, laundry, door to the garage, and the family room beyond. To the right, a living room with a southwestern-style area rug, cream-coloured couches, Navajo sand art, and a large metal Kokopelli silhouette on the wall that seemed to draw his eye—the theme taken from her time pursuing her doctoral degree at University of New

Mexico in Albuquerque. He stepped into the living room and approached the Kokopelli silhouette. Lightly, he ran his fingers over it, a little smile on his face.

When he moved away from the artwork, she followed him through the living room and into her library, with its floor-to-ceiling bookshelves, fireplace, and well-worn black leather couch.

"We seem to share a love of stories," he said as he browsed the titles.

She nodded, thinking back to his flat. "Yes, I noticed you have your own library."

"The one in my London flat isn't as extensive as the one I have on Asgard, but yes, I enjoy books. Whether stories are written in a book, visualized in movies, spoken on the radio, or told sitting around a campfire, I love a good tale." He chuckled and flashed her a grin. "Wouldn't be the God of Stories if I didn't."

"True."

After entering her large open-concept kitchen and family room, again, he was drawn to the West Coast First Nations artwork on her walls. There was the painted drum, with Coyote prominently featured in the centre, several paintings and line sketches of salmon, a facemask carving of Raven, and another yellow cedar carving of Raven bringing the moon to the people. Lightly touching each one as he circled the room, he turned from the last one to stare at her with a stunned look of wonder.

"These are all... these are all me... your home is decorated with art of me."

She considered his earlier smile. "The Kokopelli as well?"

"Yes."

Wow. Her heart thudded. Thor had mentioned Raven and Coyote were Loki, but Kokopelli too? That was... a lot to take in, and it made it damn hard to deny the connection between them. She walked over to him and cupped his cheek, gazing up into his green eyes as his arms wrapped around her.

She bit her lip, then told him, "My mom told me the stories from a young age. These particular gods were always my favourites. Clearly, part of me recognized you, has sensed a connection with you, from as early as I can remember."

"Soulmates," Loki breathed, and his lips found hers.

The kiss started tender, with featherlight touches. It deepened quickly as tongues met, stroked, and caressed. His hands held her tight against his long, leanly muscled length. Gods, she'd missed the feel of his body, so strong against hers.

Wanting more, she slid her hands into his hair, tugging and scraping her fingernails up his nape. The tremor of his body against hers filled her with elation. She wanted, no—she needed, to feel it again. She dragged her fingernails over the back of his neck and scalp repeatedly, heady with his shuddered, groaned reaction.

With a growl against her lips, he lifted both her legs to wrap around his waist. Her hold tightened and she ground his rigid length against her core, teasing them both. Gods, it had been so long. She needed him inside her desperately. She ached.

Whether Loki read her thoughts or was equally desperate, a flash of black later and he surged inside. Shannon didn't care where their clothes had gone. She was too busy keening at the fullness inside her again, stretching her, filling her to that point of pleasurable pain. Fuck, it was so blindingly perfect.

Not yet moving, except for that initial thrust, he broke their kiss to growl, "Are you okay?" He peered into her eyes.

"*Yes!* Gods, yes," She tightened around him and tried to move, to buck. She wanted that delicious friction, to feel him driving within her. But even with her newfound strength, he was far stronger than her, easily holding her still while supporting her weight around his hips. Frustrated, she whimpered, thwarted in her efforts.

Loki smiled that little wicked half-smile of his that had her core contracting, tightening on his thick length.

Shannon ran the fingertips of one hand down the back of his head, yanking his hair when she reached the nape. To hell with teasing. She wanted him to *move*.

Green eyes darkened, and he began lifting and slamming her hips down on him.

"Yes, like that. Oh gods, just like that," she whimpered at the delicious spikes of pleasure.

The friction was perfect. So perfect that it had her writhing in minutes. At the mercy of his savage strokes building a fiery intensity inside her, she couldn't hold his gaze as she panted and spine arched.

His teeth tugged on a pebbled nipple. Lightning flared.

"Gods, Loki! So fucking good!" Another long cry escaped.

The exquisite dual assault had her rapidly cresting. Heat expanded out from her core, firing nerve endings to burst outward. As she screamed, Loki groaned his release and staggered.

The next minute found them collapsing upstairs onto Shannon's bed. Together, they cuddled, facing each other while they caught their breath.

"That was intense."

"It took the edge off at least," Loki agreed, lips twitching in amusement.

Their smiles widened, and before she knew it, they were laughing.

Shannon was still chuckling when Loki flipped her onto her back, rolling on top. His eyes darkened as he conjured a length of black silk. Taking her left wrist, he tied it so the silk was snug, but not cutting into her.

"What are you doing, Loki?"

He conjured another length, tying it around her right wrist, then raised a black eyebrow. "I should think it would be obvious." He took both lengths and tied them to her bedposts. With a shift downward, Loki conjured another two lengths of silk that he tied around her ankles and to the bottom bed posts.

"I understand *what* you are doing. What I'm wondering is *why* you are tying me up?"

He gazed down at her, thin lips pressed together in satisfaction.

Experimentally, Shannon tugged on the silk with one arm. She couldn't reach her body, but if she wanted to, she could escape the ties.

"It's time to discuss your penchant for running off, abandoning me with no word, and leaving me to worry about you." His voice held a dark threat.

A thrill shot through her abdomen. "Ohhh... bring out the whips and chains. I'm ready for my torture," she sassed and wiggled her hips.

"Are you now?" His eyes glinted as a wicked smile grew "Perhaps next time."

Her sex clenched. Maybe she was in more trouble than she thought.

Taking her right foot in his hands, he massaged his thumbs into her arch. Holy hell, it was heavenly. At first, it was simply relaxing, easing tension she hadn't known was there. Loki watched her, eyes not leaving hers as he gauged her reactions. But as he moved his thumbs around, testing and seeking her response, it shifted to erotic. Arousal built, flaring up her body and tightening her nipples.

Shannon had had no idea feet were an erogenous zone.

Restlessness plagued her, her skin tingling, as his talented lips joined his too-clever fingers in their assault with kisses to each toe. But he didn't stop there. Phantom fingers lightly stroked over her wrists. Ripples of sensation flowed down her arms and up her leg at the same time. She squirmed on the bed as heat built in slow waves.

Turning her leg in his hands, he ran his tongue up and over the back of her knee. She jerked in his hands, and he smiled as he blew air over the moist skin. Stronger waves of arousal surged up her body, centring in her core.

The phantom strokes on her wrists shifted to her inner elbow, and she turned her arms, trying to increase the sensation. Loki smiled, his eyes glinting as he lowered his wicked mouth to her thigh, spreading her legs as he kissed his way up her inner thigh. She squirmed. Gods, he was driving her wild.

Higher. Just a little higher.

He bit down, and she gasped, body bowing in reaction.

Loki chuckled, a satisfied evil sound that felt like a caress, then moved to her other leg, starting at her foot before moving to her knee and again kissing his way up her inner thigh. Holy fuck. She was going to lose her damned mind at this rate. How was he so patient?

The phantom caresses advanced up the tender skin of her inner arms, down the side of her torso, and to the sides of her breasts, creating half-circle strokes on the sides and undersides, but never her aching nipples. Shannon panted, chest heaving at the arousing touches that never quite went where she most needed them.

"Loki, please." Why did that come out as a whine? She didn't whine. Ugh!

"Please what, darling?" he asked with a little smirk.

"Touch me." There. A demand. Not a whine.

"I am touching you." Loki kissed her stomach, his actual hands replacing the phantom caresses along the sides of her breasts, holding them, sweeping his thumbs near, but not touching her nipples.

Fuck. She squirmed, her skin prickling and breath rasping.

"*Please* make me come." Shit, did she beg? Her heartbeat thumped a heavy rhythm in her core. Gods, she did, but she couldn't take it. She'd needed him, missed him for so long.

He surged up her body, hand pinning her throat as his rigid cock slid thick against her wet heat, teasing, tantalizing, but not entering her. Damn it.

Chapter 26

MINE

Loki snarled, holding back through sheer relentless will. Yggdrasil's branches and leaves, Shannon smelled amazing. Lush, wet, willing woman. His woman. His goddess. His soulmate. The one person he'd not dared hope for and would never give up. A shiver rippled down his spine, his cock a blacksteel rod aching to sink into the soft clench of her sex.

But she'd run from him. His fault for fumbling how he'd told her, sure, but still, she'd fucking *run*. She'd been in *danger*. She'd risked everything, and the primal core of him roared in fury. He was Asgard's deadliest warrior, blooded and proven on battlefields so lethal, Sidhe populations hadn't yet recovered from the last war. Shannon *couldn't* die like Sigyn, couldn't risk herself. She was *his*, damn it. And he would fucking make sure she remembered it.

"No, you aren't even close to where I want you yet." He moved his hips, deliberately hitting the sensitive bundle at the apex of her thighs and sliding over it with a wet slick that tormented them both.

Shannon moaned, writhing, clutching at the sheets. Her heartbeat fluttered under his fingertips as he held her throat and pinned her to the bed. With his other hand fisted in her hair, he stared into the widely dilated pupils of her hazel eyes. This gorgeous goddess was his, and if the soulmate bond wasn't enough, he'd bind her to him with pleasure, drenching her in it until she couldn't breathe without craving him. The way he felt for her every bloody second of every bloody day.

But first.

"I'm going to bring you to the edge, over and over," he growled, not letting her escape his gaze. He teased, grinding against her as she squirmed. She was close, her breath catching and back arching.

Gritting his teeth, Loki stilled, catching her hips to immobilize her movements.

"Damn it!"

"You will *not* come until I allow it," Loki promised. Dark, erotic menace filled his eyes and roughened his tone, but better his beautiful soulmate see the real him, understand the ruthless male in her bed, playing her luscious body like the incredible instrument it was.

Tilting her face, he seized her mouth in a passionate, proprietary kiss. A claiming. No, he wasn't being subtle. She was his, and he'd imprint his possession on every fibre of her being, as she'd done on his.

Her taste taunted his control. His hips rocked, lightning flaring up his spine as her wet heat kissed his cock. By the Nine, he ached to thrust inside. He caught one nipple in a hard pinch. Body tightening into a bow, she screamed into their kiss, and he stilled as his fingers dug into the curve of her hip.

Shannon tore her mouth away, panting and swearing.

Amusement pierced the fierce arousal within him. Bor's beard, she was gorgeous with her eyes flashing fire at him, cheeks rosy. "That's quite the mouth you have on you, darling," he purred, then laughed when she snarled.

Mouth descending, he kissed the fury from her, again bringing her to the trembling edge and testing his control. Having her in his arms, even spitting curses at him and trying to hide her reactions so he'd misjudge how close she was—as if he couldn't read her body, feel her arousal in the bond—soothed the savage need to hold her, keep her, protect her from harm. Over and over, he brought her to the brink, then halted, waiting for her thwarted orgasm to subside.

"Fuck me!"

"Not yet," Loki purred, immobilizing her at hip and throat. He petted her racing heartbeat, the trapped fire burning through her veins. By all the realms, he fucking loved being cradled by her thighs, pressed against her soaked, flushed folds, gazing into her passion-glazed eyes. Eyes that turned watery as he once again started grinding his aching length against her sensitized clit. As much as it pricked his conscience, another, fiercer side of him roared at his success, at her surrender.

Finally.

"Are you going to run from me again?"

"No," she whimpered, a tear sliding free to fall into her hair.

"What was that? I don't think I heard you."

"*No!* I won't run!"

Relief almost turned him light-headed, almost had him slipping inside her to give them both what they wanted, but fuck, he needed her to admit it. He had to resist just a little longer. "Are you going to talk to me when we disagree so we can work it out?" he demanded in a harder tone as he pinched her nipple.

"Yes! *I promise!*" She panted, so close to the edge her entire body trembled.

Voice turning soft, he asked, "What do you promise?"

"Gods! I promise to talk things out with you. *Please,* Loki!" More tears escaped her welling eyes.

Norns, hold her to her word. He shifted slightly, teasing at her entrance with tiny thrusts. Fuuuck, she felt amazing, sucking him in and gripping so tight. As if her body never wanted to let him go. Gritting his teeth, he growled to get the words out. "Who do you belong to?"

"*You*, Loki."

Her body shook, small contractions squeezing the head of his cock, and he couldn't wait any longer. Ripping the silk ties, he scooped her legs over his shoulders and slammed deep. She cried out, eyes rolling as waves of her orgasm clenched around him. Fingers digging into the bed, he growled and fought the need to follow her into bliss. No, not yet. But bloody everlasting fuck, she was spectacular.

Awareness gradually returned to her gaze.

"Are you back with me, darling?" he purred as her rippling aftershocks milked him, tempting his control.

"Yes," she gasped.

He started to move, slowly thrusting into the Valhalla of her tight body. The friction was incredible, gripping him in perfect wet heat.

Shannon yanked her wrists, lifting a hand to his neck and tangling fingers into his hair. "If I understand this soulmate thing, I'm yours, Loki, but you are also *mine*," she demanded, holding his eyes as she joined their fingers with her other hand. "And I don't fucking share."

Joy bubbled like champagne in his chest. "Of course I'm yours. Only yours." His mouth descended to capture hers, not to plunder, but to coax and pleasure. Tilting his hips to glide over that ridged flesh inside her, he revelled in bringing her to orgasm twice more before he couldn't hold back the building pressure within him. With increasing speed, he chased the rising tide. Stiffening, he demanded, "Again, come for me once more!"

Trembling, sex clenching as she peaked, Shannon screamed.

Sparks burst behind his eyes as black seidhr swirled around them. His. She was his. His roar echoed, filling the room as the hot flood of his release claimed his soulmate in the wildest, most primal of acts.

Chapter 27

WEIGHTY CHOICES

When Shannon woke, her body hummed with energy. Wow. That was the best sleep she'd had in months. Finally, the godsdamned lingering exhaustion was gone. Reaching over for Loki, it took her a minute to realize he wasn't there. She tossed back the covers to sit at the edge of the bed.

<Loki?>

A second later, he appeared beside her.

"I was getting concerned. You slept for fourteen hours!" He handed her a cup of tea and a banana chocolate chip muffin. "I tried to wake you earlier." He smirked, then kissed her. "You're grumpy when you don't get your sleep."

Shannon took a sip. It was her favourite, and he'd even added lemon. Such thoughtfulness. Warmth heated her chest as much as the tea did.

"Yeah, well"—she shrugged—"it was a long ass day between Thor discovering me in Egypt, going to Asgard and meeting your mom, then finding you at my brother's place." Her stomach twisted. Gods, *so* many things happened yesterday. They hadn't discussed the whole soulmate thing. She still didn't know what it meant. Were they truly bound for eternity? He wanted her now... but what about when he got bored or she grew large with their baby? Didn't she get any say in this?

A lump formed in her throat, and she swallowed.

And what about the royalty situation? Was that only if they stayed together? How would it impact the baby? The baby. Gods. Was having a child with him even a good idea? She knew so little about him beyond his media-driven public persona. What kind of father would he make? Did he want to have kids? Was he capable of being responsible? Reliable? A child would need that.

The life he'd seemed to lead here on Earth… well, it wasn't exactly child-friendly with constant parties and different women, never mind the ever-present drugs and alcohol. Not that he seemed to fall into the substance-abuse trap typical of many rock stars, thank heavens.

Still, to make such a life-altering decision on three days' acquaintance seemed… well, more than risky. How many women had he been with since August? How could she trust a relationship with a man, a god, who changed women as often as he did boxers? Shit. She hadn't even asked him to wear protection. Not that he could get her *more* pregnant, but had he been telling the truth when he'd said he couldn't catch or pass on a sexually transmitted disease?

Fuck.

He was a player and a much better liar than she'd ever be. And like a lonely, pathetic fool, she'd fallen right back into bed with him. For fuck's sake, could she be more gullible? She wrapped an arm around her belly, a flutter there cutting off her thoughts. She sucked in a breath. Oh gods. Was that… was that the baby? Her heart raced. No—no, she wasn't ready to tell him. Not yet. Not while she had no idea how he'd react or if she wanted him in her life, in her child's life. This baby would be protected and loved, no matter what.

"You were in Egypt?" Loki asked, frowning slightly as he searched her expression.

Was he picking up her conflicting emotions? With determination, she forced herself to stop her mental spiral and sipped her tea before answering him. "Yes. Isis found me on a Greek island. She taught me how to use my powers, how to defend myself."

Loki sprang to his feet, pacing and thrusting his hands through his hair. "Bor's balls, Shannon! Isis hates me! She could have killed you!"

Shannon clenched her teeth and took a measured breath. He wasn't wrong. She'd seen the warning signs, but still, she'd stayed with the mercurial goddess. It wasn't like she knew so many immortals that she could take her pick of safe mentors. And damn him, but Isis had been fine with Shannon. It was Loki she hated. "She was fantastic to me until Thor showed up and blabbed that I was your soulmate."

He scrubbed his hands over his face. "She has reason to hate me," he muttered.

"Yeah, Thor said something about Osiris. You killed her husband?" She took a sip of tea, peering at him through her lashes. Why did Loki kill him? If they'd been enemies, perhaps it was understandable. Would he tell her the truth? Her shoulders tensed. If he came up with a lie that made him look good, it would give her another glimpse into his character... and suggest he wasn't a person she could trust. Who was the real Loki, the rockstar bad boy or the considerate lover and god?

Loki put his hands behind his neck, staring down and kicking a foot against the floor. "I did. It was stupid. The foolish arrogant jealousy of a boy barely in his teens." Meeting her eyes, he continued, "Osiris was also known as Baldur. He was our half-brother from Odin's first marriage. My oldest brother. I looked up to him, but in my anger after discovering I was adopted, I was stupidly jealous of the attention he got. I didn't kill him myself, but my childish prank was his downfall. His death was my fault." He winced and mumbled something under his breath, too low for her to catch even with her new, sharper senses.

Shannon sipped her tea, giving herself time to absorb what he'd told her and restrain her inappropriate smile. He hadn't held back, and it sure sounded like the truth, as raw, painful, and ugly as it was. Part of her understood what he must have felt at his familial revelation. Even with her dad dead, she was angry with him and her mom for hiding that she was adopted. Angry and hurt. And she wasn't a teen hormone bomb with the emotional control of a gnat. An immortal teen? With powers?

Her fingers tightened on her cup. How was she going to handle raising this child? A child with abilities?

She met Loki's hesitant gaze, a piercing ache in her chest. So many layers to the man, the god in front of her. Who was he, really? Could a relationship between them work?

"Well, I guess I won't be visiting Isis again." Shannon tried to smile, a need to comfort him welling from within her, yet she couldn't completely eradicate the disappointment in her voice. Isis had been mostly good to her—Shannon's first friend in this new world of gods and immortals—until Shannon's soulmate connection was revealed.

If she was going to build a life as a goddess, going to raise an immortal child, she needed friends she could talk to, friends who would understand the challenges. And Lynda... well, Lynda wasn't going to fill that need. While Shannon had stayed in contact with her, their relationship had suffered. Lynda knew Shannon well enough to know she wasn't telling her everything. Constantly lying was wearing away the threads connecting them. Shannon found herself avoiding calling. It was easier to hide behind emails and texts. To not hear the accusation in Lynda's tone. How was she ever going to repair their friendship?

Alarm widened Loki's green eyes, and he shook his head. "No, please don't. Isis will *never* forgive me and would love to see me suffer." He returned to sit beside Shannon, taking her hand with worry lining his face.

"I'll stay away from her," she reassured him. "Now your mom, on the other hand, offered to help me kick your butt... and then she invited me to pop by for dinner whenever was convenient."

His eyebrows drew together, and she laughed, the weight on her chest lifting slightly. It was such fun to tease him. Even when he scowled, she sensed the sparkling bubbles of delight from their connection.

"I'm not sure about you and my mother ganging up on me."

"I'm sure, trickster, that you'll survive it," she teased, then leaned around him to glance at her nightstand. According to the clock, it was after eight already. "Since we are going to spend Christmas with my family, we need to go shopping for presents."

Loki tugged Shannon against him, relishing the feel of her in his arms. He couldn't believe he'd admitted his greatest failure and she hadn't rejected him. How was she so understanding? So forgiving? Norns, he was a lucky bastard. "Where do you want to go shopping?"

She sighed and laid her head on his shoulder. "Everything will be a zoo today, with it being Christmas Eve. We need to take my car so we can carry the presents and don't have to explain how we got there. My family *will* notice if we keep arriving and departing without a vehicle for what is normally a two-hour drive."

He brushed a strand of red-gold hair from her face. "What does your family like?" He could conjure gifts for her, then they could skip the shopping and spend more time in bed.

"Heather likes pretty things—jewellery, scarves, that sort of thing. Sarah collects cookbooks, so that's always a good option for her. Liam likes anything relating to history, particularly books. My mom loves her Chinese teas. I usually pick that up because she rarely gets into Vancouver."

Hmm... without knowing the specifics, he wouldn't be able to conjure the tea, especially if she liked a particular brand. But the other things, those were doable. "Any particular era of history?"

"No, Liam's a fan of all of it. He would have loved to have seen what I explored in the Mediterranean." Excitement filled her tone and her eyes sparkled as she told him about exploring the ancient ruins and the fun she'd had playing with the dolphins.

What would she say if he shapeshifted into one to play with her? "I'm so very proud of how fast you've mastered your abilities. It's incredible." He ran his hand down the silken weight of her hair.

"Thank you. There was certainly some trial and error involved." She wrinkled her nose.

Damn, she was adorable. He wanted to hear more of her stories. With a chuckle, he touched a finger to her nose. "Yeah, I'm sure."

She stuck her tongue out at him, and he laughed again, light bursting in his chest. She was *playing* with him.

"Okay, so if we stop at a bookstore first to pick out Liam's present, we should be able to get the rest with a quick swing through Chinatown."

Loki froze, his hand paused mid-stroke. Chinatown. Did they dare risk it? The last time he'd run into the brothers was... well, a few hundred years ago here at least. But Lü and the other Eight Immortals had signed the treaty on behalf of the Shen. Surely the dragon gods would abide by it. "That's probably okay," he said slowly as his hand continued its movement down Shannon's hair. Besides, he'd be there to protect her and would whisk her away at the first sign of those arrogant assholes.

Yeah, it would be fine.

"What's the concern?"

His head rocked side to side as he pursed his lips. For her protection, Shannon needed to learn about the different races of immortals, the treaties, and the history of conflict, but how much should he tell her now? He didn't want to scare her away by dropping it all on her at once like he had when she transitioned. "The Shen aren't on great terms with Asgard. We have a treaty, but mostly, we try to avoid each other."

"Thor told me about the Shen. They are the Eastern gods or immortals?"

He smiled and exhaled a thankful breath. He owed his brother for breaking that ice, and hell, for finding her. "Yes, the Shen are from the realm Kunlun, but they've interacted here on Midgard predominantly with the mortals of the Far East. Occasionally, they are here in the Americas as well. I had a few run-ins with them as Tezcatlipoca, the jaguar god, in what is now Mexico, or as Raven here off the coast."

"Again, with the cats."

Her playful smile had his widening. Yes, he loved that she teased him. "You met a couple of Shen when we went to the UK premiere. It's in all our interests to not rock the boat. Thor and I are on speaking terms with them. I wouldn't trust them, but we're friendly enough with those few to keep up appearances at the movie releases and events."

"Wait a minute. I just thought of something. Were you other panther gods, too? Like that one in Egypt?"

Loki chuckled. "Yes, my clever girl." It was fascinating how humans took his actions thousands of years ago, turned them into mythology, and then created new stories from them in ways he never would have predicted.

Shannon laughed, then stopped and blinked. "Uh… isn't Bastet a female goddess?"

Loki held back his wince. It wasn't something he was hiding, but Shannon had already dealt with so much in such a short time. He'd not planned on shoving it in her face that not only was he a shapeshifter, but he was also genderfluid—a natural consequence of his half-Jotun heritage from a parent he'd never met. Would she mind? Surely the Norns wouldn't have paired them if Shannon wasn't compatible with him on such a basic level.

Still, his smile was cautious when he answered, "Yes."

"Damn. You're already so outrageously sexy as a man. I think I'd be incredibly self-conscious of how ordinary I am if I had to measure up to you as a woman."

How could she possibly doubt herself? She was everything. Tension uncoiled from his gut, and he framed her face in his hands. "Darling, you are extraordinary. If you were any sexier, I'd never let you out of the house."

"Will you still want me when you are in a female form?" Her arm wrapped around her middle as if she was protecting herself.

Struck momentarily speechless, Loki stared for a second, then rubbed at his breastbone. She really worried? But... but how? How could she think he wouldn't want her? She was his soulmate, his other half, a fire in his blood. He'd want her until the end of days.

Voice hoarse with emotion, he said, "I am still me, whether I'm in another shape or presenting as another gender. And Shannon, I will never, *ever* stop wanting and desiring you. It will not happen." He kissed her until she was breathless, then pulled back and smiled wickedly as he held her passion-fogged gaze. "I also guarantee I will have you coming and screaming my name for all eternity."

A blush coloured her cheeks and she searched his expression for a minute before finally nodding. "Let's get ready so we can get this shopping done and head to my brother's place."

Loki stood and led her into the ensuite bathroom with its blue marble counters, matching Jacuzzi tub, and large walk-in shower with blue and white tiles. Shannon turned on the hot water and stepped in, closing her eyes. Steam billowed as water caress her curves, but as much as he enjoyed the visual feast, Yggdrasil's roots, he wanted to touch her more. To show her with actions how he felt about her. She needed to never doubt how much he loved and desired her.

Not that he'd tell her he loved her. Not yet. She was so skittish. No way did he want to send her running again.

After stepping behind her, he poured body wash into his palms from the white and yellow bottle on the ledge. "Let me wash you," Loki whispered in her ear as his soapy hands glided over her. But restraint wasn't in him this morning. Not after the long hours of patience last night. He needed her, needed the connection, to feel her surrounding him. Stroking and caressing every gorgeous inch of soft skin, he relished the sounds of her pleasure, and while she still shuddered, he lifted her leg to thrust inside.

Fuck. She was perfect, and he didn't hold back. Water flowed over their heated bodies as they found their release, and if his knees were a bit weak, well, he'd accept a weakness if it meant he had the joy of his soulmate.

Contentment suffusing every fibre of his being, he lathered her silken hair, playing with the length as he worked first shampoo, then conditioner into the glorious mass. Shannon moaned at his touch. Yeah, he loved pampering her and playing with her in the water.

But he didn't dare challenge his control when her fingers strayed to his chest to wash him. Damn it. If only they hadn't agreed to go to her brother's. "Not this time, darling, or we'll never get out of here." They'd have time later. He'd fucking make time if he had to. He grit his teeth, clinging to his restraint as he rinsed the soap off his body, then firmly shut off the water.

He eyed the thin white towels folded on the rack and conjured his own. There was no need to suffer inferior materials just because he was on Midgard.

"You don't like my towels?" Shannon asked with a smile.

"Mine are better." Loki took his time drying her hair. By the Nine, he could spend hours delighting in the feel of it on his skin, but once it was mostly dry, he carefully rubbed the moisture from her skin. It was an excuse to explore, to caress, to kiss every inch. Fuck, she was tempting.

Shannon gave a throaty moan, and heat flashed to his groin. "It's true. They are far more effective than mine." Eyes half-lidded, she seemed to be enjoying his ministrations as much as he relished giving them.

"All done." He stood, tossing the towel onto the rack. "Now, go put some clothes on that sexy body before I drag you back to bed," he threatened, only partly teasing. She was seduction personified. Curved in all the right places, glowing with an internal light. He could hardly bear to release her. Although, he needed to feed her more. She'd appeared so tired yesterday, so drawn.

Shannon laughed, a joyous sound that filled the bathroom with light and warmth. With a wink—sassy woman—she walked into her bedroom and removed a matching blue bra and panty set from her drawers. Loki followed, conjuring black jeans to restrain his constant erection around her, then added a black button-down shirt, socks, and boots. Maybe dressed, he'd be able to resist her allure long enough to take her shopping.

Fuck. Maybe not.

He leaned in the bathroom doorway and admired that biteable ass and those plum-coloured nipples as she put the lingerie on. Mouth watering, he bit back a protest when she added dark-blue jeans and a royal-blue cowl-necked sweater from her closet.

"Do you have everything you need so we can leave from shopping to head to my brother's?"

Loki conjured Shannon's backpack from the energy he'd stashed it as when he couldn't stand looking at it in his flat in London, a constant reminder of her absence, then conjured a second one for him. It wouldn't do for her family to wonder why he didn't have any luggage.

Shannon quirked an eyebrow. "Is that *mine*?"

He smiled. "Yes." Even with what she'd told him she'd discovered of her powers, he had so much more to show her. Bor's beard, he couldn't wait to get her to Asgard.

She replaced the clothes inside with warmer ones. He was tempted to browse her drawers, to explore the fabrics and fashions she preferred, but she finished before he had the chance to do more than open a couple.

"All set. Let's go."

Abandoning his snooping, he followed Shannon downstairs to the foyer where she added black-heeled boots and a long black leather jacket. Fuck, she looked sexy as sin in leather, and he imagined her in jewel-toned blue silk with thigh-high leather boots. Damn.

Distracted by his fantasy and the different outfits he'd love to dress her in from the styles of his home, he hardly noticed getting into her vehicle or the drive through city streets. Yet, part of him remained alert, aware of every potential danger.

After parking, Shannon led him to Smith Rare Books on Cambie. Just the scent of the books was comforting. He could have spent the rest of the day there, browsing the stories, but found the special edition 1942 *The Gods Are A-thirst* by Anatole France on the second aisle. Great name for a French Revolution epic.

"What about this for Liam?" he asked as he showed it to her. She leafed through the yellowed pages and nodded. The clerk gift-wrapped the book, and despite Loki's concerns, they set off to walk the half kilometre to Chinatown.

At the Pacific Village Mall, Shannon found a colourful silk scarf for her sister and picked up a gift bag and tissue paper in another shop. Leaving the mall behind, Shannon stopped at a tiny little store with various odds and ends. Buried on a back shelf, she found an old Hong Kong-style cookbook. As the elderly shopkeeper wrapped it in tissue with ribbon, the hair on Loki's nape rose. He peered at the other shoppers, but none seemed to be paying any attention to them. What was he sensing?

After they exited the store, the prickling on his skin increased and he shifted Shannon away from the street side, moving her to his right as he glanced behind him at the crowded sidewalk. Was someone cloaked behind them?

<*What's wrong?*> Shannon glanced around, frowning.

Did she not feel the surveillance? He checked the nearby roofs. Nothing was visible, but with the street so crowded, he couldn't pinpoint where the danger was coming from. <*We may have someone following us. Make sure you keep your hand on my arm in case we need to teleport.*> He passed her the bags to keep his hands free, just in case.

Shannon peered at their reflection as they passed shop windows. <*A fan, looking for a photo or autograph?*>

<*No, this feels different.*> Nothing mortal would alert his senses like this. His skin crawled and seidhr pressed at his control, trying to erupt around him. He fought his instincts to not call his armour. Fuck, this was bad. He had to get her out of there. Off this fucking street.

It was only half a block until they reached the Tea Leaf Emporium, with his tension rising every step. Opening the door for her and ushering her inside, Loki glanced up and down the crowded street before following her. Damn it. He hadn't spotted anyone who looked like they were paying particular attention, but he trusted his battle-honed instincts. They'd never let him down.

Shannon shopped and he paced alongside her, eyes scanning their surroundings. Bor's balls. If there weren't so many people around, he'd teleport her right out of the store.

"Are you done? You got everything you needed?" he asked as she paid. If he could find an empty alley corner, he'd cloak them from sight and teleport. To hell with walking back. He wanted her away from whomever or whatever seemed to be stalking them.

"Yes," she murmured, eyes wide as she searched nearby faces.

Fuck. He was scaring her. With a wince, he opened the store's door, keeping her behind him as he stepped out. But before he could leave the shelter of the entrance and slip them into the busy streams of pedestrian traffic, three massive shapes shoved their way forward.

Loki's heart clenched, then dropped into his gut. Of all the fucking bastards to find them, why the bloody Helheim did it have to be the pompous asshole Quetzalcoatl and his brothers? Seidhr swirled around Loki's fingers, yet Asgardian energies had little effect against their dragon scale, whether the fuckers were in their humanoid or dragon form. Not without pouring everything he had into it and not against three of them, damn it. His hands flexed as he drew the seidhr back inside. He couldn't unleash chaos in these close quarters. It was too effective at destroying everything, and there was no way he'd risk Shannon with his unruly, unpredictable Jotun energies. He'd never forgive himself if he hurt her.

Fuck. Fuck. *Fuck.*

And of course, he didn't have Laevateinn with him, his only weapon that could pierce their hides with ease. What the fuck had he been thinking, bringing her here without it? Could he call his sword from his rooms in Asgard in time?

Or perhaps... could he talk their way out of this?

"Tezcatlipoca, you ugly fucking bastard. What brings you to my part of town?" asked the deep rumbling voice Loki had hoped to never hear again.

Chapter 28

HERE BE DRAGONS

At the stranger's voice, Shannon pressed herself to Loki's back, feeling the tension in his muscles. Was this one of the Shen, one of the ones he'd been concerned about? Surely with the treaty, they'd be fine?

"Quetzalcoatl, it's been a long time," Loki said carefully.

"Please, it's Ao Guang now. We must keep up with the times, yes? And you haven't yet answered my question," the deep rumbling voice demanded.

Loki inclined his head. "Just shopping for Christmas presents, actually."

"Really? *You?* Celebrating a holiday dedicated to another god? Now why does that sound unlikely? I see no purchases," the voice sneered.

Shannon rolled her eyes. Had this arrogant blowhard lived under a rock the last fifteen years? Raven's Chaos had put out a fucking top-of-the-charts Christmas song for that action-packed holiday movie six, maybe seven, years ago. It was no wonder no one suspected Loki's true identity. His mortal cover of Tod Corvus was brilliant.

She pushed the bags into Loki's hand, and he brought them out in front of him. "It's as I said, just shopping. I'm keeping up appearances with local traditions," Loki said.

"Well I learned the lesson to not believe your lying tongue, trickster! The mortals revered me as a *hero* until you showed up with your insidious mischief! Who is there behind you?" the voice snarled.

<*Slowly,*> Loki warned, fingers tightening on hers. <*Stay behind me as much as possible. Do not let go of me. Don't believe what I'm about to say, either.*>

<*I trust you.*> At least to protect her—them. Her free hand lowered to her belly then fisted. Despite the bad-Bond-villain caricature vibe this Ao Guang asshole was giving off, the anxiety coming through her connection with Loki had already warned her this was a dangerous situation, even without his words. She'd not second-guess him.

"My latest conquest. A bit of fun." Loki drew her around to his side.

Shannon got her first look at the speaker. A massive Asian-appearing man, he was taller and broader across than Heimdall—a feat she hadn't believed was possible. His dark-blue eyes, pure blue with a vertical pupil, glared, and a sneer twisted his face. Two men flanked him, almost as large as he was. They shared features in their dark short-cropped hair, dark umber skin tone, the roundness of their cheeks, the shapes of their noses, and their thin lips. All three with those unusual eyes, although red for the man on the right and black for the man on the left. Definitely not human. Pedestrians flowed around them, almost like they didn't see the huge men towering over them. Not a single person gawked at their size... except for her.

<*Shen?*> she asked, recovering from her surprise.

<*Yes, three brothers. Dragons. Resistant to my magic. Affinities for the natural elements, like you, but particularly fire and water.*>

Lip curled, Ao Guang said, "Huh. No accounting for taste if she's with you." His eyes narrowed. "I still owe you for getting me drunk and causing an orgy with my priests and priestesses. You got me banished! While I was gone, they destroyed my temples, replacing them with edifices to *you*!"

Shannon would have laughed but a surge of alarm came through the bond, just as Loki said, <*Fuck. I'm going to telepo—*>

Faster than she could blink, Ao Guang lunged for Loki, grabbing his shoulder. His brother seized Shannon's upper arm, thick fingers biting into her like rigid bands of iron. She bit her lip to muffle the yelp of pain. With a sharp tug, he yanked her forward, straining Loki's grip on her wrist.

Loki snarled but released her, rather than turning her arm into a tug-of-war between them.

The brothers forced Loki and Shannon down the street, rough fingers digging into the tender flesh of her inner arm. She tried to make eye contact with the pedestrians in front of her, but their gazes skated off her like she wasn't there. Every person who got within a metre dodged out of the way as if Shannon and her captor were normal obstructions in the sidewalk, like a mailbox or light post.

Why didn't Loki say anything? Why didn't he fight?

She was going to have one hell of a bruise, but she focused on keeping her feet as she tried to ignore the painful grip, her thudding pulse, and the frantic fluttering in her stomach. Was it the baby? She fisted her hands to keep from cradling her abdomen. The brothers pulled them through the gated entrance of the nearby gardens and into the inner courtyard. Out of sight of the public. A chill washed over her skin. Not that being in public had seemed to help her any.

Loki was shoved down onto a wrought iron bench. Ao Guang held him there, towering over him with a firm grasp on Loki's shoulders, until his brother switched places. The other brother, the one holding Shannon, dragged her in front of the bench as Ao Guang stood between them, sneering.

"Maybe she's just a bit of fun. Maybe she isn't. Either way, you are going to watch as my brothers and I fuck her in front of you." Ao Guang laughed in a sinister rumble. "Since I know how much you like to share."

Nausea churned, climbing her throat as Ao Guang continued to spew horrifyingly graphic details of his revenge that included eventually chomping off bits of her to eat while she still lived. No godsdamned way would she'd let these Shen assholes with the bad form to monologue touch her. Fuck, could they *be* any more of a villain stereotype?

Loki opened the bond wide, wider than it had ever been, letting her into his thoughts as he strategized. This wasn't his first run-in with these particular brothers. His conjured blades wouldn't pierce their thick hides, and he couldn't teleport with them holding him. They weren't susceptible to either the frost or fire he could summon. His telekinesis bounced off them.

And none of his worry was for himself.

No, it was entirely for her. Despite their dire situation and her fear-fuelled fury, warmth curled around her heart. No one had ever put her first before.

<*If you can get out, you need to leave me,*> Loki insisted, his voice a desperate drumbeat in her skull. <*Please, Shannon. I couldn't bear it if something happened to you. I can't risk releasing chaos so close to you, and I can't stop them any other way. Not the three of them together. Please!*>

Despite the inner turmoil their connection allowed her to hear, his face was impassive, not giving the Shen a visible reaction other than his glare.

<*Not going to happen, Loki. I'm not leaving you with these overgrown lizards,*> Shannon snapped. Loki's fear for her and her visceral disgust at their threat combined into a volatile inferno churning like a toxic stew within her. Swallowing, she fought to keep from showing it, from allowing it to trigger her abilities. Loki might be looking out for her, but she'd be damned to the depths of the darkest hell before she left him to these fucking bastards.

"You really don't care?" The dragon god ran his hand down her body, trying to get Loki to react. "These mortals are so fragile. I'm not sure she'll survive our cocks. We'll likely break her beyond repair."

Godsdamned disgusting fucker. The muscles in her jaw flexed as she gritted her teeth. She'd show him who was fragile.

"There are always more. They live such a short time, after all." Loki shrugged. <*I'm so sorry. Yggdrasil's roots, I'm so sorry, Shannon. Please! You've got to escape! I'll try to distract them so you can get away. I'll follow, I promise.*>

"But they taste so damn good afterward." The dragon god leaned down and licked her face, then grinned at his brothers.

A wave of revulsion shook her. Unable to swallow down her loathing, Shannon wrinkled her nose. "Get your fucking paws off me!" Clenching her teeth again, she tightened control of her abilities as they surged alongside her emotions. <*We are* both *getting away, Loki!*>

Ao Guang's eyebrows flew up. He looked at her like a bug that had decided to talk, and his brother tightened his grip on her arm. Lack of circulation was turning her limb numb.

"The little mouse speaks! What a filthy mouth it has! I'm sure I can find a better use for it," he threatened with a leer as he cupped his crotch.

Molten fire raged within her, even as the sick bubbling in her stomach had her fighting not to heave. She wanted to obliterate these fuckers. Her fists tightened to the point that her fingers tingled.

"Let go of her, brother. I'm going to bring her to heel and teach her a woman's place." Ao Guang gestured to the one holding her, who released her at the same time as the air became dense, pressing down. The asshole started unbuttoning his pants, and in a flash, she understood. He was trying to push her to her knees in front of him.

<*Get out! Now, Shannon! They can fly like you. Be fast! Go! Leave me!*> Loki demanded, shoving his will through the bond.

"Not... going... to... happen... assholes!" Temper condensed to a tight point then flared to a white-hot burst, and Shannon shoved the air back in a sudden explosive wave, lightning crackling from her body to strike them. The dragon gods staggered, the brother losing his grip on Loki.

Heart in her throat, Shannon dove at Loki.

He lunged for her.

Their hands met.

In an instant, he'd teleported them to her car, blocks away from the garden.

"We need to go. Now. Right now. It won't take them long to find us again," Loki urged as she unlocked the vehicle with shaking fingers.

Holy fuck. Her heart pounded, chest heaving. Air sawed in and out of her lungs. "That was more excitement than I was expecting!" Understatement of the century. Adrenaline surged through her nervous system, every sense sparking. Somehow, she'd hung onto the bags. She tossed them into the backseat, and they jumped into the car.

"You were brilliant. They weren't expecting it. They know it's not in my powers to manipulate air. It was really smart, Shannon." His tone was both admiring and relieved when she turned the key to start the engine, even though it had taken her three tries to get the key into the ignition.

"They pissed me off. I—I didn't plan it. Don't give me too much credit. I just reacted." Shannon laughed with a nervous, almost hysterical energy. Her hands trembled as she clung to the steering wheel and drove them away from Chinatown.

"Still, it worked. That's what counts." Loki put his hand over hers and squeezed reassuringly.

Rainbow lights swirled around the vehicle.

Her heart lurched and she almost missed stopping at the red traffic light. Oh gods... what now? Was her entire car going to get sucked to Asgard? What the fuck had her life turned into?

Loki opened the window and thrust out a hand in time for a long silver sword with glowing black runes on the metal to smack into his palm. He snorted, drawing it inside and flipping it into the backseat. "Sure, *now* the damn thing arrives."

Shannon gaped, glancing between him and the backseat while keeping an eye on the road as the light changed and she hit the gas. "What the actual fuck, Loki?" Where the hell had that come from? Had that been the Bifrost lights? Did Heimdall toss him a *sword*?

He pried her fingers of one hand off the steering wheel and lifted them to his mouth, kissing each one. "Laevateinn can travel between realms to get to me, the same as my brother's hammer, Mjolnir. It's keyed to my blood and one of the few weapons capable of chopping off a Shen dragon's head."

She grunted and pulled her hand back. Would have been nice to have had that earlier, but she certainly wasn't going to object to the weapon's presence now. She glanced down at her speedometer and slowed. Although fuck, she didn't want to get stopped by the cops with a huge sword on her backseat. Did one require a permit to carry around a sword?

It took over an hour to escape the downtown core's traffic and pass over the Port Mann bridge, but when they reached Langley, she finally deemed them far enough to pull over for a few minutes. They'd seen no sign of pursuit and she'd started to shake so bad, she was worried she'd crash the vehicle.

Loki came around to her side and opened the door to pull her trembling body into his arms. She had to peel her white-knuckled grip from the steering wheel before she could sink into his hold.

"We're okay. You were amazing. I'm sorry. I'm so sorry," he murmured while he held her tight, one hand stroking over her hair and down her back, soothing both of them. She closed her eyes, tucked her head into his neck, put her arms around his waist, and inhaled the woodsy orange-leather scent that was so uniquely him.

Despite the training Isis had given her, she hadn't been prepared. Not even close. They'd only escaped because the dragons didn't know about her abilities. That wouldn't happen a second time. The element of surprise was lost.

And fuck, the dragon gods had terrified her. She'd never had anything like that happen to her before. Not Trent's assault. Nothing. Even Isis's attack, as painful as the slashes had been, hadn't scared her down to her soul. Fear still churned in her belly and a chill ran down her spine. Luck would only last so long. She needed to do better, to learn to defend not just herself, but also her child. Oh gods. She was so not ready to defend a child! Another chill shivered over her skin, and she shuddered, taking comfort when Loki held her tighter.

"I'm so sorry, Shannon. That was my fault." His voice cracked. "I'm sorry I put you in that position. You were endangered because of me." Loki's regret poured through the bond.

His scent sank into her pores, settling her nerves. "I've been warned that the immortal world is dangerous. It was bound to happen. At least I was with you. It took both of us to get away." She nuzzled his neck, taking comfort in his tight hold and the strong beat of his heart.

How long they stood there, holding each other, she wasn't sure, but they both seemed to need the contact. When her heart slowed from its rapid, panicked rhythm, her limbs ceased trembling, and no more adrenaline surged through her system, Shannon drew back to gaze into Loki's eyes. "I need training to learn to better defend myself. Next time, my luck might run out."

He nodded. "Yes. Not that you didn't do awesome, because you did." He kissed her before continuing. "But I agree. After we spend Christmas with your family, we need to go to Asgard and get you offensive and defensive training with your abilities and weapons. I won't have you unable to defend yourself."

Loki's quick agreement and support had her exhaling the breath she hadn't realized she'd been holding. Maybe this thing between them *would* work out. "Sounds like a plan to me." She leaned in to touch her lips to his, and he cupped her cheeks, deepening their kiss before pulling back.

"Okay, back into the car. Let's do this." He opened her door, helping her into the seat and buckling her in.

She smiled, remembering how he'd done up her seatbelt during their flight the night they met.

Too close. That was too damned close. Loki had had her back for not even one fucking day and almost lost her again. His instincts screamed to take her to Asgard now, to not wait another minute. He needed her to be safe. Maybe behind guards, palace walls, and his own protections, he could finally relax.

Damn it.

The surging adrenaline in his veins had him fighting to force himself to sit in the car, to not escape this realm with her. He couldn't lose her the way he'd lost Sigyn. Not Shannon. Not after the Norns had blessed him—him of all unworthy gods—with a soulmate.

As they drove, Loki hid his clenched fists, tapping legs, and uneven breaths with an illusion of calm. He'd tightened down their connection, keeping his thoughts private and preventing the leak of emotion. He couldn't chance scaring her away again by being stupid. Bloody fucking hell. Stupid in a completely domineering, overprotective way.

Think of her, you damn git.

Still battling his instincts when they arrived at the farmhouse, he did his best to participate in the discussion with her brother and his wife over dinner. Fortunately, Liam wanted to discuss storytelling and engaged Loki in a lively debate on how writing styles had changed over history. Her brother didn't need to know that Loki had experienced it. Liam's passion for the topic and his willingness to argue with Loki was exactly what Loki needed to pull his mind away from his worries.

After midnight, Shannon led Loki upstairs to a nicely appointed bedroom with a nineteenth-century four-poster cherry wood queen-sized bed, night tables, and a dresser set. A handmade quilt adorned the bed. She pulled the chains on stained glass lamps that sat on the matching night tables, sending a glow through the room.

"I like your brother and his wife." Loki removed their clothes. "They're fun, interesting people."

"I'm glad you like them." She raised an eyebrow. "What have you done with our clothes? I kinda want to wear them again. Where *do* they go when you do that?"

Loki chuckled. "You'll find yours in your backpack. Mine get converted to energy, which I re-use when I want to conjure new clothes, or new versions of the same clothes next time."

"I wish conjuration was one of my abilities. It seems so useful." She sighed wistfully.

"Darling, I am more than happy to conjure whatever you would like, whenever you would like." He pulled Shannon into bed with a tug, tucking her curvy form against him.

If only he could always keep her in his arms. More than anything, he wanted to sink into her warmth and reassure himself that she was alive and safe. But given the way she'd been uncomfortable when he'd drawn her into his lap after dinner, she'd be anxious with her family on the other side of that thin wall. Her brother's and his wife's conversation was a low murmur coming through even now.

But if he reassured her he could keep any sound from travelling... He winced. He wasn't entirely sure he'd be able to stay in control. Especially after almost losing her today. Embarrassing her would *not* be a great way to convince her to stay with him.

And he needed to convince her.

She had no way of knowing the meaning of a soulmate connection. How could she, after only months as a new goddess? Mortals had no equivalent. As deep as love could get on its own, it couldn't compare to the connection Shannon and Loki shared—their emotions, thoughts, and very beings entwined on a multi-dimensional level.

At least he got to hold her.

He bit back his sigh as she shifted, then shifted again. "Go to sleep before I change my mind about ravishing you with your brother in the next room. I only have so much willpower where you are concerned," he groaned, trying to still her movements with his arm. "For the love of my sanity, stop wiggling that sexy little ass of yours."

Shannon snorted out a laugh but settled down. It didn't surprise him when she drifted off to sleep quickly.

Yet that blissful oblivion eluded him. With the house quieting around him, his mind was anything but. Over and over, he saw Ao Guang and his brothers grab her and recalled the terror of her slipping from his grasp. His thoughts tortured him with what could have happened—what had almost happened—if his goddess hadn't been so clever and surprised them. Too easily did he remember Sigyn's broken body and the devastating scatter of smaller body fragments beside her, all that remained after the ravages of the dark elves and their sick tortures. Four hundred years by the Asgardian calendar might be two thousand here, but time hadn't lessened the impact of those horrific memories. The loss of his wife... and his child.

Despite his affinity with chaos, Loki found himself less tolerant of the idea of unpredictable events compromising Shannon's safety. She *had* to be protected. He needed to get her to Asgard and convince her to not leave. Whatever it took.

Chapter 29

CHARMED

Shannon woke hot, wet, and restless with a muscled male body wrapped around her. No wonder her dreams had been one long erotic fantasy—Loki's thigh pressed between her legs, his hand cupped her breast, and his rigid cock nestled against her ass. If the walls in her brother's home hadn't been so paper-thin with no damned insulation between, she would have done something about the heat her amorous cuddly god had stoked within her. Damn it. Maybe they could... No, she'd never be able to look her brother in the face if he heard them. Not ever.

Still, it wasn't a bad way to wake on Christmas morning. Definitely nothing wrong with the physical side of their relationship—she was almost whimpering by the time she wiggled out of his hold. Of course, he followed her into the shower. Fending off his hands left her aching and giggling. His playful touch and murmured flirtation soothed the jagged edges within her, that part of her feeling rejected and a little lost after the recent revelations. It helped that he'd also been adopted. He knew what it was like to have his foundation rocked.

She relaxed into the massage as he washed her hair. If he wanted to pamper her, who was she to object? Frankly, she wanted to see how long this honeymoon phase would last.

In the back of her mind, that ticking clock reminded her she only had a few weeks at most before her pregnancy started to show. She had to decide whether to trust Loki enough to try to raise a child with him, or whether she needed to disappear, this time, for years—however long it would take to teach her child to survive as an immortal. Neither choice was without risk, but gods, she wanted to trust him, to believe his words of commitment yesterday, to believe they could make a relationship work. He'd break her heart if she allowed herself to think he'd be faithful, be supportive, and then he shattered her trust. But every time she considered the possibility of raising her child alone with dangers like the Shen dragons or Isis, the spit dried in her mouth and her soul shivered, ice coating her bones.

After a quiet breakfast with Liam and Sarah, the four of them drove the fifteen minutes to her mother's house across the Fraser River in Hope. Shannon rarely visited since Uncle Colin moved in a few years ago. Supposedly, it was to keep her mom company, but he was an asshole whenever he drank. And he drank often.

"Shannon! About time you visited," Colin boomed, swaying on his feet at the front door of her mom's red-brick-and-cream-stucco Tudor-style home, the house Shannon had grown up in that hadn't felt like home since her dad died. In a rumpled, stained T-shirt, and checkered pyjama bottoms, his black hair sticking up everywhere, and with a distinct odour of booze and stale cigarette smoke about him, Colin had clearly made no effort whatsoever to clean up for Christmas.

"Hey, Uncle Colin. This is Tod Corvus, my b—boyfriend." Shannon fumbled over the introduction, glancing at Loki for his reaction. It wasn't like she could call him her soulmate, after all. Outside of Hallmark specials and romance books, humans didn't talk like that, and they'd only spent a grand total of five days together so far. Gods... only five days? It felt like so much longer with everything that had happened.

Loki extended his hand and Colin took it, shaking it vigorously. Fuck, was that avarice she saw in her uncle's bloodshot eyes? Heather leaned against the taupe-coloured wall farther down the hallway, a smug expression on her face. What the hell had she been telling Colin? As Shannon glared at her sister, her mom came around the corner from the kitchen.

"Come in, come in. Colin can do his impression of a doorstop later." Mom rolled her eyes and elbowed her brother in his beer gut. Colin glared at her and stomped away to flop on the couch in the nearby family room, mumbling curses. The Christmas tree stood in its usual place of honour by the family room bay window, a scattering of presents wrapped in red, green, and blue snowflake paper underneath. Handmade ornaments from childhood mixed with store-bought balls, lights, and tinsel in a mishmash of old and new.

"Thanks, Mom." Shannon followed Loki inside, with Sarah and Liam behind them. After placing the gifts under the tree, she joined Loki at a loveseat across from Colin.

"Eggnog," Heather said, returning from the kitchen and holding out two white mugs with snowmen dancing on them.

Loki took his, but knowing the amount of rum Heather would have added, Shannon shook her head. "No, thanks. I'll just have tea."

Heather gave an exasperated huff. "Sure, I'll just wait on you hand and foot then, shall I?" She tossed her head and flounced away with the rejected mug to sink into a chair by the tree. Scowling at Shannon, she downed half the mug in one go.

Shannon sighed. Why did it always have to be this way? "I'll get it."

"No need." Mom placed a teacup and saucer on the table beside Shannon. "I've got it already. You visit so rarely, it's no trouble to spoil you."

Shannon ignored the bite in her mom's words and picked up her tea. Passive-aggressive guilt trips were the norm around here. Taking a sip, Shannon watched Colin add more rum to his eggnog from a flask beside him. Her stomach churned. Whether it was her nausea or her baby's vote on the rum-soaked eggnog, she wasn't about to put any of *that* in her belly.

"Not a fan of eggnog?" Loki murmured too low for the others to hear.

"Not this early in the day when it's more rum than eggnog."

Once everyone had settled with drinks, Liam read labels and passed out presents from under the tree. The sound of ripping paper filled the room.

Loki sniffed his mug. "Hmm... I see what you mean. Perhaps not," he agreed, setting it aside on the nearby oak side table and shocking Shannon into halting with the teacup almost to her lips. He was a god, with an immortal constitution. He could drink an entire mug of straight rum and wouldn't feel it. Was he abstaining because she was?

She took a sip and set the tea down, smiling as Sarah and Liam thanked her then handed her a tin of homemade shortbread cookies. Heather opened her present next and shrieked, launching herself over to hug Shannon before sitting with the scarf wrapped around her neck, admiring herself in the mirror over the fireplace.

Colin and Rose got into an argument, getting more heated by the moment. Gods, why did they have to do this today? So embarrassing. Shannon tried to avoid listening to them as Loki placed a small silvery-white wrapped box in her hand. She blinked, staring down at it. They hadn't discussed presents between them. Fuck. She hadn't gotten him anything. Were they at the gift-giving stage? She almost snorted. What the hell did one get a god who could conjure anything he wanted?

Her hand clenched around the box. Did she want to open it? His gifts came with consequences. The Asgardian mead. The transition to goddesshood and immortality. A child.

"Aren't you going to open it?" he murmured in a tone that caressed her senses, and she met his gaze. Damn it, he was way too good at that, at undermining her willpower. He could get a saint to sin with that voice, and shit, she was no saint.

"I'm a little scared to. The mead packed quite the wallop."

Loki smiled and brushed a fingertip over her forehead, pushing a strand of hair away from her eyes. "I promise this present won't bite."

"Hmm..." Staring down at the silvery-white box, she wasn't convinced, but the idea that they could actually be building a relationship was still sinking in. They might be soulmates, but if Loki turned out to be abusive like Trent, or he couldn't keep it in his pants around other women, she would *not* stay.

No way.

Her hand twitched towards her abdomen before she stopped it. She had a child to protect, even if it meant protecting their baby from its father's bad choices. She would not be forced into some toxic relationship or sit idly by as he fucked someone else. A wave of fury swept over her as an image formed in her mind—a visceral rejection of Loki cheating on her—and a breeze jangled the ornaments on the tree, setting them swaying.

As Rose and Liam searched for an open window that Shannon knew wasn't the cause, Loki put his arm around her, fingers at her chin to turn her to meet his pale-blue gaze. A gaze that hid his true nature. Would she ever see the real him? How could she know?

<I'm sorry, darling. I honestly didn't mean to upset you.> He searched her face as his soft words stroked her mind.

With a small smile she didn't feel, Shannon tore the wrapping from the box, dragging her gaze away from his. Beneath the silvery-white paper was a dark blue jewellery box, and Shannon gasped at the silver charm bracelet revealed inside. Three charms were attached to the delicate chain—a platinum set of movie reels with diamonds, a shot glass with a chunk of amber, and a coyote in such detail that she could see his fur and glittering emerald eyes. Tears welling, she traced over each tiny work of art with trembling fingertips.

"It's perfect," she managed through the emotion clogging her throat. A mix of elation and relief surged through the bond, and she turned her face into Loki's firm chest, his other arm coming around her as well. "Thank you."

"I was thinking we could add special memories to it over time," he murmured, kissing her forehead. *<It could be a physical reminder that you aren't alone when you're feeling overwhelmed by everything you are learning. I know you're going through a huge adjustment. It's got to be a lot.>*

Gods, he'd put so much care into it, far more than she expected. Even with his own experience of being adopted, how did he know that something tangible would help? Her fingers clenched around the bracelet. She'd never received anything so thoughtful before.

She met his gaze, smiling. "Put it on me?"

"Absolutely."

With nimble fingers, he had it latched around her left wrist in moments. The charms jingled against the chain in a delightful tinkle that had Shannon shaking her wrist again. It was musical... well, of course it was. He was a god of music, after all.

The wrapping paper was cleaned up and her mom ushered everyone into the dining room with its rectangular maple table covered in a cheerful red linen tablecloth, green placemats, and her mom's best china. Although more drinks flowed, Shannon ignored the slurred words from Uncle Colin at the end of the table as they feasted on perfectly baked salmon, skillet-fried bannock, roasted potatoes, turnips, brussel sprouts, and candied butternut squash. Heather was amazingly pleasant, sitting across from Loki and Shannon, telling them funny stories about customers in her hair salon.

Liam was passing around slices of apple pie, made from fruit on their farm, when the doorbell rang. Rose abandoned the argument with her brother to go answer the door.

"Shannon," Mom called. "It's Lynda here to see you."

Shannon frowned down at her pie. How the hell had Lynda known she was here? She glanced up in time to see a guilty expression on Heather's face as her sister put her phone down beside her plate. Heather had been on it occasionally, but not constantly like she usually was. Still, the damn thing was never far from her fingertips, and she loved to gossip.

A sinking sensation in Shannon's gut had her taking a slow breath. "Have you been posting pictures to Instagram?" Hard to keep her voice calm, but she resisted the urge to scream.

Heather shrugged, but a sly smile crept onto her lips. "And TikTok. It's gone viral already. Two million views and rising."

Fury turned Shannon's veins molten and her heart thundered, circulating and building the anger in her chest. The candles in the centre of the table blew out as the decorations hanging from the china cabinet swayed. With her fists clenched, she shoved back her chair, Loki rising with her. Almost shaking, she couldn't answer her sister. Of course, Heather had sold them out. What the fuck did she care about their privacy? Loki put his hand on her lower back, not saying anything as they approached the front door.

Rose took one look at Shannon and retreated to the dining room, leaving them alone with Lynda.

Arms crossed at her chest, in a vivid blood-red skirt, a perfectly fitted matching suit jacket, a snow-white blouse, and red heels, her best friend was the epitome of style and sophistication. Never would Lynda show up anywhere without her makeup immaculate and every hair of her chin-length streaked-blond bob in place. Yet the sneer on her pale face destroyed the image, turning pretty doll-like features into something far uglier.

"You lied to me." Turning her gaze to Loki, Lynda held out her hand. "Hi, I'm Lynda Warden of Warden Marketing dot com. I'm Shannon's best friend, but you probably haven't heard of me." She tossed a glare at Shannon.

Chapter 30

A LEAP OF FAITH

Shannon winced when Loki's eyebrow rose, but he didn't take Lynda's hand. "Is this the way you treat all your friends?"

Eyes narrowing, Lynda pulled her hand back.

Crap. Here came the explosion. "Why don't we step outside, Lynda?" Shannon opened the door and her friend stepped out. <*Please, let me deal with this. Stay here.*> She closed the door on him before he could follow her, then leaned against it.

"Seriously, Shannon? You fucking *told* me you hadn't seen him again! Yet here you are, in your mom's goddamned house having fucking *Christmas dinner* with him. You lying bitch!"

Shannon flinched at the venom in Lynda's tone. She hadn't lied about seeing him, not when she'd last spoken to her a week ago. But she had been lying to her best friend for months, and the barb struck true. What kind of friend lied constantly?

"I'm sorry. I actually hadn't seen him until I bumped into him in Vancouver"—she fought the instinctive blush that wanted to erupt at the new lie. Gods, she hated, hated lying—"just a few days ago when I got back from Greece"—another squirm as her hands clenched around the bottom of her sweater—"and since the sparks were still there, I invited him to dinner."

Lynda rolled her eyes. "Right. You just *happened*"—her fingers air quoted the word—"to bump into him, a celebrity?" She snorted. "As if. *You. Are. A. Liar!*" Her manicured fingernail stabbed into Shannon's chest with each word.

Shannon flushed, shrinking against Lynda's anger and unable to refute her friend's argument.

"Fuck you, Shannon. You know I need the business. It would be *so* easy for you to just mention my name around all these rich people you are meeting, yet I'm not even important enough for you to tell your new rich, famous boyfriend about me! Your best friend! Who has been there for you every time Trent has shown up? Who drove you to the hospital—"

<*I can change Lynda's memory. Let me help you, darling,*> Loki offered.

"—when he gave you a concussion? You bitch! Who fucking held your hand when you got your restraining order? Me! It was me, every god damned time."

<*No, I have to deal with this myself.*> Shannon took every hit, hunching her shoulders. Lynda was right. She had been there when Shannon needed her. It was little enough of an ask to mention Lynda's company, but Shannon hadn't. Even if she wasn't meeting a bunch of famous people as Lynda thought, Shannon was a terrible friend. All she'd given her was lies, constant lies, over and over for the past five months.

"I'm sorry, Lynda," she murmured.

Lynda snarled and threw up her hands. "I'll believe that when you prove you mean it. Bring me some fucking customers, bitch. Then we'll talk."

Jaw clenched, Loki fought to keep his temper as he listened to Shannon's so-called best friend through the door. Why wouldn't Shannon let him help her? It would be so easy to change her friend's memory. And she didn't defend herself from the harsh words Lynda spewed.

But he knew. He sensed her sorrow, her heartbreak as the heaviness in her spirit came through the bond.

More than ever, he wanted to whisk her away from all of this. To protect her from the pain. Fingers flexed as he paced while they spoke outside. By the Nine, he hated being unable to help her.

Shannon was quiet when she returned, but her downcast eyes and tightened lips told the story as clearly as the ache in his heart. Her friend had left, which was probably a good thing. If he'd seen that vile woman right then, he might have killed her like he had Trent. No one hurt his goddess and got away with it.

Her ex's fate had been sealed when Loki heard his crimes and saw the evidence on Shannon's flesh. The sharp blade of Asgardian justice didn't wait for constantly changing mortal laws to fail again when it came to crimes against their people. Not after he'd confirmed the truth from Trent's disgusting memories. Shannon hadn't been the first woman the mortal had hunted. Loki's only regret was that he hadn't caught Trent before he'd deliberately driven two other women to suicide. No, that sadistic fucker was Hela's problem now.

Instead, Loki drew Shannon into his arms. He held her for hours as they visited with her family, even her drunkard of an uncle. Although to be fair, Thor could be worse when he was celebrating. Shannon didn't object when Loki convinced her to come to bed early that night.

The next day, they took their leave before breakfast and drove her vehicle back to the city. When she teased him with a little smile on her face in her secluded backyard hidden by towering conifers, some of the tightness in his chest eased.

"Could we stop somewhere in the city for appropriate clothing for the palace? I felt underdressed when I met your mom before. I can't imagine my jeans and T-shirt are usual palace attire," she said, letting her fingers slide from her hips, up to cup her breasts as she watched him with half-lidded eyes.

"Temptress." Loki gave her a slow perusal from head to toe and back again, trying to not grin at the way her hips swayed and her weight shifted from foot to foot. "Unless it is some kind of formal event or you are going to the throne room, jeans and a T-shirt are fine in the palace. But if you like, I can conjure you Asgardian-style clothing typical for the elite?"

"Yes."

The husky drop in her voice almost had him dragging her inside her house, but he resisted and conjured an emerald, black, and gold empire-waisted dress. Jewel tones complemented her olive complexion and brown, red, and gold locks. By the Nine, she was stunning in the style of his realm.

Loki didn't restrain his purr of approval. Shannon looked like home. He couldn't wait to get her behind protected borders and to show her everything.

He hadn't had enough time to weave more than basic protections into the charm bracelet. With an arm around her to hold her sexy little body against his, he opened his mouth to call on Heimdall.

Shannon covered his lips with her fingers before he could speak, and Loki frowned, searching her expression. What was she—

A sparkle lit those beautiful hazel eyes as she said, "Heimdall, please open the Bifrost."

Yggdrasil's roots, it lightened his heart to see that mischievous little twinkle, and he chuckled. Even so, he jolted slightly when the rainbow lights swirled around them. His mother must have given Shannon Bifrost privileges. Part of him was proud of his goddess for adapting so quickly, but damn it, he'd hoped to keep her reliant on him so she wouldn't leave Asgard—and safety—as easily.

Still, he buried that thought as the portal deposited them on the platform.

Heimdall nodded at them, lifting his hand from the control pad. "Welcome back to Asgard, Princess Shannon, Prince Loki. The All-Father and All-Mother would be pleased if the two of you would join them for dinner."

Bor's balls. Not just Bifrost privileges. Fortunately, Shannon was facing Heimdall and didn't see the involuntary wince Loki didn't quite manage to suppress. But damn it, he'd not wanted to pile more on her after everything she'd dealt with during the last couple of days. *Norns, please don't let her freak out.*

"Thank you, Heimdall. Close your mouth, Loki. You're going to catch flies." She tossed Loki an amused glance and sashayed out of the chamber and onto the bridge.

He blinked at her tone. She seemed fine? How could she be fine with all of this so fast? He scrambled to catch up to her. "Princess?" he asked, cautiously.

"Your mom didn't waste any time once she found out we're soulmates." She shrugged one shoulder. "I'm told it makes me part of the royal family."

An icy shiver crept up Loki's back. Something in Shannon's tone belied her casual words. "You aren't... angry? Or feeling rushed?" Like walking through an antlion scree slope, he stepped with care. He wasn't certain what might cause her to flee again and bit back the impulse to tug at his hair. Why had his mother dropped all this on her at once?

Shannon halted and her hand rose to his cheek. A little smile flitted at the edges of her mouth, yet her gaze was serious. "Loki, I'll be honest. Yes, this shocked me. It's a lot. Before I met you, I thought I needed a change in my life." She shook her head, a wry twist to her lips. "This wasn't exactly what I'd envisioned. Everything about us has upended my life. It's why I ran before." She glanced away, toward the city.

Her hand started to drop, and he caught it, turning it to kiss her palm, but she didn't meet his eyes.

Was she thinking of running again? *No. Please, Norns. Don't let her leave me again.* His heart thundered in his chest, his fingers unsteady as he reached for her chin, tilting it up to make eye contact. Part of him wished she hadn't learned to shield her thoughts so well.

"Please, Shannon. Please talk to me?" It was rough, forcing the words out past the lump in his throat.

She swallowed, eyes softening. "I haven't had the best experience with romantic relationships."

His jaw clenched on the growl that wanted to erupt. Yeah, he still remembered injuries her ex had given her, the pleasurable memories the sick fucker had had of beating her mentally and physically. It had taken him a while to track that bastard down, but getting rid of Trent had helped Loki's sanity during the months he'd searched for her.

"And... I wasn't ready for the depth of our connection. I still need time and space to come to terms with all the changes. This is all happening very fast." She glanced away for a few seconds, this time down at the charm bracelet on her wrist, but then met his gaze again with a directness that reassured him. "I'm trying to deal with it all. Sometimes, I need a bit more time to think about things before I'm able to discuss them with you. But I *do* care about you, Loki, and I like what I've seen so far." She swallowed. "I'm... I'm willing to see if we can make this soulmate thing work between us."

At her words, relief surged through Loki with the force of floodwaters scouring a canyon, and he had to lock his knees to stay standing. "I was scared, Shannon. Scared to tell you, because I didn't want you to run again. Those months of not knowing where you were, it was torture. I don't want to lose you again. It was..." The remembered dark, gaping pit in his chest had him blinking away moisture from his eyes.

"I told you I wouldn't run again," she teased, a small smile flirting at her lips as she caressed his cheek.

Desire gripped him hard and fast, tightening his groin as the memory of her bound, writhing and pleading, flashed through his thoughts. So fucking gorgeous. "Yeah, I got that promise from you under duress. I wasn't sure if you would consider that fair."

She laughed softly and tugged his head down, kissing him deeply and thoroughly until they were both breathless. His pulse pounded in his veins, need for her riding him with every beat of his heart.

When their lips parted, she asked, "Does that answer your question?"

Loki groaned, his fingertips flexing in her hair and on her ass as he held her warm, curvy body tight against him, so soft compared to his unyielding form. The temptation to lift her dress and wrap those legs around him surged and his hips jerked, grinding and straining to sink into her hot, wet sex. "Yes, darling, I do believe you have convinced me. Bor's balls, you have me harder than dragon scale. Let's go before I attempt to mask us from all of Asgard and take you right here on the bridge. You have a way of making me lose my head and control of my magic. Abstaining at your brother's was torture."

Forehead pressed to hers, it took several calming breaths to ignore the throbbing ache in his groin before he could force himself to release her.

And fuck, she looked tempted, biting her lip as her gaze flickered between his lips and meeting his eyes.

Damn, but she drove him wild. The churning cauldron of desire built as the seconds continued to tick and he vibrated with the effort to hold himself back. Loki was close to throwing caution to the wind when she shivered, straightened her shoulders, and pushed her hair back away from her face, holding him at bay.

A groan escaped him and damn it, he almost pouted. As he held his elbow out to escort her and offered, "Shall we?" he considered teleporting them to get there faster.

Yet Shannon seemed a little distracted when they reached the far side of the bridge, so instead, he pointed out some of his favourite sights and shops as they walked to the palace. Although she murmured polite acknowledgements, her mind was elsewhere. Was she having second thoughts? Was she worried about being here? Being part of the royal family? Meeting Odin? Loki clenched his jaw. Did she have doubts about him? Yggdrasil's roots, but he hated not knowing her thoughts.

Once inside the palace's white halls, he led her directly to his suite of rooms. They didn't have long to get ready for dinner with Odin and Frigga, and damn it, he wanted dessert first. If she was limp with orgasms, surely she'd be too relaxed to dwell on her worries.

As soon as he closed the heavy oak-and-blacksteel door behind her, Loki pinned her to it, claiming those soft, full lips.

The arousal that had been simmering since their kiss on the bridge ignited and flared along their bond. Shannon arched against him, even as he plundered her mouth and discarded their clothes. Delving between her folds to find slick heat had him growling with savage need.

Her moans were music to his ears, and when she gasped a breath, Loki shifted to kissing and biting his way toward her ear. Fuck, he could not get enough of the taste of her skin. He was ravenous.

While he stroked and taunted her tender flesh, her hips pushed against him restlessly. She was as eager as he. A shiver crawled down his neck when her nails scraped over his scalp.

"I've got to be inside you," he groaned, circling and flicking a thumb over the hard nub at the junction of her thighs.

"Now," she moaned in agreement, lifting her legs to climb and wrap around his hips as he drove his cock deep.

His eyes almost rolled back in his head with her wet quim clenched around him. He couldn't restrain himself and thrust in vigorous, pounding strokes, with her braced against the door. It was glorious, absolutely fucking glorious.

Heat and squeezing friction surrounded him as he drove into her again and again. The coiling tension built. Her cries of pleasure sang in his ears and his breath rasped.

Hotter and higher, it surged up his spine as she tightened around him, quivering with her orgasm. As her walls fluttered, she screamed, "Gods, Loki! I'm—"

"*Shannon*," he roared, unable to hold back as his own climax blasted through him.

He stayed like that, panting and holding her against the door, until his pulse no longer raced and he could breathe without gasping. Leaning his forehead on the door and gazing sideways down at her, he caressed her soft cheek. Shannon was such a miracle to him. Norns knew, he never wanted to let her go.

When she'd recovered her breath as well, Loki picked her up under the ass and carried her over to the bed, keeping them joined. If he could, he'd forgo dinner to pleasure her over and over. Fuck, she was dinner and dessert all rolled into one, feeding both his soul and energies. What did he need food for when he could feast on her?

Shannon wrapped her lithe arms around his neck and peered up into his eyes as he walked. A smile tugged at the corners of her lips and her eyes danced with inner light. Before he reached the bed, they were laughing together.

Turning, he sat with her on top of him.

"My wicked, impatient god," she said.

"Always, when it comes to you, darling." How annoyed would Mother and Father be if they skipped dinner? Their disapproving expressions popped into his mind, and he stifled a groan.

Unable to resist, he kissed Shannon again. "Now, as much as I hate to say it, and damn, I really hate to say it, I need to pull myself out of your deliciously tight, wet body." He flexed inside her, hard and ready to take her again. "We absolutely *have* to get dressed for dinner."

Shannon moaned and lifted herself off in a sensuous slide, to stand straddling his legs. Her fingers buried in his hair and she tugged at the strands until Loki dragged his eyes from her glistening sex to meet her gaze. "We will be picking this up where we left off after dinner. I expect you to fuck me until I can't move," she commanded in a sultry tone.

So bloody perfect. "By the Nine, I am a lucky damn bastard. Your wish is my command, Princess." Reaching up to hold her hips, he drew her closer. He needed a taste of his glorious goddess to tide him over until he could feast on her again. Loki bent to kiss her wet folds and flicked his tongue over her little pearl. She was better than ambrosia or the finest Asgardian meads. And fuck, he loved the flavour of them together, his seed and scent claiming her.

"Loki," she moaned, tugging his hair as her hips jerked towards his mouth.

Hearing her moan his name was a warm glow, lighting him from within. With agonizing slowness, he released her aroused flesh. "Just a preview, darling," he promised.

Eyes glazed by passion, her body language seemed torn between wanting more now and duty, echoing his own conflicted state. Reluctantly, he released her when she stepped back.

As her eyes cleared, she took note of her surroundings. It made him wonder what she saw from her perspective. He had modelled his London flat after his rooms here, with the same colour palette, plenty of space for his books—although, admittedly, they still spilled over the many tables, chairs, and sofas—his piano, lute, guitar and wall of instruments, and gardens to walk, read, and enjoy. A glance outside had him wincing. Bor's beard, they were going to be late.

"You should jump in the shower first. If I join you, well, we'll definitely be late. I'd rather not deal with Odin in a bad mood." Loki gestured toward the open door so she'd know where the bathroom was. Father did *not* like to be kept from his meal, and Loki didn't want to prejudice him against Shannon by jumping on one of Odin's pet peeves with both boots.

"Are we really that close to dinner?"

"Yes, we're pushing it."

"Okay, you can use the shower, then. I don't need to." With a slight frown as her eyes unfocused, she summoned a layer of water that she rolled as a thin wave over her body, cleaning herself. She dispersed it with hot air, leaving her skin dry.

Pride swelled in Loki's chest. The precise control over her seidhr was impressive in so few months. She'd come a long way since that first day. "That is some very nice magic, darling. Now do me, and I'll conjure us the appropriate clothes." He winked at his pun, and she laughed as he stood and held his arms out.

Shannon ran water over his body, and his little minx teased him with it, even as she cleaned then dried him. By Yggdrasil's many branches, he loved that she wanted to tease.

To clothe her, he conjured a fitted green and gold corset that curved up over her collarbones and around the back of her neck. Long pointed sleeves with bare shoulders, a floor-length velvet green skirt with gold stitching, and a long gold cape with green piping completed the look. After nodding approval of his choice, she asked him to conjure her a gold hair clip, which she used to pin up the sides of her hair. She left two long strands to frame her face.

His goddess was stunning.

For himself, he'd put on his usual black and silver Asgardian attire—black leather pants, and a liquid silver-black scale-mail-accented tunic with black leather. Since dinner with his parents required formal attire, he added his blackened silver chest armour with the royal crest of Yggdrasil in gold, vambraces, and a high collar with its long black cape edged with silver.

Shannon's eyes glinted. "Now that looks nothing like those costumes the fictional Loki wears in those movies or video games. Where are your horns?"

"Darling, please. *That* is entertainment. *This* is battle-tested Asgardian armour," he replied with a smirk, gesturing to the interlocking scale weave of liquid metal protecting his torso. Self-repairing and with the ability to change colours for stealth so he didn't have to expend energy on illusion, it flexed and flowed with his body's movement. "I know Norse mythology is popular on Midgard right now, but Shannon"—he caught her chin in his fingers—"little about it is real. Don't make the mistake of putting yourself in danger because you've assumed something from fictional tales. Stories have their place, but not when it comes to educating you about the reality of the immortal worlds."

PART 3

Immortal Is the New Normal

"Reality is created by the mind. We can change our reality by changing our mind."

Plato

Chapter 31

BEWARE OF GODS BEARING GIFTS

Despite their dressy attire, Shannon let out a relieved breath to find it was just the two of them dining with Frigga and Odin.

"I'm happy to see you again so soon, Shannon," Frigga said, enveloping her in a hug as they entered the dining area within Odin and Frigga's suite of rooms. "Have you told Loki about the baby yet?" she murmured in Shannon's ear before releasing her.

Shannon gave a small shake of her head. "Thank you for the invitation, my queen."

Frigga and Loki shifted to either side of Shannon, presenting her to Odin. He'd hung back as he observed them. And *oh my gods*, he was *far* more imposing than any Hollywood version. Entirely in liquid gold armour and black leather, with long braided white hair and a neatly trimmed white beard, he sported a golden eyepatch but his remaining blue eye seemed to penetrate deep into her soul. He radiated an energy that was impossible to not notice.

"This is Loki's soulmate, Princess Shannon of the Aos Sí, but raised as a mortal on Midgard," Frigga told him.

"Come here, child," Odin commanded in a deep, richly resonant voice.

Behind her, Loki and Frigga greeted each other. Shannon swallowed, gooseflesh rising on her skin as she stepped closer to Odin.

"My king, I apologize. I'm unfamiliar with Asgardian etiquette. Do I curtsey?" she asked bluntly. Better to simply ask than to offend by not knowing.

A small smile appeared on Odin's face, and he held out a hand. She took it, and a rush of energy poured into her, tingling over her skin. It wasn't unpleasant, just unexpected.

"When we are in public, yes, you should greet me with a curtsey or bow, depending on your attire. Loki and Frigga will help you learn our ways, I'm sure. Here in private, we do not need to be so formal. Instead, I'm pleased to have a worthy daughter for my mischievous son. Frigga tells me you're an excellent match. I know the Norns would not have paired you otherwise."

To say his warm welcome and kind words surprised her was an understatement. She'd had a preconceived notion of his personality based on fictional accounts of him. Exactly as Loki had warned her, she quickly realized how flawed they were. This Odin had worked out any differences with a teenaged Loki eons ago and seemed to accept and be proud of him, flaws and all. Perhaps there was some truth to the mythology that he'd given up his eye for wisdom. Although curious, Shannon wasn't about to blurt out that question. She had *some* self-preservation, after all.

"Thank you, my king," she said, trying to not trip over her tongue.

"Please, I hope you will become comfortable enough to call me Father in time."

Unexpectedly, tears came to her eyes. She'd not anticipated, not thought to receive such quick acceptance, especially with her birth parents rejecting her. A sudden realization halted her spike of joy. He was the All-Father. He didn't mean it the way she'd taken it, surely. "I... thank you... Father," she managed past the ache in her chest.

He smiled kindly as he tucked her hand onto his arm and drew them away from where Loki and Frigga conversed. They strolled out a set of doors and into a beautiful garden full of fragrant flowers, hanging grapes, and trellised fruit trees. The sweet scents of various blooms blended in the warm evening air.

"I understand from Frigga you haven't yet told my son about our grandchild? May I ask why?"

Shannon's pulse hiccupped, and a tendril of worry threaded through her belly, churning uneasily. How free was she here? Would they take her child from her if Shannon's relationship with Loki didn't work out? Her free hand fisted. No one was taking her baby, damn it.

"It's still quite a shock. I need a little time for it to settle into my brain, to feel real to me, before I tell him," she explained, searching for the right words to make sense of it all. "There's been such an overwhelming number of things to adjust to in such a short period. I haven't been able to catch my breath."

No way was Shannon going to bring up that Loki and she were still feeling their way into an actual relationship. Soulmate or not, she wasn't making life decisions based on a few days together.

"May I?" Odin asked, his other hand hovering over her abdomen.

She nodded permission. "Yes."

Odin's hand made contact, and she gasped at the energy now circling through her. It didn't hurt. Instead, the tingling was like an electric current, filling her with vitality.

Odin smiled. "He's going to be a handful. I'm looking forward to seeing how Loki handles a child as mischievous as himself."

"It's a boy?" she asked, tears trickling down her cheeks.

"Oh yes. A healthy, powerful boy," Odin said with a rippling laugh. He removed his hand from her abdomen, and although she still felt the energy flowing from his arm to her hand tucked into his elbow, it wasn't as overwhelming.

"Now daughter, as with all my children, I would like to give you a gift. I sense you are already a strong elemental goddess, so what ability can I bestow?"

His offer caught her off guard, and she blinked. He... he considered her one of his children? Already? It wasn't just lip service because he was the All-Father? For immortals, they sure decided things quickly.

Could she trust the joy blooming within? Her need for acceptance, to be wanted after finding out her birth parents had tossed her away, was a jagged gash in her centre. Still, she wasn't going to reject the offer. No way. She swept her fingertips over her cheeks, brushing away her tears to give her time to answer.

"I'm not sure. Well, I guess..." She paused, trying to consider her choices.

Odin waited patiently, not saying anything.

Finally, she added, "My goal is to learn to better defend myself, my child, and Loki against any that would threaten us. I'm not sure how that would translate to an ability."

Odin smiled with a pleased gleam in his eye. "Fighting skills are an ability, my child. Whether they are used offensively or defensively, they can be innate or learned. Even innate ability can be further honed, as you've discovered with your other abilities. It's a wise choice. I am very pleased to imbue you with innate fighting ability, to see to your and my grandchild's safety."

At his words, he took both her hands. Energy again circled through her body from the points of contact, but this time, rippled outward, down to her toes and up to her head. It was exhilarating, electrifying, sparking through every cell of her body as it sank deep into her flesh. Her hair crackled.

"It will take a few hours for the energy to settle into your genetic structure," he said, one side of his mouth curled into a half smile as he removed his hands. "Given the way your transition to goddess occurred, I believe I should return you to Loki, so you can retire to your chambers. I suspect there may be some side effects as the energy settles in." He winked at her.

Shannon's mouth dropped open. Oh, gods! She knew exactly what he was referring to. Odin was also married to a fertility goddess. Her cheeks heated, and she was speechless to respond. Holy hell, this was not how she'd expected her first family dinner with Loki's parents to go.

Odin gestured for her to lead the way, and she turned to head back into the dining room. He must have warned Frigga, because her hand covered her face, green eyes dancing as she tried not to laugh when Shannon entered.

Loki's mouth dropped open. "What... what did you do to her, Father?"

Odin chuckled. "I imbued her with an ability, my son. Just as I have given all my children an ability, in addition to their inherent ones."

Loki hurried over to Shannon, his fingers framing her fiery cheeks. "Why do you look embarrassed, darling?" He turned to Odin when she didn't answer. "She's surging with energy. Is that normal?"

Frigga and Odin shared a look, both chuckling. Loki's gaze narrowed, his brow lowering as he looked from one to the other. "What am I missing?"

"I'd suggest you take her to your rooms, son," Odin said with a twinkle in his eye.

"Immediately," Frigga added, as she gestured to him in a shooing motion.

"Please, Loki," Shannon finally whispered. <*I need you inside me now, like right now.*> Into their connection, she fed the arousal building rapidly within her, the energy coiling and surging.

His eyes widened.

"Oh!" He looked at his parents, and they nodded, smiling.

The next moment, Shannon and Loki were in his rooms, and she leapt at him.

After the first round, which was fast, intense, and had her screaming his name while leaving scratch marks on his back, they panted on their backs on the bed, catching their breath.

Loki laughed, and she hit him.

"It's not funny!"

"I beg to differ. It's hilarious!" he said, as he howled, holding his stomach. "How did Father know what imbuing you with an ability would do to you?"

"I told Frigga."

Shannon didn't think it was possible for Loki to laugh harder. She was wrong. He cried, tears of mirth streaming as he roared with amusement.

"You told my mother... about your... transition? That you... needed... me to fuck you... nine routes to the Nine Realms... for the better... part... of twenty-four... hours? You... are amazing! Truly amazing! If I didn't... love you before, by Yggdrasil's heartwood... I would love you now." He barely got the words out between gales of laughter.

Even as the energy built within her again, she grabbed a pillow from the bed and pummelled him with it.

"I hate you, you wicked god," she grumbled when he continued to chuckle.

Loki caught the pillow in his hand, tugging it out of her grip, before flipping her under him on the bed.

Eyes dark, he purred, "Oh no, my darling. You love me, and you love what I do to this gorgeous body of yours." He pinned her hands above her head and parted her thighs with one muscular leg.

She moaned in pleasure as he thrust deep.

"Allow me to remind you," he rumbled in her ear, and Shannon surrendered to his skilled embrace.

Chapter 32

WARRIOR GODDESS

Shannon blinked bleary eyes from her cocoon in the luxurious bedding. "I hate you," she mumbled.

"No darling, you love me desperately." Loki's tone was amused and alert.

Damn it. "Why are you awake?" she complained, even as she mulled over his statement. He sounded so sure, like he knew her feelings better than she did. Did she love him? This fast? How did she know if what she felt was real? She thought she loved Trent, that idiot abusive jackass. She wasn't exactly the best judge.

"Because, my beautiful, sexy goddess, it is well into the late morning, and you should start your training."

She groaned and pulled the pillow over her head. She was not a morning person. All this thinking made her head hurt.

Loki pulled the pillow off.

"Father has sent you a gorgeous set of armour. You absolutely should get up."

That piqued her curiosity enough that she opened her eyes. Loki stood over her, smiling. He really was too handsome for his own good.

"See, I knew you loved me."

Okay, *maybe*. She liked almost everything about him so far. Even if she wasn't sure she trusted her judgement, and still, there was that nagging issue of his being a womanizer. Not that she'd seen him look at another woman in her presence so far. Either way, she wasn't going to give that giant ego of his a boost right now. She sat up, letting the blankets fall.

"Now, you are the gorgeous one." He reached for her.

She batted his hand away. "I thought you wanted me to get up?"

"Maybe I changed my mind," he teased as his gaze scanned her body, leaving a heated trail she forced herself to ignore.

"Didn't I recharge your godly energy enough last night?" she retorted over her shoulder as she walked to the bathroom.

"Never, darling. I'll always want you," Loki called after her.

Smiling, she closed the door.

When she came out refreshed, showered, and dried, Loki conjured her clothes— reinforced black leather combat leggings and a dark forest-green tunic. Over the tunic, he'd added a fitted black leather corset that continued down past her hips to split into two overlapping panels that came to mid-thigh. One panel was black with silver edging. The panel on the other hip was woven with green leather strips and green edging. The corset had reinforced shoulders, extending up along the curve of her neck.

He came over with what appeared to be a thick silver-black neckpiece an inch wide. Opening a hidden fastening, he laid it on her chest where it curved up over her collarbones, slid it through two slots in the reinforced part of the corset at the tops of her shoulders near her neck, then fastened it at her nape.

Although Shannon expected it to be heavy, she didn't feel its weight at all.

"Touch your hand to it," Loki said.

Puzzled, she did as he requested, and the metal tingled under her fingertips. She jerked her hand away before she processed the sensation fully. It hadn't hurt, just startled her.

"Think about having armour."

She'd no sooner thought about it than interlocking liquid scale plates formed over her torso. They covered her arms, back, shoulders, chest, and abdomen, down to the flair of her hips.

Her pulse leapt as she gaped then blurted a breathy, "Wow!"

"This set of clothes and armour will respond and change to your thoughts. Think about adding a cape."

Immediately, she imagined a cape like she'd seen Loki wear. When she looked down, it flowed from her shoulders and she couldn't help petting it, feeling the solid material in her fingers.

"This is incredible!" Shannon told him, unable to drag her eyes from the miracle in her hands.

"You can modify it to suit your needs. Sleeves, no sleeves, vambraces or not, full jacket, no jacket, armour or not. You can even shift it to Midgardian-style clothing should you prefer. Just do not take the torc off. It will hide itself if you wish it not to be seen."

"Did you have a hand in this?" she asked, seeing his style in it as she finally looked up to meet his gaze.

Loki smiled, a fingertip gliding over the torc. "I may have had a bit of input."

She hugged him. A surge of warmth expanded from her chest. Was this how it felt to have her decisions supported? To have a true partner who cared about what mattered to her and wasn't threatened by it? "Thank you. I love it. It's perfect!" It seemed he really was completely on board with her learning to fight, not expecting her to rely on him.

Loki drew back and took her hand. "Come on, sexy warrior princess. It's time for you to start your training." He led her out of his rooms, through the palace's gleaming white-and-gold hallways, and into a large hard-packed black sand courtyard. Racks of weapons were at one end, and pairs of fighters sparred against each other. They were a mix of men and women, which she expected. Shannon was a bit surprised to see predominately women, though.

Was that why Loki was so willing to support her in this?

Still, every one of the women was fit and muscled, not carrying the extra weight Trent had so often mocked her about... even if she'd finally lost some of it. She still had a long way to go to reach their lithe strength. The way they moved... they were graceful but fierce. Gods, could she actually learn how to fight like them?

"The Valkyrie, the female warriors of Asgard, use this as their primary training ground. The Einherjar, the male warriors of Asgard, have another training ground, but as you can see, the two mix frequently," Loki explained.

He walked over to a rack holding quarterstaves, picked up two, and tossed her one.

"We'll start with these and go over basic footwork and postures." He showed her how to position her hands and had her copy him in a series of drills. After a few repetitions, she was able to follow him in the sequences flawlessly. Slowly increasing speed, Loki had her mimic him until they were moving through the footwork drills at full tempo. It felt like dancing—maintaining balance and flow from one move to the next.

"That's excellent, darling. Okay, now that you can keep your feet and balance, let's add defensive blocks and attacks." Loki took her through another series of drills that built on the previous, this time with him showing her which way to block, sweep, and attack with the staff in different positions. Again, they started slowly until she could go through the moves at full speed.

"Whether it's the ability Odin gave you, or it's your innate flexibility and gracefulness, you are a natural, my love. Let's try sparring where you need to react to another person."

Ha! Take that, Trent! Shannon couldn't help the thrill of pleasure that shot through her at Loki's compliment. "I agree, Loki, but I don't think it should be you. You'll hold back and not test me."

He nodded ruefully. "It's true. I abhor the idea of hurting you." He perused the courtyard.

"Hey, Kara!" Loki called, and a tall, bronze-skinned woman in brown leather pants and a matching cross-halter leather top turned.

"What do you need, my prince?" she asked as she started over towards them with her bouncing mane of curly red hair piled on her head.

"Would you please come spar with Princess Shannon?" he asked.

She eyed Shannon inquisitively. Shannon lifted her chin towards the leanly muscled Valkyrie who didn't have an ounce of fat on her frame despite having full breasts and curving hips, and tried to keep the wistfulness out of her voice. Gods, she'd love to be tall and athletic like her. "Nice to meet you, Kara. I need to spar with someone who won't take it easy on me."

Kara's golden eyes lit. "Well then, it's nice to meet you, Princess. Let's see if I can kick your ass, yeah?"

Shannon blinked, then laughed. "Are there any rules?" she asked as Loki tossed his stave to Kara.

"No, darling. Just as in an actual battle, everything goes. We try to avoid serious injury or death in training, but as immortals, we can take a lot of damage and heal from most things. First one unconscious or who says 'yield' is the loser of the bout. Are you sure you want to do this?" A crease formed between his brows.

Warmth curled around her heart. He wasn't holding her back, even as his worry registered. The eagerness on Kara's face had Shannon smiling. "Game on," she said.

"Commence." Loki backed away.

Kara came at Shannon in a flurry of blows aimed at her feet. Dancing, Shannon blocked and dodged. Next, Kara went for her hands, but Shannon spun and blocked her with the stave. The Valkyrie warrior wasn't following the patterns Loki had taught Shannon. Her unpredictability was exhilarating, and Shannon's reflexes fired almost without thought.

Kara tried to sweep the backs of Shannon's knees, and she blocked the strike, following it with a spin into the red-head and a body blow as Shannon hooked her stave on Kara's shoulder and heaved. Shannon blinked and almost cheered. It hadn't been a move Loki has shown her, but damn, it worked. The Valkyrie went flying, landing on her feet some yards away, with a smile and nod of respect on her face.

Their blocks and attacks got faster, becoming a blur of spins, lunges, and dodges. When Kara almost caught Shannon with a blow to her abdomen, Shannon found herself thickening the air so Kara couldn't connect.

The warrior's eyes narrowed when her stave bounced off the invisible barrier. Stepping back, she disengaged. "You're an air ability?" Kara asked as they caught their breath.

"Elemental," Shannon said, still panting.

"Ah, that's excellent. Hey, Mist!" Kara called.

"Yo!"

A petite woman with multi-hued blue hair braided down her back jogged over. In tight silver leggings and a fitted blue leather tunic, she was Shannon's height—short when most of the Valkyrie seemed at least six feet. But she also had a perfect hourglass shape and still managed to have the defined muscular limbs that Shannon wished she had. With pixie-like features and an upturned, pert nose on almost silvery skin, Mist grinned and cocked a fist on her hip, while Shannon took in the woman's unusual tricoloured blue irises with rings of pale ice, brilliant sapphire, and darkest ocean.

"Princess Shannon is an elemental. She'd be better off sparring with you so you can both use your abilities," Kara said. The warrior turned back to Shannon and inclined her head. "Thank you for the match. It was a pleasure to spar with someone as unpredictable as I am."

"Umm... Thank you, Kara," Shannon replied.

Mist quirked a navy eyebrow at Shannon quizzically. "I manipulate air and water vapour. Although, I'm shit with liquid or solid water. You?"

"All four natural elements to some degree," Shannon said.

"Dayum. Kara also said you are unpredictable. That is a high compliment coming from her since battle strategy is one of her strengths. Are you ready?" Mist asked.

Flushed with pleasure, Shannon was excited to spar again. "Yes," she confirmed, bringing the staff to the ready position. Her muscles trembled with anticipation.

Mist started similarly to Kara, with a series of blows aimed at Shannon's feet. Unlike Kara, the blue-haired warrior paired it with gusts of wind to try to throw Shannon off balance. Shannon blocked her opponent's attempts, and although her balance wasn't as steady, she mostly countered the wind the Valkyrie threw at her. It was far more of a challenge to pair them together. Mist knocked Shannon off her feet a few times.

Each time, Mist stopped, grinned, and waited for Shannon to get up, then they resumed their sparring.

Slowly, Shannon got better at combining her blocks with shields of air, or her attacks with gusts. She didn't knock Mist over but considered it a success when she made the warrior stagger.

Mist smiled and put her hand up to indicate she was done. "That was well done. You are picking this up quickly. We'll have you combining your strengths in no time."

"Thank you. I appreciate it. Loki is too gentle with me." Shannon glanced over at where he sat watching, arms crossed, foot tapping. She turned back to Mist and offered her arm.

The blue-haired Valkyrie clasped Shannon's forearm as Shannon had seen others do. "I'm happy to work with you, Princess. It's great for me as well, since we've got a couple of earth manipulators, but not air, or an elemental with multiple strengths in the Valkyrie. Same time tomorrow?"

"Yes, I'd like that. See you then, Mist."

Over the next two weeks, Mist taught Shannon different ways to combine air and water vapour with strikes and blocks, first with the stave, then they moved to a pair of long trident-shaped daggers, or sais. Versatile weapons, they were easy to wield for blocking, hooking a sword or staff, punching, and yes, stabbing if need be. Briefly, Shannon tried short swords and longer swords but came back to the sais.

"You still must be able to wield a sword if it's the only weapon available to you," Loki advised.

Much to Shannon's pleased amazement, he persisted in helping her learn, especially every time she tried a new weapon, but left the sparring sessions to Mist. Loki seemed to support her acquisition of skills as fast as possible. That he wasn't at all threatened by her successes, as past violent experiences had led her to expect with Trent, continued to surprise Shannon.

"I know, but if given a preference, I'd like to focus on getting better with these. They feel more natural in my hands than the other weapons I've tried." She twirled the sais, enjoying the balance and spin of them.

"We can work for a few hours each day to get you familiar with a range of weapons," Mist suggested. "You should also learn the basics of the bow and throwing knives in addition to the sword. Even guns, due to their frequency on Midgard. But then, focus the rest of the training day on improving your skill with the sais."

"Does that sound reasonable, Loki?" Shannon asked.

"Yes, that's a good plan," he agreed. "Let's go with the sais today as we need to stop early. We'll require time to get ready for the celebration the king and queen are hosting tonight, to introduce you to the people of Asgard." After kissing Shannon, Loki nodded to Mist and retreated to his usual position, leaning against a pillar where he watched them train.

"I have to say, my princess, I am thrilled to have you join the royal family," Mist murmured as they moved into their initial warm-up. She was using a long sword and a dagger today.

"Why's that?"

"I have never seen our prince so content. Loki's still his mischievous self. I don't know how he could be otherwise, but unlike in the past four hundred years, ever since the last war with the Sidhe, there is no edge to it."

Shannon was pretty content herself, she had to admit. The more time she spent with Loki, the deeper she fell for him. With the bond wide open, she sensed a depth of caring that amazed her. Flashes of pride and warmth surged through their connection when he complimented her on her increasing proficiency with weapons, hand-to-hand techniques, and her own abilities. And every time, the scars binding her heart cracked open wider, and the glow within her chest grew a little brighter, a little warmer.

It didn't hurt that his eyes never seemed to stray. No matter what the Valkyrie were wearing, which was sometimes very little, every time she glanced over at him, his eyes were on her. Regardless of the glares she occasionally got from some of the women and a few men in the palace hallways, or how they attempted to get his attention, his gaze stayed on her. He never flirted, except with her, and then he was completely outrageous at times, pulling her into closets or an empty room to have his way with her.

Not that she minded.

A fierce grin stretched her lips wide as she thwarted Mist's first flurry of attacks and spun to make one of her own, going for the Valkyrie's thigh and neck.

"Plus, you are a badass!" With a laugh, Mist blocked and returned to attack Shannon in a fast series of moves.

Too busy laughing at her comment, Shannon almost missed the swipe of Mist's sword. At the last second, she caught it with the sai lying along her forearm and intercepted the warrior's dagger thrust with a shield of air.

"What are you doing?" boomed a voice like thunder across the training ground. Thor landed with a loud thud and a spray of gritty sand, pushing Mist away from Shannon. "You could hurt my nephew!"

"Thor! I'm training! Your nephew is fine, damn it!"

Chapter 33

CAT IS OUT OF THE BAG

Fuck. Shannon's eyes closed, her jaw clenching when she realized what she'd just shouted. Although she was ready to tell Loki, she hadn't yet found the right time. When she wasn't training with Mist and Loki, Frigga was teaching her about the realms and customs of Asgard. Somewhat reluctantly, Shannon had agreed to the formal introduction ceremony as Loki's consort and to take vows to Asgard as a member of the royal family. She wasn't sure she was ready for that commitment, but as Frigga had pointed out, she was going to start showing any day now and the ceremony would quiet any controversy when her pregnancy was revealed. Better to get ahead of it.

But ugh. She'd planned to ask Frigga's help later today in planning something, wanting it to be special when she told Loki. Not blurting it out like she'd just done.

So much for that idea.

"I'm sorry, little sister. It scared me when I saw—"

Shannon tuned Thor out as she faced Loki. He was staring at her, eyes wide, mouth open.

Without looking at Thor, she punched his shoulder, hard.

"Ouch," he complained.

"Thanks a lot, Thor," she grumbled, before making her way over to Loki.

He remained as still as a statue. His pupils were dilated, only a small ring of green still showing as he blinked rapidly. Butterflies—no dragonflies (those huge Jurassic-era ones) flew, spun, and bounced off Shannon's insides in a tumultuous tumble. A chill coated her cooling skin and air seemed in short supply. Maybe he wasn't happy about their baby?

When she reached Loki, his hands went to her abdomen hesitantly, almost like he was scared to touch her.

<*Our baby?*> His mental voice was barely a whisper. <*We... we have a baby?*>

<*Yes, our son.*>

Loki fell to his knees, wrapping his arms around her middle and pressing his face to her abdomen. It took a minute for Shannon to understand what she was hearing with his words garbled by overwhelming input from the bond. Chaotic flashes of multiple emotions tangled and spun, changing too fast for her to track.

<*Oh Norns, I love you. My child, our boy. How am I so lucky? By the Nine, I love you. Our baby. Oh Norns, our baby boy.*>

Dizzy, her legs almost collapsed, and she locked her knees as she blew out a shaky breath. She slid her hands into Loki's dark locks as he kissed her abdomen over and over. Tears welled, then fell from his eyes.

"I love you, Loki." It scared her a bit to say it out loud. Oh hell, it fucking scared her a lot. Her pulse pounded in her ears, acid climbing her throat. The last time she'd said those words—

In a surprisingly fast move that had her instinctively flinching, he stood, hands sliding up to cup her head as he kissed her senseless. Her nerves were forgotten, the maelstrom of passion swirling between their mental and physical connections. Her head spun and thoughts scattered with the careless abandon of leaves in a stiff autumn breeze.

Behind them, Thor cleared his throat.

Loki lifted his lips from Shannon's as she panted, a brilliant smile on his face. "I love you, darling. I am *ecstatic* at the news." His happiness shone from every pore as he turned them to face his brother.

"Congratulate me, brother! I'm going to be a dad!" Loki shouted. Thor grabbed his brother in a big bear hug, making Loki grunt and laugh. "Maybe don't squeeze me to death before the baby's born."

After releasing him, Thor thumped Loki hard on the back, almost making him stumble. "I can't wait to see what mischief your child causes you!" Thor laughed in his thunderous voice. Eyes gleaming, he turned to Shannon. "I'm sorry, little sister. I didn't realize you hadn't told Loki yet."

With the glint in those pale-blue eyes... Yeah, she didn't believe that apology. At all. She scowled. "I'll remember that when you want me to keep a secret for you, Thor."

He grinned and gave her a much gentler hug than the way he'd manhandled his brother.

"Go find your own woman," Loki told him, punching Thor in the arm.

Thor laughed and released her.

"I'm overjoyed for you both. Now, I'll go tell Father and Mother that they can announce the baby, too!" Thor said. He turned to head into the palace halls.

The wide grin and jaunty step to his walk had Shannon growling. He'd done it on purpose, the big jerk. Damn it. She wasn't sure she wanted the rest of Asgard to know about her pregnancy yet. Hell, she hadn't talked to Loki about it. She hadn't even told her own family yet. Although, it wasn't like someone here was going to race to Earth to tell them ahead of her. Still.

"Thor Odinson!" She sent a narrowly arrowed blast of dense air at him. It knocked him over, and he sprawled face-first in the black sand of the training arena.

With a good-natured chuckle, Thor picked himself back up. "Nice one, sister!" he called with an arm wave as he passed through a white stone archway, exiting the arena.

No one was training. They either smiled outright or tried to hide their grins behind their hands.

"Ugh!" It was all Shannon could do to not stomp her foot.

Loki laughed and wrapped an arm around her. "Yeah, we're done for the day. We'll see you later, Mist."

Amusement dancing in her tricoloured eyes, Mist grinned and gave them a little finger wave.

Loki teleported them to their rooms and sank onto a black leather sofa, pulling his beautiful goddess into his lap. In awe, he couldn't help resting a hand over her still-flat abdomen. Although with what he knew now, perhaps there was the start of a curve under her toned muscle.

Their son. Norns, he was the luckiest bastard ever. They were having a *son*. The words repeated in his head as a constant refrain, and he grappled with the reality of his new future. He wanted to sing, shout, and dance for joy all at once. "When is our baby due, darling?"

"In about eighteen, no... seventeen and a half weeks."

"The night of your transition?" It had to be. No question that this was his child. By the Nine. Their son.

"That's what Frigga thinks since you *told* me gods couldn't get mortals pregnant without conscious magic, and I was on the pill. Clearly, *that's* useless against magic. Unless you are going to tell me you were trying to get me pregnant the first time at the theatre?" She raised an eyebrow.

He lifted his hands in surrender. "Honestly, I swear I did not deliberately get you pregnant. Not that I am not thrilled that you are, but it wasn't intentional."

Although, if he'd known it was possible this early in her immortality, he would have absolutely done everything in his power to get her pregnant and keep her with him—probably best he not admit that. While the more enlightened, rational side of him knew it'd be wrong, darker, more primal instincts roared with proprietary satisfaction to have his mate tied more closely to him, to have his child growing inside her, evidence of his claim, his possession. Yeah, he fucking *loved* that he'd gotten her pregnant.

Shannon narrowed her eyes slightly, and Loki kept his expression mild—a thread of concern welling. Had he'd somehow given his thoughts away?

"Frigga figures I must have a fertility god in my background, given how my transition went. According to her, after that, she would have expected me to be pregnant."

Huh. That was what he got for not paying enough attention to childhood lessons. Probably something he should have known. He wrapped his arms around her again, fingers spread on her abdomen. *Mine.* "Why didn't you tell me earlier? How did Thor know before me?"

Had she worried he wouldn't be delighted? Yggdrasil's roots! This couldn't be more perfect if he'd planned it. Shannon finally told him she loved him, *and* she carried his child. Tonight, she'd formally take vows to protect Asgard.

Surely, she'd never leave him now.

"I only found out when the healers did the genetic profile. Thor brought me to Asgard and was with me." She looked away and crossed her arms, holding her elbows with her hands. "I just... I just needed a bit of time to come to terms with it. We haven't known each other all that long, Loki—barely more than three weeks in actual time spent together."

Was he moving too fast in asking her to take the vows to Asgard? He wanted her acknowledged as his consort, protected by the shelter of the royal family so those few they'd encountered—the ones who didn't like to hear he was no longer available—would stop their attempts at getting his attention and no demon-spawned fool would try to flirt with her. Thor had already rescued several idiots from Loki's temper and newly possessive instincts. Killing his own people was frowned on, after all, but he had no patience for those who eyed Shannon lasciviously when they thought he wasn't looking. The rumour mill was *not* working fast enough to ensure they knew she was his soulmate.

And okay, he'd wanted her focused on Asgard so she wouldn't feel the need to return to her career, to return to Midgard where she wasn't safe. But their child changed the equation. A thrill shot through him with a savage sense of satisfaction. She was *his*. Motherhood would tie her to him more effectively than any commitment to Asgard.

Loki caressed the soft skin of her abdomen, cupping her cheek to turn her back to him. "Of course, I can understand that, my love. You've had a lot thrown at you in a short amount of time, a lot of changes."

The wariness in her hazel eyes disappeared and she smiled, a soft curl of her lips, as she watched his fingers move over her skin. "Odin says our son is strong."

"He would know. Father and Mother must be ecstatic to have their first grandchild to spoil." Loki grinned, imagining their reactions.

"Thor's mortal children don't count?" Her voice was perplexed, a frown furrowing her brow as she met his gaze.

It had to be confusing to her, and he hurried to explain. "Since Thor has no plans to give them Asgardian food, no. Odin and Frigga haven't travelled to Midgard for centuries, so unless Thor changes his mind, Mother and Father will never meet them. Mortal lives are short, the equivalent to only seventeen years here if they live to the age of seventy on Midgard."

He winced, thinking of the mortal children he'd had in the past. Despite how he'd loved them, their lives were the flickers of glowflies, here today and gone tomorrow. Even knowing that, he'd mourned each of their deaths.

And Sigyn had died before... but he wouldn't think about that now. Not given the joy of this day. There was no way he'd spoil this happiness with that memory.

Shannon and he were having an immortal son... Loki swallowed as emotion choked him. Their child would live as long as Shannon, and hopefully, outlive them. The realization had him blinking back tears.

His voice was a little hoarse as he continued to explain. "There is also no guarantee they have enough god genes to become immortal. The magic used to allow mortals and immortals to interbreed is unpredictable. It's not as simple as the current Midgardian understanding, according to Mendelian genetics."

"So they could end up being mortals with powers if they don't have enough genes?"

"Yes. If you look through Midgardian mythology, you'll find references to them. Before Father and Mother found each other, Odin had numerous mortal demigod children."

"Are you talking about Hercules and Perseus?"

He smiled. Of course, those two would come to mind. "Yes, they were mortal sons of Odin whose legends survived into tales for the ancient Greeks to incorporate into their mythology as sons of Zeus. Both were dead before Thor and I were born, but as you still know the names today, you can imagine it is no small decision to give a mortal food of the gods when the outcome is so unpredictable. Their lasting impact on Midgardian history and culture has to be considered."

"But you treated it as no big deal when you gave mead to my friends and me."

Damn. She would pick up on that, wouldn't she? His goddess was too clever sometimes. He kissed her, hoping to get her thinking about something else.

Her hands rose to his cheeks as she leaned away. "Wait, stop distracting me. Why did you give me the mead when you knew the risks?" Shannon held his gaze as she waited for his answer.

Sighing, he admitted the truth. "Darling, you are my soulmate. I had faith the Norns knew what they were doing when they paired us. As it's extremely rare for someone to have enough genes to activate, the risk to your friends was infinitesimally small."

And he'd been desperate to prove she truly was his soulmate.

"That's logical, I suppose."

Loki raised an eyebrow. Of course, it was logical.

"So you didn't birth an eight-legged horse, a world serpent, a giant wolf, or the Goddess of Death?" she teased, eyes full of mischief.

He snorted and rolled his eyes. "Bloody hell. Those legends are going to haunt me forever. Midgardians are hilarious with the way they get reality and stories intertwined." He kissed her when she laughed. "Remember what I told you about trusting information from myths and legends? The so-called *world serpent* is one of the Shen, a dragon god, and not nearly as large as portrayed in the stories, unless you count his ego... although Ao Run *is* far better than his older brothers, the ones you met."

Shannon wrinkled her nose.

Loki bopped her on that cute button and continued, "The horse, Sleipnir, is a nuckalavee or fae demon horse, and the wolf, Fenrir, isn't a wolf at all, but a Cŵn Cyrff hellhound. Both are dark Sidhe, Unseelie, and part of the Wild Hunt of the Aos Sí. Obviously, *none* of them are my children when I'm half Jotun and half Vanir."

She grinned. "And what about the Goddess of Death?"

He sighed. "Hela is the Goddess of Death, or Hades when they are presenting as male, but either way, half Aesir, half Jotun, one of the fire giants, and *no* relation to me as far as I'm aware. They do rule Helheim, the dimensional realm of souls, though."

"Come on. You know you like the stories. You're the God of Stories."

She wasn't giving this up, and he had to admit, he loved her teasing. "They are creative, it's true. But damn, Thor laughed his ass off for centuries when they first started circling." He shook his head. "That the Celts tended to get the details right, and the Norse got it so backwards... I suspect a fellow god was trying to pay me back with some mischief of his or her own in planting the seeds of those stories with the ancient Norse." Frankly, although he had no proof, Loki suspected his brother was behind it. Bloody git.

Chapter 34

WELCOME TO ASGARD

Loki had outdone himself. He'd conjured a gorgeous fitted gold brocade dress with emerald-green velvet trim for Shannon. Her armour provided the cape and gold metallic corset that perfectly complemented the styling and colours of the dress. She'd added smoky eyes in shades of green and gold, then brushed her long hair back over the cape. Emerald-green leather thigh-high boots peeked out the side slits of the dress as she walked from the bedroom toward the door exiting Loki's rooms. Between the rich fabrics, armour, and boots, Shannon felt like the badass princess Mist had called her.

Turning to Loki, she admired his form. He was always sexy to her, but there was something about him in formal court attire that she found breathtakingly attractive—black leather boots and pants, black tunic with woven silver threads, and black cape. His intricate silver armour, with gold inlaid Yggdrasil design and accents, was far more ornate than his everyday Asgardian wear. It made her want to do wicked, wicked things with him.

"I do love the way you think, darling," he purred, with a glint of lust in his eyes. "You, my gorgeous princess, are the breathtakingly sexy one." His eyes lingered on the slits in her dress and her thigh-high boots.

"Gonna have to disagree, my love," she murmured as she ran her hand down his armoured body.

Loki grabbed her wandering fingers. "As much as I want you to continue, Mother and Father will kill me if we are late. They'll never believe it wasn't my fault."

That almost made her want to make him late on purpose.

The look on his face had her laughing. He'd caught that thought. "Very well. I'll behave," she reluctantly agreed.

"How did I get so lucky as to have a goddess as mischievous as I am?" He kissed her hand, tucking it into his elbow as he steered them out of his suite of rooms.

Shannon smirked.

"I was just about to fetch you," Thor boomed as he walked toward them decked out in his own finery of black leather boots and pants like his brother, but a royal-blue ornate silver armour with the inlaid golden Yggdrasil design. It was the first time Shannon had seen Thor dressed in formal court attire. He cleaned up well. "Mother didn't trust you would arrive on time."

"Hey!" Loki protested. "I'll have you know it is my glorious goddess here who was trying to waylay me to make us late. It's not always my fault."

Thor looked at him skeptically, while Shannon snickered.

"Will you please defend my honour?" Loki exclaimed in mock offence.

"I don't know what you are talking about, love." She blinked innocently up at him.

Thor laughed, his amusement echoing down the hallway. "You really are perfectly matched." Thor held out his elbow for her other arm so she could walk escorted between them.

They made their way through the palace to the entrance of the royal auditorium. It was a massive, open-tiered space with brilliant white stone pillars that allowed thousands of Asgardians to see the raised dais and golden thrones. For those farther back, a live image of the dais with Odin and Frigga was projected on some kind of cloud or mist-looking screens hovering in the air in numerous locations. They reminded Shannon of the illusions Loki projected when he wasn't putting any effort into making them solid. She couldn't see any obvious technology, but she'd discovered the distinctions between science, technology, and magic were non-existent in Asgard.

The enormous crowd was boisterous, cheering loudly as they came into sight.

<*This is nuts! They're so loud. How do they even know who I am?*> she asked when she recognized her name. Fear and delight combined to churn in her stomach. It'd be a lot harder to leave after this if things didn't work out between them. Maybe she should have waited longer before accepting this step. What if Loki changed? Trent had been wonderful at the start, too.

<*They love you,*> Loki replied, smiling and waving to the crowd. <*Do you think the Einherjar and Valkyrie haven't been talking about you? Gossip spreads like wildfire here in the capital city, especially when it is about the royal family.*>

Together, they walked through a corridor formed by the palace guard—their bodies creating a path to the dais. Shannon swallowed down the lump growing in her throat. Copying Loki, she waved and smiled at the audience as they approached Odin and Frigga. She couldn't believe how welcoming and excited the crowd seemed to be. Where was the dissent? The objectors who would be present in a human crowd? Despite searching, she saw nothing but joy on their faces.

When they reached the steps of the dais, she curtseyed as Thor and Loki bowed to their father and mother, who'd risen from their thrones.

"Rise." Odin's voice thundered out over the noise of the audience.

Taking her hands, Thor and Loki walked up the steps with her until she was in front of Odin. He'd stepped forward, the thrones and Frigga behind him. The brothers moved away to each side, leaving Odin and Shannon in the centre.

"Shannon Murphy, of the Tuatha Dé Danann, Aos Sí, formerly of Midgard," Odin projected out to the now quiet crowd.

Her pulse pounded, a metallic taste coating her tongue as a cold shiver raised the hair at the back of her neck. Formerly? She hadn't been expecting that. What did he mean? She wasn't giving up her home! She narrowed her eyes slightly, hoping she wasn't doing something she'd regret. She barely knew these people. How could she—

A flutter in her abdomen distracted her. She inhaled a shaky breath and released it slowly. Her child deserved the chance to know his heritage, to know his father. Now was *not* the time to freak out or panic. Nothing was wrong, damn it. *Don't screw this up in front of all of Asgard, Shannon. Pull yourself together.*

With another shaky exhale, she inclined her head, as Frigga had instructed when Shannon had practiced the protocol. Frigga had been so patient, teaching Shannon various royal customs so she didn't make a fool of herself.

"Are you soul-bound to my youngest son, Prince Loki?" Odin held her gaze, a small smile on his lips.

"Yes, All-Father," she answered and heard her voice projected throughout the massive space. It was a weird sensation.

There was a moment of pure silence, of shock, and then the crowd roared their approval. Had the rumour mill not included that bit of intelligence, then? It almost made her grin, but she kept the serious expression on her face.

After waiting for the noise to die down slightly, Odin continued. "Do you agree to abide by the royal family's duty to serve in the best interests of Asgard and the Nine Realms?"

"Yes, All-Father." Both Odin and Frigga had taken the time to talk with her about what it meant to be part of the royal family. They weren't figureheads. She'd be expected to pull her weight. As long as they didn't force her to stay if she didn't want to, she was excited about the challenge. A little intimidated, but still, thrilled. Although she had much to learn about Asgard and the other realms, they'd reassured her she'd have lots of time before she needed to represent Asgard on diplomatic missions.

The audience roared again.

Odin patiently waited for them to quiet.

"By the choice of the Norns, who rule fate itself, I, Odin All-Father, bind you to serve Asgard and the Nine Realms. I bid you welcome to our royal family." He placed a delicately branching gold, silver, and diamond tiara on Shannon's head—a symbol of the great world tree Yggdrasil—before kissing her on the forehead. Energy surged into her from the point of contact.

Again, the crowd's approval rippled through the air.

Clasping her fingers, Odin turned her to face the people and held his other hand out to Loki, who joined them.

"Not only have the Norns seen fit to bless us with Princess Shannon, soulmate and consort to Prince Loki. They have also blessed us with the next generation of the royal family, a healthy and strong son. The child of Princess Shannon and Prince Loki's union, our first immortal grandson, will be born in just over four months. Upon his birth, we will rejoice and commemorate with a month of celebrations across the realm!"

Damn. She hadn't expected him to announce it like that. But if she thought the crowd was loud before, it was deafening at Odin's proclamation. Asgardians seemed to love their royal family. This wasn't the odd love-hate for most current Earth monarchies. Instead, the wave of happiness and excitement rippling through the masses was an almost visible energy. There were tears of joy, people hugging, cheering, and jumping. Shannon's eyes watered at the acceptance and enthusiasm washing over her. It was indescribable.

Gods, she hoped she could live up to their expectations.

Chapter 35

SHELL GAME

The energy of the crowd was intoxicating, and Shannon seemed to glow as the crowd shouted her name. Still, Loki kept an eye out as he and Thor guided her between the rows of guards and exited the auditorium. His instincts were humming, prickling at his nape, but he couldn't identify any specific threats. When they reached the large feast hall, string musicians played and servers walked around with trays of beverages, while the hall slowly filled with the Asgardian elite, the powerful gods and goddesses of the realm, and the skilled Valkyrie and Einherjar, their top warriors.

Together with his brother, Loki led Shannon out to the attached gardens. Odin and Frigga joined them with drinks as they waited for the guests to arrive.

"Have you thought of names yet?" Odin asked, lips twitching in the corners.

"Odin!" Frigga chided, then smiled fondly.

"Well, considering Loki just found out today, no, Father, we haven't," Shannon replied with a grin. His smile broadened at her words.

"Thor makes a good name," Thor teased.

Loki rolled his eyes—as if—and punched his brother in the shoulder. Dickhead could name his own kid after himself if he wanted an ego trip.

"Boys!" Frigga scolded, sharing an exasperated look with Shannon while shaking her head.

Shannon's laughter rippled through Loki, sending bubbles of light into his soul. Her eyes sparkled as she asked about the various gods and goddesses entering the hall. While Odin kept her entertained by telling a story involving a group of five Asgardians that Loki knew tended to be pompous idiots, Loki scanned the gathering, trying to pick out what had his senses jangling. Something wasn't—

<*I love you.*> Shannon squeezed his fingers as she talked with Thor and Odin about her training.

Loki's heart leapt at her words. <*Darling, I love you endlessly.*> He resisted the urge to steal her away for the rest of the evening. His mind still buzzed with unexpected joy. He could scarcely believe she carried his child. Fuck, he was so fortunate. Beyond his wildest hopes. Unable to resist his instincts, he turned her so he could cradle her abdomen and the small bulge of their baby. Norns, he couldn't wait for it to grow.

She cuddled against him, her hands over his. <*I'm very grateful for the way your family has accepted me.*>

<*They are grateful you've taken me on, my love. Of course, they think you are wonderful.*> He kissed the top of her head.

The musicians stopped and the elite formed a corridor to the far end of the room that held the royal family's table. As all eyes turned to them, Loki searched faces and shifted Shannon between him and Thor. Together, they led Shannon through the cheering crowd, getting good-natured ribbing from some, and accepting respectful nods from others. None ogled Shannon... wise, given he scowled at a few faces he'd growled at over the last week when they'd flirted with her. Still, nothing stood out or explained the tension singing in his spine.

After Odin and Frigga took their chairs at either end, Loki seated Shannon between him and his brother. Whatever was bothering Loki, he knew Thor would protect Shannon with his life.

"Let the feast begin!" thundered Odin.

Servers entered with large trays of roast auroch, grilled skewers of fowl, and the current late summer vegetable harvest of corn, tubers, beans, and squash. Frigga had arranged for Mist and Kara to sit across from Shannon, giving her some familiar faces to talk with, but Thor had also invited a few of the warriors he and Loki considered friends. He needed to remember to thank his brother for that as he hadn't taken the time to introduce Shannon to very many Asgardians yet.

"Have you met our friends Roskva and Sigrdrifa on the training pitch, little sister?" Thor asked as he introduced the two Valkyrie sitting beside Mist and Kara.

"I haven't had that pleasure." Shannon nodded to each of them.

"Sig and Ros are fierce foes on the battlefield. We've fought together many times," Thor said.

"Meh, Ros isn't that tough, Thor. She just looks pretty while doing it," scoffed Thjalfi, the silver-haired, blue-eyed male on the other side of Thor who more often than not, managed to get himself in trouble... okay, perhaps Loki instigated the trouble much of the time.

His twin, Roskva, rolled her eyes. "Ignore my foolish brother, Princess. Thjalfi wouldn't know fierce if it smacked him upside the head."

Shannon laughed at their taunts, and then Thor introduced Vidar. Loki wasn't as familiar with the Einherjar. Twice as old as Thor and Loki, he hadn't gotten into teenage hijinks with them the way the twins had. Nor had Loki had occasion to conduct a mission with him, although he knew Thor had recently gone to Niflheim with him. Vidar wasn't particularly boisterous, but he seemed polite enough. Still, Loki frowned at him. The warrior was an odd choice. Why did Thor invite him when there were lots of Einherjar they knew much better?

"You seem very familiar for some reason." Shannon frowned at Thjalfi.

Eyebrows raised, the rogue smirked at her. "Now I know you aren't making a pass at me, Princess," he teased, eyes glinting. "Soulmates have eyes only for each other."

Loki snorted and laid his hand on Shannon's, glaring at Thjalfi. "You got that right. Stop your flirting, hradr."

Shannon met my gaze, then looked back at Thjalfi. "Hradr? Speedy? Fast?"

Loki nodded, encouraging her with his smile. His lovely goddess had both beauty and brains. "A nickname. Thjalfi and Roskva joined my band a couple of years ago."

Recognition lit up her expression. "You're the drummer, John Olive! Oh... then that would make Ros..."

Roskva had long, blond hair, instead of auburn, and her face was more rounded, with fuller lips than the leaner-looking Beth Olive, the mortal image of the musician who played keyboards and joined Loki in vocals. Would Shannon figure it out?

"Keyboard?" She looked at Loki for confirmation.

He smiled. "My clever girl. What do you think Roskva's abilities are?"

"Can an earth elemental change their appearance the way I manipulate plant growth?"

Thjalfi smiled as he nodded. "Our princess is clever, not just beautiful. Damn, but you are a lucky bastard, Loki."

"Yes, love, they can. It's possible you can as well, although please don't try it with being pregnant. We don't want you manipulating your body right now, just in case," Loki warned her gently. Even the thought of her attempting it now had him shuddering.

"Huh. Something to try later, then," she reassured him.

The musicians started playing. Good. Except for the one blisteringly hot dance when she'd won the bet, Loki hadn't had a chance to dance with his beautiful soulmate. He rose, holding his hand out to her. "Darling, shall we start the dancing so everyone may enjoy?"

She quirked an eyebrow, confusion in her hazel eyes.

<As this feast is in our honour, it's our role to start the dancing,> he reminded her.

<Ah, of course.> "I would love to."

Taking his hand, she stood and followed him to the clear area in the centre of the room. He didn't hesitate to tug her into his body, revelling in the way she moved against him as he led the waltz. Other couples filled the dance floor after a few minutes, but Loki didn't release her. Norns, she was perfection in his arms. When Thor swept her away at the end of the song, Loki growled. That big oaf better not step on her toes, damn him.

But when he went to reclaim her, she was stolen by Odin. There seemed to be a conspiracy to keep Shannon parted from him. No sooner was one song finished than another would start, with a new partner whisking her away and thwarting Loki's attempts to regain her hand. Despite trying to keep an eye on her, he lost her in the crowd as he danced with Frigga.

The song ended and his mother chuckled. "Go find her, darling. You're going to be distracted until you do."

Loki murmured his apologies and set out through the twirling couples. But no matter where he searched, he couldn't spot her. The creeping worry plaguing him all evening shifted to alarm when he circled the dance floor twice and couldn't find her. When he made his way to the table, she wasn't there either.

Tension vibrating in his limbs, he snapped, "Where is Shannon?" to Thor, Roskva, and Kara, all sitting at the table.

They stood, scanning the crowd. Roskva and Kara set out through the room to search as Thjalfi strolled up and frowned. "What's going on?"

Loki grabbed him. "Where is Shannon?"

Eyes widening, Thjalfi pointed back the way he'd come. "Dancing with Vidar."

Loki spun, searching the dancers.

No Vidar.

No Shannon.

Chapter 36

A SECOND TOO LATE

Dancing with Loki had been an absolute feast. Light on his feet, he'd led Shannon with firm direction and expert skill. With no worry about steps or rhythm, she relaxed and enjoyed herself. Her love. Her soulmate. The thought still shook her. Loki kept her tucked against his tall, athletic frame. In complete harmony, they'd moved as one. Every so often, he'd raised her palm to plant a kiss on it, sending a delightful shiver through her.

If only the others hadn't stolen her away. Not that she truly minded dancing with Thor, Odin, or Thjalfi. But when Vidar took her hand, she had to fight an uncomfortable prickle that broke out on her skin. What was so off-putting about him? He wasn't rude or loud. He didn't flirt but held her at a distance. Still, she couldn't look him in the eye and talk like she had with the others. Their conversation stalled.

Too busy trying to control the needle-like sensation at his touch, Shannon didn't notice they'd moved to the edge of the room until he swept her out into the gardens.

"Wait... what are we doing out here?" she asked as Vidar tugged her around a set of hedges. Shannon stumbled on the edge of her dress, then yanked her hand free.

But the tall, slender Asgardian with dark eyes and close-cropped short hair, so different from most of the heavily muscled Einherjar with their warrior braids, stepped back. His narrow lips pressed together, and he didn't speak. Instead, he glanced behind her.

Before she'd fully turned, Shannon knew she was in trouble. An instinctive air barrier caught the first slash toward her face but as she called her armour and raised her hands defensively, the sight of Isis's face hidden in the shadows shocked her into a moment's hesitation.

Moonlight caught the glint of talons swiping toward Shannon's abdomen as Isis snarled, "No way is that fucking bastard getting his happily ever after."

Sharp agony stole Shannon's breath as her armour covered her from neck to thigh a second too late. She didn't have time to figure out how bad it was. She was too busy fending off the six-inch black talons as Isis attacked. Gods, what she'd give for her sais or even a sword. Keeping Isis from taking out her eyes or any other vulnerable spot took every bit of her meagre training.

<*Loki!*>

Backing up, Shannon tried to get space between them. But Isis was relentless.

<*Loki!*>

Desperately, Shannon shouted through their mental bond, unable to get more out between the ferocity of Isis's attack. The distraction cost her. Stabbing at Shannon's leg then swiping up towards her face, Isis flayed open Shannon's cheek. It was only the last-minute jerk of her head and an air deflection that saved her eye.

"They're coming. We have to leave now." Vidar spoke from his position where the hedge turned a corner towards the feast hall doors.

"I'll be back. Enjoy your last days, Shannon," Isis snarled and stepped back, nodding to him. Panting, Shannon watched in shock as a swirl of energy surrounded Vidar and Isis. In the next moment, they disappeared.

With a bellow, Loki rounded the corner, Thor, Thjalfi, Roskva, Kara, and Mist right behind him. Shannon's knees weakened, black creeping in at the edges of her sight.

Chapter 37

IDUN'S APPLES

Loki roared, lashing out with his power to stop Isis and Vidar from teleporting away. But they'd already disappeared and his energy crackled through empty space. Racing to Shannon's side, he caught her as she collapsed.

His heart stopped. Blood poured from her cheek, the bone visible, but her hands had grabbed her abdomen. "No... Norns, no... please," he murmured, pressing a thumb to her torc to retract her armour. Horror froze him as the red ruin of her dress and abdomen came into view.

Their child!

"Healer hall," he gritted out before teleporting Shannon there, knowing Thor would pass on the message. "Healer Moja!" he shouted even as he strode towards an alcove with Shannon in his arms. Warm blood soaked his hands and the stench of copper filled his nose. *Please... please... Norns, please.* The calm, green-smocked healer was there before he laid Shannon on a sensor bed.

The beam washed over Shannon's body, highlighting the jagged tears in her abdomen and the blood flooding the bed in a red river. Moja's fingers flew over the holographic pad. As Loki watched, scarcely able to breathe, Shannon's muscle and tissue began knitting back together.

"She'll be fine, Loki," the diminutive healer promised.

"What about our baby?"

"You son is okay. A little rambunctious perhaps, with the adrenaline racing through Shannon's system, but it won't hurt him."

Loki staggered, his knees weakening before another healer pushed him down into a chair beside the bed where Moja continued to work on Shannon. Over the next hour, Moja sealed up the four slashes that had cut Shannon open diagonally from ribs to hipbone and just missed her belly button. They'd gone deep enough to nick her liver by her ribs—the hardest and longest repair—but turned shallower farther down and hadn't penetrated all the way through the muscle of her abdomen by the time they were over Shannon's womb.

But the intent was clear. Isis had tried to kill Shannon and their child. And she'd come far too close to success. An inch deeper... he shuddered.

Unbidden, the memory surfaced before he could halt it. Sigyn's blue eyes blank with death, mouth still open in a soundless scream. Her blond hair sticky and streaked with darkest red in a halo around her ravaged, bloody body. The story of her suffering told in the bruises, bitemarks, and foul fluids polluting her nakedness. And the ultimate insult left her womb raggedly slashed open with their daughter's tiny, dismembered form cast like horrific dice upon the Unseelie's sacrificial stones.

His fists clenched. He would *not* lose Shannon. Would not lose another child. It was not happening. If he had to surround Shannon with guards until he hunted down that vicious bitch, Isis, he would. No longer would the fact that she was his sister-in-law protect her. Not after going after Shannon.

And Vidar... that traitor would pay.

Loki's eyes met Thor's. His brother had arrived shortly after Loki, a silent show of support. Frigga and Odin had both been in, but waited outside, not wanting to crowd the space.

Thor nodded. "We will hunt them down. We won't stop until we catch them. I promise, Loki."

When Shannon woke, her abdomen and cheek were tender but not the fiery agony of before. Still, her hands flew to her abdomen. "Our baby... is our baby okay?" Loki squeezed her in a tight hug, and she gasped, pushing at his arms. "I need to breathe."

He shuddered but loosened his hold. "Sorry... sorry. Yes, our son is fine. I just... that was a little too close, Shannon. Don't do that again."

She snorted. "Sure. I'll get right on telling your psychotic sister-in-law to attack you instead, shall I?"

Loki lifted his head, tears in his green eyes, and Shannon cringed at her nasty words. Isis had scared her, but using Loki as a target wasn't okay. "I'm sorry," she murmured, cupping his cheek. "I didn't mean that."

Loki nuzzled her hand. "You're right, darling. It is my fault she attacked you."

Shannon scowled. "Hell no, it isn't. You are not responsible for her choices, Loki. What you did was an accident. It's nowhere near the same."

"Still, you should never have been caught without weapons. I'll modify your armour to create them." He took a shaky breath, then kissed her fingers. "I'm so sorry."

She smiled and slumped back into the bed, her eyelids drooping. Fuck, she was tired. "That would be good."

"Okay," Thor interrupted. "Now that the mushy stuff is over"—Loki punched him on the shoulder—"Healer Moja says you can leave as long as you eat one of Idun's apples to give your healing a boost." Thor smirked as he handed a familiar golden apple to Shannon. "No training tomorrow, but after that, she says it's fine as long as you rest when you get tired and don't overdo it."

Shannon bit into the fruit that was an unexpected mix of cherry and apple. She offered Loki a bite as she chewed, eyes closed. Gods, she could sleep for a damn week.

"No, love. You eat it. It has a boost of vitamins, minerals, and specific energies that are geared towards immortal metabolisms. I'm not the one healing from four gashes to her abdomen and a cheek split open to the bone."

Shannon's eyes flew open, and her hand dropped back to her belly. "You are sure our baby is okay?"

Loki smiled. "Yes, he's fine. He'll be even better when you *finish your apple*." He eyed her until she took another big bite and chewed.

While she ate, Loki told her about everyone who'd come to visit her. She might have expected Odin and Frigga, but that Mist, Kara, Roskva, Thjalfi, and Sigrdrifa had come too had warmth curling around her heart. Her jaw dropped when he mentioned Heimdall had popped in briefly.

"Heimdall came to see me?"

Loki nodded. "Yes. He's furious that Isis and Vidar escaped his sight and seem to have escaped Asgard. He doesn't know how Isis got to Asgard, either. Vidar is a teleporter, but perhaps he has broader powers than he's made known."

Shannon finished her apple, not quite as sleepy as before. "As much as I appreciate Healer Moja and Asgardian medicine, I'd love to get out of here."

Loki stood. "Agreed." He scooped her up in his arms. "But you are relaxing for the rest of today and tomorrow. Healer's orders so don't give me grief. If you are a good girl, I'll give you your next charm that I'd planned to give you at the end of the feast."

In the next moment, they were in Loki's rooms.

"Sofa or bed?"

"Sofa. Where's my charm?"

Loki smirked. "Did you miss the part about being a good girl?" He opened a palm to reveal a delicate golden tree, complete with fruit and leaves, that matched her tiara... Yggdrasil, the world tree. "Rest the way Healer Moja wants you to, and I'll give it to you as soon as she clears you. Deal?"

Shannon huffed. "I suppose. If I can't have my charm, then how about you tell me more about the realms." If she was stuck resting, she might as well be learning, because sure as water ran down to the sea, Isis was coming for her again. This time, Shannon would be ready.

Chapter 38

RUTHLESS SCIENCE

With teeth-gritted determination, Shannon resumed training and learning. Building on what she already knew, Loki taught her the fundamentals of Asgardian science and technology. The more she understood, the better she could defend herself and her child. That treacherous capricious goddess wasn't besting her again.

"Since your field of science is living things, what do you know about what you'd call physics?" Loki asked when they sat down for breakfast on the garden terrace off the bedroom.

"Well, I took the usual year of introductory physics during my bachelor's degree. But I didn't need additional training beyond that."

"What did they cover?"

Shannon took a bite of the fluffy mushroom, some kind of green similar to spinach, and cheese omelette Loki had made from the eggs of a local waterfowl. Asgardian foods, she'd discovered, were made with many similar ingredients to what she was used to on Earth, although they were closer to heirloom versions. Still, her god did love to pamper her and made sure she ate regularly with dishes he prepared in the small kitchen nook within his suite of rooms. She enjoyed another bite as she considered his question. Her first year of university was seventeen years ago. Damn, that was a long time ago now.

"Hmm... Newton's laws of motion, momentum, and gravity. We covered Einstein's theories of relativity."

Loki fed her a bite of bacon, and she nipped his fingertips before kissing them.

His lips twitched at her playfulness. "What about quantum physics, subatomic particles?"

"Yeah, we had an introduction to that, as well as electricity and magnetism."

"Have you heard of string theory?"

"Heard of it, but I don't recall the details."

"It's the idea that the subatomic particles Midgardian physicists are trying to identify and understand, like electrons, gravitons, photons, quarks, and others, are not individual points, but rather ribbons of energy, or strings, that have different orientations and vibrations."

"Okay, yes, that sounds familiar."

"These vibrations occur along different dimensions, not just the three spatial dimensions and time that are easy to perceive. Some of these other dimensions can be considered like a webbed field the strings attach to, such as one they have named the Higgs field that gives mass to particles. Depending on which types of dimensional connection points they have, their orientation and specific vibrations influence the characteristics of the different ribbons. For example, photon ribbons that have no mass do not connect to the Higgs field dimensional matrix."

With a wave of his hand, Loki created a silver grid in the air, floating in a single flat plane. He added a green grid floating above, then a blue grid below, so it appeared as three parallel flat grids of different colours.

"If these are three different dimensions, each flat like a piece of paper, if you were also flat and tiny, you would only be able to perceive one of these dimensions, right?" He added a miniature Shannon crawling along one grid.

She laughed. "Yes, I'm following you."

"Now imagine there are strings that connect the different dimensions." Gold strings shot up, breaking the plane of all three floating grids. Some strings were straight lines that went through all three grids. Others, he'd made into loops joining the grids, and the remaining were wavy or irregular.

He positioned the miniature of her beside one string where it came out of the grid next to it. “From your perspective on the grid, each string appears like a single point on the grid, right?”

“Yes.”

“That is the perspective of Midgardian physicists viewing subatomic particles as points, where they perceive one or a few of their properties depending on which dimensions they see, such as its spin, mass, or even spatial location. But if I were to expand my image”—Loki added more grids at different angles to the first three, creating a web of grids in the space above them, with the strings penetrating and linking the different grids in all kinds of ways—“they are missing the full scope.”

She traced a fingertip along a string. “So, there are many more dimensions than they are perceiving, and this limitation means they don’t see the complete picture of how different strings interact with different matrix fields like mass, energy, magnetism, and gravity?”

Loki gave her a pleased smile. “Exactly.”

“Okay, so Asgardian science perceives all of these dimensions, and thus the full range of the interactions?” As she returned to her seat and picked up her fork to resume eating, the charms on her bracelet jingled, and she smiled down at the miniature Yggdrasil Loki had added to it the morning she’d been cleared to resume training.

“Yes, darling. With the ability to perceive the entirety of the ribbons that make up our reality, from their smallest forms to greater interwoven structures, we can manipulate their connections, their energies, and dimensional structures, depending on our affinities for different ribbons.”

Loki expanded the floating structure so the small section he’d shown her now appeared as a miniature version of itself, a cluster of strings in a larger overall fractal model, with repeating clusters of different types, with various degrees of connection. It reminded her of cosmic web images or brain neuron clusters.

“You’ve expanded the model up from subatomic particles to atoms? Depicting the elements of the periodic table?”

“Right you are, my clever darling.”

A thrill shot through her. Still, she didn’t fully understand how they could perceive it all, but even her rudimentary grasp of it felt like a breakthrough. “When you conjure something, how does that work?”

"Our bodies and minds are not separate from this interconnected web of multi-dimensional reality. It weaves through us and makes us what we are. I use those connections to transfer some of my energy to manipulate the subatomic ribbons into new woven elemental combination clusters that then create the item I am conjuring."

"So it's your energy that limits how much you can conjure?"

"Yes. What you call magic is the ability to manipulate specific forms of energy or subatomic ribbons within us. These abilities interweave into our genetic structure in different ways, which gives each immortal unique abilities. Individual immortals have different reservoirs of energy, which are naturally maintained by sufficient rest and nutrition. The older the immortal, the faster their energy reservoirs recharge. Those immortals who are gods and goddesses have the greatest reservoirs, with additional ways of replenishing those internal stores, such as I can with stories, music, sex, or chaos."

As they continued to eat, she considered what she'd learned so far. "Okay, how does the telepathy between us work?"

Loki smiled, picked up her hand, and kissed her fingers. "That, my darling, is easier explained by building on what I've already told you and adding in a related theory Midgardians have discovered. Are you familiar with Einstein's spooky action at a distance, or quantum entanglement?"

"Isn't that the idea that subatomic particles can be linked across great distances, so something that affects one also affects the other instantaneously?"

"Yes, love, exactly. Now, given what I've explained to you about subatomic particles actually being ribbons of energy that weave across multiple dimensions, what do you think a soul bond is?"

Her eyes widened. "Wow, really? We are woven together, sharing ribbons of energy across multiple dimensions?"

"That's my smart goddess." Loki turned her hand over to kiss her palm.

She shivered in reaction. "You are distracting."

He laughed and kissed her palm again.

"Loki! I'm trying to learn!" she scolded, even as she couldn't help but smile at him.

"Remember, there are many more dimensions than just the physical spatial dimensions, darling. Our bond is woven across some of those other dimensions, so the perception of distance is a false idea that doesn't account for additional dimensions. Our bond allows a small manipulation of the shared energy ribbons between us to transfer thoughts and feelings. Telepathy is an ability some immortals have, but they will always require the use of far more personal energy to read someone's mind or share thoughts than it takes us with our bond. If I physically make contact with someone to form the connection, I can read their mind or implant ideas, but it requires a lot of energy on my part pushed through that physical contact."

Turning her hand over to capture his long fingers with hers, she drew his hand to her lips, kissing each of his fingers before sucking one into her mouth. Loki's eyes darkened as his pupils expanded, and she gave him a smirk, releasing his finger.

He opened his mouth to speak, and she put a finger over his lips. "How do my powers work? Why do I manipulate the four natural elements?"

He cocked his head to the side, considering. "I've been meaning to test that. Since you aren't able to conjure, teleport, or create illusions, as those abilities are tied to manipulating all types of subatomic ribbons to a more generalized degree, it's likely your abilities are tied to the manipulation of specific clusters that comprise different elements."

"Specific elements... you mean specific elements of the periodic table?"

"Yes, darling. Consider that water is composed of one molecule of oxygen and two molecules of hydrogen. Air also consists of oxygen and hydrogen, as well as nitrogen and carbon. The simplest form of fire requires oxygen, hydrogen as a fuel, and energy in the form of heat. The Earth's crust and growing things are primarily carbon-hydrogen bonds, with nitrogen, silicon, and sulphur."

"Oh! I see what you are saying. Maybe I simply manipulate oxygen and hydrogen in various ways that allow me to manipulate what we call the four natural elements of water, air, fire, and earth."

"If we test you to see which types of basic element clusters you can manipulate, we'll have a better understanding of the range of your powers to help you develop them more."

Shannon was almost jumping in her seat, so excited to understand what she could do.

"Okay! Bring it on!"

Loki laughed.

The rest of the day was spent with Loki conjuring basic elements, or elemental combinations for her to try to manipulate. Her head pounded and her muscles trembled by the time they'd gone through not only the periodic table she'd learned but more elements humans hadn't yet discovered.

She flopped back onto his bed as her phone pinged. "So what's the verdict, oh wise sensei?" She swiped it up to check the text message. It was Lynda. Her heart started to beat faster. Was she finally talking to her again?

> LYNDA: —I know I was a bitch at Christmas. Sorry. I'd just lost a big contract. I didn't mean to take it out on you. Drinks on Saturday? The usual place? U can buy the first round since it's my birthday :)

Shit. It was almost mid-March? How the hell had time gone so fast?

Loki chuckled as he lay down beside her.

"You, my beautiful, clever, and talented goddess, can manipulate all the non-metals as we suspected, including gases like fluorine and chlorine. That gives us some offensive abilities to explore. Unfortunately, you don't have any affinities for any metals, or earth elements like magnesium, despite your affinity to metalloids like silicon and arsenic."

"Those gases are so corrosive and toxic." She shuddered, recalling images of mustard gas used during the First World War. "I don't know if I could use those."

Loki rolled over, caging her under him and pinning her with his gaze. "You can't be squeamish. If you are defending yourself from immortals like Isis, you need to be vicious. We have tremendous abilities to heal ourselves and can be very difficult to stop. You *have* to strike first," he insisted.

She wrinkled her nose. "That's pretty horrifying, Loki."

"I want you prepared for *any* eventuality, to protect yourself and our son. You need to be absolutely ruthless if the situation calls for it," he growled sternly, no give in his tone.

His hand caressed the gentle curve of her abdomen, now showing the first distinct signs of pregnancy. Still, his eyes were hard emerald chips as he said, "I won't risk the two of you to sentiment. If you are in danger, strike hard and fast so you can escape." His lips pressed together, a scowl darkening his face. "If you aren't willing to use every weapon available, then you won't be leaving Asgard. You're a target, Shannon."

She narrowed her eyes. She was a godsdamned adult and could go wherever the hell she pleased. How dare he threaten her? "I *will* be leaving Asgard. I need to go spend an evening with Lynda."

The need to repair her friendship was an ache in her heart. Gods, it had been way too long since she'd enjoyed time not thinking about immortals, danger, and this bizzare new life. A simple evening with Lynda would be refreshing. And her baby bump wasn't very noticeable yet. Surely she could hide it to go spend a few hours with her best friend. It wasn't like Isis had her lojacked and knew exactly where she would be or could predict her visit with Lynda.

"*Lynda!*" He rolled his eyes, lips twisting in a sneer. "We haven't caught Isis or Vidar yet. It's *way* too dangerous."

Shannon clenched her fists, restraining the urge to shove at him. "It's her birthday."

"You'd be putting her at risk as well, painting a bull's eye on her back. She doesn't have immortal healing or any abilities to defend herself." He shook his head. "And before you say it, we couldn't bring her to Asgard if she were injured. The Bifrost is dangerous to mortals. Their bodies can't take the strain. Promise me," he demanded, as his gaze burrowed into her, unrelenting and fierce. She couldn't even blink. "Promise me you won't leave Asgard right now. Not until you get more training. It's not safe, Shannon, for you, our child, or her."

This was the dominant, dangerous immortal who had fought on numerous blood-soaked battlefields and defended Asgard for hundreds of years. For the first time, she saw the dark depths of his ruthlessness. His usual mischievous twinkle was gone. This was the Black Prince Asgard's enemies feared to rouse from its slumber. Kara and Mist had mentioned his nickname and lethal reputation, but Shannon had never seen him like this. Although not directed at her, she shivered at the unyielding threat of annihilation in his eyes, even as her pulse pounded a furious tempo at his threat to trap her here.

No fucking way.

Even so, a sinking sensation in her gut came with the realization that she couldn't pull Lynda into this mess. He was right that it was too dangerous for her best friend. No, Shannon would be smart and bide her time. But she *would* learn enough to defend herself and her child, to take back her freedom.

"I won't," she promised, pushing him off her as she rose. Damn him. He was right. There wasn't anything she wouldn't do to defend her child. Isis would *not* defeat her a second time.

Chapter 39

MORE PROTECTION IS BETTER

Why did he agree to this? What the fuck was he thinking? Loki's heart refused to settle as he lifted the flat dark-blue box from the hidden drawer in the bedroom wall. With a touch, the chamber retreated into the stone, appearing as nothing more than a vein in the marble. Keeping the box behind him, he turned to watch Shannon.

She sat on the edge of the bed, fastening the strap of a silver stiletto heel around a slender ankle. "Where will the Bifrost set us down? Harry's movie premiere is in London, right?"

"In the patio of my flat. It's the tallest building around. No one can look down into my gardens to see the Bifrost lights." Plus, it was the most protected place for them to arrive, given the safeguards he had worked around the building.

Although he hadn't told Shannon, Loki's paranoia had gotten a thousand times worse since Isis's attack had almost killed her and their child a few weeks ago. He couldn't save Sigyn and his unborn daughter, but by the Norns, he would *not* let anything happen to Shannon and his son.

Despite their searching, they hadn't located Isis or Vidar. Still, he couldn't get away with locking Shannon in Asgard, as much as he'd like to. Although it was safer than other places, Isis and Vidar had gotten to her here.

But he'd take every possible precaution before bringing Shannon to his friend's red-carpet event.

After helping her stand, he took in the view of his beautiful goddess. Damn, he was a lucky bastard. Long limbs were shown off to perfection in royal blue chiffon. Cut high, the slit of the empire-waisted gown revealed a sexy leg before the fabric curved over the swell of their child. Enraptured, he could spend hours gliding greedy hands over her soft skin and the miracle of their growing baby. Of course, that assumed he wasn't distracted by those sumptuous breasts, so nicely displayed by the square neckline of her gown.

Muffling his groan, Loki fought the impulse to strip off her clothes and take her back to bed. She was safe here in Asgard... okay, safer. Taking her to Midgard was far riskier. More than Isis and Vidar would salivate at capturing or killing Loki's soulmate and child.

He forced a shaky breath, fingers tightening on the box behind his back.

He'd be with her. And Thor was joining them. As were Roskva and Thjalfi. Shannon was gaining skills daily.

It would be okay.

"You are absolutely ravishing, darling. It needs something, though." With his arms outstretched, he presented the dark-blue box and held it for her to open.

Lying on the navy lining was a platinum necklace with a large sapphire teardrop pendant, surrounded by diamonds embedded with protective spells that had taken him a day's energy to craft. It was paired with a set of dangling earrings with a smaller version of the sapphire teardrop surrounded by diamonds and an anklet of diamonds and sapphires that included a powerful tracking spell.

No way was he losing her again.

With Shannon wanting to join him at events on Midgard, Loki had delayed her leaving as long as possible, until he couldn't come up with a reasonable excuse to keep her from coming to Harry's premiere. Not with Thor opening his big mouth about it. Yggdrasil's mighty branches and leaves, it'd been brutal keeping her from visiting her so-called friend Lynda last week. Frankly, he'd be happy if Shannon never saw that mercenary shrew again. After caving in to agreeing to bring Shannon tonight, he'd panicked at the thought of her vulnerability, then strategized ways to keep her as protected as possible.

Short of tying her to his bed.

Fuck. If he thought he'd get away with it, he would. But she'd never put up with that for days on end. Especially if he wasn't there to seduce her.

Constantly, he was torn between his need to protect her, and knowing he couldn't cage her or she'd try to leave him. Not that he'd let her. By the vast Nine Realms, he loved his strong-willed, independent soulmate. Yet her very self-sufficiency terrified him.

Sigyn had also been headstrong, and Loki couldn't—he *wouldn't* let history repeat itself. That loss was still a jagged hole inside him, and while he'd forever mourn the daughter he never got to know, what he'd felt for Sigyn was a pale shadow compared to the interwoven tendrils growing between Shannon and him. Sigyn had been a lover. Shannon was the other half of his soul.

Shannon's pregnancy was a blessing from the Norns. At some point, she'd need to slow down and take it easy. And once their son was born, he was the perfect reason for her to stay in Asgard to care for him. With her already away from her career, it shouldn't be too difficult to convince her to pick it up again once he was older. Perhaps when he turned fifty, the equivalent of a child passing into adolescence on Asgard. She'd have no complications reinventing a mortal identity as two hundred and fifty years would have passed on Midgard. No one would be left to remember the mortal scientist and professor she'd once been. Even better, she'd have decades of training with her abilities and be less vulnerable.

Yes, that was a much more desirable path forward.

Although... Loki wasn't sure he wanted her to pursue her career even then. Too many immortals walked Midgardian soil. Maybe he could keep her busy in Asgard, away from the worst of the other immortal races that might harm her.

Shannon sucked in a breath. "Oh my gods! These are gorgeous, Loki! Thank you," she gushed. Quickly, she removed her charm bracelet, pearl earrings, and necklace and held her long tawny locks off her neck. "Will you put them on for me?"

"I realized"—Loki kissed her slender neck while he fastened the necklace over her hidden torc armour repository and gently inserted the earrings into the holes in her ears—"that other than your charm bracelet, I hadn't given you any jewellery yet. I apologize, darling."

After bending to one knee, he wrapped the anklet around her slender ankle, exposed by the slit in the dress. He fastened the clasp, then slid his hands up her silky leg slowly as he stood.

"Mmm... wicked. Trying to get me hot and bothered before we leave?" She raised an eyebrow, even as a shiver raised the hairs on her arms.

If only he could convince her to stay in bed with him, he'd happily seduce her all evening. "I can't help myself. I can't keep my hands from you."

Shannon ran caressing fingers over his two-button, notch-lapel black suit jacket and black band-collared dress shirt beneath. In a possessive little display, she straightened his textured pocket square. A warm glow suffused his chest. No way would he discourage her from these loving, tender touches.

"You, my love, are the one who is too sexy for words. Not sure I want your fans seeing you looking this hot. You might kill them with a single look," she teased, even as her eyes dilated and darkened with desire.

"Temptress. Keep eying me that way and we won't make it to the premiere." Norns, if only. "Just one more thing, love." He pressed his thumbs to the hidden torc on her neck. "Another upgrade to your armour. Tell it to give you bracelets for both arms, picturing what you want."

Her head cocked to the side, eyes narrowing slightly. After a minute, delicate silver Asgardian scrollwork bracelets appeared on her wrists.

When she lifted her arms to examine them, the pattern had him blinking, then smiling as satisfaction curled in his gut. Did she know the Asgardian symbols had meaning? It was a protection spell interwoven into her charm bracelet. There was no way he'd dissuade her from using it. If he could layer more protection around her, he would.

"Perfect. Just as with the rest of your armour, these are stronger than any metal on Midgard. They expand to vambraces faster than you can call the rest of your armour to block a weapon strike or provide a shield if needed." It took him a minute to speak past the lump filling his throat. "Maybe you think I'm overly paranoid, but I can't lose you, Shannon. I wouldn't survive." Even the idea had him tensing, his muscles primed to fight.

Shannon smiled and cupped his cheeks. With slow thoroughness, she kissed him. When she pulled back, those gorgeous hazel eyes locked with his. "Loki, I love you. If it makes you feel better to give me more protection, I'm okay with that."

Almost dizzy, Loki held her for a few minutes. The tension gradually receded, and his pulse returned to normal. "Okay, we'd better go. I'm going to teleport us so you don't have to walk far in those sexy heels." He glanced down at said heels.

"Deal!"

Two teleports later they were at the bridge, and within another moment, they'd reached the Bifrost chamber.

"Set us down at my flat in London, please," he asked Heimdall.

The rainbow of lights swirled and when they dissipated, Loki and Shannon were in the garden by the infinity pool. As they entered his flat, Shannon glanced around. "What happened to all the damage from my transition?"

"I repaired it with my seidhr." She seemed to forget how easily he dealt with that kind of chaos. Something happening to her or their son, now, that would be a different story. The swath of destruction he would cause would be planet-changing. "My manager arranged a car service. We're expected to make the rounds of after-parties." He guided her into the foyer.

"Of course, love. I'm looking forward to spending time talking with your friends. Is Roskva bringing a date? Will I finally get to meet Thor's wife?" she asked as the elevator descended.

"Like my brother, Ros has a Midgardian spouse at present. They were married last year, a few months before we met, although I haven't met him yet. I don't know if they are bringing their significant others, but if they do, you'll get to meet them."

A black town car waited at the curb, and after Loki helped Shannon in, they set off for Leicester Square.

Shannon glanced at the dark-haired driver, then met Loki's gaze. <*I know it requires more energy, but can you make the illusion hiding our baby convincing enough to allow me to hug your friends?*>

He smiled. <*Yes, darling. I'd already planned to do so. With all the recording I've been doing, I have no shortage of energy. I won't notice the expenditure tonight.*> Even if it caused a drain on him, he would have done so. Shannon would be safe at all costs. There was nothing he wouldn't do to protect her.

She reached over to squeeze his hand and he tucked it into his elbow. <*Thank you. I'm relieved I won't have to think about accidentally giving my pregnancy away. You haven't told any of them, right?*>

He frowned slightly. <*No, love. Not even my management team knows yet. How would I explain a pregnancy that takes far more than nine months on Midgard? Apparently, getting married after only attending a single public event together last year would be considered reckless and irresponsible.*> His mental tone lowered to a disgusted growl as he fought not to scoff. <*We haven't been seen dating, despite the Christmas pictures your sister posted. According to my manager, it would make me appear to be a risky choice for producers so I'm calling you my* girlfriend.>

Loki rolled his eyes, lip curling. Bor's beard, he hated not claiming her in every possible way. No damned asshole had better think she wasn't taken. <*He's concerned investors will pull the funding for the sequel we're filming this summer. He wants me to wait until we've been seen dating at least a year, preferably two, before we announce our engagement.*>

Chapter 40

FRIENDS & WHITE LIES

With difficulty, Shannon resisted yanking her hand from his elbow as her jaw tightened. She fought to not grind her teeth at his presumption. Once again, Loki was steamrolling right over her emotions and choices. For fuck's sake, she was barely used to calling him her boyfriend after a measly five weeks together, and he assumed they'd get married? It wasn't something they'd discussed. Maybe it was old-fashioned of her, but she'd like to at least be *asked* first. Not fucking be taken for granted.

Joining the royal family, being called a princess and his consort—those were political decisions revolving around their soulmate bond and his status. It wasn't personal, and once Frigga had explained the importance, Shannon understood not really being consulted or waiting until she was ready for a lifetime commitment between her and Loki. Instead, it was a cultural expectation by the Asgardians when it came to soulmates. But actually getting *married*—that would be an individual choice to demonstrate their commitment to each other. Not a mystical connection out of her control. And sure as fuck not some cursed *image* for his damn career.

Godsdamn it, Shannon wanted to be asked, to know her opinion and emotions mattered to the man who wanted a lifetime commitment from her.

He didn't seem to notice her reaction as he gazed out the car window.

Shannon bit back her growl.

This wasn't the time or place for that discussion. If they argued, she might lose control of her abilities. Better to just shove those feelings down and not talk about it for now. Despite the thundering of her pulse, she didn't want to ruin their evening and her rare break from training.

Especially not her first time back on Earth since Christmas, five months ago. That five-to-one time difference between the immortal realms and Earth was still hard to wrap her mind around. She wanted to tell her family about her pregnancy in person, but he continually argued it wasn't safe to visit.

Still, she didn't reply to his *pronouncement*, not sure she could keep from biting his head off. Since Isis's attack, he'd grown more protective and more controlling to the point of ridiculousness. It wasn't like the damned goddess was standing on every street corner, waiting to leap out at Shannon. While Shannon was willing to accept armour upgrades and protection spells clinging to her clothes and jewellery, and even allowed him to talk her out of visiting Lynda, she was also a grown ass woman. She was fully capable of acting sensibly. She wasn't about to plop down on Isis's estate in Alexandria, or jump willy-nilly into Shen territory.

<Any idiot hitting on you, thinking you aren't already mine... there won't be enough left for burial.> Loki's tone savage, he turned from the window and gazed at her with narrowed wolfish pale-blue eyes.

As much as she wanted to roll her eyes and snort, she didn't. Instead, Shannon reinforced the walls around her anger so it wouldn't leak out into the bond or influence her powers. Given his possessiveness and tenuous control regarding danger to her and their son, she was planning on keeping her distance from everyone except his closest friends anyway. No need to poke the Black Prince's buttons.

Still, distracting his thoughts from their current dark direction was possibly the better, smarter response... especially as her own temper seemed to be ping-ponging all over the place today.

Shannon took another few slow breaths and nodded, gliding her hand over his chest, then let her fingers trail down.

His lips quirked and he caught her hand. *<Wicked goddess.>*

The car stopped, and the driver opened Loki's door moments later. The fans roared as they spotted him rounding the car to help her out. With his arm around her, Loki went to reach for her abdomen, remembered, and pulled his hand back with a grumble. A small smile tugged at her lips. It satisfied some need in Shannon to see him complain about hiding their baby.

Gah, her emotions were all over the place today. Damn hormones.

After tucking her hand securely into his elbow, Loki waved to the press and fans, and they started down the carpet. As she took in the shouts and camera flashes, the implication of his earlier words finally penetrated and had her almost stumbling.

She caught his eye. <*Gods, Loki. How are we going to handle it when our child doesn't age at the rate humans will expect?*> Not the most opportune moment, granted, but given their surroundings, she couldn't ignore the implications of his current fame when it wasn't just her pregnancy, but her baby's entire childhood at stake. How... oh fuck... how could she explain to her family? She had to tell them something.

Loki held her gaze, brushing a strand of hair back from her face. <*I haven't thought that far ahead yet, but we'll work it out. Don't worry.*> He hoped to avoid Midgardians ever knowing about their son by keeping Shannon on Asgard as her pregnancy advanced, but admitting that to her... Yggdrasil's roots, he knew it wouldn't go over well. Already she wanted to tell her family. And fuck, he felt like a bloody git giving her all the reasons why they couldn't.

It had been hard keeping her on Asgard these past weeks.

Yet the longer they went without letting anyone but Asgardians be aware of her pregnancy, the better. Bad enough fucking Isis and Vidar were out there, already targeting her, waiting for a chance at her again. At least the Shen dragons didn't know she was his soulmate. He drew in an unsteady breath, body tensing. What the fuck was he thinking, bringing her to this? Bad enough being his consort, but now pregnant, Shannon was an irresistible prize for so many enemies. He couldn't let them find out.

An image of Sigyn's ravaged body, broken and bloody, flashed into his mind and his heart thudded. With teeth-gritted determination, he shoved the memory away, locking it behind walls, trying to keep a smile on his face for the flashing cameras and shouts for his attention. Those bastard dark elves would *not* get their hands on Shannon.

He growled, a low snarl below human hearing.

Or those fanatical Jotun sects. And no fucking way was he exposing her to the Dwarven sons of Ivaldi or thrice-cursed Hreidmar and Fafnir.

Deliberately, he controlled his breathing, taking deeper inhales and slow, careful exhales. Those enemies weren't on Midgard. Keeping Shannon away from Alfheim, the home of the elves and dwarves, would minimize exposure to many of his enemies. Still, he leaned into the comforting presence of Laevateinn strapped to his back and hidden from sight and touch by illusion. Never again would he be caught without the ability to protect Shannon.

That reminder calmed his pounding heartbeat, and when Shannon quirked an eyebrow at him, squeezing his hand, the glow of their connection soothed.

<*Nope, no worries for me.*> She flashed a wide smile for the media. <*I'm not going to think about that. Tonight is all about fun! I've been looking forward to this for days.*>

Her playful words prodded him. She needed this. She'd shouldered so many changes so fast. The least he could do was to give her some fun, some enjoyment to balance out her new responsibilities and constant training. He sucked in another breath and forced his limbs to relax. <*Sorry to disappoint, but I'm turning your wine and shots to juice, love. No getting our baby drunk.*>

Shannon glanced sideways at him, a slight crease on her forehead. <*As if I would! Of course you are turning my alcohol into juice.*> She paused, lips pursed. <*I could probably do that myself, couldn't I?*>

<*Yes, but you should practice before trying it in a room full of Midgardians. Some things you've tried so far have a tendency to... explode.*> He managed a straight face, but remembering some of her misfires and resulting outbursts had him struggling not to reveal his amusement. When she didn't learn as quickly as she wanted, Shannon got frustrated and impatient. Yet really, she was making incredible progress.

She nodded ruefully. <*Okay, that's fair.*>

Although he wasn't scheduled for any interviews, Loki couldn't resist stopping to talk to the press about the new album Raven's Chaos was recording and the upcoming Assassin sequel this summer. When they came across studio executives, various directors, producers, and fellow musicians and actors, Loki introduced Shannon. They were like a slow-moving boat, with the faster flow of people going around them, but it was his fault for catering to the fans.

Their appreciation made his music and acting so much fun, even if it was the initial action of telling the tale or producing the song that created most of the energy, not the digital reproductions. Still, the tiny influx from every person who watched or listened always buoyed his reserves whenever he was on Midgard. As they moved along and he signed autographs and posed, he kept a sharp eye out for any danger to Shannon.

An arm thumped him on the back and he spun, muscles tensed to launch an attack… then, "Hey, old man!" reached his ears through the black churning chaos pumping through his mind and body.

Loki forced his limbs to relax and snorted. Basil had no idea how close he'd just come to annihilation. "Hey, puppy. How's it going in nursery school?"

Basil laughed then punched Loki in the arm before turning to Shannon. "Love, I'm sorry your boyfriend is so rude that he can't introduce you. I'm Basil O'Keefe."

Basil held out his hand, and when Shannon went to shake it, he tugged. While Loki could have held on and she was more than strong enough to keep herself where she was, she was in no danger from his antics. Loki released her and let Basil pull her into a hug.

"I'm—oof—I'm Shannon Murphy," she said around her laughter and impact with his whipcord-lean body.

With a shit-eating grin and arm around her waist, Basil turned her to face Loki. "I'm stealing your girl, Tod. She's far too good for the likes of you."

Loki quirked an amused eyebrow. *<All right there, darling?>*

<He's funny and a bit chaotic,> Shannon reassured him. *<I see why he's your friend.>*

"And how does Serena feel about you two-timing her?" Loki teased while nodding to Basil's girlfriend and fellow actor, talking to the press a few feet away.

Basil shrugged, his grin widening.

Shannon chuckled when she glanced at Serena, who'd also rolled her eyes at Basil's antics, and then gave Shannon a thumbs-up.

Thor fist-bumped Loki when he arrived and caught Basil with his arm around Shannon. "Unhand my sister, thief, before I squash you."

Shannon smiled up at Thor, who then frowned down at Basil. The look of alarm on the young man's face had Loki chuckling. Thor wasn't even really scowling.

"Okay, okay! I'll give her back! No need for violence, Tempest!" Basil released Shannon before leaping at Thor to hug him. "Sorry, Shannon," Basil said, somewhat abashed after Thor was through scolding him. "It's very nice to meet you. Cor, but you're mad to get involved with this lot. Just saying!" he yelled the last when Thor cuffed him lightly on the head.

"Out of the way, squirt." Thor picked the much shorter man up and moved him, making Shannon laugh.

Thor carefully folded Shannon into a hug. "Loki has a good illusion on you to hide the baby." When he added, "Are you okay after that puppy's rough handling? I can still wring his neck for you," in a voice pitched to immortal ears, Loki covered his smile. As large as his big brother was, the God of Thunder and Battle turned into a complete teddy bear around pregnant women. It had driven Thor's wife around the bend when she couldn't do anything without him trying to get it for her first. Loki had already suffered through numerous lectures about taking care of Shannon from his well-meaning brother.

"I'm good. No worries, Thor. I appreciate it," Shannon whispered.

"Let's get her out of this madhouse, brother," Thor suggested with an affectionate smile.

"Right there with you, brother," Loki agreed, as they moved to either side of Shannon. Better to get her inside. Surely he'd satisfied his fans by now.

With him on one side and his brother on the other, the press wanted even more photos, but fortunately, they weren't far from the theatre entrance. In relatively short order, he and Thor had Shannon through security where he could get her a drink before they needed to find their seats.

While Loki went to get her a beverage, Shannon chatted with Thor. "No Amelia?"

Thor shook his head. "She and the twins are at home in Australia. It's too much to drag them around for all these things, and she prefers to be around her siblings when she needs a break from our rambunctious offspring."

Shannon crossed her arms. "When will I get to meet her? You are going to let me meet your wife, right?" Bad enough Loki didn't want her visiting her own family right now, but surely he couldn't object to Thor's spouse and kids. Especially with both brothers there as protection.

"Of course, Shannon! We've got my movie's premiere in Sydney in two months. That will be two short weeks for you. Depending on how recording for Loki's new album is going, maybe the two of you could spend a few days visiting us?"

"Absolutely, I'd love that. I don't know..." As Loki returned with a glass of red wine for her and two glasses of scotch for himself and Thor, she asked, "Love, could you get a couple of days before or after Thor's red carpet in Sydney to spend some time with his family? So I can meet Amelia and the kids?"

"Of course, I'll see what I can do, darling," he reassured her.

Cautiously, she took a sip. True to his word, there was no alcohol, but the wine was still surprisingly full-bodied and flavourful. When she nodded her approval, he gave her a little half-smile. Of course, he'd make sure she'd enjoy it. He loved pampering her. It was part of what made his constant overprotectiveness bearable. She took another sip and rolled her shoulders, irritated with herself and her thoughts. That snipe hadn't been fair. After Isis's attack, he had a right to worry. She sure did.

Gods, she was cranky today, bouncing from one mood to the next.

"Ros has arrived." Thor peered over the sea of heads to the entrance of the theatre. He gave her a quick wave so she could locate them.

"By the Fates, this place is packed! What a zoo it is outside!" Roskva exclaimed as she reached them, making the rounds for hugs. "Nice illusion. Loki's?" she murmured when she hugged Shannon.

"Yes, not part of my skill set."

A handsome blond man with bright brown eyes and a wide smile joined them, handing Roskva a glass of red wine and wrapping his lean arm around her waist.

"This is my husband, Bobbie. Bobbie, I know you've been wanting to meet the rest of Raven's Chaos. My brother is on his way, but this is Tod Corvus, the Raven and lead singer, and his brother Tempest. Gods on and off the stage and pitch."

The raw truth in Ros's introduction had Shannon blinking and biting her lip to keep a shocked laugh from emerging as Ros continued by introducing Shannon. The Valkyrie had said the words without the slightest hint of a wink or nod. When it came to unflinching deception, these immortals had no qualms whatsoever. It made Shannon wonder how long it would be before she could lie without guilt.

Bobbie held out a hand and shook each of theirs, polite but clearly clueless. Shannon couldn't imagine. Just maintaining the relationship with her best friend was difficult enough.

<*How do Thor and Ros do it? How do they maintain a relationship that hides so much of themselves?*> she asked Loki as the conversation flowed around them.

<*It's hard. It wears on them. But they are in love, so they try to focus on the positive, on the good things they can share since the mortal's life is so short in comparison.*>

Damn. Somehow, she kept forgetting that aspect, that she would outlive every human she knew. Yet Loki would still be there. Their child would still live. With a lump in her throat, she clasped his hand and squeezed. <*We are so incredibly lucky.*>

<*Truly, we are blessed by the Norns. Not a day goes by that I don't thank them.*>

The theatre house lights flickered, signalling it was time to find their seats. Ros and her husband left to find Thjalfi, and Loki guided Shannon to a seat between him and Thor. As they waited for the movie to start, Shannon gazed around the huge red-and-gold gilt space. It was a veritable who's who, with more celebrities from outside the UK than she'd expected. Eventually, her attention was drawn to the front stage when a man introduced various studio executives, then the director, screenwriters, and lead actors. With a brief pause for effect, the star of the film was introduced—Harry Chapelsworth, a classically handsome, tall, dark-haired Caucasian man who happened to be Loki's close mortal friend. Harry spotted Loki, nodded in acknowledgement, and told everyone to enjoy the show.

The movie was fantastic, of course. Full of humour and action, as expected. As the lights came up, Shannon tried to get Loki to tell her what the end credit scene hinted at. Surely, being Harry's close friend, Loki had *some* idea. But he refused to say anything.

"Ugh, you are such a sphinx!" she complained.

Both Thor and Loki chuckled, and Loki teased, "But darling, I wouldn't want to ruin the surprise for you."

"And actually, the sphinx isn't Loki. It's based on Helios, or Horus, the son of Isis and Baldur. We don't see our former nephew very often, as he's spent the last eight hundred Asgardian years on Vanaheim. Odin struck him from the royal family, stripped him of his Asgardian status, and banished him when he sided with the Sidhe in Freya's war," Thor murmured, once the surrounding seats had cleared out.

Another family betrayal? Isis had also been stricken from the royal family and banished after she attacked Shannon. Had the son's treachery been a foreshadowing of Isis's actions? Shannon definitely wanted to hear more.

Her phone pinged, and she withdrew it from her clutch.

LYNDA:—2 busy 2 come see me, but not 2 busy for the red carpet I see! WTF? I don't rate a single evening in the last 5mo?

Shannon winced at the condemnation in Lynda's message. Not that she blamed her. It was true, even if it wasn't the whole truth.

SHANNON:—I've mentioned your company to multiple people here, I promise. I'll see how many more I can tell this evening.

Would that satisfy Lynda? Shannon hated feeling like she was selling something, but if she couldn't see her friend without endangering her, what else could she do?

"Huh. You are such a cradle robber, Loki," she teased, putting her phone away and trying to recapture her lighthearted mood. He leered at her playfully.

Thor laughed. "You aren't wrong."

Another ping sounded, but not her phone this time.

Loki glanced at his screen. "Harry will meet us at the Mall Galleries' after-party." He stood and met Thor's eyes, with some understanding passing between them.

"Sounds good. I'll ride with the two of you if that's alright?" Thor rose to his feet. "I assume you won't make Shannon walk there."

"Of course not. Not in those shoes, nor with the crowds outside. No way. Yes, you can ride with us. I didn't drive, so you'll fit," Loki teased.

His words created a mental image of the two brothers in their taller, broader Asgardian forms trying to fit in Loki's low-slung sports car, heads sticking out of the windows and knees jammed into their chests. It had definite clown car vibes. She bit her lip, grinning as Loki helped her stand. "How far away is it?"

"It's less than a ten-minute walk, but this is a really busy, touristy area, even without a premiere happening. It's not worth dealing with the crowds and the paps, darling." Loki guided her to the aisle with a hand on her back. "There is no way I'd risk you or our son."

A smiling dark-haired man approached as they neared the theatre's exit. Long and lean, with the body of a greyhound in his navy suit and white shirt, his round face, tilted eyes and wide mouth were familiar. It took a few moments for Shannon to remember where she'd seen him, then she jolted—Derick Lang, the actor playing Jin Xiang in that martial arts-based monster flick she'd met briefly on the red carpet, then seen on the screen that first day with Loki, the date that rocked her world.

"Hi, Tod. I was hoping to talk to you. Would it be alright if we found a quiet corner?" Derick asked politely, maintaining his distance and not offering to shake their hands.

Not expecting it, Shannon almost stumbled when Loki pulled her back and tucked her partially behind him. His face was carefully blank as he inclined his head to Derick. Thor nodded as well, flashing a brief smile, but then shared a look with Loki and stepped away through the doors.

Why were they both on edge around this actor? Loki hadn't behaved this way when he'd introduced her in August. She searched the man's expression but found only mild interest.

"We can talk over there, and anything you need to say can be said in front of Shannon." Loki swept his arm toward the front of the now almost-empty theatre, back the way they'd come. A flash of black seidhr accompanied his arm and some kind of fragile, almost translucent mist rose around the three of them.

PART 4

Chaos Theory

"Something unknown is doing we don't know what—that is what our theory amounts to."

Sir Arthur Stanley Eddington

Chapter 41

PARTY CRASHERS

Derick nodded and headed down the aisle, with Loki and Shannon following. No one was within listening distance when they reached the screen, with the odd mist accompanying them. Once there, he turned and bowed from the waist, again surprising Shannon. His actions were oddly formal.

"Please forgive my previous lack of formal greeting, Prince Loki. On behalf of the Shen, I would like to apologize for the grievous behaviour of Ao Guang, Ao Qin, and Ao Shun to you and your companion, Doctor Murphy. The Shen wish to keep our current treaty with Asgard and know the inexcusable actions of our three dragon lords may have jeopardized the relationship between our two peoples. What reparations can we offer to make up for our insult?"

Oh shit. Shannon's spine stiffened. She'd forgotten Loki said she'd met other Shen before.

Loki held Derick's gaze for a moment, then inclined his head. "Before we discuss reparations, let me formally introduce you to Doctor Murphy. Lü Dongbin, Xian Leader of the Eight Immortals, this is Princess Shannon of Asgard, *my consort*."

Shannon inclined her head, copying Loki's movements, and watched as Dongbin registered Loki's words. His dark-brown eyes widened, and his golden-brown skin paled noticeably.

"Our insult has been grievous indeed." He bowed deeply to her, maintaining eye contact. "My deepest apologies, Princess Shannon."

<*What do I do, Loki?*> Shannon knew nothing about diplomatic relations between the Shen and Asgard, other than the treaty Loki had mentioned. She hadn't gotten that far in her studies with Frigga yet.

<*Usually a gift and a concession are the appropriate responses in an instance like this. The Shen value jade, so something made of jade would make a good reparation gift, as well as a guarantee of safe passage in all North American Chinatown areas,*> he said, then added, <*And don't say thank you. It's considered rude.*>

She inclined her head again. "I wish I was making your acquaintance under better circumstances, as I very much enjoyed your movie. It would be appropriate to guarantee us safe passage in the Chinatown areas across North America so this doesn't happen again. As far as reparation, a jade statue to commemorate the bonding of Prince Loki and I would be acceptable."

Dongbin bowed again, graceful in his movements. "Princess Shannon, you are as gracious and kind as you are beautiful. Ao Guang and his brothers have been restricted to Kunlun for the near future, and the Shen are pleased to offer safe passage in North American Chinatowns. I will have a jade statue commissioned from the Yáochí, the Jade Pool of Kunlun, which instills a blessing for those fortunate enough to be gifted with it."

Loki and Shannon inclined their heads again, accepting the offer, and that seemed to be the cue for everyone to relax, as the mist around them disappeared and Loki asked him how he'd enjoyed the movie.

Dongbin grinned, eyes lighting. "It was such fun! I very much hope to be in one with you, Loki. Perhaps we could team up."

Shannon laughed. "Yeah, that would be quite the movie with the two of you. I can see the wild action sequences now with the two fighting styles they've given your characters."

Dongbin nodded, enthused. "Oh yeah! It'd be great!"

Loki's phone pinged again, and he glanced at the message. "The car is waiting. We should get going or we'll hold up the process. We'll talk again soon, Dongbin."

Dongbin nodded, smiling. "I would like that. It was wonderful to speak with you. I'm so pleased to make your acquaintance, Princess Shannon."

She smiled and gave him a little wave as Loki led her away.

The place was packed. How they'd find Harry and his wife Elise in the sea of people at the party, Shannon had no idea. Loki and Thor were in huge demand and seemed to be acquainted with every person there. A bit overwhelming, as there was no way she'd be able to remember even half the people they'd introduced her to.

"How are you doing, darling?" With his arm around her, Loki kept her tucked protectively against his side.

"You sure know a lot of people."

"Yes, it's the nature of acting. We work with a new group of people every new project."

"Okay, that makes sense."

"I'm going to go get us drinks," Thor announced when he finished the conversation he was in and turned back to join Loki and Shannon. He'd been blocking anyone from bumping her from her other side, both brothers ensuring she stayed in a sheltered bubble. She didn't think they even realized the way they coordinated their movements with each other. It was just ingrained protectiveness, combined with hundreds of years of training and fighting together. Although it wasn't something she was used to, she couldn't deny the warm glow it gave her.

"That sounds great. Thank you." She smiled as she held out her glass. Neither of them wanted her to fetch her own drinks and ensured she had a refill to stay hydrated in the warm room, overflowing with body heat from the large crowd. To keep herself at a more comfortable temperature, she used her power to cool the surrounding air.

Loki nodded. "If you see Harry, let him know where we are. There's no way I'm dragging Shannon through this crush."

"Of course." Thor set out after a reassuring pat on her back.

It was amusing to watch him carve a path. Being close to six-and-a-half feet in his Midgardian form and broad-shouldered was part of it, but it was also simply the dominant alpha-male aura that had people moving instinctively out of his way. He moved as if he were in his wider, taller Asgardian body. Before the crowd closed in, Shannon glimpsed Harry and a sleek, dark-haired woman, his wife, making their way in this direction. It must be nice to be tall, to be able to see over more people. Even in her heels, she only came up to Loki's chin, yet that was an improvement over not reaching his shoulder when at his natural height.

"Harry and Elise are over there." She jerked her head in the direction Thor had gone as her phone pinged.

LYNDA:—Who? Did u get their contact information so I can follow up?

Shannon stifled her groan. Seriously? Couldn't Lynda be happy Shannon was mentioning her company?

SHANNON:—No, I didn't. Sorry. But I gave them your website address.

Turning, Loki must have spotted Harry and Elise, because he raised a hand in greeting. A few minutes later, they appeared close enough that Shannon could see them too. Still, Harry and Elise were waylaid several times by others before they reached her.

"Tod, it's been too long." Harry gave Loki a backslapping hug.

"Indeed. You remember Shannon?"

Harry smiled, brown eyes alight, and pulled her into a tight hug. "Sure do, and this time, Tod's not keeping me from hugging you. So rude last time, not letting us talk. It's nice to see you again. Thank you for coming."

Amused at his needling of Loki, Shannon hugged him back. "Absolutely. The movie is fantastic! Really loved it. I'm sorry I wasn't available to come to the previous premiere."

"Work is just so inconsiderate, isn't it?" He chuckled. "I'm glad you could come tonight." Pulling back, he held his hand out to his smiling wife. "This is Elise, my better half."

"Shannon, I'm so pleased to meet you. When Harry said he got to meet you last August, I was so jealous." She gave Shannon a tight, full-body hug and a genuine, enthusiastic greeting.

"Unfortunately, it was all a bit of a blur. It was my first red carpet. I was a bit shell-shocked. This time is better. Maybe by the time it's a movie of Tod's, I'll actually be prepared." It wasn't completely a white lie, but other events of that day had pushed the memory of the red carpet from the forefront. Loki ravishing her and revealing his true identity was indelibly stamped in her memories in sharp sensory detail. Just remembering was enough to have need thrumming up her spine, goosebumps spreading over her skin.

Loki caught her eye, a slight smirk on his face. Shit. Had her emotion slipped through the bond?

Elise smiled in commiseration. "It does take some getting used to, doesn't it? Harry mentioned you're a professor?"

Although such a normal question, it jolted Shannon like a splash of cool water. While she'd been scrambling to learn enough to defend herself and survive, she hadn't yet resolved what to do about her career. Since finding out about her pregnancy, she'd turned over primary supervision of her grad students to a colleague. But she needed time to figure out what she wanted.

Ironic that despite becoming immortal, she never seemed to have enough time. Either way, she didn't know how to answer a question she hadn't worked out for herself yet.

<*What's wrong, darling?*> Loki reached over to rub her back while he continued to talk to Harry.

<*Elise asked about my job. I don't know what to say.*> She scrambled for something, anything, to say while keeping her confusion internalized.

<*Even on leave, you're still a professor, right? No one needs to know you're changing careers as a royal kick-ass immortal goddess.*>

Loki's assumption that she'd be quitting her job sent annoyance spearing through her. First, his fucking comments about marriage, then Lynda pressuring her and making her feel guilty, now *this*? She fought back a snarl, and her gut churned as she shifted on her heels. Heat crept from her chest to flush over her neck and face.

Damn him!

She knew her job-related responsibilities would have to change—she needed more flexibility—but if he could have a mortal career, Shannon didn't see why she couldn't, too. She just hadn't decided what that would look like, and for fuck's sake, this wasn't the time or place to have that discussion.

Not trusting her tenuous control and temper, she ignored Loki's quirked eyebrow and finally said, "Yes, at Victoria Charles University in British Columbia."

Elise's forehead wrinkled slightly as she tilted her head.

Shannon flinched. The odd tone in her voice had given her away. She wasn't the actor, the liar, Loki was.

"My apologies, Shannon. I didn't mean to upset you." Gently, Elise put a hand on Shannon's arm.

Shit, if only Lynda was nearly as compassionate. Appreciating Elise's gesture, Shannon gave the kind woman part of the truth and a small smile. "Oh no, you didn't. I'm at a bit of a crossroads with my career, not certain how to move forward. It threw me for a minute."

"Ah. Yes, I understand." Elise gave her a commiserating smile, eyes warm. "When I stepped away from being in front of the camera, it was a big decision. But I love it. Next to marrying Harry"—she winked at him, and he kissed her, before returning to his conversation with Loki—"it was the best decision I've made. Vancouver looks lovely. I've never been there."

The tension in Shannon's shoulders loosened. "Oh, it is. Absolutely. I'm biased since I grew up just outside the city, but the blend of mountains, temperate rainforest, and ocean is spectacular. If you ever get out that way, you'll have to visit me." And wow, Elise's welcoming personality was such a delightful change from Lynda.

"I would love to! Are you staying in London long? Perhaps we could get together, with or without the boys." She nudged Harry with her elbow and grinned at Shannon.

Shannon matched her grin, enjoying the mischievous sparkle in Elise's brown eyes that lit up her creamy complexion and sprinkle of freckles. Yes, this woman was Shannon's kind of people, for sure. With Loki already maintaining a close friendship with Harry, perhaps a friendship with Elise wouldn't be as challenging as it was with Lynda. "Not this trip, but Tod is going to be filming in the UK during July and August. I'm sure I'll be out to visit him. Why don't I ditch him for some girl time?"

"I love it! Give me the dates and I'll make it work."

"What's this? Ditching us and making plans on your own?" Harry asked during a pause in his and Loki's conversation.

"Maybe we want in on the fun, too," complained Loki with a slightly sulky pout that belied the amusement in his eyes. *<I'm glad you seem to be hitting it off with Elise, darling.>*

<She's fun. I can see myself getting into trouble with her.>

Elise and Shannon linked arms. "Sometimes, us ladies just need to have a girls' night. It's not always about you," Shannon teased.

Harry turned to Loki with a scowl. "Your Shannon is corrupting my Elise."

Loki snorted. "If you believe that, then Elise sure has you fooled."

The men laughed. Shannon met Elise's gaze and both rolled their eyes.

"Let's get out of this crush and head to the north gallery room set aside for us. It's more exclusive and there should be food. I'm starved!" Harry suggested.

They agreed, following as he led the way. Elise and Shannon continued to chat, while Harry and Loki stopped every few minutes to greet someone. Progress through the main gallery was slow.

The doorway Harry aimed for appeared ahead through the crowd, with two burly security men preventing anyone not invited or escorted from entering. With a nudge to Elise, Shannon indicated the direction.

Elise laughed. "Now, if only we can wrangle our men to actually reach there."

Harry was stalled in front of her, talking to an attractive couple. The man was half a foot taller than Harry's six feet, with short, well-cut blond hair, sea-green eyes set in a pale, narrow face, and a lean but athletic build. He smiled as they chatted, yet his eyes were cold and distant. A chill shivered over Shannon's skin despite the evening's heat. The woman was Harry's height, with unusual long silver hair drawn up into a high ponytail, emphasizing her stunning features with razor-edged cheekbones in a perfect milky complexion. Her blue eyes matched the icy blue of the sleeveless sheath dress she wore draped over a slender body—the ideal Trent had always pushed Shannon towards, although even as a pre-teen, she'd never been that small in the hips and bust. It made Shannon wonder if the woman was a model. She certainly had the height, face, and body for it.

Behind Shannon, Loki was turned around, chatting animatedly to a boisterous red-haired, ruddy-cheeked man about a project they'd done together a couple of years ago.

"Shannon, Elise, come meet Rhiana and Dion," Harry said as he turned to include them in his conversation. "Dion is a writer, and some of his work might be right up your alley, Elise."

Elise shook Dion's hand as Shannon stepped over to shake Rhiana's. The woman gave her a small, insincere smile that suggested Shannon was beneath her notice and should be grateful to meet her. So, not just a model, but an egotistical one. Despite her off-putting attitude, Shannon strove to be polite and restrained her eye roll as she held her hand out.

"Hi, I'm Shannon," she said as their hands met. There was a jolt, like an electric shock as soon as their skin touched. An odd look crossed Rhiana's face before she focused on Shannon with slightly narrowed eyes.

"It's nice to meet you, Shannon," she replied in a soft, lyrical voice that was at odds with her cold exterior.

Not certain what to make of the look and weird shock, Shannon gave her a polite nod. After withdrawing her hand from Rhiana's long, narrow fingers, Shannon turned to Dion.

Just starting to introduce herself, Shannon gasped as their hands connected with the sudden shock of touching a live wire.

Instinctively, she jerked back from the pain, only for him to lunge and tug her towards him. She stumbled, just managing to halt her forward momentum before she crashed into him. The illusion over her shattered, leaving her pulse thundering as she froze, stunned. His iron grip on her hand had fire ants climbing up her arm in biting shocks, and a pulse of blue seidhr flared from her necklace.

Chapter 42

THERE'S ALWAYS CAKE

Dion clenched a hand that snapped the seidhr back like he'd punched Shannon in the throat. "Who are you, really?" he demanded in a low snarl. As she struggled to breathe, he glared with furious narrowed eyes, taking in Shannon's curved abdomen.

<*Loki!*> It all happened so fast that she didn't get out more in her mental shout before Loki was there, pushing his way between them. With difficulty, Shannon yanked her hand from Dion's tight grip and shifted further away, gasping as the constriction choking her disappeared. Loki re-established the illusion, hiding her pregnancy.

<*Are you okay?*> he growled, even as he spoke to Dion in a tight, low snarl.

Fingers patting her throat, Shannon sucked in a few big breaths. Nothing seemed bruised, but the sensation lingered. Leaning into Loki's rigid back, tucked mostly behind him, she inhaled his familiar citrus, leather, and wood scent. The contact with his body centred her, and the tightness in her lungs dissipated.

<*Yes, he surprised me. What is he?*> Because there was no fucking way he was human, not after that.

Wide-eyed, Rhiana tried to coax Dion away, but he wasn't budging. Dion and Loki locked gazes, neither giving ground as each strove to intimidate the other.

<Tuatha Dé Danann. Unseelie Court. They both are. They are forbidden from being on Midgard and the bloody bastards know it.> His mental tone cut with the savage aggression of an unsheathed blade. A dangerous black fury surged in pulses through the bond.

Holy shit. Elves. She'd finally met elves. And they were assholes. Shannon's stomach churned, her skin prickling with goosebumps. She swallowed.

Waves of tension permeated the air.

It didn't bode well for the mortals around them, particularly Harry and Elise, whose eyes had widened. Harry had an arm around Elise, shifting her away from the confrontation as much as the packed crowd allowed.

She sucked in another quick breath, fingers digging into Loki's jacket. Damn it, she didn't want Loki's friends in the line of fire if this came to blows. In a swift survey of their surroundings, she spotted Thor making his way back to them. He caught her wide-eyed expression. Face darkening, he moved faster through the crowd as they scattered out of his way.

Glancing around Loki, Shannon caught Rhiana whispering something in Dion's ear. He broke eye contact with Loki, staring past Shannon's shoulder. Had they spotted Thor?

With a quick word and polite smile to Harry and Elise, and a last glare toward Shannon that sent a warning note shivering up her spine, Dion and Rhiana made a rapid exit through the crowd, away from Thor's approach.

<Stay with Harry and Elise. Ros will be here within the next minute,> Loki snarled as he turned, motioned to his brother, and set off after them. Thor shifted to follow.

"What was all that about?" asked Harry, frowning in the direction of Loki's disappearing back. "I almost thought they'd come to blows."

Shannon barely held back her wince as heat climbed her skin. "Tod took exception to Dion's handling of me. He's quite protective." Would that excuse fly with Harry? It was the best she could come up with on the spot. Holy flying flapjacks, she sucked at lying.

He raised an eyebrow, and she tried not to squirm under his perusal.

"Are you joining us inside?" Ros asked from behind Harry and Elise.

Thank go—maybe she needed a better freaking expression if she was a damned goddess herself now. Shannon released a silent, shaky exhale and sent

Ros a grateful look when Harry and Elise turned to greet her. A fluttering pain in her chest had her fighting the urge to rub at both it and her throat.

Ros flashed a Valkyrie hand sign acknowledgement.

"Yeah, Tod and Tempest know where to find us. I'm with Harry. Let's get some food," Shannon suggested, needing to get off her trembling legs.

Although she hadn't wanted to admit it to Loki, she was more than a bit shaken by the encounter with Dion and Rhiana. Finally, she'd met people of her race, and it had been nothing at all like she'd expected. Why had Dion taken such an immediate, strong dislike to her? Her arm still ached where he'd gripped her, with pins and needles stabbing her nerve endings all the way to her shoulder. It was hard to hide her discomfort.

Harry's expression lightened and he laughed. "Yes, quick, before Tod comes back and eats all the cake."

Despite her distress, Shannon smiled and shook her head in amusement. Loki *did* like his desserts. They followed Harry past the security and into the much less crowded north gallery. She hung back from Harry and Elise so she could talk to Ros.

"Are you okay? Who were they?" Ros demanded as soon as the others were out of range of her whisper.

"Yeah, just uncomfortable." Shannon winced, giving in to the need to shake the pins and needles in her arm, rubbing at it and her chest. "Unseelie. They gave the names Dion and Rhiana, but Loki knew them at a glance."

"Those inbred bent-stem pisswaters are forbidden from being on Midgard!" Shannon couldn't help but be impressed by Ros's creativity as she turned the nearby air blue, blending Asgardian, English, and Dwarven curses seamlessly. Maybe Shannon needed to adopt some of the Valkyrie's linguistic style. "Stay close to me, Princess. Please. The princes would kill me if something happened to you."

"I can take—"

"Yes, I know you can take care of yourself," Ros interrupted, "but these are immortals, and you're pregnant. Please! Even Loki and Thor have backup. My twin is out there, keeping an eye on the perimeter in case Isis or Vidar show up."

With a raised eyebrow, she eyed Shannon's continued massaging of her arm, shoulder, chest, and throat. Shannon shrugged a few times and tried to ignore the unpleasant feeling, lowering her hand and waving toward the others.

"Okay, okay... Let's get some food. I wasn't kidding about being hungry."

They joined Harry and Elise at the buffet table spread along one wall. If she couldn't have wine, Shannon wanted chocolate, damn it. It was her next favourite stress food. With the events of the last half an hour, it was all she could do to resist rubbing her abdomen to reassure herself everything was fine.

Bloody fucking dark elves! The thrice-damned crowd swallowed Gwydion and his hag of a mate only feet from Loki, blocking him on every side. No matter how he pushed, he couldn't close the distance. How, in all the vast realms, did they manage to squirm past people to make headway in this crush?

His fists clenched, he fought to keep his temper as black edged his vision—a sure warning sign his seidhr was clamouring at his control. But disgusting Unseelie had put their polluted hands on Shannon. Fucking filthy sadistic bastards that had raped and killed Sigyn, had sacrificed his unborn daughter.

And now they knew Shannon was pregnant!

A growl of rage poured from his throat. Even though the sound was pitched below mortal hearing, people took one look and tried to get out of his way. Good. He didn't give a flying fuck if he scared them as long as they fucking *moved*.

A glint of silver hair ahead near the leftmost door had Loki shifting toward it. Sure enough, there was Gwydion's blond head in front of Arianrhod. Snarling his apologies, Loki elbowed, pushed, and squeezed his way to the door. Those who tried to talk to him paled and scrambled aside.

Only thirty seconds passed before he reached the exit where he'd spotted the elves, but it felt like eons. Thor joined him moments later.

"Heimdall, do you see Gwydion or Arianrhod? They just left from this door," Loki murmured, knowing the God of Boundaries, Road, and Sight was keeping a closer eye on them this evening with the danger of Isis and Vidar looming.

<*No, they remain cloaked to my senses,*> Heimdall answered in Loki's mind. <*Even when you said they were in front of you, I was unable to get a lock on them.*>

Standing in the flow of people waiting to get in, Thor and Loki searched for two heads going the other way. A line of cars waiting to drop-off or pick-up shone headlights at them from the right, with the road blocked off for the event. The tree-lined street made it hard to see, and they moved out to the edge of the roadway, searching through the media with their lights, microphones, and cameras, the fans hoping for a glimpse of their favourite star, and the security holding them back.

"Do you see them? Anywhere?" Thor asked, his head swivelling.

"No. Bor's beard! How the fuck did those manky redcap-loving death dealers get to Midgard? Did we miss some of the circles?" Loki snarled.

"If we did, we'll find them and close them. They won't get a foothold here again," Thor rumbled. "Thjalfi's coming."

In the silver blazer, black T-shirt, and tight black leather pants of his musician persona, Thjalfi strolled up to screams of nearby fans. He gave them a little wave and flashed a smile, but continued until he reached Thor and Loki.

"I'm sorry, Loki. I tried to follow them, but the slimy blood fuckers went around a tree"—he gestured to the nearest one to the entrance—"and by the time I got around it, they were gone. He had to have disguised them with illusion. I've searched, but I haven't been able to spot them again."

Too furious to answer, Loki jerked his head in agreement.

Thor gave him a long look. "I know you're pissed. You have every right to be, but you appear like you are a hair's width from losing your shit in front of the media."

Loki dragged air in through his nose, held it for a few seconds, then forced himself to exhale slowly. Concentrating on the entrance behind them, he laid an invisible trip ward keyed to Elven signatures. Even disguised, the Unseelie should set it off if they re-entered the building.

Thor thumped him on the back. "I'm going to stay out here with Thjalfi. We'll do more sweeps, see if we can reacquire them and keep an eye out for Isis or Vidar"

"Stay frosty," Thjalfi added with a punch to Loki's shoulder. "Watch over our princess."

Loki glared at him, and Thjalfi laughed, raising his hands and backing away.

Thor shook his head, grabbing Thjalfi in a headlock as he dragged him away. "Fool. You like to live dangerously, poking at him?"

Loki took another calming breath before reaching out to Shannon. <*The fucking dark elves got away. Gwydion is a strong mage. He must have hidden himself and Arianrhod as they left. We lost them outside the entrance when they eluded our sight briefly.*> He knew his rage had to be swamping her through his tone and the bond, and he gritted his teeth, ratcheting it back under rigid control.

Shannon's mental voice was hesitant when she asked, <*Gwydion and Arianrhod are their actual names?*>

Loki swallowed the curses that wanted to erupt. After the shock of those fuckers, she didn't need his shit, too. <*Yes. I've cast a spell that should alert me if they attempt to return, but I don't think they will. Heimdall will tell Odin what's happened. He needs to be aware they've found some way to sneak into Midgard again.*> Loki forced himself to take another few calming breaths. <*You are safe?*>

<*Yes. I'm with Ros, Bobbie, Harry, and Elise in the north gallery, having some food.*>

He grunted. As a consolation prize, it wasn't a bad one. <*Don't let Harry eat all the cake.*> He turned and re-entered the Mall Galleries and worked his way through the crowd. His soulmate was safe and unharmed. She was having a good time. He needed to focus on that.

The unexpected comment had Shannon choking on a bite, and Elise asked if she was okay. After all Loki's snarling and growling, fury so thick she could almost see it surrounding her in a black wave, he was asking about *cake*?

"Yeah, I just swallowed wrong," Shannon told Elise as Ros frowned.

Cautiously, Shannon took a sip of the wine she'd carefully, and successfully, removed the alcohol from, without exploding either the glass or the wine. *Yay!* Although it wasn't nearly as nice as when Loki converted it for her, it would do. Flashing subtle hand signs, she let Ros know Loki was returning. Despite not being fluent in the Valkyrie silent battle communication yet, she was getting better. Kara made her practice daily.

Harry and Elise were telling them about an upcoming holiday to Mallorca when Loki rejoined them.

"What was that all about, mate?" Harry's eyebrows rose as he paused with his fork partway to his mouth.

Loki kissed Shannon, then turned to put an arm around both Elise's and Harry's shoulders as he peered down at Harry's mostly empty plate. "Absolutely nothing. Just got waylaid talking to some folks. Did you eat all the cake on me?"

Loki's tone was calm and teasing—diametrically opposite to his snarled words only minutes earlier. Shannon's jaw almost dropped. How the hell had he hidden the dangerous immortal so completely? No sign of it leaked out from his appearance, expression, tone, or even through their bond. Somewhat dumbfounded, she caught the subtle black flash with his hands on the backs of his friends' heads when he changed their recollection of events.

But if she hadn't known it was coming, she wouldn't have seen it.

No wonder she'd only seen fleeting glimpses of that side of him. A shiver ran up her spine, raising the hair at her nape. Trent, too, had started as a caring, considerate partner. It was well over a year, closer to two, before he started showing he was an abusive, violent, controlling asshole. If Loki could change his demeanour so completely, hide an integral part of himself that easily, that fast, how could she know which was the real him? Even with the bond, how well did she really know him after only five weeks?

"Are you kidding, Tod? I had to make sure I got some before *you* ate it all and left none for the rest of us!" Harry fired back with a snort, shovelling his last bite into his mouth.

Loki laughed and winked at Shannon. "Well then, I'd better get started on making a dent."

She shook her head as they headed to the buffet table.

Elise sighed. "I don't know where the two of them put it. It certainly never ends up on their hips like it does mine."

"I know, right? It isn't fair, is it?" Shannon commiserated, and Ros laughed.

"Shannon, I've seen you eat. I don't know where *you* put it and keep your figure," Ros teased.

Shannon blinked and glanced down at herself. Ros thought she had a good figure? But this was Loki's illusion, not truly her... with her big boobs and ass, and thick thighs Trent had always disparaged. Still, this pregnancy did have her eating a lot. "Tapeworm." Shannon smirked. "But you, Elise, you've had four kids and still have your beautiful, slender figure."

Elise laughed and gestured to herself. "Yeah, a great dress hides all sorts of flaws."

"What flaws? There are no flaws," Harry disagreed as he rejoined them with another loaded plate. "You're gorgeous."

The blush that came to her pale-cream complexion at Harry's completely nonchalant remark had Shannon smiling. It was clear he wasn't saying it as an attempt to compliment his wife, but instead, a simple statement of facts from his perspective. To see them interact in such a warm, honest way brought a lightness to Shannon's mood.

Others came and went as they talked for the rest of the evening. Shannon understood why Harry was Loki's best friend in the mortal world. They had a deep affection for each other, grounded in mutual respect. She hadn't realized how much of a troublemaker Harry was, but with the two of them together, they were constantly zinging each other. Elise and Shannon were in stitches, giggling at their antics.

Yet it had her wondering. Loki's friendship with Harry seemed effortless like there wasn't this massive gulf between them due to Harry's lack of knowledge and lack of immortality. What was Shannon doing wrong? She looked down at the messages that had blown up her phone a few minutes ago.

LYNDA:—WTF? That's it? That's all u did? How am I supposed to work with that?

LYNDA:—You are such a selfish bitch, Shannon. Can't believe you are surrounded by all those celebrities like ur a BFD. U don't deserve it.

LYNDA:—Why the fuck couldn't u have invited me?!

Why was her friendship with Lynda so fractured and difficult? Was it her? All the changes she'd been through? All the lies? She'd finally gotten Lynda to believe Shannon hadn't lied about not being with Loki during her time in Egypt, although Lynda thought she'd been in the forests of Greece and Turkey. Keeping her lies straight was exhausting, and it was hard to protest her innocence when Shannon was actually lying. Just not about what Lynda thought.

Gods, what a mess.

Chapter 43

ASK, DAMN IT

Loki planted kisses on Shannon's forehead, cheeks, and nose. "Wake up, love. Do you still want to come to the studio with me, or head back to Asgard?"

"Why are you so awake?" Shannon grumbled and half-opened her eyes to glare at the blue ones a few inches from her face. After staying up late getting to know Elise and Harry, Shannon and Loki had spent the night at his London flat, re-christening his king-sized bed. At least his bedroom wasn't destroyed this time.

He chuckled and kissed her, a quick peck on the lips. "Come on, sleepyhead. I've already worked out, and I'm about to jump in the shower. I have to leave within the hour."

"I'm going back to sleep. You go ahead." Bad-tempered, she tugged the blanket over her head. It was too bright, he was way too damn cheerful, and although her stomach gnawed a bit, the throbbing at her temples had her closing her eyes again.

He pulled it down again. "Nope, no way. I'm not leaving my pregnant wife here in London alone, without me."

Yesterday's anger surged anew with white-hot intensity, and she glared slit-eyed at him. "One, there is no ring on this finger. You haven't married me yet, buster. Frankly, you haven't even *asked* me yet, so stop assuming! Two, I can take care of myself. Isn't that why I've been training with Mist for the last month?"

Taking her face in his hands, he kissed Shannon breathless, despite her annoyance. He really was far too good at that. Damn, but it was hard to stay angry with her brain scattered. It took her a minute to pay attention to what he was saying.

He smirked and shook his head. "Darling, you are my soulmate and consort. Of course, you are my wife. As soon as my manager says it won't cause a scandal, I will put a ring on you just like Beyoncé's song, satisfying your Midgardian tradition. Paparazzi are a necessary evil I'd like to keep from swarming you whenever we're here. They're like circling razorbeasts at any hint of scandal, doing stupid things like peeping in windows and spying at inopportune moments. We don't want to accidentally expose the immortal world."

"No, Loki. I am *not* your wife," Shannon snarled, shoving at his unmoving form. Godsdamn it. Why was he so fucking big? "*Ask* first. Give me a fucking choice. Maybe I don't want to marry you." His assumption pissed her off, and her pulse pounded, sending pain flaring bright in her head. Heat grew within her chest, climbing her throat to her cheeks. Maybe her fucking opinion should actually matter to him? There was no way she'd be taken for granted. If she was so godsdamned important, then shouldn't she get a say on whether they got married and when? Why did his career get the final say instead of what she wanted?

Loki laughed and kissed her scowl, tugging gently on her lower lip. "Rest assured, love. When the time comes, I will ask properly. Now, you've made tremendous progress with Mist, and if it was just you, I'd be more willing to contain my worry. I know you can take care of yourself against mortals."

Unsuccessful in pushing him off her, Shannon turned on her side and crossed her arms. He wasn't listening to her concerns, but at least he'd said he'd ask... eventually. Maybe she'd say no. Bastard.

Loki's tone lost its playful lilt, turning starkly serious. "But it's not just you, darling. You are carrying our child. If Isis and Vidar, or now Gwydion and Arianrhod, were to come across you without me... I can't bear the thought." His next words were barely audible, and she strained to hear, "Please, Shannon, don't ask me to do that. We don't know if they left London or not. Those ruthless fuckers could still be here."

Fear percolated through their bond, sending a chill skittering down her back.

Shannon's resistance melted. She could get some damned sleep in his palace suite just as well as here if it made him stop fussing at her. "Fine, I suppose I could go back to Asgard and train with Mist." Although she'd wanted to visit his recording studio, she was in no temper to do so today. Not with him completely unwilling to see her point of view. Some space from her stubborn prince would be good... before their fight worsened.

And frankly, she felt the need to hone her skills after the unexpected encounter at the after-party. The Unseelie had scared her. She rubbed the arm Gwydion had sent painful sparks through, then touched her throat, as if she could still feel the choking bite.

"Thank you, darling." He kissed her cheek, relief in his tone.

Shannon sat up and he tugged her out of bed, leading her to the shower. Searching for something that wouldn't set off another argument, she asked, "How do you keep track of time, moving between realms?"

It made her head hurt to figure out the conversion. Okay, so it probably wasn't the calculation causing her headache after only four hours of sleep, but still, math first thing after waking was cruel and unusual punishment. Loki had been popping to Earth multiple times a day, for a few hours each time, over the last week when recording started for the new album. The difference in how time worked between the realms was to their advantage, giving Loki an entire workday as Tod each time he went to Earth. It was strange to get used to.

Jet lag had nothing on travelling between realms.

"Not sure." Loki shrugged. "Somehow, I just seem to know without thinking about it. Do you want a spelled timepiece that will display the passage of time in both realms? When Asgardians need to travel back and forth to make specific commitments on Midgard, our mages provide them. I made one for Thor. I'll make one for you if you'd like?"

No sooner had she thanked him than he had her up against the shower wall, a rainfall of steaming water streaming over their bodies. Damn him, she wanted to be furious, but she just couldn't hold on to it in the face of his relentless carnal onslaught. And afterwards, headache dissipated in favour of humming energy and heaving breath, she braced unsteady legs against the slick tiles.

The last remnants of anger were swept away, down the drain with the orange-scented body wash, by the solicitude in his touch as he washed her, cared for her. His satisfaction and pleasure came through the bond, swelling the lightness in her chest.

Once out of the shower, she dried off and dressed, only to catch Loki smirking. "Happy with yourself, are you?" He followed her out to the rooftop garden.

"Absolutely, darling. I love having you scream my name in ecstasy. It gets me hard, remembering." To emphasize his point, he tugged her against him.

A snort of amusement escaped. "You're always hard."

"Only for you," Loki whispered as he kissed her neck. The truthfulness of his statement intertwined with love and desire, flowed through their connection to fill all the spaces inside her. Despite doubts that popped up to plague her at times, she didn't question that. Not any longer. He'd shown her in so many ways.

Wide awake, her body loose, limber, and energetic after their shower, Shannon kissed Loki once more before stepping away. "Stay over there, unless you are planning to skip recording today, you sex fiend."

Eyes glinting, he assumed a mock hurt expression. "Why darling, I love you too. Such beautiful words you call me. In a couple of hours, when I'm done here for the day, I'll see about proving them true."

"Heimdall? I'm ready." Loki blew Shannon a kiss as the rainbow lights surrounded her. "Seriously, he's such a fiend," she told Heimdall as the lights faded.

Heimdall smiled. "Prince Loki loves you. He can't help himself."

"Oh!" Heat flushed her cheeks as a thought occurred to her.

"No, Princess. Never would I invade your privacy that way." He held up a large hand, stepping away from the hovering panel to duck down and meet her lowered gaze. "Please don't feel embarrassed. I monitor your safety without hearing and seeing the details of your intimate moments. Think of it as an unconscious alert system that notifies me of keywords, phrases, and dangers in your surroundings, without actually monitoring you myself, until you call on me. My conscious mind is not watching you unless something pings that alert system. Does that make sense?" he said in a kind and understanding voice.

Her shoulders dropped, tension dissipating at his words. "Yes, that does make a good analogy. Thanks, Heimdall."

"Of course, Princess."

With a wave, Shannon set out across the bridge, the energy thrumming under her feet. Her son was doing flips inside her. To settle him, she rubbed a hand over him as she walked. Instinct told her he was going to be just as energetic as his father.

Holy shit, that was a terrifying thought. How would she handle it?

Chapter 44

THE FOREST FOR THE TREES

The green light of the healing table clicked off and Shannon sat up. If she thought she'd spent considerably less time with Loki when he'd first resumed recording with his band, she'd barely seen him at all over the last two weeks. With filming of his movie due to start mid-July—the latest Loki could get the producers to push it—Raven's Chaos was cramming long recording sessions to wrap their album before Thor's premiere.

She hadn't even told him she was due to see Healer Moja for a check-up today. Not that she'd had the chance. He'd known about and not shown up for the last one, nor acknowledged that he'd missed it. Was he losing interest already? Or just swamped with his career, trying to accommodate the vacation with Thor's family she'd asked for? She wasn't sure, but either way, she wasn't going to chase after him to demand his attention like a needy groupie. He had to decide on his priorities himself, or a relationship between them would never work. Still, the pit in her stomach belied her nonchalance at his continued absence only scant weeks into being together.

The round-cheeked healer frowned as she handed Shannon one of the golden apples. "You are losing too much weight, Princess. Your son is fine, growing exactly as he should. But I'm concerned about you. Pregnancy is energetically expensive, and you are a young immortal, still settling into your goddess energies."

"What does that mean for me?" Shannon stared down at the fruit.

"Pay closer attention to your energy levels. Recharge more often. Don't skimp on sleep. Eat more often, especially high-calorie foods. At a minimum, I want you eating one of Idun's apples each day."

"I can do that," Shannon agreed, hopping off the bed and taking a big bite, brandishing her compliance. "Thanks!"

Moja put a hand on Shannon's shoulder, holding her gaze as Shannon chewed. "If your energy depletion doesn't start levelling off, we may need to restrict your activities."

Shannon's eyes widened, alarm tightening her chest. That didn't sound good. She needed to be ready, to be able to defend herself and her child. Gods, she had so much to still learn, to master. She didn't have time to languish on bed rest, a tempting, helpless victim for Isis. "I'll be careful." She waved to the healer as she continued eating the apple and left to find Mist.

Recharge more often. What did that mean? Take more food breaks?

Shannon was training with Mist and Kara when Loki returned to Asgard. Norns, but she was gorgeous in motion and his heart swelled to see her safe, sweat gleaming on her skin with a determined frown on her face. Like a dancer, her graceful armour-clad form launched into the air as if a staircase rose in front of her. Even as she fell at the fourth step, he knew she'd conquer the skill in no time. Her progress was nothing short of remarkable. In all his years, he'd never seen an immortal master their abilities so quickly.

She picked herself up from the black sand and put her hands on her hips. "What am I doing wrong?" Despite this being a training session, she bristled with weapons—a pair of sais on thigh sheaths, a long dagger at her hip, and throwing knives in forearm sheaths.

He smiled. The latest modification to her armour seemed to be working the way he'd envisioned, compensating for her inability to conjure or manipulate metal. Never again would she be left without a weapon as she had been when Isis had attacked.

Mist shook her head. "You are thinking too far ahead and letting your concentration lapse too quickly on the current air stepping stone. It's dissipating on you before you move to the next one." Mist demonstrated, using visible cloud steps. "You want to remove it fast enough so your opponent can't use it, but not so fast that you lose your balance and fall. Until you have practiced it over and over, it won't become instinct. For now, you still need to concentrate to maintain and dissipate each one."

"Ugh!" Shannon landed on her hands and knees partway through her next try, and Loki fought to stay in place, to not catch her. Bor's beard, it was hard to watch her fall.

Kara laughed and extended a hand, helping Shannon to her feet. "Stop beating yourself up. It takes practice, which is what you are doing. You are making excellent progress."

With the next try, Shannon managed to stay aloft, and Mist tested her with slower-motion mid-air hand-to-hand. Kara shouted suggestions up at them and stood below, shaking her head at their antics when both started giggling like loons, hanging upside down, with Mist murmuring to Shannon's belly.

As proud as he was of her, his uneven heartbeat had him asking, "Are you two going to come down anytime soon?"

When Shannon tilted her head from where she and Mist floated, she spotted him and shoved Mist's head off her abdomen.

Mist shoved Shannon back playfully as they landed next to Loki. "Shannon's skills have really advanced."

"Indeed," he agreed. As Loki tilted his head down, Shannon leaned up to kiss him with a quick peck on his lips that left him wanting more.

"I'm hungry! Let's eat!"

Loki held back his sigh and nodded. As much as he'd anticipated stealing Shannon back to the bedroom, she and the baby needed fuel after training.

"You are always hungry," Mist complained. "Your son is a bottomless pit!"

"By all means, let's feed both of you. We could all use a break." Kara led the way to the warrior's lounge off the training grounds. Long tables on the far wall held a buffet-style meal the kitchen staff replenished throughout the day.

"What are you in the mood for?" Loki pushed Shannon to sit on a bench at a scuffed and scarred wooden table.

"Your son and I would kill for a roast hen, bacon, tomato, greens, and cheese sandwich on sourdough, with extra mayo and pickles."

Loki smirked. "Pickles? Is this the start of the weird cravings?"

"Hey! Pickles are *not* weird on sandwiches!"

Teasing her with a raised eyebrow, he chuckled and quickly assembled a plate, adding a pile of raw yellow and red sweet capsicum, green cucumis, and orange daucus. Wasn't she supposed to eat a multitude of vegetable colours to get all her nutrients and minerals? He added chopped sticks of raphanus, a spicy white vegetable that was his favourite. She liked that, didn't she?

As he reached the drinks, he paused.

Water? Apple cider? It wasn't made from Idun's apples, but still, the fresh cider was good. Oh wait... milk. The image of Shannon, their babe at her breast, shot fiery heat through his abdomen and he clutched the plate. Yggdrasil's roots, he couldn't wait for her lush body to fill. Biting back his groan, he stared at the drinks for a long minute, caught in the fantasy until another warrior came to fill their mug.

Hastily, he filled a tankard and crossed the room to set the plate and drink in front of Shannon. Her lips twitched as she thanked him. Had he given her too much? Heading back to the tables, he filled his plate with greens, raphanus, cheeses and meats, and a slice of gooseberry pie.

When he rejoined Shannon, she'd eaten half her sandwich. Good.

Mist started tucking into a bowl of noodles when Kara joined them with her plate of roasted vegetables and meats. "I didn't think you drank milk," Kara nodded at the untouched tankard in front of Shannon.

Loki frowned. She didn't drink milk?

Shannon's lips curled into a little smile, and she patted Loki on the thigh. "I don't. Not unless it's in a smoothie, milkshake, or with copious amounts of chocolate."

Oh... well, he could fix that. With a black flash of seidhr, the milk turned into a chocolate milkshake, complete with straw.

Immediately, Shannon took a big sip. "Thank you, love." She gave him a big grin.

Loki took a bite of his salad. "Of course, darling. I'm just trying to make sure you get all your micro and macronutrients."

"Have you been reading pregnancy books?" she teased.

Auroch shit... had he said that out loud? Shannon had read that *What to Expect When You're Expecting* book three times. Of course, he'd read it too. And, okay, maybe he'd read it five... ten... more times, when Healer Moja remained closed-lipped about immortal pregnancies. But Norns, it had been a thousand years on Midgard since he'd last fathered children. Granted, he'd spent more than half of those years on Asgard—a measly hundred years here—trying to not hurt from their loss to the ravages of time. Still, none had been immortal children. There had to be some differences, didn't there?

Heat rose across his face and he bent his head to take another bite of his food, not looking at any of them. Shannon's fingers touched his chin lightly, turning his face towards her. When she kissed him, the slight tension in his shoulders disappeared.

"I love you, Loki."

"All teasing aside, Loki, I think we need to figure out what Shannon is the goddess of. She needs more recharging her energies." Mist slurped the last of her noodles. "I'm concerned about her energy usage. She's lost weight. Her face has seriously thinned out, and she's losing curves."

Shannon snorted. She'd actually been pleased to lose a few pounds, Trent's years of insults ringing in her ears. He'd mocked her "baby-fat cheeks" and "big ass." Still, if both Mist and Moja were concerned, maybe it was a bigger deal than she'd thought. Especially with Moja's looming "restricted activities" threat.

"I completely agree. Have you noticed feeling more energetic in certain circumstances or environments, Shannon?" Loki met Shannon's gaze as he forked up his pie.

"Sex with you always revs me right up," Shannon quipped and laughed as Mist and Kara clapped their hands over their ears. Damn, it was so easy to get a rise out of them. Yet they weren't prudish at all and razzed each other about their varied conquests frequently.

"Oh, for the love of all the realms! We don't want to hear about your kinky sex life!" Kara complained, wrinkling her nose.

Shannon snorted and almost choked at the bald-faced lie the Valkyrie managed with such an earnest expression—Kara was a *massive* gossip, the juicier the better.

Loki grinned and winked. "But we have such fun!"

"Ugh! Shut up! Seriously!" Mist threw a bread roll at Loki even as her eyes glinted.

He caught it and bit into it, chuckling. "Okay, *other* than sex with me, since we know you must also have a fertility god or goddess in your ancestry. Anything else? You might notice it not so much as feeling energetic, but perhaps a sense of calm, peace, or just rightness. I'm not sure how else to explain the sensation."

Shannon thought about it, considering what he meant. "In the past, I'd have gone for a hike in the forest around my home, or a swim in the ocean when it's warm enough. That's where I've felt the most content."

"We have a few hours before we need to leave for Thor's movie premiere. I haven't taken you out of the capital yet. Why don't we go for a walk in the Mimameidr Woods? It's a forest of towering redwoods even Heimdall can't put his arms around, out past the western gate of the city," Loki suggested.

"I'd love that," she agreed as she finished her food. "Let's go!"

"Do you two want to come?" he asked Kara and Mist.

They looked at each other for a minute, then smirked.

"Nope, we don't need to witness any of your freaky sexcapades. There is only so much brain bleach in the world," Mist teased in a mock disgusted tone, nose in the air… before she winked.

Shannon huffed and rolled her eyes with great exaggeration as she stood to leave, cocking a hand on a hip that still had too much padding as far as she was concerned. "Whatever, losers. We are going for a walk, not sex against a tree!"

Loki's eyes glinted. "Why darling, I love how your mind works. Later, ladies!" He tucked Shannon's hand in his elbow, leading her from the room.

After walking down the corridor, up two sets of stairs, and down another long hall, Loki pushed open one side of a tall, double set of blacksteel doors, and they entered a massive, busy hangar. Shouts, metallic clangs, and thuds of feet created a cacophony that almost had Shannon covering her ears. Sleek black ships shaped like a pair of horns wrapping around a central sphere loomed over the majority of the space. Armour-clad warriors wove around jumpsuited technicians, or perhaps they were maintenance staff, as one opened an external compartment on a nearby ship and used a scanner on the ship's innards. Others unloaded or loaded crates, barrels, and boxes from lowered ramps in the spherical portion of various ships. These had to be the shuttles to and from Skaikaup, the Asgardian space station Frigga mentioned where trade with other planets and meetings with visitors who were not approved to visit Asgard's surface happened. Once she took up some of her royal duties, it was where Shannon would spend considerable time. She'd already seen such a diversity of beings here in the capital city. What would it be like to visit the space station? Her hand rested on her abdomen. Holy hell, she had so much to learn, so much to explore.

Loki squeezed her hand, drawing her attention. "Since we don't have tons of time, we'll take a skuta to the forest. I'd rather have the extra time to ravish you." His eyes were dark with promise as he directed Shannon over to a quieter side of the hangar and a row of much smaller ships. These skuta looked like miniature Viking longboats with curved, silver wings rising from the sides but no sails.

Heat flared between her thighs, even as Shannon attempted a token protest. "And here I thought we were supposed to be finding out if walking in the forest replenishes my energy?"

"Oh, we will." Loki showed her to a grey padded bench seat in the nearest vessel. "The two aren't mutually exclusive, after all."

Arousal shivered over her skin as she watched him ready the ship. Loki's recording schedule hadn't coordinated with the Asgardian sleep cycle over the last two weeks. With not having more than an hour together at a time, they hadn't done more than kiss, cuddle, and catch a quickie in the shower, vacant room, or wherever Loki could catch her alone on his short visits. She was missing her amorous god's more thorough attention.

The controls lit blue when he pressed something, and a silver glow surrounded them. The craft lifted into the air and shot through a golden shimmering barrier spanning the mouth-like circular hangar entrance. Once outside, Loki banked the ship to the right and they flew over the rainbow bridge and along the shoreline of the deep blue fjord separating the capital city and palace from the mountain peak that held the Bifrost chamber. A gleaming white granite home was built into the cliffs below the high dome of the Bifrost chamber. Shannon hadn't noticed it before.

"Is that where Heimdall lives?"

Loki turned to see where she was pointing. "Yes. Even in his few off hours, he prefers to stay close to the Bifrost."

With the craft speeding down by the narrow, winding inlet, Loki sent up a spray of water behind them, swerving back and forth playfully.

She laughed. "Don't kill us, you maniac pilot!"

Loki grinned and nodded up ahead at the rapidly approaching forest.

"Wow! You weren't kidding when you said they were large!" Just back from the rocky shoreline, the forest of redwoods started. The trees had to be one hundred and fifty metres tall, at least, and as wide around as a small house. Although she'd been to the redwood forests of California, these made those trees look tiny.

Loki had barely set the craft down when Shannon was out, running for the nearest trunk. She pressed her face against the rough bark. The sense of age was an ache that went right down to her bones. These trees had to be ancient.

"How old?" she asked in a quiet, reverent voice.

"This forest is older than I am, older than Odin."

Her eyes closed, feeling the ebb and flow of the tree, its energies rooted in the depths of the soil and reaching so far into the sky. Like a lullaby, it was calming and peaceful. The woody scent filled her nose, reminiscent of growing things, warmth, and the comfort of being in Loki's arms. The trees creaked, moving with gentle breezes, and waves quietly lapped on the shore behind her, with the occasional bird or chipmunk talking in the forest.

"Clearly, you are a Goddess of the Forest at a minimum."

It took a minute for Loki's words to penetrate the spell of the tree's energies.

She opened her eyes and blinked. "Sorry, what?"

"You have been mesmerized by the tree, pressed against it for the last fifteen minutes. I can see the vitality in your cheeks. How do you feel?"

His words surprised her. She'd thought she'd only been against the tree for maybe a minute at most. Unwilling to lose contact, she turned to face him, while still leaning back against the trunk. "Calm. Happy. And now that you mention it, the lingering tiredness and slight headache I hadn't noticed until it wasn't there anymore is gone. I feel fantastic."

Loki smiled, relief lightening his emerald eyes as the furrow at his brow smoothed out. Had he been worried? "Obviously, we need to get you out to nature more often, especially when I can't be around as frequently to recharge you through the day. Between our son and your training, you are using a lot of energy every single day. More than your body can recharge on rest and food. It's good we are taking a little vacation with Thor's family."

He had noticed, too? She supposed she really should pay attention. She reached out to take his hand. "C'mon then. Let's go walk while we still have the time." Abandoning the tree behind her, Shannon eagerly tugged him deeper into the forest. Why had she not come out here yet? Her heart leapt to explore a new forest on a different planet. Would all the plants be bigger versions of those on Earth?

There was no path, but the understory plants weren't dense under the towering heights evergreens. An entirely alien environment, yet plants had the same challenges to compete for light, nutrients, and space. It was easy to walk between the large ferns on the springy carpet of conifer needles and thick, rich-green mosses. Silently, they walked hand-in-hand deeper into the forest. Deep breaths of moist, resinous air filled her lungs, so distinctive of temperate conifer rainforests on Earth. A profound peace and sense of home settled into her chest. Gods, she hadn't realized how much she'd missed walking in the forest.

After half an hour, they turned to loop back toward the shoreline. As they came to a slight opening in the canopy, tall woody shrubs with small leaves and distinctive pinkish-red berries caught her eye. An excited thrill ran through her. Could it be? Here? On Asgard?

"Are these huckleberries?" So many wonderful childhood memories were of picking and eating the tart berries in the forest with her parents, climbing the hillsides above town with her siblings to harvest bucketfuls, and backing off when the bears beat them to the best patches.

Loki chuckled. "I take it you are a fan? Yes, they are."

"Oh, I adore huckleberries! Especially huckleberry jam!" Quickly, she started picking and stuffing handfuls into her mouth, blinking back tears. Those were good memories of her family. Before her dad died. Before she discovered she was adopted and realized her sister hated her.

Loki grinned as he picked berries and ate a few, but mostly fed them to her. With a playful tease, Shannon kissed his fingers and his eyes darkened. Their eyes met, held. Yeah, she'd rather he distracted her, and kept her from dwelling on things she couldn't change.

"Darling, I'd rather taste the berries on you." His voice deepened as his mouth descended on hers.

Berries were forgotten as lips and tongues met. Her back bumped into a wide tree trunk. Amusement had her breaking their kiss briefly to smirk at him.

"Time for tree-trunk sexcapades, is it?"

"Absofuckinglutely," Loki growled, kissing his way down her neck.

In agreement, she tilted her head to give him better access, moaning as he bit lightly at her nape, exactly where he knew it drove her wild, damn him. Loki scraped his teeth against her skin and she shivered.

Reaching down, she stroked Loki's rigid length through his black leather pants, gripping when his hips jerked. Holy hell, she loved the feel of him in her hands and the way he responded to her touch, pulsing hot against her palm.

"Enough of that, or I won't last a minute," Loki groaned and caught her wrists, pinning them above her head against the tree.

"But I want to touch you!" she whimpered, pulling against his hold. He never let her touch him as much as she wanted. Damn it. One of these days, she was going to tie him down and have her wicked way with him.

"Later!" Loki insisted as a band of black seidhr trapped her arms. Shit, had he read her mind? His hands made quick work of opening her tunic and freeing her breasts to his hungry touch. "By the Nine, you are so fucking sexy," he groaned, lowering his mouth.

"Gods, Loki!" Pleasure spiked with each tug of his wet mouth and clever fingers. Heat built in her core. Pregnancy had made her nipples even more sensitive of late, and the fucking wicked bastard knew it. How did he always drive her completely bonkers, so fast, so easily?

Loki twisted a tip, tugging. "I can't wait until these gorgeous breasts of yours fill. So beautiful," he mouthed before sucking hard.

She trembled. Sensation flared as the pull of his mouth and fingers drew the bowstring tighter inside her. Fuck, he should come with a warning label.

"The sight of you, swollen with my child, is so fucking gorgeous, darling. Bor's beard, I could spill right now, watching you writhe and hearing you moan for me." Loki fisted his cock through his leather pants. "Come for me like this, just like this, as I play with these beautiful tits," he demanded.

"Loki, please." Hips moving, she panted, seeking the contact he was denying her. It wasn't fair. He was so damn good at driving her wild.

"Come for me, Shannon." Loki was unrelenting in his sensual assault. She was so close. her core throbbed and her legs shook. Lifting his head, he held her gaze. "Now!" Loki demanded in a fierce growl. With a light twist and pinch of her nipples, he gave her just the little bite of pleasure on the edge of pain to kick her over the precipice.

Her vision whitened as lightning shot through her body, and his name tore from her throat. Her core clenched, achingly empty as it spasmed, and she writhed against her bound hands.

Regaining her senses, Shannon's eyes focused just in time to realize Loki held her now-naked hips in the air. He thrust hard into her still-pulsing heat. "*Gods!*" It kicked her right into orgasm again, prolonging the pleasure bursting over her senses.

Loki was breathing hard and not yet moving when her brain kicked back in. In control of her muscles again, she deliberately tightened around him.

"Yggdrasil's heart!" he swore as he panted, then looked into her eyes. Not breaking eye contact, he pulled almost out, then slowly slid in again. Loki gave a dark half-smile at her gasp and did it again. Each time, it sent a blast of intense pleasure exploding up her spine. Holding her hips, he thrust, adjusting to slide repeatedly over that sensitive spot inside her.

Shannon whimpered, trying to buck.

"You will come again for me," Loki growled.

She moaned her agreement, knowing he would have his way. Like the maestro he was, he played her body, building her arousal with each delicious stroke. She tried to flex her hips and drive him harder, but he just smiled. Loki's strength far outmatched hers. Holding her there, he kept her trembling, not quite over, until she was ready to scream.

"Harder! Loki, *please!*"

It seemed to be what he was waiting for, as her pleading triggered him to take her hard, deep, and fast.

"*Loki!*" Raw and primal, the scream burst from her throat as fireworks exploded throughout her body, shooting out of her fingers, toes, and the top of her head. Roaring with his own shout of completion, Loki's hips jerked with his release, flooding her as she panted and shook in his arms.

After releasing her wrists, Loki carried her to a thick bed of moss, and they sank to the ground, with her sprawled half on, half off his long, toned body. "How's your energy level now?" he asked in a playful tone after their heartbeats had returned to a normal rhythm.

"Fully topped up, just as you intended. Now ask me if my legs still work," Shannon groaned. Leaning up, she kissed him lightly on the lips, enjoying the sated look in his green eyes.

It was true, though. She felt full, for lack of a better description. No fatigue, no headache. Shannon could fall asleep if she wanted to, but that was due to the deep relaxation and endorphins, not any lingering tiredness. Movement was effortless as she threaded her fingers through his hair. Every residual muscle ache and bruise from training was gone, including the small scratches to her palms and knees from landing on the course training ground sand.

Loki caressed her curved abdomen, pausing to rub a particular spot when their son kicked under his touch, as he told her about the songs they'd finished recording today. His contentment was in his tone and their bond, and she basked in the warmth surrounding her, filling her. Time to just be themselves, with no interruptions, had been so rare.

Shannon sensed his reluctance when he said they needed to leave and found herself torn, not wanting to abandon their secluded bower. Yet the promised vacation and chance to meet Thor's wife and kids lured her to untangle their limbs and straighten her clothes.

The flight back seemed to take half the time of the trip there. "If we aren't going to be late for Thor's premiere, we need to be quick," Loki warned as he slipped the ship into a gap between others in the hangar.

"Can't we go right to the Bifrost? You can conjure clothes and anything we need?"

"True, that will save us some time, if you are okay with relying entirely on me? If you want, we can always go shopping after the premiere."

"I'm good with that. Put me in some sassy red-carpet number with fuck-me heels, my sexy fashion god." Shannon grinned when his eyes flashed and he scowled. Gods, he was such fun to taunt. And when he was all riled up... so fucking hot.

"What? Did I somehow leave you unsatisfied, that you need to wear fuck-me heels?"

Loki sounded offended, and she gave him an innocent blink.

"No, love. It's just to give you ideas for after the premiere. Or perhaps a closet, or side room, should the mood strike us." Full of energy, her body thrummed and she couldn't help flirting with him. She peered up through her lashes.

He cocked his head, nostrils flaring. Then he caught her gaze and his eyes glinted, humour and arousal darkening the emerald depths. "Damn woman, you know how to drive me wild." He shook his head as his hand adjusted his rigid cock straining his leather pants. "Seriously, the Norns gave me my perfect match. Now that's all I'm going to be thinking about."

A wave of black rolled over her and left her in a slinky, emerald-green full-length dress, with thin spaghetti straps, a plunging neckline, a low back barely above the curve of her ass, and a high slit up one thigh. A strand of emeralds trailed down between her breasts, and matching earrings hung from her ears. Gold stiletto heels completed the look, and an illusion hid her baby bump.

The barely-there covering over her breasts had Shannon eying the potential for disaster. "You did ensure your magic will keep me from a wardrobe malfunction, right?"

Loki gave her a darkly possessive smile. "Of course, darling. Every man will be picking his jaw up off the floor, but only I get to see those gorgeous plum nipples. They are mine." His gaze travelled down her body and back up again in a slow, heated perusal. "I may not even let Thor hug you in this."

She rolled her eyes, allowing irritation to fill her tone as she crossed her arms. "If that's the case, then you better put me in something else, because I'm not forgoing hugging him so you can show me off. I'm not a possession."

Loki raised his hands in surrender. "I know. Truly. You, my beautiful, sexy Shannon, are a strong independent goddess, and I am the luckiest god in all the realms."

"And don't you forget it!"

He kissed her, licking along her lower lip, and winked as he changed his clothes for a fitted black jacket, and a black turtle-neck to match his already tight black leather pants. Fuck, he was gorgeous. And hers.

Chapter 45

CALL OF THE SEA

The white sand was warm under Shannon's feet, with a light offshore breeze lifting strands of her hair in a fluttering caress. With Amelia beside her, they explored the beach in front of Thor and Amelia's island vacation home in the Whitsundays, a short boat ride from the airport on Hamilton Island where their private charter had landed. After the premiere, Loki and Shannon had spent the first few days visiting with them in Sydney, seeing some of the tourist sites, taking in a rugby game with Thor's team, and meeting Amelia's siblings, but this... this was perfect and exactly what she'd hoped for in discovering more of Australia. It was someplace she'd always wanted to visit yet hadn't managed to get to until now.

The two women hit it off immediately. It was obvious why Thor had fallen in love with Amelia. Funny and warm, she was no pushover. When she scolded Thor for getting their kids all riled up before bed or for giving them junk food, Shannon grinned. Amelia didn't hesitate to tell the powerful god her mind. And it was all kinds of cute the way he turned from a thundering grizzly into a mushy teddy bear around her. Shannon had blackmail material for years.

"This is stunning." Shannon took in the view of the bright afternoon sun reflecting off the green-blue water and frothy waves breaking on the long beach. Gods, she couldn't wait to jump in the water, the craving almost a heated itch under her flesh. The salt-laden breeze was helping, but Shannon's skin felt overly warm, sweaty, and sticky. And the discomfort was growing the closer she got to the water. Avoiding using her powers in front of Amelia and the kids was getting harder.

"Yeah," Amelia said in her lilting Australian accent. "Coming up here this time of year is bloody awesome. It's perfectly tropical, but not too hot and not cold either. Why deal with the shitshow in Sydney when I can be here instead?"

"I would be, too! Should we be keeping an eye on them?" Shannon gestured to the twins as the red-headed girls took off splashing along the shore.

"Growing up around water, we've made sure they are strong swimmers, nevertheless the kids know the rules. They aren't allowed to go deeper than their knees without one of us swimming with them."

"The water looks fantastic. I'm looking forward to jumping in myself." Ha. Understatement. Even as she tried to look around, her gaze was constantly drawn back to the ocean in front of her. Goosebumps rose as she fought the need.

"You want me to cook the steak tonight, right?" Thor called out to her. The guys were bringing in the groceries from the boat to stock the house for the weekend while the kids burned off pent-up energy from the flight and boat ride.

"Yeah, babe!" Amelia yelled back. "Put the beers in the esky, too!"

"Already done!" Loki shouted back.

Shannon laughed. "Of course, they took care of the alcohol before the food!"

Amelia shook her head in amusement. "No worries. Why don't we join the kids in the surf?"

A shiver rippled down Shannon's spine, eagerness rising. "Now that sounds like the best idea I've heard all day!"

They walked back to the deck and shed their layers. Quickly tugging off jean shorts and a T-shirt, Shannon revealed the black bikini underneath. Still, she had to fight not to cradle her abdomen, the move instinctive. It was weird to look down and have her stomach appear flat when she was twenty-six weeks pregnant. There would be no hiding this belly without Loki's illusions.

A whistle pierced the air and she turned to see Loki smiling, eyes roving over her body in a heated caress.

She cocked a hand on her hip. <*Checking me out, love?*>

<Always, darling. Don't worry about the illusion. It will hold in the water as well. Just don't go forgetting and flop on your sexy round belly.>

<As if I would. Despite not seeing our son, I feel him regardless. My balance and centre of gravity keep changing.> She followed Amelia into the surf with the kids. The water's first touch was heavenly, refreshing and cool. A tingling sensation washed over her skin as she waded through the surf to submerge herself. Freed from the heat, she dove, played, swam, and splashed with Amelia and the kids until arms reached around her, tugging her back into a hard chest.

"Why Tempest, I believe you have the wrong woman." Shannon bit her lip against a laugh.

Loki snorted in amusement. "Nice try, darling." With effortless strength, he lifted her out of the water and tossed her.

As the water closed over her, Shannon let herself sink, enjoying the prickling sparks that seemed to race over her nerve endings with her entire body submerged. She swam further out and sat down on the bottom, looking back at the shore. The kids swam and ran—their legs visible in the clear depths. Her heartbeat slowed and limbs relaxed. Gods, it was peaceful under the water. Her eyes closed. Maybe she'd just nap right here.

<You are freaking Amelia and Thor out. They think I've drowned you.> Loki chuckled, his mirth sending bubbles of mischief through the bond. *<Come up, Shannon, or—>*

He didn't get the teasing threat out before Thor was there, dragging her up out of the water. "Are you okay, Shannon? What did that fool brother of mine do to you?" He was clearly panicking, thinking she was hurt as he held her and lightly tapped her face, peering into her eyes.

Her lips twitched. *<I take it you haven't told Thor I can breathe underwater?>*

<Now, where would be the fun in that? It's not my fault he hasn't had time to spend in Asgard lately to learn the range of your powers.> Loki's tone was completely unrepentant, smirking at Thor's reaction.

A laugh burst out of her. "I'm sorry. I'm fine! I'm sorry, Tempest. Honest, I'm fine. I can hold my breath for a *really* long time. The water is just so relaxing." Thor put her back on her feet as she reassured him, patting his arms.

Amelia grinned. "Oi, you gave us a turn, but I should have known Tod would be shit-scared if there was something to fret about."

Thor scowled down at Shannon. "Okay, time for dinner. That's enough for now. You'll give me grey hair, Shannon!"

A welling of warmth burbled up inside her for this immortal who had accepted her as family so quickly, treated her as a beloved little sister, and watched out for her even when she was a brat... like now. "Well, you are *so* much older than me, old man," she teased and then swam away, giggling.

"I'm not old!" he growled, affronted, sending a splash of water over her face when she turned back to stick a tongue out at him. Amelia and Loki laughed. Thor's eyes gleamed with humour, even as he grumbled and headed towards the shore.

Reluctant to get out, she sank back into the water. The soothing caress of it over her skin was refreshing, and her body tingled with energy. Even her lower back no longer hurt as the water made her pregnant belly buoyant. Bobbing in the waves, she let herself float. Amelia already had the kids out of the water and towelling off, with Thor firing up the barbeque.

Loki swam out to join Shannon in the deeper depths. "Darling, I can sense how much you are enjoying the water. With the way you are glowing with vitality, I'd say you are a sea goddess as well."

Lazily, she wrapped her arms around his neck, fingers playing with the short hairs he was currently sporting as his Tod persona. As handsome as he was in it, she preferred his dark locks. "Mmm... It does feel fantastic to be in the water. Later, when Amelia and the kids are asleep, let's swim out and explore the coral reef."

"You can put a bubble around me to take me with you like you did for Isis? Or I can shift to a dolphin." Scooping her up into a bridal carry, Loki started wading them through the waves back to the shore. It never failed to make her feel tiny, almost delicate, when he carried her... the exact opposite of the overweight cow Trent had called her. Well, at least now that she'd gotten over her discomfort of thinking she was too heavy for Loki. He'd disabused her of that notion by raising a black eyebrow, then lifting a couch in his rooms with one hand... with her on it. She'd stopped protesting and let the toe-curling pleasure take her every time he picked her up.

She grinned. "I'll take you. You can depend on my magic for once."

Loki chuckled, leaning his head down to kiss her lightly. "I trust you will keep me breathing."

They reached the shore, and Loki continued carrying her up the sand to the patio. After depositing her in a lounge chair, he snagged a couple of towels as she removed the salty moisture from their skin. It wouldn't do for Amelia to wonder how they'd dried so completely, so fast.

"Cider?" Thor handed Shannon a bottle as he glanced at Loki. Loki gave him a tiny nod—he'd already removed the alcohol from the bottle.

"Yes, please. Thanks, Tempest."

Amelia set out a couple of trays of raw veggies and dip with another tray by the kids, who dove into the food as if she'd been starving them. After grabbing a bottle of beer, she relaxed into a chair beside Shannon, and they watched Thor and Loki debate the best way to grill the steak and prawns.

"For brothers, they get along amazingly well," Amelia marvelled. "My siblings fight, a lot."

"Yeah, I don't get along with my sister." Even if Frigga and Odin hadn't adopted Loki after Frigga's sister's death, Shannon could see Loki and Thor being close. Cousins by blood, but brothers by choice. She smiled, recalling Loki's comments about valuing chosen family, not just those linked by blood. "But these two do live on different continents now so aren't constantly up in each other's business."

Loki had given Shannon a perspective that was changing how she viewed the new relationships she was building in her life. Still, now that she knew she was adopted, she couldn't help but be curious about her Elven relatives, especially her parents. Surely her birth family wouldn't be as hostile as Gwydion and Arianrhod had been. Maybe that was just an Unseelie thing. Shannon rubbed her hands over her arms, chasing away remembered pain from Gwydion's grip and that electric jolt. When her son was born, she wanted to try to find her parents, to see if she had any existing Elven family. She needed to know not just where she came from, but why they'd given her away.

"Shit, yeah! Space certainly has a way of making the heart grow fonder," Amelia agreed.

After passing around plates of food the guys had cooked to perfection, they ate, relaxed, and talked until the sun set on the ocean in a brilliant display of fiery reds and oranges, bleeding into the deepest indigo. When the twins started yawning shortly afterwards, Amelia and Thor took them inside to tuck into bed.

Loki lifted Shannon from her chair, settling her between his thighs on a chaise lounge with his arms wrapped around her. The heat of his body was a welcome comfort as she relaxed into his strength. "How is our son behaving this evening?" He kissed her neck and sent shivers up and down her spine. Even when he wasn't trying, his touch tantalized with possibility.

"He was rambunctious earlier, but he's settled down for now. Although he's got a foot or elbow up near my ribs and gives me a good shot every once in a while."

"Where? Maybe I can coax him into a new position."

Gladly, she took Loki's right hand and, with the illusion lowered, showed him the spot on her lower left ribs. As he talked to their son, he massaged. Between the warmth coming through their bond and her own feelings, she was cocooned in warmth, happiness, and love... a feeling she'd missed of late with Loki gone so much, missing baby check-ups and only having time for the briefest of physical interactions. This vacation had been exactly what she'd needed to reassure herself that they were actually building a relationship.

When they heard Thor and Amelia returning an hour later, Loki settled the illusion on her again, hiding their child.

"Oi, you two lovebirds, I'm kinda beat so we're hitting the sack," Amelia said as Thor whispered in her ear. She laughed and gave him a push.

Somehow, Shannon suspected sleep wasn't on Thor's mind. "G'night. We'll see you in the morning. We're going to stay out here for a while longer. I'm in the mood for an evening swim."

Thor opened his mouth, and Loki beat him to it. "Don't worry. Of course, I'll make sure she doesn't get eaten by a croc or stung by jellyfish."

Thor picked Amelia up to toss over his shoulder. "Okay. G'night then."

"Put me down, you giant idiot!" she said, laughing.

Thor smirked at them and smacked her on the ass with a sharp crack. She yelped, and he carried her into the house. A moan echoed around the corner as they disappeared.

Loki chuckled. "I don't think Amelia's sleeping anytime soon."

"Nope," Shannon agreed. "Let's go explore the reef and give those two some privacy." Eagerly, she rose and tugged Loki to his feet. With a bounce in her step, they held hands as they walked down to the water she couldn't wait to submerge herself in again.

As the water closed in, his clever goddess created a bubble around Loki's head, pulling him along in her wake. Not simply shifting to an animal form was odd, but inspiring confidence in Shannon's abilities was important. Especially since they'd discovered the sea as a third source of goddess energy for her. He smiled to himself. Of course his soulmate was multi-sourced, given the range of her seidhr. It seemed a universal law that the more powerful the god or goddess, the more sources of energy they tapped into. She hadn't yet asked, but Loki was sure she wanted to find out more about her Elven parentage. Given what Rose had told her regarding her birth father, discovering her affinity with the sea wasn't a surprise. Dylan had to be an Elven sea god of some kind, although Loki hadn't heard of him. And who was her mother? What traits did she pass on to her daughter?

But that was something they'd explore after their son's birth. Cautiously. Loki had a lot of bloody enemies among the elves, although he had a few former friends and even past lovers among the Seelie. Before the war had made such relationships impossible. The dark elves though... his fists clenched. As if he didn't have enough reasons to hate the Unseelie, just recalling the way that bastard Gwydion had gone after Shannon had his vision tunnelling and a pounding starting in his ears. Loki bit back the growl rising in his throat. Had it been because she was with him? What was that electrical shock Shannon had described? Gwydion had known she wasn't mortal. How? Loki didn't want the fucking sick bastard anywhere near his goddess.

Wrenching his thoughts to their surroundings, he mused at the surprising peace under the water—a sharp contrast to the chaos churning inside him. No boat noise disrupted the gurgling sounds of their passage and the clicking of dolphins some distance away. Shannon created a light glow around them as she propelled them through the water toward the nearest section of the Great Barrier Reef, twenty kilometres offshore.

He'd managed to calm his turmoil by the time a pod of bottlenose dolphins found them. Their sleek silver forms dove around them, brushing against their bodies as Shannon laughed. Did they somehow know she was a sea goddess?

<Skinny fins want to swim? Want to play?>

<*Go fast? Dive with us!*>

Gleaming eyes meeting Loki's, she said, <*Yes, we'd love to swim and dive with you,*> as the dolphins nudged their hands with impatient dorsal fins.

After grabbing on, they shot through the water like bullets, swerving and diving. When one dolphin tired, another took its place.

<*Oops! Sorry, love,*> Shannon apologized the third time she'd not kept the bubble in place due to a sudden swerve of Loki's dolphin.

Fortunately, he could hold his breath long enough for her to get it back in place again. But it was the playful mischief in her expression that gave her away. <*Are you sure you aren't doing it on purpose?*>

Shannon grinned. <*Maybe?*>

Bor's beard, he loved her, loved this side of her that called to his own sense of fun. <*Dangerous game, darling. You'll never know when I'm going to pay you back.*>

<*Oh, look at me shaking in my non-existent boots.*>

And fuck, he loved her sass. By all the realms, it made him harder than Yggdrasil's trunk. With her being pregnant, he was hesitant to educate her in more erotic forms of discipline the way he craved, but once she'd given birth to their son... oh yes, he couldn't wait to see if she'd respond to a firmer hand in the bedroom and anywhere else he could convince her to let him seduce her.

The brilliant colours of the reef came into view. They released their dolphins, thanking them for the game. The sea mammals chittered happily, telling Loki and Shannon to come play again as the pod left to go eat. Loki swam over to Shannon and they started to explore.

Huge mounds of brain coral and staghorn coral jutted from a nearby ledge in and amongst bright pink soft corals. Vividly coloured fish contrasted with silver schools of fish as they darted in and out of large anemones and coral branches. Yellows, purples, greens, pinks, and even blues—there were so many colours, and so much life surrounding them. Shannon wove between canyons of corals that formed tall ridges, building on dead coral of the past.

Seeing the wonder on her face as she explored had his heart expanding. This was something they'd need to make time for in the future, to be sure she fed this part of her soul. Striped angel fish and a bright blue school of surgeonfish led her down a deep canyon. As he followed, she pointed to something moving in the depths when a dark shape to Loki's left caught his attention.

His pulse leapt and his gaze sharpened. Oh, bloody fan-fucking-tastic. He conjured a blade to toss at an eye of the enormous black horse-like kelpie when it darted towards him. One of the few vulnerable spots, it killed it instantly. But the damn things hunted in packs. There would be more.

<*Watch out for—*>

His warning was too late as Shannon screamed and dodged a lunging kelpie. Heart in his throat, he conjured another blade and drew back to throw, even as he knew he couldn't reach her in time. Before he released the knife, three kelpies attacked him. After calling his armour and killing the first with the blade in his hand, he was killing the second with telekinesis when his concentration shattered—pain speared through the bond like a spike into his chest, seizing his lungs.

Chapter 46

CAN'T CHOOSE YOUR FAMILY

Growling, Loki twisted back to Shannon as he blindly killed the last creature, taking a moment to absorb the scene. Blood stained the water by her leg, and a kelpie jerked at her calf with its teeth sunk in. She had called her armour, smart girl, and it covered her arms, chest, and abdomen down to her knees. She stabbed at the head of the kelpie biting her leg.

Power and rage swirled in a blazing inferno within him. With his telekinesis, he shredded one about to attack her and focused on another aiming for her. But a thick muscular tail wrapped around his neck, distracting him as his lungs tightened. The fucking kelpie attacked him from behind. He exploded it with another blast of telekinesis and conjured blades in both hands.

<Loki! I'm in trouble,> Shannon shouted.

Another wave of agony pulsed up the bond, stealing the last of his breath as her scream vibrated the water. He fought to not grip his chest. *<I'm coming!>*

Quickly killing another kelpie, and then another, Loki found himself surrounded by the long thrashing sea-horse-like bodies ending in tapered tails and short-tusked, snapping jaws of six more. Where the fuck did they keep coming from? Why the hell had he left Laevateinn at home?

He killed the ones separating him from Shannon as fast as possible. He didn't care if they bit him—he had to get to her—but more seemed to replace the bloody water demons as fast as he killed them. A glance between shifting dark bodies showed one trying to chew through the armour of her shoulder. The creature wouldn't succeed, but the fucker was still hurting her with its powerful jaws. Another had her foot, shaking her.

"Godsdamn it! Let me *go*!" she yelled.

Loki snarled, exploding another and stabbing two more as the heat igniting his veins surged. They couldn't get through his defences, but those annoying bastards were hurting Shannon and keeping him from her with sheer numbers. Through the swirling shadows, he spotted another trying to bite her other leg.

Changing tactics, Loki channelled the heat within him and sent it out as a wave. The beasts squealed and backed off. Never had he appreciated his partial fire giant heritage more. Blasting them again, he drove the kelpies further away and darted toward Shannon.

In the water next to her, his distinctive long blue hair and large, muscular physique easily identifiable, was Poseidon. He removed a kelpie's tail from around Shannon's neck, and her sai slashed up to connect with his silver sword.

With another fiery blast at the surrounding kelpie, Loki forced the demons away as he fought his way closer to Shannon.

"I'm trying to free you from these bunyip, but if you'd prefer I not, just say so," Poseidon said, his clear, deep voice ringing through the water.

Shannon hesitated, then said, "Sorry. Yes, please." Cautiously, she withdrew her sai, and Poseidon hacked the remaining kelpies surrounding her into fish bait.

After killing another half-dozen of the fucking things, Loki finally reached her. <*Shannon? Are you okay?*> He barely noticed when she put a bubble around his head and the tension in his lungs eased. His focus was entirely on her and her injuries—her pain resonated within his chest as a sharp, pulsing ache. <*Is it just your legs, darling? Is our son okay?*> Running trembling hands over her, he searched for the source of blood in the water, particularly over the obvious curve of her pregnancy. Please Norns, she had to be okay. She had to be.

<*Our son is fine. It's just the bites on my legs and the puncture on my foot. Maybe some bruises on my shoulder,*> she reassured him.

Loki used his meagre healing seidhr to close the bite wounds on both her legs, watching the flesh knit back together but unable to reduce the swelling, bruising, or fine tearing. It was a patch job that temporarily sped up her own healing, nothing more. What he would give for a fraction of Healer Moja's abilities right then.

But more blood flowed into the water in a pink cloud around them and pain continued to pulse along the bond.

Where? Where was it?

He searched lower and finally found the raw punctures on the side and soles of her precious feet. His brave goddess, fighting them off—she must have caught a tusk. Focusing on each wound, he poured his energy into her flesh, coaxing her body to heal itself.

Damn it. Why wasn't he better at this?

His fingers trembled as the last puncture slowly closed on the ball of her foot. Yet internal damage still surrounded the abused tissues and he wasn't skilled enough to do more. Not with his limited abilities and the number of injuries on her. Still, they would all heal within the day now that he'd given the energy to close them, especially with the added energy of the ocean helping boost her healing.

<I'm sorry, darling. I should have been able to get to you sooner.> Damn it to Helheim, she shouldn't have been injured, shouldn't have had to fight to protect herself with him right there. He continued to stroke over her calf and foot, needing the contact after the scare.

"You called them bunyip?" Shannon asked Poseidon. *<I'm fine, Loki. They scared me because I didn't know how to fight them, but I'll be okay thanks to your healing.>*

"Yes. In this part of the world, that's what they're called. The Celts call them kelpies. They are a predatory horse-like fae water demon," Poseidon replied.

After Loki took several steadying breaths, his hands stopped shaking and he forced his jaw to unclench. "It's been quite a while, Poseidon," he said, speaking aloud for the first time. Loki's voice was muffled, travelling out of the air bubble and into the water. But the sea god would hear him, regardless.

"At least five hundred years, I think, Prince. You rarely venture deep into the waters of the realms. I'm back to using Manannan Mac Lir again." The blue-haired sea god tilted his head. "Who is your lovely companion? She's obviously a sea goddess, but doesn't recognize water demons?"

"Princess Shannon of Asgard, my consort," Loki introduced her. "Recently of Midgard."

"Congratulations to both of you on your pairing and soon-to-be parenthood. Manannan Mac Lir at your disposal, my beautiful goddess," the far-too-attractive male said, as he held out a hand to Shannon.

Loki gritted his teeth at the instinctive growl that wanted to rise, resisting the urge to punch Manannan in his perfect smile. The sea god was *not* flirting with her, damn it. He'd just helped save her.

Shannon hesitated and something settled in Loki's gut. <*He's Seelie, a good one who was not banished with the rest.*>

She took the sea god's hand and surprise flared up the bond. Manannan's eyes also widened. Was it that weird jolt she'd described previously?

"Not just a water goddess, but Tuatha Dé Danann. How do I not know you?" he asked with a slight pinch to his brow, still holding her hand.

Huh. Elves could identify each other by touch? Why wasn't *that* in the Asgardian database? Was that what set Gwydion off?

"I've only recently discovered I'm not human. I'm still learning the full extent of my goddesshood, and I don't yet know my birth parents," she told him.

Manannan smiled and gave her a slight bow. "I am honoured to meet you. As a fellow Tuatha Dé Danann and sea god, I'd be happy to help you explore your water-based powers if you have questions. Perhaps we will find clues as to your parentage?" He released her hand and looked back and forth between Shannon and Loki.

<*Is it safe to ask him? To tell him what I know?*> She met Loki's gaze.

Loki smiled and squeezed her uninjured calf lightly. <*While you are carrying our child, I'm not comfortable with him teaching you about your water-based powers, but later, when you aren't so vulnerable, yes.*> He hesitated, hating to admit it, but of all of them, Manannan was trustworthy. He'd proven himself, stayed neutral, unwilling to support the atrocities of the Unseelie by fighting in the war against Asgard. <*Poseidon can teach you things I can't. He's incredibly powerful, the strongest of all the Elven sea gods and goddesses. You can trust him with whatever information you have about your parents.*>

"I'm very glad to meet you as well. At some point, I will take you up on the kind offer, but not yet." She gestured to her abdomen.

"Completely understandable, my dear."

"However, if you could tell me anything about my parentage, that would be wonderful. All I've learnt is my father's name, Dylan Connolly."

Manannan's eyes widened, and then he nodded. "Well, that explains your sea goddess traits. Dylan is a Summer Realm sea god, the God of Selkies."

"Selkies?" she asked.

"Seal-skin fae shapeshifters," Loki answered when she glanced down, eyebrows raised. Intriguing. It must be where she got the ability to speak to animals. Would Shannon be able to shape—

"Dylan is the only good one of his close family, though, as his brother Llew and parents, Gwydion and Arianrhod, are all Winter Court nobles. You don't want anything to do with those members of your family, I'm sorry to say," Manannan warned in a careful voice.

Loki's mouth dropped open. Yggdrasil's twisty limbs! Of all the unfortunate elves to be related to, they were up there in bad choices. Damn. What game were the Norns playing, to have Shannon and Loki just happen to bump into her paternal grandparents, the sick fuckers?

Shannon stared at Loki, and he wasn't fast enough to hide his distaste.

"Aren't Gwydion and Arianrhod the two Sidhe we ran into in London?" A frown furrowed her brow. "They're my grandparents?"

"Yes," Loki said, trying not to snarl. "Manannan is right. You want nothing to do with them, Shannon. They'd be happy to stab you in the back." He shuddered to think of Shannon trying to find out more about her background from that pit of vipers. Human sacrifice to power their realm was the least of their crimes, with Llew, her uncle, being one of the main purveyors of victims. Fucking Wild Hunt.

"You should be especially wary of them in your current condition." Manannan gestured to her pregnancy. "Never trust them. Do not let them learn you are expecting a child."

Interesting. So he was aware of their nastier... practices. That he'd warn Shannon, well, it just made Loki respect him all the more.

"I appreciate your honesty," she said, eyes wide.

Manannan inclined his head. He cupped his hands together, and a glow formed between them. When he opened his hands, a silver-and-blue spiral seashell sat on his palm. He held it out to Shannon.

"When you want to talk to me, ask questions, or are ready for me to help you learn more about your sea powers, go to the nearest saltwater body, focus on the shell and speak. I will hear and find you," Manannan promised.

She took the shell from him. "Thank you, Manannan."

"It has been a pleasure, Princess Shannon." After nodding to both of them, he sped away through the water.

<*My grandparents are evil?*> She turned to Loki as he rose in the water.

Loki winced. There was so much she needed to know, but fuck... he didn't want to overwhelm her. Not again. Not after losing her for four months last time. Let the bad news sink in first, before he told her how bad it really was. It was not a conversation he was anticipating, yet he had to warn her. Of their dangerous enemies, the dark elves topped the list—their sick proclivities put her particularly at risk right now.

Just like Sigyn.

He swallowed hard, forcing those memories away to focus on his beautiful sea goddess. <*I'm sorry Shannon. I know that's not what you wanted to find out, but at least you learned more about your father.*>

<*Yeah. I'm also kind of in shock that I met Poseidon. He was interesting.*>

Shannon's expression was drawn and lacked the usual sparkle. Now was not the time to expand on Manannan's warning. Maybe he could distract her and bring it up again when they were safely back on Asgard. Such bleak thoughts could circle and drive one to insanity. Even if he wasn't there, his mother or Mist and Kara could help her talk it out.

Yes, better to wait.

And if a part of him was pleased that when she understood the risks, she'd be more willing to stay safe on Asgard... well, no one could blame him for wanting his pregnant soulmate protected.

Loki wrapped his arms around her, kissing her through the air bubble on his head. <*It was more excitement than I was expecting on our evening swim. You manage to surprise even this God of Chaos, my love. We should head back.*>

She nodded and propelled them through the water. Although he stayed alert, he relaxed into her power and thanked the Norns when she started to play, swerving them up and down, leaping into the air and back down into the water. It helped burn away the remaining adrenaline from their bunyip encounter.

Relief surged, easing the tightness in his chest when Shannon actually whooped in glee. Bor's beard, he was glad to see her enjoying herself. When she brought them to a stop on the beach by Thor and Amelia's house, she was giggling—such a beautiful sound.

Lips twitching, Loki took in her joyous expression, eyes bright from her play. "It's no wonder you are my soulmate. You love mischief as much as I do."

"Now just think how much trouble our son is going to get into!"

Bloody Helheim. He hadn't thought of that. Fuck. She burst out laughing when she caught his expression. "Stop scaring me!" he growled, capturing her wicked lips to stop her laughter.

The last few days of their visit passed too quickly. Although she was quieter than usual, his gorgeous goddess loved the water and glowed with health the more time they spent in it, allowing him to remove his illusion from her injuries within a couple of days. Still, the revelation about the paternal side of her family seemed to weigh on her, and every time he considered telling her more, his chest tightened. He couldn't burden her further. Not yet.

"If you get tired of the gloomy English countryside while Tod is filming his new movie, come back and visit some more," Thor told Shannon as she and Loki prepared to leave.

"I will keep that in mind. Elise has already claimed part of my time when I'm there," she said.

Loki's head whipped around, his heartbeat increasing as his fingers tightened on their bags. Was she talking about the girls' night idea? He'd thought that was a joke. Surely she knew it wasn't practical right now. Not with needing to hide her pregnancy. Not with dangers like Isis and Vidar, or her bloody grandparents... or Bor's balls, Ao Guang and his brothers. He wasn't sure he believed Dongbin about them being banished to Kunlun right now. No way would he trust his soulmate's life and that of his unborn child to Dongbin's untested honour.

Thor checked over his shoulder to where Amelia wrangled the kids on the beach. He met Shannon's gaze and lowered his voice. "Just be careful, little sister. Especially if Loki can't be with you."

Loki almost snorted. Careful? She needed to be more than careful. Had he made a mistake in not being blunt with Shannon about the risks? No way was she going to Midgard without him. Not until after their son was born...

Yggdrasil's roots, maybe never. Could he shadow her unseen, to give her the illusion she was having an evening alone with Elise? Would it be wrong if he didn't tell her?

The image of her sprawled on the ground, torn and bloody, dying and reaching for him without him there to help her, had his heart pounding hard enough to escape his chest, his muscles locking, and not enough air making it into his lungs. His vision tunnelled. No. He couldn't do it. There was no way he could let Shannon go without him.

Chapter 47

HELLHOUNDS, BUNYIP & TROWS, OH MY

In the emerald and white marble of Loki's decadent bathroom in the palace, Shannon sent a flow of warm air over her and Loki's naked forms. Their quick shower to wash away the last of the sand and salt from their trip had turned into a sensual hour-long joining that left her limbs relaxed and her body humming with energy. "How soon do you need to head to London?"

Loki bent over to kiss her rounded belly. "Pretty much right away, but first I want to go with you to see Healer Moja, to hear how our son is doing."

"I'd like that." As he talked to their son, Shannon smiled and ran her hands through his dark locks. "I need to go to Vancouver to deal with my position at the university." And maybe visit Lynda. Shannon's stomach churned at the lies she'd have to tell. It probably wasn't a good sign that she dreaded seeing her best friend. Shouldn't a friendship of this many years be more enjoyable and not feel so obligatory?

Loki straightened at Shannon's words, taking her hands in his. "To give up your career is hard, I know. But you have so much here, with learning to master your skills, royal duties, and our son. If you want to pick it up again, later on, I'll help you figure out a way."

Yanked from her thoughts about Lynda, Shannon frowned. "Why do you expect me to give up my career? With you figuring out how I can access text messages and the internet, there is a lot I can do from here, as long as it doesn't require real-time communication like phone calls or live streaming."

"Even with that, you'd still need to travel back and forth a lot. It's just not practical right now when our son is going to need you."

What the hell? Her? What about *him*? After jerking her hands from his, she crossed her arms. "That doesn't make sense, Loki. The time difference works for us. Even when I need to go to Earth for a few hours, that's only minutes here. An hour here gives me an entire five-hour workday there if I needed it, and I wouldn't have to go that often."

His eyes narrowed, lips pressed together. Annoyance surged down the bond in a prickling wave. "Do you not want to be here for our son? Aren't you excited about being a mother?"

Shannon's jaw dropped at his unexpected attack, and her chest tightened. "Of course, I'm excited about being a mother. That's got nothing to do with it."

So much for supporting her successes or her right to have a career too. How typical. He'd lasted a whole seven weeks before showing he was a misogynistic asshole—a fraction of the time it had taken Trent. Oh, he didn't want to steal her success like her ex... no, instead, Loki wanted her barefoot and pregnant like the caveman he was. Should she really have expected more from someone older than the damned pyramids?

"It doesn't sound like it when you're more concerned with how you can leave our son than readying the nursery for him," Loki bit out.

Shannon clenched her jaw at the spike of pain stealing her breath. She refused to reply as heat built behind her eyes. No, she would not cry. No. Not happening. Was... was Loki pushing her into a fight? She didn't want that. Yet what was she to think with his lack of understanding and deliberate avoidance of any logical argument? Her pulse thundered in her ears, the languid relaxation long gone.

Godsdamn it. She closed her eyes. The last thing she wanted to do right now was fight.

Loki had no right to tell her what she could or couldn't do. He might be ancient in Earth years, but she wasn't going back to the woman-as-chattel times. If that was what he thought, he could pull his head out of his misogynistic ass right now. There was no way she'd spent all those years fighting for her career only to toss it away to be his gods-be-damned baby factory doll he could lock up whenever he didn't want to play with her. She was a modern woman, and for fuck's sake, Asgardian culture had equality of the sexes. Frigga ruled alongside Odin. Valkyrie fought alongside Einherjar. Loki had yet to give her *any* rational reason why an hour's absence from their son every few days would be a big deal, even if she was breastfeeding.

Was he incapable of minding their child for that short length of time? Thor had told all kinds of stories of taking care of the twins as babies. She'd assumed Loki would also want to take responsibility for his son, but perhaps she should have taken his past weeks of absence as a clue. He'd put his career before her, before his son's check-ups. It seemed he planned to do the same after their child was born. Gods. What the hell was wrong with her that she fell for such selfish men?

Loki held up a hand to stop her from saying anything further. His nostrils flared, and he exhaled a huff. "Let's discuss this later when we've both calmed down. I'd like to go to the baby check-up with you. Okay?"

Her fingers dug into her arms. Fuck him if he thought this was all okay. He'd already shown his colours. "Fine."

"How's this?" Loki conjured a comfortable long-sleeved blue tunic with thumb holes, stretchy black pants, and soft canvas shoes for her, and his usual boots, black leather pants, and black tunic for himself.

He was trying to appease her by conjuring her favourite loungewear, but she wasn't particularly impressed. Now her opinion mattered? Yeah. Right. Whatever. "It's fine," she bit out, grinding her teeth as a muscle flexed in her jaw.

Ignoring Loki's proffered elbow, Shannon left his rooms and headed through the palace to the healers' wing. She entered the bright open space with its many arches leading to individual healing rooms, and an apprentice bowed and darted off to find Healer Moja. The round-face healer appeared quickly and directed them into a room.

"Princess Shannon, Prince Loki." Moja inclined her head respectfully as she gestured for Shannon to lie down on the sensor bed.

The familiar green glow surrounded her. With a few quick finger movements, the healer had an image of their son projected in the air. Shannon's anger at Loki was shoved aside and buried, forgotten in amazement as she gazed at her son. A warm glow bloomed inside her. She could see him so clearly, right down to the fingernails on his fingers and toes. It was indescribable, watching him kick and punch as she felt his movements.

"Your son is developing exactly as he should for almost twenty-seven weeks. He is close to one-point-five kilograms in weight, and approximately forty-two centimetres in length. You can thank Prince Loki's half-Jotun heritage for your son's slightly larger than average size, although Tuatha Dé Danann are also often tall," she said.

Loki's eyes were wide as he studied the image. "Is it my imagination, or are his eyes open?"

Moja smiled. "You are correct, my prince. Watch." She shone a light on one spot on Shannon's abdomen, and their son blinked, turning his head away from the bright light.

"As you are entering your third trimester next week, I would like to see you twice a week instead of once a week."

Out of the corner of her eye, Shannon saw Loki's head whip to stare at her, but she ignored him and continued to meet Healer Moja's gaze.

"I'm going to remind you again to keep an eye on your energy levels." Healer Moja's eyebrows rose, waiting for Shannon's nod. "You are doing better than last week, but again, don't underestimate how often you need to rest or recharge. You have little in the way of reserves. Pay close attention. Don't let yourself get worn out, or too low on energy."

"I will," Shannon agreed. With no headache and brimming with energy after the swimming and sex, Shannon felt better than she had in weeks. Gods, it was nice to not feel like her limbs were dragging or to grit her teeth against spikes of pain stabbing her temples.

"Have you been eating your apple daily?" Moja pinned her with narrowed eyes.

Yeah, she knew Shannon hadn't over the last five days. Shannon squirmed and glanced away. Talk about being called onto the carpet. "I was, and I will today, but I didn't have any while on Earth for a few days."

"Shan—"

Healer Moja put up her hand to halt Loki's growl, stepped over to the basket on the counter, and lifted two golden apples. She placed both in Shannon's hand. "Eat two per day until your next check-up, and then I'll decide if you can go back down to one per day."

Shannon nodded, and Loki crossed his arms. Great. One more thing for him to scold her about.

"Given the combination of your genetics, it is increasingly likely your son will be large. Before he becomes too large for a safe vaginal birth, I want to deliver him. If possible, I'd like to avoid a surgical solution. Even immortal bodies require more healing from surgical deliveries, and you are still settling into your immortal energies," instructed Healer Moja.

"Okay," Shannon acknowledged as a ripple of fear shivered over her, and she put a hand on her belly. Surely they didn't lose women in childbirth here, not with their advanced medicine?

Moja shut off the scan, and the image of their son disappeared.

Loki helped Shannon off the sensor bed, and they headed to the training yard while Shannon ate her apples.

Just before they entered, Loki stopped her with a hand on her arm. Tension shot up her spine, reigniting the heat in her chest. Ugh. What did he want now? She needed some damn space from his infuriating attitudes and to work off the anger again simmering in her gut.

"When did Healer Moja ask you to start coming in once a week?"

She shrugged. "Three weeks ago."

It wasn't like he'd been around to tell. He'd started recording with his band and missed that appointment without telling her why. She wasn't about to fishwife him. Then after that disastrous after-party, he'd essentially been gone. She'd been lucky to see him for barely an hour once during the day, and he'd slept with her for an hour at night. At this point, he'd missed as many appointments as he'd been to. Was she supposed to arrange her prenatal visits around his band's schedule, for fuck's sake?

He drew her into his arms, and although she didn't return his embrace, she didn't fight him. She'd probably only bruise herself on his hardheadedness and annoying muscles. "I wish I'd known. I would have come."

Shannon didn't scoff, but really, if they hadn't just returned from vacation, he wouldn't have managed to come to *this* appointment.

Loki sighed. "I'd better go, or I'll be late. I'll see you in about three hours or when I'm done filming for today. First day's shoots can be a bit chaotic."

Her jaw clenched, nostrils flaring. He'd just fucking made her point for her, yet he didn't acknowledge it. At all. Asshole.

Loki still held her, as if reluctant to go and as the seconds stretched, she considered shoving him away. She just wanted him to let her go, damn it.

"I love you. You are my entire world, Shannon," he murmured, his forehead against hers.

She rolled her eyes, biting back the fury climbing her throat. How could he not see how angry she was? What a joke his damn words were. Words were fucking cheap. Actions mattered. And it was obvious he didn't respect her enough to treat her as an equal.

Finally releasing her, he stepped back and held her eyes as he teleported away.

Shannon had been down this road with her ex-fiancé. Trent had being supportive and wonderful. Their first year had been fantastic. But then, he'd grown more resentful as her successes grew and his collaboration in her research shrank. It was several years before he attempted to change her, to mould her into what he wanted. When that didn't work, he tried his fists.

A snort escaped her, and she shook her head. She and Loki had been together for less than two months. A whole seven weeks before he showed his true colours. But he'd already been successful in changing her into what he wanted, hadn't he?

On a much grander scale than Trent had attempted.

Even if she left Asgard and left Loki, she'd never be the same. She'd never be a naïve mortal again. They'd always have the link of their son and the soulmate bond. No, she'd never be fully free of Loki if she left.

Yet, there was no way she'd be happy with someone who couldn't respect and value her for her brain as well as her body. An icy heaviness settled on her chest, heat building behind her eyes as she shivered at the bleak prospect of a future as a trophy consort.

Rubbing her hands over her chilled arms to rid herself of the goosebumps, she considered her options. No way was she caving to Loki's demands. He could change his attitude, or he could sleep elsewhere. She would not be pushed around again.

Resolve growing within her, she focused on her torc, changing into her fighting leathers, armour, and boots before she entered the Valkyrie training yard. Some hand-to-hand combat training was perfect for her mood.

"Oho. Back from vacation, are we?" called Mist from Shannon's right.

Grinning at Mist's playful tone, Shannon spun a knife in her direction. Mist laughed, appearing from behind the cloud she'd used to disguise herself, flicking Shannon's knife through her fingers.

"I think you dropped this," the Valkyrie said cheekily.

A reluctant laugh burst from Shannon, easing the tension in her jaw and shoulders as she took the blade back and they embraced. "How goes the training?"

"Not nearly as fun as when you are here to spar with me!"

"Bring it on then," Shannon challenged, and they were off, diving, spinning, and climbing through the air in a wild, three-dimensional, no-holds-barred match.

After an hour, they gave up trying to best each other.

When they stopped for a break, Kara left the archery range and joined them. In her usual brown leathers, her curly hair was restrained in thick braid but attempting escape. "How are you coming with the noxious gases, Shannon?"

Grimacing, Shannon held her hands a foot apart and a cloud of pale-yellow gas formed in a bubble. She hated creating the mix of fluorine and hydrogen cyanide, shuddering at the ominous sight, but it would be an effective deterrent against an immortal. "I don't know if I can do it yet under attack, but I'm not willing to risk either of you to test it out. This stuff is extremely nasty." She dispersed the gases.

"Still, it's important to have options." Kara poked Shannon in the shoulder with her bow. "Anything interesting happen while you were on Midgard?"

"Actually, yes. Loki and I got attacked by bunyip, and we met Manannan Mac Lir." And found out her grandparents were evil and hated her. Her chest tightened as the pit in her stomach deepened. Had they somehow known who she was to them? Would her uncle and father be the same, hating her on sight? Is that why Dylan had given her up? The same questions had plagued her over and over the last three days. Part of her wanted to know more, but like Pandora, would she regret opening that box?

"Oh! Poseidon himself! Haven't seen him since I was little." A flush washed over Mist's fair cheeks and she looked away, biting her lip.

Shannon eyed her friend. Was—

"How did you fare with the bunyip? I hear they can be quite difficult when they attack in numbers," Mist blurted.

Shannon scowled, wrinkling her nose. "They were nasty. I wasn't doing very well until Manannan helped me, although I almost stabbed him before I knew who he was."

Kara cocked her head. "What did you try against them? They are weak against fire, given that water is their natural element."

"Yeah, I was trying fire when one started choking me. I'm not sure how successful I would have been. I tried my sais and using water, but you're right, the water didn't work."

"Remember to use the opposite of whatever element they are. Use fire for water-based creatures like bunyip or grindylow. For banshees, their element is air, so use earth, fire, or water. For hobgoblins and pixies that are earth and air, use fire or water. I'd try air and water for earth-based creatures like trows," Kara instructed as she tore apart her braid and redid it with nimble fingers.

Mist tapped a fingertip to her lip. "Or sunlight."

"True. They will turn to stone in sunlight." Kara patted her hair and tossed her braid over her shoulder.

"Damn. I need an encyclopedia of creatures in the immortal world that humans think are only myth or legend." Shannon wiped sweat from her brow, and her stomach growled. "Unless you mean the Harry Potter versions are actually real, I've never even heard of half of the creatures you just mentioned."

Mist smirked. "Ha! Harry Potter. No. Well, kind of. We should have something like that in the royal library. That's a good idea."

"Why don't we head there after lunch? We should eat first." Kara glanced at Shannon's belly and a glint of humour appeared in her golden eyes.

Shannon huffed. Fuck. She was always hungry, damn it. "Sounds great. I wanted to talk to you two about joining me when I head to Earth later today. Loki isn't available, and I need to go to my university."

"I'm in." Mist nodded. "I'd love to see where you are from."

"Yep, me too." Kara slid her bow onto her back beside her quiver.

After soup and sandwiches, with Mist revealing the extra large bag of Hawkins Cheezies she'd picked up yesterday on a quick trip to Midgard—what an awesome friend to stock up on Shannon's cravings—they headed to the library. After a few minutes of searching the floor-to-ceiling wooden shelves, the two Valkyrie returned to the comfortable chair where Shannon sat with orange fingertips, still munching on crunchy cheesy goodness. They laid several thick books that described various creatures found across the Nine Realms on the nearby black oak table. After cleaning her fingers, Shannon started with the book that dealt with Midgard, reading about redcaps, clurichaun, and hellhounds. She'd reached the section on boggarts when Loki joined them.

He surveyed the three of them around the table, one eyebrow raised. "Ah! Doing some light reading, are you?"

Shannon glanced up, then returned her eyes to her book. "Trying to rectify my woeful lack of knowledge about mythical creatures since I didn't recognize the bunyip as dangerous when I spotted them, nor know how to handle them."

"I'm glad, darling. The more you educate yourself, the safer you will be."

She snorted. "Still, it's not like I'm going to run into one of these at my university."

Loki scowled and crossed his arms over his chest. "You have no idea what you might encounter. Risking yourself or our son is foolish when you can simply pick up your career again once he is grown and you've had years of training."

Shannon clenched the book, restraining the urge to throw it at his hypocritical, misogynistic pig head. "Or I could simply go for a few hours when needed," she managed through her snarl.

In the next moment, an enormous creature stood before her with a bulbous nose and grey, warty skin. A round red hat on its head dripped blood down in single droplets that coated long, stringy white hair. Sharpened teeth, including two tusks, jutted up from its mouth. The coppery stench sank into her nose as Shannon inhaled a gasp then scrambled backward, falling to the floor and reaching for her sais.

"Loki!" Kara barked, shoving her chair back and moving in front of Shannon.

The image disappeared and revealed Loki in its place, one black eyebrow raised in mocking disdain as he held Shannon's wide-eyed gaze.

"Was... was that a redcap?" She swallowed, trying to calm the panicked fluttering in her chest.

"Yes." Kara helped Shannon to her feet, then scowled at Loki. "We use images, solid illusions of the creatures, to practice battling so we don't freeze at our first sight of them, but we don't use them to torment the unsuspecting in the *bloody royal library*."

"She needs to know before she does something stupid." Loki pressed his lips together, eyes narrowing.

Stupid. Foolish. Well, she knew what he thought of her, now didn't she? A sinking sensation in her gut combined with the onset of a headache. "Great. Something else to add to my list for training," Shannon murmured.

Mist hugged her. "Don't feel discouraged. You've made incredible progress with your training in a short period."

"You truly are the badass warrior princess we call you," Kara agreed, glaring at Loki. "Don't feel bad that there is more to learn. We still learn new things, even after hundreds of years of training."

Loki shrugged. "I need to head back to London." Reaching for her, he lifted his hands to Shannon's face and kissed her before she could yank herself away. With a gleam in his eyes, he stepped back and disappeared.

Crossing her arms, Shannon scowled. Egotistical, controlling bastard.

Chapter 48

THE OTHER SHOE

Stopping by the suite of rooms she shared with Loki, Shannon picked up her cell phone and checked its messages. How Loki made it work didn't matter, just that it did. As Earth technology advanced, he'd found ways of taking advantage of it. Now, keeping her phone and computer charged was a simple matter of willing some of her personal energy into the battery. A skill Loki had taught her in a few minutes.

She hesitating while debating with herself, then, with slow taps, she composed a message to Lynda, inviting her friend over to her place for pizza after Shannon finished at the university. She bit her lower lip as she hit send. Maybe Lynda would be appeased by meeting Mist and Kara. Plus, it would give Shannon a social buffer when Lynda found out about the baby.

Shannon winced and glanced down at her protruding abdomen. How was she going to explain how far along she was when just under two weeks ago on Earth, she'd appeared in photos with Loki on Thor's red carpet with no pregnancy in sight? The complications had her headache worsening, and Shannon rubbed her temples. Fucking hell, she really needed to tell her family.

After checking the weather in Vancouver, she shifted her fighting leathers into sandals, low-cut black pregnancy jeans, a sapphire scoop-necked tank top long enough to cover her bulging belly down to her hips, and a hip-length lightweight black leather jacket. The only part of her armour she kept out were the wrist cuffs, allowing the rest to retreat into her torc. She tied her long hair back into a high ponytail and set out to meet Mist and Kara.

They waited near the palace entrance closest to the rainbow bridge. Admittedly, Shannon was curious to see what they'd chosen for earthly attire. Mist was in a blue short-sleeved T-shirt, jean shorts, and sandals, her distinctive blue hair also tied up in a ponytail. Kara had her red curls piled up on top of her head, and she wore a white flowing peasant blouse, dark-green capris, and sandals. Both fit into the current fashions perfectly. No one would ever guess they were immortal Valkyrie.

Shannon grinned and gestured to their attire. "So where do your armour and weapons hide? There's no way you'd leave Asgard without them."

Mist tapped her silver belt decorated with Asgardian scrollwork that must be spells, from what Loki had been teaching Shannon before he got so busy. It was beautiful and didn't look out of place woven through the loops of her jean shorts.

Kara grinned as she brought her wrists together, clinking her bracelets, similar to the ones Shannon wore. When Shannon extended one of hers, Kara nodded.

"One more thing. Since we don't have the telepathic soulmate connection you and Loki can use, we're going to use Valkyrie earcuffs." Kara handed Shannon a small, delicate-looking silver clip. They both turned their heads and showed Shannon theirs, already in place.

"Show me how to put it on correctly?" Shannon tilted her head towards Kara.

Kara clipped it onto Shannon's ear, halfway up. "It will stay in place, and even if you whisper, we will hear you. The range is at least ten kilometres, although I'd prefer it if you weren't out of sight."

"There are a few meetings you can't come to, but you can be just down the hall from me."

"We'll take that compromise," Mist agreed.

Kara nodded.

They set out from the palace, through the city, then gates, and onto the bridge. As they walked its length, Shannon rubbed her abdomen and told Mist and Kara about her plans for the day.

"Is the baby giving you trouble?" Mist brushed fingertips over Shannon's belly.

"No. He's just really active when I walk across the bridge. Something about the bridge's energy gets him excited."

Greeting Heimdall, Shannon asked him to set them down at her house in Deep Cove. When the Bifrost's swirl of lights dissipated, she led them to her RAV4. After backing out of the driveway, they headed onto the busy streets, over the Second Narrows bridge to East Hastings Street, then up the mountain to the faculty parking lot, near the science and technology wing.

As they walked the familiar path to Shannon's department, she pointed out quirky landscaping features that were remnants of the university's start during the height of the hippie movement in the sixties. After leaving the two Valkyrie at Shannon's office with its uncomfortable chairs and piles of papers, Shannon headed down the beige hall to the dean's office.

With a nod from her secretary, Shannon knocked on Mary's door and smiled at the dark-haired Italian woman's congratulations. She'd liked her dean when the small, fiery woman was appointed to the position, and her response now reaffirmed Shannon's opinion. As they discussed her options for maternity leave, Shannon's heart jolted. Holy moly, if she stayed on Asgard, her baby wouldn't be born for another year. Damn. Right when her leave was almost finished. Still, she'd deal with it then.

"I am thrilled for you, Shannon. File the paperwork with Nancy, and she'll get your year of maternity leave processed so it kicks in after your sabbatical."

"Thank you, Mary. What are my options if I want to work primarily from the field after I return from leave? The research sites I've developed outside of Canada will take considerable on-the-ground time." Yeah, calling Asgard outside Canada was like NASA saying the moon landing was a trip outside Texas, but it wasn't as if Shannon could tell the truth.

Mary's eyes widened, and she shook her head. "Well, we certainly do not want to lose you, given your reputation and publication record. There is no impediment to teaching remotely, or offering your courses as field destination classes."

Somehow, Shannon didn't think Mary meant off-planet, but the idea had her lips quirking.

"In fact," Mary continued, "you can buy out part of your teaching commitment, although the faculty contract stipulates you teach at least one course per year. It's up to you how much you have your grad students in the field."

Bring grad students to Asgard? Yeah, that wasn't happening, but imagining their wide-eyed stares as they tried to take it all in had her biting back a laugh. Too bad humans couldn't travel by the Bifrost. "That's better than I anticipated. Thanks, Mary." Shoulders lowering and breathing easier after how well the meeting had gone, Shannon stood to leave. After Loki's attitude, this almost seemed too easy. It had her waiting for the other shoe to drop.

"Make sure you stay in touch for teaching assignments before the end of your maternity leave, so your department head can do his planning. Let me know if you run into any issues with Bill. I'm aware he's not always the most collegial with female faculty."

Right. There was the shoe. Shannon tried not to scowl at the mention of her department head. To call him a misogynistic ass was a gross understatement. He was almost enough of a reason to simply quit and start a consulting company. Dealing with his shit on top of Loki's today? Fucking wonderful. All she needed was to bump into Trent, and it'd be an asshole trifecta.

Mary smiled, understanding on her round face as she stood, holding her hand out.

Shannon shook it. "Thanks for your support, Mary."

"Well, you are one of our star faculty, so of course I'm going to support you. And again, congratulations."

Grinning as she left Mary's office, Shannon stopped to fill out the required paperwork with Nancy. Once done, Shannon took her time, walking slowly along the industrial off-white tile and admitting to herself that she was stalling. She refused the Valkyries' offers to join her. Although she dreaded the coming conflict, taking Kara and Mist wouldn't make it any better. In fact, it'd be significantly worse. Bringing three strong women into Bill's office would be like waving a red flag in front of a bull. After reassuring them she'd be fine alone, Shannon entered her department's main office.

"Is he in?"

"Yes, he's available," Christine said after congratulating her on the baby.

To calm her nerves, Shannon stopped and took a few deep breaths.

I will *keep my patience.*

I will *keep my patience.*

I will *keep my patience.*

With the mantra running through her head, Shannon lifted her hand to knock. Upon hearing a grunted acknowledgement, she walked through the door and around the corner into Bill's office.

He took one look and sneered. "So, I take it you won't be doing your goddamn fucking job anytime soon."

Great. He was in his usual mood.

"Nice to see you as well, Bill. I'm well, thanks for asking."

Bill rolled his beady eyes, curling his lip at her. Frankly, it made the short, gaunt man with his greasy comb-over look even more like the pasty-faced scarecrow he resembled. "What the hell do you want? I don't have time for your fucking bullshit."

The tension built, creeping up her back and into her neck, adding pressure to her already-pounding headache. Unfortunately, being an immortal goddess hadn't given her any new asshole harassment coping skills. Not unless she wanted to squash him like the bug he was.

It was tempting.

A bit *too* tempting.

Shannon entertained herself by briefly imagining soaking him so it looked as if he'd peed himself—a little humiliation for all the times he'd deliberately embarrassed someone at departmental meetings. Thank goodness she hadn't brought Loki as she'd initially planned. She didn't want to be in the position of having to defend the evil little shit from her overprotective consort. It was bad enough that she had to protect Bill from herself.

On the other hand, given the attitude Loki had given her this morning, maybe she should arrange to have the two meet. They could bond over their fucked-up views of feminine roles in the workforce.

Shannon blew out a breath, shifting her shoulders. She was *not* going to lose her temper.

But fucking hell, it was hard not to respond to his confrontational tone. With another deep breath to keep her voice calm and even, she replied, "I've met with the dean and filed for my maternity leave. I'll be on leave until November 1, 2023."

"You do know that completely fucks with our course offerings, right? Bad enough you went on sabbatical with little notice. Now you're busy popping out a damn crotch goblin. What the hell am I supposed to do in the meantime?" Bill snarled.

Blood red washed over her vision in a haze of fury, and she clenched her fists.

Crotch goblin? *Crotch goblin?* How *dare* he!

Papers stirred, rustling in the breeze that circled in the room as she fought for control. The coffee in his cup bubbled over and spilled across the desk in a brown wave, distracting Bill from seeing the sparks shooting out of his cell phone as it fried. He jumped from his chair to grab paper towels and wiped at the mess, swearing.

Damn, but it was hard to rein it back in. The desire to destroy his entire office, and him along with it, surged. She was so done dealing with his shit, with Loki's shit. All this shit! But she couldn't expose the immortal world, especially not to a raging asshole like Bill.

Fuck! Fuck! *Fuck!*

By the time he'd cleaned up the worst of the coffee she'd boiled out of his cup, she'd gotten herself under control.

She took the time to breathe deeply and ensured her voice stayed calm, despite the tension singing up her spine. "You should discuss those course offerings with the dean. My leaves are protected by the faculty union contract."

"I know what the goddamn contract says. That doesn't mean I have to fucking agree with it," he yelled.

At her limit, Shannon released a burst of exasperated temper that fried his computer's hard drive and exploded the battery within its case. Since he wouldn't be able to trace it to her, it wouldn't put her grad students at risk of retribution. Because yeah, he was petty like that. If she confronted him directly, it wouldn't be her who paid the price. She was tenured and protected by a union contract, just as he was.

Instead, she satisfied herself with destroying his phone and computer, knowing it would cause him all kinds of grief. Hopefully, he lost data he didn't have backed up. Anything important to the department was on Christine's computer, not his, so her loss of control wouldn't affect other faculty or students. She's the one the did the real work, after all.

Despite her taut muscles, she deliberately lowered her shoulders and straightened her spine. It pissed her off that she'd started to hunch with the stress of talking to him.

Just breathe and stay in control.

"I'll be buying out all but one of my courses when I return, and offering my forest ecosystem and climate change management course as a field destination class."

Bill grunted, sounding slightly less aggressive. "Do you have anyone in mind to teach the classes you are buying out? We'll need sessional instructors."

Deep breath in, deep breath out.

"Yes, several of my former doctoral students would be excellent sessional instructors. They have the skills and know the material. I'll give them a heads-up when it's time."

"Actually, if you could shoot me their names now, we'd like to offer some of those courses in the meantime. I'll see if the dean will spring some money to hire them." His tone was slightly more conciliatory now that he wanted her cooperation with something.

Manipulative asshole. It was the only time he was nice.

She took another calming breath. "I'll get those to you today."

Bill grunted again, waving at her dismissively. "Great. I'm busy. Go away."

Without another word, she left, relieved to escape his office before she exposed her powers more than she already had. Such a close call. A big part of her wanted to go back and squash him. Frigging hell, squash him like the evil spider he was. She circled her shoulders and arms a few times to relax the muscles, as she forced herself to walk away.

When she opened her office door, Kara's and Mist's furious expressions had laughter bursting from her.

"Tell me we can go kill that repulsive man!" Mist's eyes snapped with rage and wind whipped through Shannon's office, scattering papers.

"Why did he get away with talking like that to you!" Kara's snarled words poured out on top of Mist's.

"Thank you, both of you. I appreciate your anger on my behalf." Shannon grinned, wiping the mirth from her eyes. Gods, she'd needed that. She rubbed at the thumping drums pounding in her temples. "Trust me when I say I dealt with him. Bill is now discovering his computer and phone are fried, and he's lost everything."

Kara crossed her arms and sniffed. "Paltry. I'd like to break every bone in his body."

Mist drew a knife, motioning in the air. "Disgusting toad deserves to be pinned to the ground by his testicles. See if he'd talk that way to you when—"

Shannon hugged Mist, interrupting her flow of threats. "Thank you. Really." After releasing her, Shannon turned to Kara to hug her tightly as well.

"You are ours, Shannon. We don't let anyone get away with talking to us that way," Kara said into Shannon's hair.

Chapter 49

PIZZA PARTY

They made excellent time returning to Shannon's house. It was still early afternoon, and the evening rush hour traffic hadn't quite started. Worn out from the stressful emotional roller coaster of a day thus far, Shannon ordered more pizza than she expected they'd need and sent a text to Lynda that she was home. Asgardians might have great food for the most part, but they sucked at pizza.

While she waited for the delivery and the arrival of her best friend, she showed off her home.

Mist wandered around Shannon's family room, poking into things. "Great colour scheme, Shannon. Very you. Did you know those were representations of Loki when you chose your wall art?"

"No, not until he told me."

"Just goes to show the Norns knew what they were doing, pairing the two of you," Kara said.

Bemused, Shannon nodded. Although she'd never really believed in fate before, the evidence of it in front of her was undeniable. Yet just because they were soulmates, it didn't make everything else magically work out. Especially when Loki was being a thick-headed ass.

"What animal is depicted on these silver plates and this totem?" Mist pointed at the small black argillite carved totem pole and rectangular engraved sterling silver plates in frames on the oak shelves beside the fireplace.

"Orca. Killer whale. I've always been drawn to them as my spirit animal. They fascinate me. When the resident pod comes into the inlet, I'll sit on my dock and watch them for hours. My mom gave me handcrafted and engraved silver orca totem earrings when I graduated high school." Shannon loved those earrings, but they were valuable enough that she kept them locked in her safe in her home office, along with an Orca- and Raven-engraved silver bracelet. That jewellery only came out on very special occasions.

Mist nodded. "Not surprising with you being a sea goddess, that you'd be drawn to animals as majestic as orcas. Where'd you get that?" She indicated the quilt Kara had unfolded from the carved wooden blanket rack Shannon kept by the couch. In various shades of blues and greens, it had hints of water and forest in the subtle patterns.

"My mom made that for me. She had me pick out the fabrics, and this is what I was drawn to. She hasn't made many quilts, but each one is unique." Something about that quilt always comforted Shannon. It was her favourite to curl up with.

"It's really beautiful." Kara stroked it with her fingers. "I love how it reflects your goddess powers of forests and seas."

Yet another way Shannon's past choices hinted at her future, leading her down a path that would reflect the new realities of her life as an immortal, as a goddess. Looking back, she could see those pivotal moments, even if she didn't know that's what they were at the time. It made her wonder whether she would be any better at recognizing those critical moments in the future. Had the career choice she'd just made at the university been one of those moments?

When the doorbell rang, she jumped up to answer it. Lynda, her cap of short blond hair perfectly coiffed and designer suit in pale pink, stood on the other side of the door. When Shannon opened it, Lynda's smile turned into a scowl as she glanced down Shannon's body and fixed on the swell of her pregnancy.

Blue eyes narrowed. With one eyebrow raised, she sneered. "Forget to tell me your celebrity knocked you up? Or did you get knocked up on purpose to keep him this time?"

The words and tone sent an arrow of pain into Shannon's chest. Why was her best friend not happy for her? When did Lynda turn into such a resentful bitch? Was Shannon just that oblivious? Clinging to the door and fighting the heat building in her eyes, Shannon took a minute to respond calmly. One loss of control was enough for today. "Tod and I decided to wait to tell people," Shannon said quietly, not responding to Lynda's deliberate taunt.

"Right. So I'm just 'people' now?" She rolled her eyes, then pointed a manicured finger at Shannon. "You've turned into an elitist snob. It's clear you've decided I'm not good enough to hang with your celebrity boyfriend. And he's not here now, is he? Even after almost a year, you can't be bothered to mingle with him and any of your so-called friends." She tried to peer around Shannon, but it was Mist and Kara who approached. Lynda's lip curled as she eyed them.

Stabbing started behind Shannon's eyes as her migraine kicked into a new ice-pick level of agony, and sudden exhaustion had her sagging. Why? Why was nothing ever good enough for Lynda? Hadn't it been enough that Shannon tried to put the word out with people about Lynda's company at both red carpets she'd done in the last few weeks? For fuck's sake, why was her friend never satisfied? How much did she owe for the help Lynda had given her with Trent? Shannon's fingers tightened on the doorjam. Their relationship shouldn't have a cost-benefit ratio like a godsdamned business transaction.

"Well, it's clear you don't need me when complete strangers know about your pregnancy sooner than lifelong friends," Lynda sneered. "Even if they don't have the taste to know weird dye-jobs went out with the eighties."

Every bone in Shannon's body began to ache as if Lynda's words had drained the life out of her. Frigging hell, she didn't want to deal with this shit anymore. She had apologized so many times over the past year. It was never enough. Why was she trying to maintain a friendship with Lynda? It didn't make either of them happy.

"That's enough, Lynda. If you want to be angry at me for not telling you sooner, fine. But don't start insulting Mist and taking your hurt feelings out on her." Shannon crossed her arms to keep from rubbing her temples. "If you want to come in and talk, we can, but I'm done with your snide, resentful comments. Either accept that Tod is busy and we'll try to get together with you when we can, and that I'll share things in my own time, or walk away. I'm not responsible for your desire to use him to prop up your failing business, and I'm not apologizing for having a busy schedule that takes me away from Vancouver for months at a time right now."

Lynda drew back, sucking in a breath. Shannon held in her wince. Damn it, she hadn't meant to blurt all that out quite so bluntly. The pain was making it hard to think.

"Fine. If that's the way you feel, we're done. Don't come crawling back when he dumps you or treats you like shit, whaling on you like the last one did. Enjoy single parenting, Shannon," Lynda snarled, then turned on her heel to shove past the hapless pizza boy coming up the walkway.

Part of Shannon wanted to run after her former friend, to apologize, but exhaustion dragged at her limbs and she remained motionless. As much as Lynda had been there for her when Shannon needed her, since Shannon's transition, they'd constantly been at odds. Shannon was always going to have to lie to her friend about the immortal world. Maybe it was better if they parted ways. Maybe some things just couldn't be repaired, couldn't survive her new reality. Was this a glimpse of what she had to look forward to with her family as well?

The lanky teenager with a ball cap and a large red thermal bag kept his balance, not dropping the pizza despite Lynda's push. Shannon gave him a small smile when he reached her, and she overtipped him while Mist and Kara took the pizzas into the house. The food smelled fantastic. Her stomach growled, reminding her how hungry she was.

"Eat here, or take it to Asgard?" Shannon asked.

Kara ignored Shannon's question and instead gave her a narrow look. "What did she mean by 'whaling on you like the last one'?"

Crap. Shannon sighed and rubbed at her temples.

Mist explored cupboards until she found plates. She put a few slices on one and handed it to Shannon while Kara continued to wait, a muscle ticking in her jaw.

Shannon bit, chewed and swallowed, then answered, "Three years ago, I broke off a relationship with a man who'd become abusive."

Mist took her by the shoulders and steered her to the couches in her family room. She sat beside Shannon. "Tell us the whole story."

Shannon looked down and ate another bite, even as her stomach churned. Crapola, she did *not* want to admit how stupid and gullible she'd been. Her vision turned watery, and she blinked, a tear falling to her plate.

Kara moved to Shannon's other side, her arm around Shannon. "Please," she asked quietly.

Shannon's voice shook as she started speaking. "Trent and I met at a faculty Christmas party seven years ago, just a couple of years after I was hired. He's in a different department, a biochemist. We went on a few dates, hit it off, then started getting together more regularly. A year and a half later, we got engaged. I thought my life was perfect. I'd gotten tenure and been promoted to associate professor six months before, a year earlier than expected. I'd received several large grants, Trent and I were collaborating on a few projects, my research as a whole was taking off, and the media seemed to love what I was doing. My dean put me up for an early career award. It was everything I'd hoped for, and I seemed to have a man who celebrated my successes with me." She swallowed against the lump of emotion that rose to choke her, remembering how happy she'd been before it had all crashed around her.

"What happened?" Mist asked.

"Over the next year, he changed. It started when he didn't get the grant he was counting on and had to let some of the staff go from his research lab. I quit telling him about my successes. I didn't want him to feel bad, but it didn't help. He grew resentful and abusive. Everything became my fault. He started criticizing the way I dressed, where I went, who I saw, and my weight... Actually, he'd started that much earlier, but I didn't really notice it as much until then. It got to the point where he accused me of embarrassing him at faculty events, then saying I'd cheated and slept with someone to get a grant I hadn't known he'd also applied for. He stole my data and claimed it as his, but it wasn't his area of expertise. The grant panel saw and censored him." She shuddered and swiped at the tears dripping down her cheeks. Leaning forward, she snagged the box of tissues from her coffee table and blew her nose.

She picked at her pizza, then put the plate on the table. Nausea rising, she gripped her thighs to tell them the rest. "That was the first time he struck me, but he didn't stop there. It was the classic hit me, then apologize cycle. I fell for it every time, making excuses for him and hiding the bruises. Fortunately, we weren't living together. After... after he beat me badly enough that I needed to go to the hospital, I told him I wanted some time apart. I changed the locks so he couldn't get into my home, but he broke in. I couldn't prove it, but I knew it was him. He went after me at a faculty party, screaming obscenities, and I threw the ring at him, breaking it off completely between us. That was over three years ago. Yet still, he tries to come by my house or my office every once in a while."

Other than rubbing her back, Kara and Mist had been quiet while Shannon spoke. With her shoulders hunched, she waited for them to tell her how stupid she'd been to fall for such a man.

"Has Loki killed him yet? If not, may I?" Mist growled.

Kara patted her arm from behind Shannon. "Oh no. Death is far too good for him. The punishment should fit the crime. Let's break his hands and his vocal cords, then castrate him."

Shannon gaped, staring from one to the other.

A red eyebrow rose as Kara returned her look. "What? You didn't think we'd blame you for his abusive behaviour, did you?" She searched Shannon's face. "Shit. You did." She grabbed Shannon for a hug as Mist hugged Shannon from the other side. "Honey, you are not to blame for his evil actions."

"But—"

"Now, I know you aren't about to compare us to Lynda... are you?" Mist pinned her with a look. She reached out to brush Shannon's hair back from her face as Kara handed her another tissue. "Seriously, let's go find him. I want to hold your bag while you pummel the shit out of him." Mist grinned in a toothy smile, eyes gleaming.

A laugh burst from Shannon, surprising her. She shook her head, sitting up straighter. "No, he's not worth it."

Kara rubbed Shannon's back. "No, he isn't. But don't you dare let him put a hand on you again, right?"

She smiled. "I won't. You've taught me more than enough to defend myself against him." Her stomach rumbled, the nausea replaced by hunger.

Mist handed Shannon her plate of pizza. "Good. Now eat. You always have us girls, Shannon."

Her words reminded Shannon of the other topic she'd wanted to discuss with them. "So, I was hoping I could convince the two of you to come with me on a girls' weekend in two weeks, at the end of July here," she said, after finishing her first slice. "It's only a few Asgardian days from now." Although she'd considered inviting Lynda, Shannon was relieved she hadn't. Elise was too nice to be subjected to Lynda's spitefulness.

Maybe ending their friendship was a good thing.

So why did Shannon have a sinking feeling at the thought of never talking to Lynda again? Her friend hadn't always been like that. They'd had a lot of great times together over the years.

"Where to?" Mist asked, bringing her out of her circling thoughts.

"Who with?" Kara added.

"The wife of Loki's best friend, Harry Chapelsworth. Elise is in London. We thought we could head out to the Lake District for a weekend, while Loki is filming in London."

"She's not like your former best friend who was just here, right?" asked Kara. "I'm sorry to say, Shannon, but Lynda is a hag and not worth your friendship."

"Yeah, I have to agree with Kara. Lynda was a user. You are definitely better off without her in your life," Mist agreed.

She didn't disagree with them, but still, the loss hurt.

"No, Elise is great, and we hit it off well. She's nothing like Lynda, I promise," Shannon reassured them.

Mist shrugged, then got up to get another slice of pizza. "It's a little more challenging to protect you with a mortal underfoot, but if you say she's great, then it sounds fun to me. Although I've heard the term 'girls' weekend,' and I'm not exactly sure what that entails."

"Essentially, no guys allowed, but otherwise, the activities are up to us. It's likely to include alcohol, although not for me. Elise doesn't know I'm pregnant, so if I can figure out a way to hide my pregnancy, I'll be converting mine to juice as needed."

If that didn't work, she was just going to tell Elise and damn the consequences to Loki's career. He could deal with it. A sudden thought caught Shannon mid-bite and she halted with the pizza at her mouth.

Fuck. *Lynda knew.*

Lynda knew, but Shannon hadn't told her family yet. Her stomach twisted. She'd have to tell them. Oh gods... once her sister knew, the world would know. There'd be no stopping it at that point. She had to warn Loki first, before she told her family. Surely Lynda was too pissed to go haring off up the valley to tell Shannon's family.

"We will do touristy things. Perhaps visit a castle or two. I enjoy historical stuff, but I know that probably isn't as interesting to you two. Actually, how old are you?" She took a bite and forced herself to eat the rest of the piece.

Kara laughed. "Mist is still a youngster, only eight hundred, but I'm eighteen hundred. Those are Asgardian years, though, so both of us have watched the UK develop from before the time of the Celts."

Shannon blinked, then grinned. "So, I can just ask you about historical stuff while we are there?"

"Cheeky baby immortal." Kara poked Shannon then laughed. "Of course you can, but it's not like we know everything. Neither of us has spent as much time on Midgard as Thor or Loki, although I've spent a fair amount here. Will this girls' weekend involve pampering? Tell me there's a good mani-pedi, and I'm in."

Shannon chuckled, trying to get into the spirit and ignore the churning within her. "That can be arranged, I'm sure. Elise probably has ideas. I'll text her to let her know we're in." With a quick text, Shannon confirmed their weekend, letting Elise know Kara and Mist were joining them.

Elise replied within minutes, and Shannon read the message aloud. "She's going to book us into a private cottage at a five-star luxury resort outside Keswick for the four nights. Monday is a holiday, same as it is here in Canada, so we'll arrive Friday and leave the following Tuesday. They have a spa on-site. She's booking us all-day packages for Saturday, but we'll be able to access the pool, sauna, and hot tubs the entire time."

"That sounds awesome!" said Mist, and Kara agreed.

"Yeah, I think so, too. I can't wait. Are we done with the pizza?" Shannon rose and peered in the boxes. They'd eaten two of the three pizzas she'd bought, and despite her uncertain belly, she'd eaten heartily. She moved the remaining slices into one box.

Kara patted her stomach. "Yeah, I'm stuffed."

"I want one more slice." Mist got up and joined Shannon at the counter.

Shannon gestured to the box. "Have at it."

When Mist finished, Shannon took the box, and they headed outside.

"Heimdall, please open the Bifrost," Shannon asked, and the swirl of colourful lights swept them up. Landing gently, she held the box out to Heimdall. "Do you want a slice or two?"

He smiled at her. "Thank you, Princess. I do." He took two slices of pepperoni, and they waved as they headed out across the bridge.

After leaving Mist and Kara at the training ground, Shannon headed to Loki's rooms for a nap. Bouncing between times made her tired, or maybe it was the bouncing bundle of joy she was carrying. The agony spiking behind her eyes and pounding at her temple certainly didn't help.

Nor did the heaviness in her heart.

As good as it had felt to unburden herself by telling Mist and Kara about Trent, losing Lynda, dealing with her department head, and the fight this morning with Loki had made this day an emotional roller coaster. She was ready to be done with it and not think about the next hurdle: telling her family.

Feet dragging, she dropped the box of pizza on a dresser in the bedroom, took off the Valkyrie earcuff, and sank into the king-sized bed.

Loki rubbed his chest as the mix of anguish and anger in the bond eased. Was Shannon asleep? He'd flubbed his lines in the scene several times over the last couple of hours when spikes of emotion had hit him, stealing his breath and concentration. Yggdrasil's roots, he hated that Shannon was still angry with him, that he'd scared her to try to get her to see reason. But what the bloody fuck was he supposed to do? He couldn't let her endanger herself and their child.

"That's a wrap for today. We'll pick it up Monday," the director called out.

Lifting a hand, Loki acknowledged the words and within minutes, he'd removed his costume, entered a bathroom, then teleported to his flat.

"Heimdall, open the Bifrost."

Not saying anything to the massive guardian who greeted him, he teleported twice to reach the palace and then strode the remaining distance to his rooms. Yet entering his bedroom, he stopped dead at the distinctive scent in the air. His gaze landed on a white box with red lettering, but he didn't need to read it to know what it contained.

She'd gone to Midgard. Without him.

His fists clenched and a blazing fiery surge welled from within him. *Bloody fucking...*

Black seidhr swirled around him, and he found himself beside the bed, looking down at his rebellious soulmate. In the dimness of the room, lit only by the glow of the double moons outside on the patio, she was curled on her side under the green and gold quilt. In ominous symbolism, her hair spilled like blood across the pillows. She murmured in her sleep, nuzzling her face into the bedding pulled up to her chin, and he found his fury dissipating like smoke.

His fingers traced lightly along her silky cheek. What the fuck was he going to do to keep her safe when she refused to listen? Had she quit her job? Was that the reason for the spikes of emotion today? By the vast Nine Realms, he was of a mind to paddle her ass until it glowed.

Even just thinking of her alone and in danger sent his pulse skyrocketing, his teeth clenching. With a flick of seidhr, he shed his clothes and climbed in behind her, tucking her into the curve of his body, feeling her warmth against him. Bor's hairy balls, she pissed him off and drove him absolutely barking mad.

Reclining against her, holding her, he gave himself four hours before he rose again, too restless to lie in bed any longer. She needed her sleep, and his oscillating thoughts wouldn't let him relax. Instead, he joined the Einherjar for a pre-dawn workout and returned to his rooms having expended enough furious energy that he'd managed to calm his snarling chaos. With a swipe of his sweaty forehead, he glanced toward the king-sized bed visible through the archway from the large main room with its sofas, chairs, entertainment system, and overstuffed bookcases.

Shannon wasn't there. The covers were thrown back.

Quickly, he strode into the bedroom and spotted her silhouetted in the rising sun's light by the two glass doors that led out to his private gardens. The box of pizza was open, and she removed a couple of slices before turning toward him.

Heat ignited in his chest at the sight of the pizza. He raised an eyebrow, glaring at the evidence of her recklessness. Damn her. Not only putting herself in danger but eating like a child? She was ridiculously young, compared to him, but he'd thought she had *some* sense. Where were her damned apples? He crossed his arms. "You went to Vancouver without me. Eating like a student again, are we? Breakfast of champions?" He made his voice as taunting as possible.

She scowled and took a big bite, giving him a wide, fake smile, her cheeks stuffed with food as she chewed. "Yep! It's got all the food groups, so don't knock it."

"Really? Where's the fruit?" he asked sarcastically. She had access to the most nutritious, energy-boosting food in the Nine Realms, and instead, she chose this crap to eat? To feed their son?

She growled—a cute little sound that at any other time would have him grabbing her to kiss her senseless, but no, not this time. Not after her precipitous stunt. She had no idea just how bad it could get, how a quick death was rarely the outcome for immortals. He'd been too soft on her. How deluded was she? It was an adorable attempt to assert herself, a baby goddess, but against his strength and prowess? Norns help him, what would it take to make her see reason, to see the reality of her situation?

"Tomato, of course. You'd think a god would know the difference between a fruit and a vegetable," she scoffed and rolled her eyes.

Yes, she was *far* too sassy this morning. His eyes narrowed as he stalked her. Her gaze widened, and she backed up, biting and chewing the pizza faster. Was she worried he'd take it from her?

There was only a chunk of crust left when she coughed and wheezed, hands flying to her throat.

Fuck! Loki teleported to her, patting her back. "Breathe, Shannon. Breathe." Bor's beard, did he need to reach into her mouth? Tip her over? Use his seidhr? Get her to the healer hall?

She burst out laughing.

He growled. That little minx was *playing* with him? She shrieked, darted away, and threw the crust at him. The molten anger and worry heating his veins shifted and lowered, firing his groin. Oh, he'd teach her to worry him like that.

In seconds, he caught his sexy little troublemaker and scooped her up, holding her against him. "We need to discuss your penchant for scaring me, darling. Making me think you were choking was not nice." He narrowed his eyes, and his voice dropped into a deep, dominant growl as tension held him in its grip. "I think that deserves a punishment."

Those gorgeous hazel eyes dilated, and she shivered in his arms. He almost roared, seeing her arousal at the idea. Fuck, he wanted—no *needed* to paddle her ass. To see those firm globes flush with heat. To see her quim soak, desperate for his attention. So many erotic things he had yet to teach her, try with her as he'd been careful with her newly immortal and pregnant body.

She glared but pressed her hips to his, grinding. "Do your worst, Loki," she taunted.

Yes, he'd been far too soft on her.

Chapter 50

Never Go to Bed Angry

A thrill ran through Shannon as those dangerous, predatory eyes of his darkened with sinful promise. Had she taunted him too far? They'd never had angry sex. And Loki was definitely still furious with her. His lips pressed together, his nostrils flared like a raging bull, and his leanly muscled body was rigid with tension. Yet, unlike Trent, he still handled her carefully. His fingertips didn't dig into her arms, leaving bruises.

And hell, Shannon didn't need her stress headache worsening *again*, on top of dealing with it all day yesterday. Anger was exhausting. She didn't have the energy to shout at him, and she'd cried enough yesterday. Angry crying was absolutely the worst.

Surely, sex was a *way* better idea than fighting. Maybe it'd cure this damn nagging headache.

Loki spun and set Shannon on her hands and knees at the end of the bed facing away from him. "Stay exactly like that," he snarled, a firm hand on her back when she went to move. Her clothes disappeared, and his hands coasted over her body.

Her pulse quickened in anticipation. While she wasn't sure what he had planned, she was sure it'd be what she needed right then to work out her frustrations and his. Her wicked god could be quite inventive when he was in the mood for sensual torment.

And he was clearly in the mood.

Good. So was she, damn it.

His hands ran lightly over the backs of her thighs, up over her ass, before a hand descended on one cheek with a sharp slap.

Oh. My.

It was a sharp sting, but not truly painful. He was moderating his strength. Heat flooded her lower body as she relaxed further, the last of the cautious tension disappearing in favour of delicious desire.

With a caress where he'd slapped, he soothed the sting before another sharp smack landed on the other cheek.

Again, she gasped at the impact and then moaned at the contrast when his tongue lathed the spot. The tingling heat grew, spreading from the points of impact.

Holy hell. Maybe she should have pissed him off sooner.

Twice more he repeated it, closer to her core each time. Why did she ache to have him smack her there? Was that a normal thing? She'd never been spanked in sex before. Fuck, it was so hot. Her nipples tightened as teasing fingers traced lightly over her swelling flesh. Every part of her focused on the inferno building within and the light touch of fingertips, wondering where he'd strike next.

"You like that, don't you?" he asked, his voice a deep and sensual purr on her senses.

Shit, yes. Craving it, she lowered her head to the bed, arching her back and leaning towards his touch.

"Answer me, Shannon. I want to hear you say it," Loki demanded.

"Yes, yes, I like it. Don't stop, please," she agreed in a breathless whisper. She didn't want gentle, damn it. No, give her this blazing passion, edged in sensual danger.

This time, he smacked right over her core, the bright sting turning to intense pleasure as his clever tongue traced around her opening. Her shriek turned to a long, low moan.

When he repeated it over her clit, her spine bowed with the shocking flash of lightning. She jerked towards him with a loud whine. Insane. Totally insane, but every part of her strained towards him, eager for the next.

Two more quick, hard slaps, with his tongue teasing her in between, had her trembling. Fuck. Her body was on fire, aching, empty. Blankets gripped in her fists, she shoved back towards him at every touch of that clever mouth.

Gods, she was so close.

With one more slap that had her jerking and shrieking in response, he sealed his mouth over the nerves at the apex of her thighs to suck hard as his hands reached around her legs to tweak pebbled nipples. The intensity of sensation flared through her body, sparks searing, igniting... and then he flicked his tongue, hard and fast.

The shockwave of nerve endings exploding roared up and out with the force of an uncontrollable forest fire.

"*Fuck* me, Loki!"

As she quivered, body spasming, he entered in a hard thrust, stretching her walls with no time for her to adjust. It was right on the edge of too much, perfect for her mood, and she screeched her approval.

Not waiting, Loki set a ruthless, brutal pace that kept her trembling, prolonging the rippling waves as the flared head of his thick cock repeatedly stroked over the hyper-sensitive front wall of her soaked core. Shannon lowered her head to the mattress, fisting the bedding as she widened her stance. Gods, she couldn't get enough, arching her ass higher in his grip. The wet slap of flesh meeting flesh echoed off the stone walls. The bed shook beneath them, wood creaking.

Moaning with each pounding thrust, she jolted at the unexpected feeling when his thumb rimmed her back entrance, pressing in, and adding to the dark, twisty pleasure sparking up her spine. Oh fuuuck... he'd done that once before, the night of her transition. And it was as sinfully perfect then as it was now—more than her trembling body could resist.

"*Loki!*" Shannon was blind to everything but the overwhelming ecstasy. Mind lost. No thought in her head. She was entirely a being of sensation, a slave to the tides of pleasure swamping every inch of her with wave after wave.

Despite the blood rushing in her ears, she heard Loki groan long and low. He held her in place as he pulsed, finding his own release in her clenching core.

Tipping them onto their sides, he held her as aftershocks quaked her body. "Yggdrasil's heart, my goddess. You drive me absolutely wild." He ran his hands up and down her body.

Too spent to answer, she panted. That had been wild, intense, and more savage than he'd been since he'd discovered her pregnancy. He'd been so careful, taking her gently. Hell, she hadn't realized how much she'd needed his fury, his raw passion. Maybe she needed to piss him off for make-up sex more often. Damn.

After moving them up farther on the bed, he pulled the blanket over their sweat-slick skin. "You scare me when you take chances, Shannon. We don't know if Ao Guang and his brothers are still in Kunlun, or if Isis knows where you are from. If Gwydion and Arianrhod are still on Midgard, no doubt they've learned about you from the media. It was dangerous to go to your university on your own."

Seriously? Anger flared anew, white-hot and scalding as it washed through Shannon's body in a rogue wave that turned her voice sharp. "Why are you assuming I have no more sense than a child? Kara and Mist came with me. Just as they are coming with me on this girls' weekend Elise has arranged."

"They did?"

The surprise in his tone had her clenching the blanket in her fists, restraining the urge to smack him. Unfuckingbelievable.

He leaned over her shoulder to see her expression. "You are? I thought we'd decided it was too dangerous to go on this girls' night. And when did it turn into a weekend? That's even worse."

Shannon rolled her eyes, then growled, "*Yes*, Loki. They did." Her post-coital bliss had evaporated with his idiotic assumptions. "And no, *you* decided that. Not me. With Kara and Mist along, I'll be just *fine* at our luxury resort in Keswick, enjoying saltwater pools, the spa, and hiking in the nearby forest." She didn't bother to address his complaint that it was now a weekend instead of a night. This entire conversation had her gritting her teeth.

"Oh... um. That's great. Yeah, that's really great that they went with you. But uh... I also wanted to be there to console you. Quitting your job had to be hard." Loki's eyes searched hers. "Though I'm still not sure about this girls' weekend."

She glared. His conciliatory tone rubbed her the absolute wrong way, like sandpaper down her skin. The asshole was only saying it because he thought she'd done what he wanted after he refused to have a real discussion with her about it. Well, fuck him and his high horse. If he didn't want to discuss it before, then why the fuck should she tell him now?

"*Right.* Thank you for worrying about me, but I'm *fine*. Everything has been worked out with my job," she snarled, turning further away from him. She wasn't lying, but neither was she confirming his ridiculous assumption. Loki could think whatever he wanted. It was his own damn fault for assuming.

Jerk.

"And I *will* be going on my girls' weekend." Shutting him out, she closed her eyes. If he could simply insist on things, refusing to talk them out, then so the fuck could she. She was so fucking done with this discussion. There was no way in hell she was losing even more friendships. She needed time with friends away from all this godsdamned shit. Away from him.

He laid back, wrapping his arm around her. "Sleep. Let's discuss the girls' weekend again after we've rested. We have a few hours before I need to be up."

Before *he* needed to be up. Everything revolved around his spoiled ass. She shoved his arm off. Moving away to get some distance between them, Shannon wrapped the blanket around her body and slammed the bond closed. No way did she care to share anything more, and she sure as hell didn't want to feel him. His patronizing, controlling attitude and foolish assumptions made part of her regret that she'd given in and had sex with him, despite the delicious humming in her body. She closed her eyes.

She didn't remember falling back asleep, but when she woke later, the headache and tiredness were gone, even as her anger remained.

Chapter 51

FACING THE MIRROR

Fucking Helheim. That was what this was. The burning lava pits of Tartarus. Loki yanked at his hair, pacing a ragged path on the woven carpet in front of the fireplace and bookcases, and around the furniture that formed comfortable seating and side tables in the main part of his rooms. For fuck's sake, he'd been to Helheim. Seen the nightmarish depths of that realm. Shannon closing the bond with him wasn't his worst nightmare, although it was close. The distance between them had his heartbeat racing one minute and freezing the next with the weight of a bull auroch sitting on his chest.

He was losing her.

But she refused to talk about it. Yesterday, he'd tried when he found his pillow on the sofa in their rooms after returning from a break in filming.

Reluctantly, he'd napped on that damned sofa, tossing and turning the entire hour. Kind of like the way he circled it now. He swore, shattering one of the wooden tables with a burst of seidhr, then clenched his fingers, pulling it back under control.

This morning, he'd again tried to talk to her, and when that failed, he'd kissed her. Shannon had stood there like a statue, not responding. It scared him down to the depths of his soul and left him unable to breathe as the room spun, his vision darkening. Yggdrasil's roots, but he'd rather have her anger, have her yell at him, than have her be indifferent. If she truly didn't care, it was a death knell to their relationship.

For a soulmate to feel that way about their partner was... bloody hell, was it even possible? With the bond closed, he had no way of knowing for sure.

Surely this wasn't just over the girls' weekend. Was she that upset about losing her career? It was just a temporary setback for her. Did she blame him? He wracked his brain as he paced, eyes drawn to that damn pillow on the sofa. Nausea churned in his stomach every time he saw it.

Of course, he knew she was annoyed he'd made a bad assumption about her going to Vancouver on her own, but this had to be a deeper issue. It had to be. He tugged at his hair again, yanking the roots.

Shannon had been angry with him before, but not like this. Never like this... well, except for when he'd fumbled to explain her new reality after her transition. She'd closed the bond then too.

Loki stopped in his tracks, heart pounding. That had also been about her career.

With the change in her circumstances, he'd thought she'd adapted to new priorities. But maybe her science was still more important than he'd realized.

It wasn't that he didn't want her to have a career. Lots of women on Midgard were working mothers now. Their culture had transformed dramatically over the last century, finally approaching the equality exemplified by most immortal races. He just didn't want her to have a career away from Asgard right now.

He'd hoped she would embrace her royal family responsibilities to Asgard, would see it as an exciting new direction. But she still had so much to learn. It wasn't practical for her to take on diplomatic duties yet.

Had he pushed her to take on those responsibilities?

He started pacing again, kicking at the slate floor and edge of the rug.

Maybe? Yes? No. Damn it, he wasn't sure.

Certainly, he'd focused on helping her develop her fighting skills—her battle, weapons, and monster knowledge. Those critical skills were the priority to make sure she was safe. That they were both safe. Staying in Asgard was the best way to ensure that. He yanked at his hair. Norns, he just needed her to be safe.

The memory surfaced before he could halt it. Sigyn's accusing blue eyes, unseeing, filmed over in death and her mouth still open calling for him, for a rescue that came too late. Her long golden hair a rusted ruin surrounding her. And the glistening white fluids splattered over her bruised, bitten, and torn body like sickening icing. Clawed and slashed, the rawness of muscle and bone gleamed in her upper thighs and hips, with her intestines wrapped around her arms and neck like vile pink ropes. But the worst, Norns curse them, the worst he could never stop seeing… the tiny fragments of his daughter's still-forming body shattered and scattered in a red rain of barely recognizable tissues over the black stone and carved symbols.

"*Fuck!*" Clenching his fists, he shouted a few more times and desperately shoved the image away, but the trembling in his muscles, cold sweat clinging to his back, and nausea churning with a bitter aftertaste left him panting.

Again, Loki's eyes were drawn to the sofa. With a shaking hand, he shoved his hair back. Damn it. He just needed Shannon to be safe. Were his expectations so unreasonable?

That damning pillow and everything it represented taunted him.

Teleporting to the Bifrost, Loki asked Heimdall for Thor's location.

"He's with his family, still at their beach house in Cairns. It's the middle of the night," Heimdall reminded him.

"Please drop me on the beach," Loki requested, and when the lights receded, he recognized his surroundings.

Cloaking himself with invisibility, he quietly crept into his brother's bedroom. Thor woke, sensing his presence even without seeing him. With a quick touch, Loki telepathed a request for Thor to meet him outside, then left.

"What is it? Am I needed in Asgard? Is Shannon okay?" Thor asked as soon as he joined Loki on the beach.

"Shannon kicked me from our bed, shut the bond down between us, and won't talk to me about it," Loki said bluntly. As much as they razzed each other, he trusted his brother. Thor would help him figure this out.

Crossing his arms over his chest, Thor scowled. "What the fuck did you do, Loki?"

Loki shrugged, then yanked his hair. "Fuck if I know for sure. She went to Vancouver without me to quit her job as a professor. Even though I'd asked her to wait until I could accompany her. So, yes, I was angry with her when she didn't. I told her it scared me and was dangerous to go on her own. We don't know if Ao Guang and his brothers are back there or where the hell Gwydion and Arianrhod are. Nevermind Isis and Vidar."

Loki threw up his hands and paced back and forth, kicking the sand. "How was I to know she'd had Mist and Kara accompany her? And she was angry that I assumed she'd gone on her own, but I apologized when she told me they'd gone with her. Although, she might... she might also be angry that I don't want her to go on this girls' weekend with Elise. Even though she's got Kara and Mist joining her, I still don't think it's safe. So I told her I wanted to discuss it more with her. I thought we were fine, but then when I woke, she'd shut the bond. When I returned from filming yesterday, my pillow was on the sofa."

No way could he tell Thor about the failed kiss this morning. The pain of her indifference was like a jagged knife, tearing into Loki every time he recalled how she just stood there, unresponsive.

Thor frowned and put his hands in the pockets of the jeans he'd thrown on. "Well... you are mired in the bog, that's for sure. Has she reacted this way to anything before?"

"Only when I tried to explain she couldn't expose her new powers to the scientific community right after her transition. Remember? She shut the bond and took off in storm winds," Loki reminded him.

Thor nudged a rock with his foot. "Hmm... you told me then that she defined herself by her career. Has that changed?"

"Wouldn't it have to? She's part of the royal family, an immortal goddess, and soon to be a mother."

"Is that your assumption, or was it her idea to quit her career?" Thor asked, eyebrows raised.

While Loki paced, he replayed their conversations. Damn. Shannon never once said she wanted to quit. In fact, they'd argued over it the morning before she'd gone to Vancouver. She'd been reasonable in pointing out the advantage of the time difference.

The realization had him wincing. "My assumption. She didn't want to quit and pointed out how the time difference meant she'd only need an hour or so every few days. But I... fuck, Thor... I guilted her about our son needing her, said maybe she didn't want to be a mother and that we'd talk more later. Then I left to go to the set." He cringed as a sour taste coated his tongue.

Thor stared at Loki, mouth open. He shook his head after a minute. “Have you completely lost the plot? Let me ask you this—how would you react if she told you that you needed to give up acting to be a father or if you didn’t, you were a shitty father, then bailed on you to go to her own chosen career when you wanted to discuss it?”

Chapter 52

TOUGH LOVE

Loki's shoulders slumped. Bor's balls. He'd really done that to her. Treated his intelligent, independent goddess like she was less than he was, that her choice of career was less valuable than his, and that she was less capable of managing her time. Attacked her ability to be a parent. Guilt was a Dwarven iron weight in his stomach.

Damn. He was such a bloody git.

"Yeah, you're getting it now. She should have handed you your head in a fucking basket or ripped out your fool tongue. What I don't understand is why you would do that?" Thor frowned and shook his head. "It's not like you, Loki. More than most, you know a female form doesn't make one less. What's going on?"

Loki sank to his knees, hands clasped behind his head. How had he been so stupid? Was he so lost to reason that he couldn't see the chaos of making decisions based on fear?

His vision blurred with tears, and he had to clear his throat several times to answer past the lump of emotion rising to choke him. "I'm afraid, Thor. You know what happened to Sigyn. After those months of not knowing what had happened to Shannon, then her getting attacked by Isis... I'm scared of losing her again. And with her pregnant, just like Sigyn was when she was taken,

I'm terrified of history repeating itself. Shannon is part of my soul. I wouldn't survive her loss."

With seditious force, his fear churned like the deadly black sands of Jotunheim under his feet, ready to suck Loki down into paranoid depths that would have him chaining Shannon to him, regardless of her wishes. And like those razor-edged sands, it would tear them apart piece by piece if he let it.

Thor yanked Loki to his feet, then slung an arm around him. "Fear isn't rational. We aren't at war with the Sidhe. The risk isn't the same, Loki. You need to remember that."

"I know that in my head, but my heart doesn't agree."

"So, instead you've tried to cage her, tearing into her sense of self-worth to do it, and that's not exactly working out in your favour. It seems to me she's acting responsibly by taking Kara and Mist with her when you can't accompany her. Do you doubt their abilities?"

"No."

"Do you doubt their loyalty to her? To Asgard?"

"No, of course not."

"Well, you have the choice of taking the risk of something potentially happening to her, which could still happen regardless of you being there. Fucking Isis got to her on Asgard right under our noses, after all. Or losing her for sure through your own idiocy by pushing her away and not trusting her. If I were you, I know which one I'd choose. Shannon is smart and learns more every day. If you explain why you were being stupidly misogynistic and overprotective, perhaps she'll forgive you."

Rapidly blinking moisture from his eyes, Loki nodded.

"And if you can figure out how to help her keep her chosen career, she'll be even more inclined to forgive you." Thor gave him a small smile. "I'm betting you can come up with some reasonable ideas... and sufficient grovelling."

"Yeah, I could do that," Loki answered as his voice cracked. A few ideas percolated. "Thank you, brother."

"Hey, you've straightened me out a time or two," Thor retorted, thumping Loki on the back.

"I'll let you get back to Amelia before she wakes," Loki said, and Thor released him with one more heavy pat on his shoulder.

Crapola. She had to tell her family. While Loki was right that she couldn't explain why their son took so many more months to be born, she knew with absolute certainty that Lynda would tell them. With the August long weekend approaching, Lynda would be going home to the town's annual celebration. Shannon was out of time. She had to tell them first.

And fuck if she was going to warn Loki. Not after the shit he'd pulled.

"Please set me down in my backyard, Heimdall." She smiled up at the massive god with his hand on the holographic control pad. As the lights began swirling around her, she said, "You'll keep an eye on me and pull me out if Vidar and Isis show up?"

"Absolutely, Princess."

In the next minute, she strode up the embedded stepping stone path in her back garden to the French doors off her kitchen. Once inside, she gazed around the familiar space and the tension in her shoulders lowered.

Gods, it was good to be home.

She made a cup of tea and sank on her couch, tucking her mother's quilt around her. It was still early in the day in Vancouver. She could afford to wait a bit before she drove to her brother's house, to give herself some time to just relax, to breathe in peace. The past two days, she'd kept busy training and learning the diversity of mythological creatures out there. There were a lot. More than enough to keep her mind preoccupied. At least, that's what she tried to convince herself when she started to mope and the heat of tears built behind her eyes... or when she cried herself to sleep while Loki was gone filming all day and all night—busy with the career that was acceptable for him to have when hers wasn't.

Glancing at the phone on the table beside her, she sipped her tea. In the past, she would have called Lynda to vent about Loki, but that wasn't an option anymore. As much as she was getting closer to Kara and Mist, she didn't know where their loyalties lay when it came to badmouthing their prince. She glanced at the phone again. Although they hadn't talked since last fall, she still had one friend she could call, even if she couldn't talk about immortal life with her.

Decision made, Shannon set her cup down, grabbed the phone and dialled.

"Hello?"

"Hey, Kristen. How are you?"

"Shannon!" Kristen almost shrieked her name. "I'm fine, but holy hell, let's not talk about me. How is that super sexy rock god I saw you with on the red carpet just two... three weeks ago? How is that fine hunk of stud?"

Shannon sighed.

"Oh... oh dear. It's going to be one of those conversations, is it?" Kristen's voice turned sympathetic, losing its bubbly enthusiasm. "I've got time. Lay it on me, roomie."

"He's a great guy, if it wasn't for the fact he prefers me at home, barefoot and pregnant." She winced. An oversimplification, to be sure, but true enough in its essentials.

"Uh... what? Are you being metaphoric?" Kristen squeaked.

Shannon snorted and rubbed her temple. "Nope. Our birth control failed, and he wants me to move to his place and quit my job."

"Holy fuck. Part of me wants to say congratulations since I know you want kids and had pretty much given up on that happening, but that's just... what the *hell* is he thinking?"

Shannon laid her head back on the couch. It wasn't completely fair the way she was explaining it, but perhaps... "He has stalkers, some seriously sick individuals. He's worried that I'll be at risk. You know how anyone can just walk onto campus and into our offices."

"Okay, I get wanting to take precautions, but asking you to quit entirely is a bit extreme. There are such things as security companies and bodyguards, especially for a rich asshole like him."

"Yeah, I didn't handle it very well when he refused to even discuss it."

"What did you do?"

Shannon grinned. "Also refused to discuss it when he realized how pissed I am."

Kristen sighed. "Not that I blame you, but isn't that the same move your mother and sister pull that drives you absolutely mental?"

"I also put his pillow on the couch."

A bark of laughter came through the phone. "I'm sure that went over like a lead balloon. That man is sex on a stick. Damn."

Shannon giggled. "Yeah, he's not happy about it."

"Still."

"Yeah, still." Shannon sighed. "I take your point. You're right. I do hate that passive-aggressive crap," she admitted. Maybe that was why it had infuriated her so quickly when Loki had done it.

"So what are you going to do?"

Shannon groaned out, "Compromise," then laughed as Kristen echoed her. Still, just talking it out made her feel more settled and less antsy. Why hadn't she called Kristen earlier? They weren't as close as they used to be during grad school, but still, they talked a few times a year.

As they continued to chat, it struck Shannon that perhaps she could keep her balance between the mortal and immortal worlds. Even though her friendship with Lynda had imploded under the weight of Shannon's new life, maybe that wasn't such a bad thing. Being mortal hadn't been what put the nail in the coffin of Shannon's relationship with her former best friend, although the need to hide things hadn't helped. Instead, it was the lack of healthy balance, boundaries, and expectations that sank them. Just because she hadn't shared the absolute truth with Kristen didn't mean their friendship wasn't valuable. Different levels of sharing truths didn't have to mean keeping all mortals at arms-length.

Sharing truths.

Yeah, she needed to get to her brother's place before she returned to Asgard to clear the air between her and Loki. While she'd live on, she was going to lose her family at some point, and their deaths would come faster than she could bear. This was one of those things Loki was just going to have to compromise on.

She hated the division between them. It left a dark pit in her centre, her chest aching with it. But fuck if she was going to cave on this. No way would she let a man tear her down again. If Loki wanted to be with her, he could learn to respect her choices and work with her to make them safe, not treat her like some princess stuck in a godsdamned tower. Or attack her self-worth and ability to be a wonderful mother just to manipulate her into what he wanted. Every time she remembered his words, fury surged through her like molten lava.

No. She would *not* be torn down again. But if he could be reasonable, maybe she'd rethink the wisdom of going on her girls' weekend.

Compromise.

After hanging up with Kristen, Shannon finished the last of her tea, now gone cold, then headed to her garage. She put her RAV4 into gear and backed out onto the driveway.

Thud.

What the hell? Shannon hit the brake, eyes flashing between the mirrors and the backup camera. There was nothing. What had she run over? She opened her door and stepped out, bending to peer under the vehicle.

A blue plastic shopping bag full of dirt?

Shannon blinked. Why the fuck was there a bag of dirt on her driveway? Had the gardener been here? She glanced down the brickwork toward the road. How had she not seen it as she backed up?

A scent wafted towards her, and she coughed, stepped away from her vehicle, and waved her hand in front of her nose. It was a fucking bag of shit, not dirt. Who would—

As she turned towards her house, a form moved out from the shadows at the side of the garage and Shannon's lungs froze.

Chapter 53

PAYBACK IS A B!TCH

Thor was right. Showing Shannon that Loki trusted she'd make smart decisions was important. After returning to Asgard, Loki focused on making financial arrangements to give Shannon choices with her career and creating a gift that would help his beautiful goddess, give her some freedom back, and take away one of his worries.

Although it took an entire day of painstaking concentration in his workshop to craft his gift, it was worth it. There was no way he was going to let his fears destroy their relationship. When it was done, he tucked it into his pocket and prayed to the Norns that he wasn't too late to make amends for his idiocy. He set out searching for Shannon.

She wasn't in their rooms.

Nor was she on the training ground or in the warrior's lounge.

She wasn't in the palace library.

<*Where are you at, darling?*> He hoped she'd answer his mental call, but his lungs froze at the thought that perhaps she'd restricted the bond so far that they couldn't communicate.

She didn't answer.

Heartbeat picking up as his gut tightened, he tried again. <*Shannon?*>

Still, there was no answer.

A fine trembling in his limbs, he fought the panic rising in his throat. <*Shan—*>

<*Prince Loki, I've lost sight of Princess Shannon at her home on Midgard,*> Heimdall's voice interrupted.

Loki's spine stiffened and he grabbed the nearby wall. <*Midgard? What was she doing on Midgard?*> he demanded, and a moment later, he teleported the two jumps to the Bifrost chamber. "You can't see her?"

"No, my prince."

After taking a calming breath and ignoring the squeezing tension in his chest, Loki held out his hand. In seconds, his sword thunked into his fingers then disappeared as he hid it with an illusion. "Drop me at her home."

"Yes, my prince."

The lights swirled around him, and he considered what would cause Shannon to disappear from Heimdall's sight. The last time was with... Bor's balls, Isis.

The lights disappeared.

Screeches and the clang of metal rang out. Oh everlasting fucking Helheim. It was Isis. Shannon was *fighting* Isis. He started to teleport between them, then halted as he blinked. Shannon had called her armour and weapons, and by the Norns... she was *winning*.

Cuts peppered Isis. Blood dripped from her cheek, forearms, and back, staining the white of her dress. She snarled, slashing with razor-sharp talons, but Shannon batted the attack away with ease. There wasn't a mark on his goddess, just fierce concentration.

With a spin after the deflection, Shannon ran up into the air and sliced down with her sais from above, severing two of Isis's talons. An ear-splitting shriek pierced the air and Isis staggered back, blood spraying from her hands.

Shannon landed lightly, poised to attack again.

Neither of them had noticed Loki's presence as he gaped at them. He hadn't watched Shannon train much in the last month. She'd improved more than he'd realized.

Isis jerked back, trying to avoid the next slash of Shannon's sais as she advanced, driving Isis down the driveway towards the road. Yggdrasil's trunk and leaves, Shannon was a force to be reckoned with. More than holding her own, she was kicking Isis's ass.

His lips turned up in a proud smile. Bor's beard, his soulmate was impressive. He was such a lucky bastard.

With a final cry, Isis shifted fully to a black kite and flew off.

For a moment, he considered chasing her, but then he met Shannon's eyes and every thought disappeared from his head. "You were amazing, darling." The words tumbled out in a reverent whisper.

Shannon's cheeks flushed, and she swiped her hair back from her face as she thrust her sais into the thigh sheaths. Her chest heaved, her breath panting. "Thanks," she wheezed, then moved toward him.

But compared to her usual gracefulness and the coordination she'd displayed during the battle, each step was a scuffling shuffle. Her armour receded and her hand supported her back. She winced and lines creased her forehead.

Bloody hell, she looked exhausted. Was it the fight? Maybe she hadn't slept enough or missed eating her apples again. "Did the fight wear you out?" He reached for her as she got closer. Fuck, this was his fault. If he hadn't upset her, he could have recharged her yesterday and this morning.

"Yeah," she sighed as he caught her around the waist.

Too light. His goddess was too light, too drained. Her eyes closed and he took in the pallor that had come to her usually golden olive skin. "Heimdall, open the Bifrost. Let's get you some energy, yeah?" What a selfish git he was to have deprived her when Healer Moja had emphasized how important energy was to her right now. But he could get her to the forest, to the trees she loved.

"Okay," she murmured as the lights surrounded them.

When the lights dissipated, Loki nodded to Heimdall, then teleported them to the palace hangar and a skuta. In the next minute, he had them launching and flying over the fjord.

"We're going to the forest?" she asked from where she lay on the bench seat.

"Yes."

Although silent on the flight, when they arrived, Shannon scrambled out to head into the trees. Right there behind her, Loki had a hand on her back to help her over the uneven ground as he bit back the need to pick her up and carry her.

After stopping amongst the trees, ferns, and mosses, she closed her eyes and took several slow breaths. The colour gradually returned to her cheeks, and when she opened her eyes twenty minutes later, the drawn look was gone.

Guilt at her condition had his muscles tensing. She should have had enough energy reserves to battle Isis and have plenty of energy left over. That she didn't was his damn fault. "Darling, I'm so sorry. Given how much it helps you to be out here, I should have been bringing you to the forest every day."

Yet another example of how he'd failed her. She shouldn't have had to battle Isis in the first place. He was supposed to track Isis down. The weight of the balance against him was heavy indeed. Bor's beard, there was so much he had to make up for.

"The exhaustion kind of creeps up on me. Thank you. I needed to be out here."

The unintentional blow struck home, and he winced. Hearing her thank him for something he should have made a priority left a sinking feeling in his gut. It wasn't like Healer Moja hadn't warned them more than once that Shannon needed to watch her energy resources. She said it at every check-up.

"Especially now, as our son uses more and more of your resources, I think you need to recharge your energy at least once a day, maybe twice a day, if you are training as well, or like today, using the skills you've learned to defend yourself. Norns, I'm so proud of you. You were amazing, darling." Loki let his fingertips glide over her cheek, relishing the contact when she didn't pull away. "Since I've spent so much time recording, and now filming, I haven't been taking care of you the way I should."

Shannon gave him a small smile. "I didn't ask. And I should have. I'll do better to pay attention to what I need."

Fuck. And he'd had the utter gall to imply she wasn't taking her role as a mother seriously enough. What a damn hypocrite he was.

"No, I'm the one who hasn't been paying attention." Loki yanked his hair. "All these changes you've had to make… I've been thinking about what you said before. You're right. When I couldn't accompany you, you asked Mist and Kara. You should be able to stay safe while visiting Midgard. You just demonstrated you can fight off immortals of Isis's strength. Not that I want you to have to, but it's a relief to know you can. If you want, you should be able to continue your career as a professor."

Air whistled in raspy breaths as he tried to keep his anxiety at bay, to keep the nightmare images from swamping him, to not remember Sigyn's broken body and the fate of his unborn daughter. "Certain things would have to be hidden from mortals, as I do with my career, but I'd like to help you find a way," he told her.

Eyes widening, Shannon blinked a few times, with her eyebrows rising. "Wait... what?" She seemed shocked, and the churning within his stomach increased.

Loki hurried to explain the idea he'd come up with. "As you have seen, I work. It helps that the time difference between realms is to our advantage, as you rightly pointed out. Maybe you could do only the parts of your job you really like. Or if it's simply the research you want, we could always set up a consulting company as a front for whatever you want to do. It's not like you'd need to apply for grant funds or report to a funding agency. I have more than you could possibly spend."

"Really? You'd do that for me?" Her voice trembled, squeaking on the last word.

It was an arrow to his heart, and a prickling heat built behind his eyes. How had he been so ignorant as to miss the importance of this to her? No wonder she'd cut herself off from him. That she wasn't sure of his support now was entirely his fault.

"Darling, I love you. I want you happy. If research makes you happy, then of course I'll make sure you can continue it. The funds are already set aside to ensure it." With his pulse pounding a frantic tempo, Loki paused, knowing he needed to bare all if he had any chance of repairing the damage he'd done.

Shannon opened her mouth to reply, and he put his finger to her lips.

"Please, let me finish. I'm sorry. So, so sorry that I've made you believe I didn't support you. My fears of losing you blinded me. In my terror that something would happen to you, to our son, I pushed you to make the choices I wanted. Instead, I should have been thinking of your needs." Loki's voice cracked as he blinked back tears. "It wasn't fair to you. It took you closing our bond and rejecting me to see what I was doing. Darling, I'm sorry."

Her expression softened, and he gathered her in his arms.

When she relaxed against him and hugged him in return, he couldn't hold the tears at bay. Streaming down in hot trails, they soaked her hair as he buried his face in it and inhaled her lemon vanilla scent. "Please Shannon, I'm so sorry I was such a bloody idiotic git," he murmured into her ear in a ragged exhalation of sound.

Chapter 54

MOSS IS THE NEW BLACK

It certainly had been a morning of surprises. No way had Shannon expected Loki's outpouring of emotion and heartfelt apology. When she'd caught sight of him during her battle with Isis, she'd expected him to step in, to take over, not to stand there with that little smile on his face.

He was *proud* of her. And he wanted to support her in continuing her career. Gods, it was everything she wanted to hear from him.

The warm glow within her chest had her opening the bond between them. His remorse and love flooded her, and her breath caught. "Wow... I. Thank you, Loki. That you are supporting my right to choose... it, well, it means a lot. I wish you'd been a little more upfront about your fears," she said quietly. "Other than my inability to defend myself, is there a specific reason why you've worried for my safety?" It was a question she'd wanted to ask for a while, but he'd never seemed open to it. Would he answer?

Loki swallowed hard. "I married an immortal not long before the last war with the Sidhe four hundred years ago. She was taken, killed in a gruesome ritual sacrifice before I could rescue her. Her and my unborn daughter."

"I'm so sorry, Loki." Shannon's heart clenched and she pulled him in for a hug. Holy hell, she couldn't even imagine the horror, but his actions made so much more sense now. She swallowed, feeling him tremble. He was proud of her ability to defend herself, to defend their baby. He really had turned his attitude around.

What an amazing man. Why had she ever compared him to Trent? He was nothing like that jerk. In a lighter tone, she teased, "And here I thought you were just being a misogynistic asshole."

"An overprotective, misogynistic asshole," Loki confirmed. "Thor agrees with you."

A surprised laugh burst from her, and she pulled back to meet his gaze. "But I should probably tell you that Frigga already ensured I'd have access to whatever financial resources I need to continue my career. She made sure I wouldn't be trapped in Asgard. Before I went to Vancouver, she helped me come up with options so I knew what I wanted to ask for from my university. Although I didn't quit my job, I got the duties modified."

Loki winced. "I'm glad you found a way to get what you wanted. And I'm sorry I was an obstacle instead of part of the solution. Mother's probably not thrilled with me either, is she?"

Shannon chuckled. "Let's just say she was very understanding when I heaped insults on your head, including wishing you'd been eaten by a bunyip, shat out, and then stomped on by a troll."

"Damn. Note to self: don't piss you off. Darling, you're inventive in your anger." Loki shook his head.

Shannon laughed again. Gods, she'd missed him. "Loki, I promise that I'll take every reasonable precaution we can think of, starting with this girls' weekend, but if you don't want me to go, I won't." He'd shown her he was more than willing to compromise, to fight to overcome his fears, that he was willing to apologize and mean it. How could she do anything less?

"Thank you." Loki breathed out a long exhale, closing his eyes for a minute. When his green eyes met hers, she smiled. He reached into his pocket then took her right hand and slid a ring onto her finger. "I want you to go, darling. I'm really glad Kara and Mist are going with you. But, since I won't be with you, and neither of them are skilled in illusion, I made this for you, to show I honestly mean it about not trying to make you stay in Asgard."

Shannon stared at the silver scrollwork ring with its beautifully entwined runes. "What does it do?"

"Think about hiding your pregnancy."

As she looked down, her curved belly disappeared. Instead, her abdomen appeared flat. She touched it and still felt the curve of their son, but it looked like her hands hovered in the air.

"Obviously, it's not as strong as the illusions I can give you when I'm with you. Although it won't stand up to touch, it will keep anyone from seeing your pregnant belly if you don't want them to. Just don't hug someone," Loki cautioned.

Shannon's real abdomen reappeared, and she cupped his cheeks, kissing him. "Thank you, Loki. This is perfect. I'll remember your warning." She looked away for a minute, exhaling. Yeah, she needed to come clean. Meeting his gaze, she said, "I was going to go tell my family. That's why I was on Earth today, but instead, I think you should go alter Lynda's memories so she doesn't remember I'm pregnant." As much as she wanted to share this with Liam and Sarah, and even her mother to a certain degree, it was a selfish desire. She'd trust in Loki and believe he'd work out a way for them to tell her family at some point.

Loki frowned. "Lynda knows?"

"Yes. She..." Crap, it was so hard to say it. "She came to my house when Mist and Kara were there, and I called her on the nasty things she said. We're no longer friends, but I don't trust her to not tell my family over the upcoming holiday weekend. And if my family knows..." Shannon winced. "Well, you remember what Heather did at Christmas."

Loki nodded. "Yes, darling. I'll take care of that later today, and I will figure out a way to tell your family before our son is born. If we tell them closer to your due date, it will be easier to disguise the time differential."

A weight lifted off her chest as she agreed and told him about her upcoming maternity leave and what her duties would be when she returned. She hadn't realized how much it had bothered her to think Lynda might tell her family. Her dean and department head, as well as the secretaries, knew, and so did Kristen, but while the gossip might eventually spread, it wasn't the type of thing academics would get overly excited about. They had the time to work out a way that didn't reveal the immortal world.

"Now with your girls' weekend"—Loki held her gaze—"promise you will either take a walk outside in the forest or spend time in those saltwater pools each day since I assume I'm not allowed to come recharge you."

Shannon smiled, her hand rising to cup his cheek. "Yes, I will. In the meantime..." She kissed his neck, biting on the lobe of his ear and drawing a groan from him—this powerful immortal that had shown her with his actions that he truly loved her. "How about you make sure I'm completely topped up before I leave?"

"Norns, yes!" Loki growled. With her encouragement, he lowered her down onto a bed of soft moss to drive her wild. He'd missed her moans and screams, and primal satisfaction roared through him as she lay there afterward, gasping for breath and recovering from their vigorous coupling. Yet, he couldn't keep a chuckle from escaping as he reached up to pick moss out of her hair. "Darling, you might want to shower before you meet up with Mist and Kara."

She huffed in annoyance, although her gaze remained soft, so he knew it was just for show. When he didn't stop grinning, she rolled her eyes.

"Come on, sexy wench, or I'll tumble you again and make you late," he said with a playful growl.

Shannon shoved him over, then stumbled as she tried to get to her feet, ending up on hands and knees, chest draped across his face. Of course, he wasn't slow to take advantage.

"Well, if you insist," he quipped, before tugging one nipple into his mouth.

"Loki! I need to—" Her words ended in a moan.

"Clearly, I didn't satisfy you and must rectify the situation before you go," he teased, as his fingers got busy sliding in and out, with his thumb circling.

Shannon moaned again.

Yggdrasil's heartwood, but he loved that sound. Drawing it from her again, and again, he played with her, bringing her to the trembling cusp, quivering around his fingers.

"Loki!" she moaned.

"Patience, darling," he murmured against her shivering, dewy skin. "I've missed you."

Lifting her, Loki turned her to brace her hands against a tree. After caressing her silky, toned back with reverent palms, he slid into her, stroking long, smooth, and deep. She was Valhalla, taking him to the cosmos and back, with the taste of her pulse on his tongue, breasts filling his cupped hands, and hot, slippery quim wrapped so tightly around his plunging cock.

Slowly and thoroughly, he built her arousal until she whimpered and pleaded.

"You sound so incredibly sexy like this," he growled, as he changed the angle of his hips to ensure he rode that extra sensitive ridge and lowered a hand from her breast to tease her little pearl.

Within seconds, she shook within the cradle of his arms, and he joined her shortly after.

They stayed like that until their pulses calmed, before Loki withdrew, turned her in his arms, and kissed her tenderly. "I love you, Shannon," he murmured.

"I love you too, Loki."

The words had him light-headed, even as warmth grew in his centre. With the bond open between them, he basked in the heat of her light, chasing away the icy darkness in his soul. Never again. By all the realms, he never wanted to feel that loss of connection again. Reluctantly, he clothed them and led her out of the forest.

"I'd apologize for making you late, but I wouldn't mean it." He flashed her a half-smirk as he started the skuta.

"You can at least conjure my backpack and fill it with appropriate essentials for me."

The glow inside him grew at her request, fulfilling his need to help her with something. If he could slay all her dragons, he would. "What do you need?"

"Toiletries, a swimsuit, as well as the multi-realm watch you made me, my cell phone, and wallet. Oh, and the Valkyrie earcuff." She changed her current outfit into shorts, a T-shirt, a leather jacket, and hiking boots.

Loki loved that she got so much use out of the torc he'd designed with his father's help. Gladly conjuring what she'd requested and adding a surprise into one of the pockets, he handed her the packed backpack. "Have fun, darling. Will you miss me?" Unable to resist touching her, he caressed the beautiful curve of her belly. After parking the craft in the hangar, he took her hand and teleported them to the palace gates where she was meeting Mist and Kara.

"No, I'm going to be having too much fun with the girls to miss your hot, sexy ass," Shannon teased. "I guess I'll have to ask one of them to keep me warm at night."

Heat flared within him and he narrowed his eyes. Little minx. "If it's female hands you want on your body, you know you have only to ask."

Shannon burst out laughing. Tugging his hair to tilt his head down, she kissed him in a passionate melding of lips and tongues. "The only one I want is you, my love. Regardless of your shape and gender. My preference is this incredibly sexy male body you are currently sporting, but if you want to experiment with me sometime, I'm open to that. I love you. Yes, of course I'll miss you. I won't close off our bond, so you'll feel me here."

Her hand rested on his chest as love and warmth flowed between them. Norns, but he'd missed that feeling. Loki smiled, cupping her cheek with long fingers, his thumb stroking. "Sorry, I know that. But I've just never had so much to lose before. My love. My soulmate. My son. At times, it scares and overwhelms me. I love you, Shannon. In this wide universe, there isn't anything more important to me than you."

Her love was a warmth in his chest, wrapping around his heart, and their lips met in a slow, thorough exploration full of tenderness.

Mist snickered when she arrived and took in Shannon's appearance.

Kara rolled her eyes. "You could at least fix her hair when you take her out to the forest to tumble her, Loki. Some prince you are!" Kara scolded.

Loki looked at Shannon's hair and snickered. "Oops. I actually meant to do that." With a quick flick of his fingers, her hair lay flat and smooth on her head.

"I will not be happy if there is still moss in my hair, Loki," she warned him, even as her eyes betrayed her amusement.

Loki grinned unrepentantly, then winked. "No moss, except on your knees and elbows."

Chapter 55

FINDING BALANCE

After a brief cab ride, Mist, Kara, and Shannon stood in front of Harry and Elise's London home. Harry answered the door, ushering them inside. "She's just saying goodbye to the kids. How was your flight?"

"Good. No delays. An easy trip," Shannon said, avoiding any details. Even understanding the necessity, she still wasn't entirely comfortable lying. It wasn't something she managed quickly or spontaneously with any real skill. "How have you been?"

"Great! Enjoying the time off with the kids and Elise. It's been a busy few years."

Elise came into sight, descending the central staircase to the foyer. "I'll say! Sorry to keep you waiting!" She led them through the house to their garage and the RAV4 inside.

Shannon tossed her backpack in the back. "I have the same vehicle! Do you have the hybrid, too?"

"Ha! See, yet another reason we were destined to be friends." Elise started the vehicle. "Yeah, we have the hybrid, and I love it."

Mist and Kara piled into the back seat.

Elise backed out of the garage. "It's a five-and-a-half-hour drive."

Even with a few stops to see various sights and to have lunch, it passed quickly. Shortly after the three o'clock check-in, they arrived at the resort.

"What do you ladies think about heading to the spa for a soak in the hot tubs to recover from our journey?" Shannon suggested as they dumped their bags in their rooms and explored the cottage.

"That sounds *brilliant*," Elise agreed.

Mist nodded.

"Kara?" Shannon asked.

"I'm game!" she shouted from her room.

Gathering their swimsuits, they walked down the paths to the spa. After changing, they followed directions to the outdoor hot tubs nestled among rock formations with greenery that made it feel like being in a natural hot pool. Well, except for the posh waiter who came over to give them a menu and ask if they wanted any drinks. Stomach growling, Shannon ordered a virgin piña colada and several trays of appetizers.

With her ring disguising her pregnancy, Shannon relaxed in the hot bubbling saltwater, letting it soak into her body. It was heavenly. As she listened to Elise, Kara, and Mist talk about hair and clothes, she closed her eyes.

"Wake up, Shannon." Mist lightly shook Shannon's shoulder. "Don't go drowning yourself."

Shannon opened her eyes. Had she drifted off? "Sorry. It was just so relaxing."

"The food's arrived. Hungry?" Kara held a plate toward her.

Shannon took handcrafted crackers and local artisan cheeses of various kinds. The water had provided enough energy that she wasn't as hungry as when she'd ordered it, allowing her to enjoy the food for its flavour. Relishing the decadence, she ordered another piña colada.

After soaking in the hot water for a bit longer, they got out, showered, and changed. Once back in their cottage, they relaxed and enjoyed the scenery while dinner baked in the oven. With drinks in hand, Mist and Elise joined Kara and Shannon on the patio. The sun was low on the horizon. There was a gorgeous view of the nearby lake and rolling green mountains, with patches of forest on their lower slopes.

"It looks like there are some nice hiking trails on the nearby mountains," Shannon pointed out. "Would anyone be up for a walk tomorrow morning before we start our spa day?"

"I'm in," offered Mist.

"Depending on how many of these I have, I might sleep in." Elise smiled, holding up her drink.

Kara laughed. "Sorry. Am I making them too strong?"

"Nope! Perfect." She winked. "But since I'm kid-free this weekend, I'm going to indulge, so you feel free to hike without me tomorrow morning."

"I'll see how I feel in the morning, too," added Kara.

Shannon smiled. She knew Kara would be up, but her chest lightened at the way both Valkyrie were effortlessly fitting in with Elise.

In a short time, their food was ready, and they headed inside to eat. The cottage had a gorgeous open-concept kitchen, dining area, and family room, with arched ceilings, skylights, hardwood floors, light oak cabinets, stainless steel appliances, and dark granite countertops. The round dining table was light oak, large enough to seat eight, with well-cushioned chairs.

Switching to sparkling wine for their dinner, Kara handed Shannon a glass of sparkling apple juice. As the conversation ebbed and flowed around her, Shannon considered how much her life had changed. In a couple of days, it would be August first. A year ago, she'd boarded her flight to London, a flight that put her in the arms of a god and changed her reality in more ways than she could ever have imagined.

Loki had blasted into her life like the hurricane-force God of Chaos that he was. Everything that had come before was swept away in a cataclysmic shift of not just what she'd thought she'd be doing with her life, but her very identity and place in the universe. The chaos of evolution could be a destructive force, neither inherently good nor bad, but everything afterward was forever different. She would never be that naïve mortal girl again, so unaware of the wider universe around her.

When she'd first been confronted with it, all she could think about was everything she'd lost. She hadn't yet appreciated how much more she had gained.

She still had her mortal family, at least for now while they lived their lifespan, but she'd gained an immortal family as well. As wonderful as Odin, Frigga, and Thor were, she also knew she wanted to find her biological parents, the Sidhe who were her birth mother and father. She might not find the answers she was hoping for, especially given Gwydion and Arianrhod were her grandparents, but Shannon still wanted to know.

Not only did she have Earth, but she had also gained Asgard as a home. She'd barely seen the whole of the palace, and there was so much still to see and discover in this new realm. With thousands of years of life ahead of her, there were so many new places to explore, learn, and understand. She had abilities to continue to develop and decide how to use. She'd just scratched the surface with them in the few months she'd been learning. Thinking about how advanced Asgard was in its understanding of science, so far advanced that to her, it was all magic, made her excited. It thrilled the scientist in her to no end. New science, new research avenues to explore. It was so much more than she'd ever imagined.

And Loki... holy hell, Shannon loved him. Her heart pounded in a frantic rhythm when she considered the depth of her feelings. She had so much more to lose now. He could hurt her far worse than her ex ever did.

The connection between them grew stronger every day they were together. Not only were they able to share thoughts, but she felt him, his emotions carrying through their bond, even when they weren't trying to send anything to each other. It was a constant warm thrum in the back of her mind and her chest.

She shook her head.

Gods, he sure had spun her head these last few days. Yet, the way he'd bared himself today, showing her the truthfulness of his regret, sorrow, and shame, while admitting the depth of his fears... There was no way she could hold a grudge. Not when she knew what it was to act out of fear. Hadn't she run from him out of fear, after all? Hadn't it been her worry that he was like Trent that had caused her to react the way she had?

Yes, she understood having fears.

That he'd faced them, and was doing his best to support her now, despite still being afraid something would happen to her, or their son, well... it eased her worries of not being valued or desired as a woman, not being supported for her choices and career successes. Those scars from her ex couldn't hold her back with Loki at her side, showing her with word and deed that she could trust him with her vulnerabilities.

She looked down at the ring on her finger and the new crossed sais charm on her bracelet, and sent a pulse of love down the bond, smiling as a heated wave returned to wrap around her, flavoured with his unique essence. How had he known that she'd need more than words to reassure her? Just when she thought he didn't understand her, he proved her wrong. She loved him all the more for it.

Yeah, she couldn't blame him at all for struggling with fears.

After all, she still had her own worries about protecting their son, but those grew less each day as she gained confidence in her abilities. Defeating Isis had gone a long way to boosting her confidence. There was much more she needed to learn, but she trusted Frigga, Loki, Mist, and Kara to teach her.

Shannon couldn't help but smile, watching Kara and Mist tease each other—Kara trying to guess the plot of the current episode they'd put on the television when dinner ended, and Mist taunting her with her knowledge. Mist handing Shannon the two bags of Hawkins Cheezies she'd packed, knowing how often Shannon craved them.

They were fast becoming close friends, the sisters she'd always longed for.

She'd learned and continued to learn so much from them. Not just battle strategy, weapons, and fighting skills, but also how to be part of an immortal sisterhood. She could count on them in any situation.

As they each headed to their respective rooms and beds, Shannon's hand slid down to cradle her belly. Their child. Would he have Loki's gorgeous green eyes? His dark hair, or her brown locks? Her olive skin or Loki's pale complexion? Her mind's eye pictured a mischievous little boy with his father's green eyes and mother's brown hair.

Although it had taken Shannon time to adapt to all the changes both within herself and surrounding her, she finally had her solid footing. Between her Asgardian family, her immortal friends, and her soulmate who loved her enough to challenge his fears, she could tackle any future challenges.

Maybe even discovering the rest of her immortal family.

Chapter 56

STONE HENGES

Something was watching them.

Kara, Mist, and Shannon had gotten up bright and early the next morning, just after sunrise, to hike along the ridge tops through the nearby forest until they were out of sight of the nearby town and had descended into a valley. Shannon practiced tossing gas balls at rock targets, and amid one throw, she stopped, with the hairs on her neck rising. When she looked around, Kara and Mist continued fighting hand-to-hand. Shannon couldn't spy anyone on the nearby hills or trail. Still, something bothered her. It was unnerving, like there were eyes on them. Early morning mists swirled and shrouded parts of the hills.

Kara and Mist stopped.

"What's wrong, Shannon?" Mist asked.

"I'm not sure. But I swear we are being watched."

Mist sent out a wave of air, hunting for disturbances. "Animals, but I'm not detecting any mortals or immortals. Kara?"

Kara scanned their surroundings as well. "No, I'm not picking up anything either. What exactly does it feel like, Shannon? You have abilities we don't, so you could very well be picking up something we can't."

"The hair on the back of my neck is standing up. Almost like there is an electricity in the air, but I can't tell from where. Kind of like that sense you get when a thunderstorm is building. Do you know what I mean?"

"I do," Mist nodded. "But I'm not picking up anything in the water vapour. This isn't weather-related."

"We should head back," Shannon said, and they agreed. Despite their vigilance on the trek back to the cottage, they never spotted anyone or anything that explained the sensation.

Elise was awake and cooking a full English breakfast when they arrived.

"Perfect timing! How was your hike?" she asked with a smile.

"Rejuvenating. It's a beautiful, misty morning, but the sky is blue and not a cloud in sight. It should be another warm day," Kara replied as they set out plates.

After breakfast, they spent the rest of the day visiting Keswick, the lake, and taking in a show at the live theatre. Despite the relaxed pace, Shannon was tired and had little in the way of energy by the time they relaxed on the cottage patio in the cooler evening air. With glasses of wine and slices of decadent chocolate cake, they compared notes about what they'd enjoyed most in exploring the town. They'd each found something slightly different, making it an ideal day for everyone.

"Being from Canada where we don't have castles, I'd love to visit some. Apparently, there are several less than thirty minutes away towards Penrith," Shannon suggested as they discussed their plans for tomorrow.

"I have to admit that I take them for granted. Other than the typical school trips as a kid, I've never really visited them. Sure, I'm game," Elise agreed.

"Yup, I'm up for whatever," Mist stated.

"Sure, I'm old. I like old stuff," Kara joked.

Elise rolled her eyes. "Oh please. I'm older than you. You are *not* old!"

While Mist coughed, Shannon bit her lip to hold back her grin. Kara just smiled.

Too tired to stay up with them, Shannon headed to bed before everyone else. As soon as her head hit the pillow, she was out.

After a good night's rest, she was up with the sun. Kara, Mist, and Shannon headed out for another early morning hike. This time, they walked towards Dodd Wood and spent more time in the evergreen forests. The trails had more use—they couldn't stop to train—but she enjoyed the walk, regardless. With no repeat of the uncomfortable watched sensation, energy sang through her veins by the time they returned to the cottage and she set about making omelettes for everyone.

"Oh! I meant to be up earlier," Elise apologized, joining them just as the food was ready.

"Not at all. I'm glad you enjoyed your rest," Shannon told her, handing her a plate.

Once they were done, they loaded up the RAV4 for the day of visiting castles. King Arthur's Round Table, an earthen henge believed to be of prehistoric origin, was their first stop. After reading the information posted at the site, Shannon pulled Kara aside to ask her what it was really used for.

"Midgardian scholars are mostly correct. People used the stone henges as calendars to mark the seasons, but the Tuatha Dé Danann also used them as gateways, similar to our Bifrost. Because of this, many mortals believed these to be holy sites and held rituals here, worshipping many of the Sidhe, and the Tuatha Dé Danann in particular, as gods, goddesses, or demons, depending on their characters. We sealed as many of the gateways as we could find when we exiled the Sidhe from Midgard after the last Sidhe-Asgardian war. Although, we obviously missed at least one since Gwydion and Arianrhod were on Midgard." Kara scowled. "It was an ugly, brutal time, but I was glad when Odin finally stepped in to stop the Unseelie atrocities. It was worth the Asgardian losses to protect the mortals."

"Wow. I have a lot of history to catch up on, to understand the politics between the Sidhe and Asgard. What about King Arthur?"

"He was an actual king in this area, and it's entirely possible they used this as a meeting place for him."

"It's cool to find out he was real. What about the legends..." Shannon started to ask, but Elise rejoined them.

"Can you imagine living like that?" Elise asked.

"Disease, poor hygiene, women treated like property. Yep, fun times." Mist wrinkled her nose.

Knowing she spoke from experience and wasn't just speculating, Shannon bit back her smirk.

Leaving the ruins behind, they travelled to Lowther Castle and gardens. It was a more recent castle, with parts of it rebuilt, and they spent a good couple of hours exploring it before stopping for a late lunch and then exploring the one-hundred-and-thirty-acre gardens, including orchards. Compared to the ruins themselves, the orchards were energizing, and Shannon found herself not wanting to leave. As fun as it was exploring, it was exhausting, too. Although she'd always wanted to see the tangible history of castles, she seemed to have very little in the way of stamina. She'd have to come back again when she wasn't almost twenty-eight weeks pregnant.

"Shannon, I don't like the look of that storm rolling in." Mist pointed to the northwest where dark clouds filled the sky.

Shannon spun, eyes widening. Damn. She hadn't noticed the storm building, clearly more tired than she realized. "Well, we've had such beautiful weather. Hard to complain that it's going to rain on the last bit of our trip."

Elise sighed. "Yeah, we've been lucky compared to the gloomy rain it often is. Let's head back. There's always indoor swimming at the spa."

"Now, there is a great idea," agreed Kara.

Shannon seconded it. The soak in the saltwater sounded heavenly as her feet had begun to ache. She needed the boost of rejuvenating energy. This pregnancy thing was really starting to have downsides.

But the storm front moved faster than Shannon expected.

By the time they made it to Elise's vehicle, it was already raining. Electricity crackled in the air. Lightning struck nearby hillsides in blinding flashes, leaving the stink of ozone surrounding them. Thunder rumbled, shaking the car. The wind picked up, making the flags mounted by the castle snap in the breeze.

Elise drove cautiously down the Old Coach Road back toward the resort. It was slow going with the wind buffeting the vehicle. They'd made it most of the way back when the rain turned into a torrential downpour, forcing her to slow even further. Even at maximum, her wipers couldn't keep up with the onslaught.

Shannon coaxed the worst of the rain away from the windshield, to allow Elise's wipers to clear enough to increase visibility, but not enough so she'd notice. Focused on her task, Shannon didn't notice the large shape until it sideswiped the car with a horrific crushing impact, knocking them across the road and into the far-right ditch.

Instinctively, Shannon cushioned her body with air as the airbags blasted out of the dash, knocking Elise out mid-scream. She twisted to check on Kara and Mist in the backseat, and the door beside her was wrenched off its hinges with a metallic squeal.

Even as massive dark hands reached for her, Shannon called her armour and put up a barrier of fire. The hands didn't hesitate or slow down. Instead, they reached right through the flames and yanked her out of the vehicle.

Or tried to.

Pain seared her neck, wrenching it as the seatbelt cut into her hips and throat. The tough fabric held against the force pulling on her, and fingers dug deeper into Shannon's shoulder and thigh. Blood vessels burst, compressed by the force, and she screamed. She was trapped, stuck partly in and out of the car.

Mist crawled between the seats to help Shannon while Kara cursed and kicked at her crumpled door, the site of the original impact with whatever had hit them.

Slashing at the vice-like hands with her daggers, Shannon tried to see what had a hold of her. But with the pounding rain, she couldn't get a good view. It shifted its grip to both of her shoulders, twisting her in front of its torso, with her back out of the vehicle as she clung to the doorframe and seat with her hands and feet.

It thunked her head against the top of the SUV, once, then twice as it continued to drag her out.

Mist reached for Shannon.

Another yank tore another scream from Shannon's throat, pain spiking along her spinal cord and shoulders. Panting, heart pounding, she tried to fight the pressure. She was being pulled in half by the seatbelt strap and whatever had grabbed her. Either her neck or her lower spine was going to snap if this creature pulled harder.

Desperately, she hacked at the seatbelt with one of her blades. As the fabric parted, Shannon was jerked the rest of the way out of the vehicle, smacking her cheekbone on the doorframe's edge.

Mist scrambled out after her.

The creature shook Shannon like a rag doll, holding her several feet off the ground. Her vision blurred, nausea climbing her throat. She tried shoving with air and shooting water at it. Yet, she couldn't pry its grip off her. Neither were her daggers able to cut the thick black-and-grey skin. Gods, what was this fucking thing?

"Mist! Kara! My daggers aren't having any effect! Neither is fire, water, or air! It's too close to me for poison gas!" she yelled, fighting her panicky thoughts to come up with options.

Mist appeared in front of Shannon, slashing with her sword at the creature's legs before darting in behind her. Through the earcuff, Kara told them she was coming through the seats too, since she couldn't pry her door open.

Twisting, Shannon tried climbing the air to flip around in the creature's grasp. Too strong. Its grip was too strong. Ruthlessly, it shook her again.

Hard.

Agony knifed her neck at the harsh movements, the crack of vertebrae popping. A yelp escaped as she tried to use the air to cushion the violent jerking of her body. The world spun, making it hard to focus. Her stomach lurched as her lunch climbed her throat.

Just as Kara escaped the car, a headless horseman appeared between them. His bone whip lashed out, wrapping around her neck. Growling, she slashed, cutting it with her dual blades.

Before she could move toward Shannon, another headless horseman took its place.

"It's a troll, Shannon. Try sunlight!" Mist yelled as she was driven from Shannon by two massive redcaps, dripping with blood and as fearsome as the one Loki had shown her in his illusion. Mist's sword gleamed in the lightning flashes as she fought, spinning and dodging their blows while using the rain to blur her image.

"What the fuck is going on?" Shannon screamed, swiping the vomit from her mouth as she concentrated on combining elements into a miniature sun. It wasn't something she'd tried yet. Hydrogen. Oxygen. Compression and heat. Although she was pretty sure that was all she needed, the surrounding chaos and throbbing pain in her head didn't make the most fucking ideal environment for experimentation.

A small glow appeared and expanded in her narrowed vision.

The troll shook her violently again. Agony speared through her head and disrupted her concentration as she gagged once more. Gods, it felt like the troll was smashing her brain against her skull.

The light winked out.

"Shit! What are they?" Shannon cried in frustration, setting her teeth to try again.

"The Norns-cursed Unseelie! The fucking Wild Hunt!" Kara yelled, battling three white hellhounds with red ears. Two headless horsemen lashed at her with their whips, slashing across her armour.

A huge white stag with flaming red eyes came into view, just watching. It snorted and tossed its head.

"*Mist!*" Shannon shrieked, seeing Mist collapse as a headless horseman's whip took out one of her legs and a redcap landed a crushing blow to her head.

An enormous black horse with a tall white-bearded gaunt rider stopped beside the stag. They exchanged looks, and the man nodded. Dismounting, he walked over to Shannon with a cruel smile twisted on his face.

"Call Loki *now*!" yelled Kara.

Shannon's heart leapt into her mouth, trembling overtaking her limbs at the stark desperation in Kara's voice.

<LOK—> Shannon got out, as the man snapped an iron ring on her leg. Agony seared her body, and everything went black.

The story continues with *Taken*, Book Two of the Triquetra Prophecy within the Gods Among Us universe.

ABOUT THE AUTHOR

Melody Grace Hicks writes spicy science fantasy romance. She'd apologize for the increase in your lingerie replacement budget, but really, we both know it's those darn wickedly sexy characters that bring you back for more, right? Born and raised on Canada's West Coast, Melody has travelled the world and brings the diversity of her heritage and travels into her fiction. An award-winning internationally published scientist and professor in her day job, she's an enthusiastic masher of mythology in the evenings, using her pen name to tell tales of soulmates, secret identities, unknown origins, betrayals, and magical powers.

For updates and new releases, please subscribe to her newsletter at www.melodygracehicks.com.

Melody loves interacting with her readers and you can follow her on Twitter/X (melodyghicks), Tiktok (@melodygracehicks), Instagram (melodygracehicks), and Facebook (melodygracehicks). Or, if you want to check out the first draft of her stories as she writes them with all kinds of bonus content, including uncensored one-shots and excerpts, join her on Ream (reamstories.com/melodygracehicks).

Also by Melody Grace Hicks

GODS AMONG US – TRIQUETRA PROPHECY

Hidden
Taken
Origin

BREAKING THE 4TH WALL SEASON ONE

A Writer's Commitment – Episode 1
Delayed Gratification – Episode 2
Don't Taunt The Trickster – Episode 3
Ladies' Night – Episode 4
Seductive Characters - BT4W Season One (Episodes 1-4) *(available in paperback, ebook, and audiobook)*
Fury Of The Storm – Episode 5
Birthday Party – Episode 6
After Party – Episode 7
Sub Drop – Episode 8
Ephemeral Pages – BT4W Season One (Episodes 5-8) (*available in paperback, ebook, and audiobook*)
Road Trip – Episode 9
Giant Complication – Episode 10
Jealous God – Episode 11

Confessions of Mischief – Episode 12
Fiction's Embrace – BT4W Season One (Episodes 9-12)

OTHER BOOKS

30 Days To Save The World – Short Story Anthology

ACKNOWLEDGEMENTS

Thank you to my many beta-readers who provided feedback during the development of this story. Your comments and reactions helped me take my first draft and weave the threads into a cohesive series. Thank you to the sensitivity readers who helped guide my word choice for authenticity regarding specific cultures, dialects, and diversity groups. I can't express my appreciation enough for my editor, Brenna Bailey-Davis at Bookmarten, who was absolutely invaluable in tightening the conflict and helping me find where to enrich the worldbuilding and character interiority to immerse my readers more deeply into Shannon and Loki's tale.

This book wouldn't exist without my daughter's steadfast enthusiasm and support. She helps me create the covers and critiques my designs. She listens to my ideas, laughs at my puns, and always wants to hear what happens next, even as I fade to black through every spicy scene when I read to her. Because come on, who wants their parent to read *that* to them, no matter their age!

To my oldest brother who inspired my love of science-fantasy, myths, legends, world-building, epic quests—oh, and Shakespeare—thank you for starting me down this road and challenging me to write diverse characters with depth.